GHOST LAKE

…and for Nokomis
who warned me not to play with fire

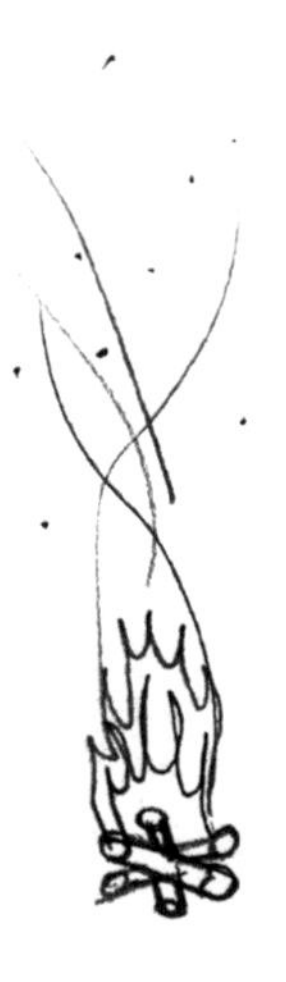

A version of "Valediction at the Star View Motel" first appeared in *Love Beyond Body, Space, And Time* published by Bedside Press, 2016.

A version of "Tyner's Creek" first appeared in *Those Who Make Us ~ Canadian Creature, Myth, and Monster Stories* published by Exile Editions, 2016.

One strand of the plot from "Intermediaries" first appeared as a version called *The Ghost Rattle* in *Playground of Lost Toys* published by Exile Editions, 2015.

A version of "Offerings" appears in *Food of My People*, published by Exile Editions, Nov. 13th 2020.

GHOST LAKE

chilling, mysterious tales of Anishinaabe culture and legend…

"A memorable, necessary read, Nathan Adler's remarkable collection *Ghost Lake* delves into the life-changing passages of love and loss, revenge and redemption, survival and discovery. His vital, authentic characters journey through a world in which the boundary between the so-called real and the illusory—the realm of mysteries, spirits, and myths—is itself revealed to be the illusion. These imaginative, expertly crafted stories are guaranteed to illuminate and stir, to challenge and entertain."

—Daniel Scott Tysdal, author of *The Writing Moment: A Practical Guide to Creating Poems*

"*Ghost Lake* is the border to all things known—but not in the way wider society conceives them: there is no lighthouse imposing its dichotomy on the darkness. It invites recovery and connection from its characters beautifully; story, memory, and relationship build the landscape for them to walk on. The people of *Ghost Lake* move through experiences with a curiosity and bravery that I hope all readers have—where there are no experts to place rules on a community's desire to remember. We need more collections like this."

—Tyler Pennock, author of *Bones*

GHOST LAKE

Nathan Niigan Noodin Adler

Published by Kegedonce Press
11 Park Road, Neyaashiinigmiing, ON N0H 2T0
www.kegedonce.com
Administration Office/Book Orders: P.O. Box 517, Owen Sound, ON N4K 5R1

Printed in Canada by Sotek Graphics
Editor: Kateri Akiwenzie-Damm
Book Design: Chantal Lalonde Design
Illustrations: Nathan Niigan Noodin Adler

Library and Archives Canada Cataloguing in Publication

Title: Ghost Lake / Nathan Niigan Noodin Adler.
Names: Adler, Nathan Niigan Noodin, author.
Description: Short stories.
Identifiers: Canadiana 20200404369 | ISBN 9781928120247 (softcover)
Classification: LCC PS8601.D526 G56 2020 | DDC C813/.6—dc23

For Customer Service/Orders
Tel 1–800–591–6250 Fax 1–800–591–6251
100 Armstrong Ave. Georgetown, ON L7G 5S4
Email: orders@litdistco.ca

We acknowledge the support of the Canada Council for the Arts which last year invested $20.1 million in writing and publishing throughout Canada.

We would like to acknowledge funding support from the Ontario Arts Council, an agency of the Government of Ontario.

All my relations…

ACKNOWLEDGEMENTS

I'd like to say chi-miigwetch to everyone who helped me to write these stories.

All the folks at Kegedonce Press: Renée Abram, Christy Telford, Patricia Campbell, and Kateri Akiwenzie-Damm.

The instructors and writers who workshopped three of these stories in the Creative Writing MFA program at UBC: Annabel Lyon, Sara Graefe, Caroline Adderson, Lee Maracle, Jill MacKenzie, Georgina Beaty, Margaret Nowaczyk, Stephany Aulenback, Michelle Glennie, Scott Randall, Galadriel Watson, Heather Ramsay, Danielle Daniel, Sarah Richards, Matthew Lawson, Haley Shaw, David Geary, Julia Teeluck, Kyle McKillop, Nicola Wistanley, Jessica Torrens, Owen Schaefer, Esther Griffin, Jacqueline Firkins, Hope Thompson, and Margaret Doyle.

As well as the editors who worked on specific stories as they appeared in other anthologies: Ursula Pflug, Colleen Anderson, Kelsi Morris, Kaitlin Tremblay, Hope Nicholson, Erin Cossar, Sam Beiko, Michael Callaghan, and Candas Dorsey.

To cousin Shirly Chapman for telling me stories about giants, windigo, and memegwaysiag, and helping with some of the Ojibwe words. To my brother Howard for letting me bounce ideas off him, artistic input, and brainstorming titles. Matt Massa for helping resolve a plot issue in "Coyote." My sister Sharon for insight into the inner workings of a horse racetrack. To the Canada Council for the Arts, and to Shirley Williams and Isadore Toulouse for some Anishinaabemowin language consultation.

Miigwetch also to my parents Bill and Mae for all their support, and to all the community members of Nezaadiikaang, Lac des Mille Lacs First Nation.

CONTENTS

INCENDIARIES

Gar has to pee. Bad. Made worse by the pressure of the seat belt on his bladder. *Need to go! Need to go!* Dede must have pulled over, because the next thing he knows, Gar is standing in the ditch, fly down and wiinag hanging out as the urine flows in an arc. It's an almost pleasurable sensation after suffering so long. But then the pleasant sensation is overshadowed by another, less pleasant, sensation—warmth and wetness.

Oh right, dreaming, but he can't seem to put on the brakes, the feeling of wetness spreads and quickly grows cold. Bedspread, comforter, and sheets are soaked. *Not Again!* Gar hops out of bed, removes his wet shorts, and pulls the sheets and blankets off before the moisture has a chance to saturate the mattress. His flesh pimples with goosebumps on contact with the air. This is the third time such a dream visited recently—the familiar pressure on his bladder, and the resulting accident. *Almost fifteen, way too old for this!*

He refused to drink anything after eight o'clock, and made sure to pee before bed, but it didn't work. Maybe it's psychosomatic? Gar blames the dreams. He'd be peeing in the dream, but he didn't know it was a dream, and he'd wake up peeing for real.

Gar gathers the soiled bedding and carries it to the furnace room where the washer and dryer are stashed, doubling as the laundry room. He stuffs the blankets, sheets and his underwear into the machine, pours in some liquid soap, turns a dial and presses it in to start the machine. Cold wash, three-quarters load. The basin begins to fill making an alarming racket, but he knows that the sound won't travel far, it only seems loud because it's so late, and the house is so quiet. It hadn't been loud enough to wake anyone before. His mum, stepdad, and grandmother are probably all still sound asleep upstairs. The furnace roars to life, and the noise helps disguise the sound of the filling basin. He drops the lid on the washing machine with a metallic clang. He forgot to pull on another pair of underwear so he has to make the return trip commando. Just as well, he needs a quick shower before putting clean sheets on the bed.

The garbage bags he placed under the sheets after the first mishaps protected the mattress from dampness. They make a crinkling sound when he turns over, or sits down, but it's better than the alternative. He pads quietly back to his room, bare feet making almost no sound on the tiles. It's chilly with the urine drying on his skin.

He rinses off quickly in the shower stall, water alternating between scalding hot and freezing cold as the pipes war with the washing machine for water. Gar soaps up, lathers, rinses, dries off. Tries not to pay too much attention to body hair growing thicker in new places. He is starting to feel like a sasquatch. Catches his face in the mirror. Round nose. Puffy lips. Messy mid-length dark hair that falls into his brown eyes. Face like a rock.

He pulls clean sheets from the hall closet, then goes back to his room, closing the door firmly behind him as he hears the washing machine enter its rinse cycle. The spare blanket is thin, he'll be cold for the rest of the night, but it's better than wet blankets.

He pulls on a clean pair of tighty-whities, makes the bed with new sheets, the new blanket, and new garbage bags in case of another re-occurrence of the peeing-dream, and then climbs in—chilled from his quick shower, and the cool air in the basement. His mom always turns the heat down at night. He is grateful for the feeling of cleanness and fresh sheets even if they make crinkling sounds. His body heat will soon warm the sheets, and he won't be as cold. The sound of the washing machine is white noise lulling him to sleep. In the morning, he will transfer the clean bedding to the dryer.

"Don't play with fire or you'll wet the bed," Nokomis warns him the next day, forehead creased with wrinkles. His grandma Delilah is standing at the screen door as he bounds down the steps of the front porch. Soft lace-up leather boots. Otter-fur medallion. He has a preference for browns and greens. Forest colours. And orange camo.

"I won't, Nokomis." His late-night laundry run hadn't gone entirely unnoticed. But it's just some old Indian superstition. There's no causal relationship—unless it's subconscious. Maybe that's the intent? The saying itself a self-fulfilling prophecy? Still. Gar pats his pockets to make sure he has his matches, lighter, and pack of cigarettes.

Check. Check. And check.

"God it's so tacky." Cadence inspects her purple nail polish. Today she wears black lipstick, yellow eyeshadow, and a turquoise scrunchie on her wrist. Her black hair is cropped too short to actually wear the scrunchie.

"Can anyone say Pan-Indian." Peyton rolls grey eyes skyward, grinds his cigarette butt into the ground with the toe of one All Star. Blue jeans, white shirt, Seattle plaid.

"I guess." Gar eyes the totem pole in question. He's never really thought about it much. It's been there for as long as he can remember. Eagle wings outspread near the top like a crown, gouged lines indicating vaned feathers, curved beak turned to one side in profile. A universally understood symbol of Indigeneity—though it made little sense for Ojibwe to construct such a thing. It had accumulated a certain sense of permanence. "It's not really a 'Nish thing is it?"

"Wrong tribe, wrong nation, wrong side of the bloody continent!" Zeke exhales a cloud of smoke. Tie die, sandals, long hair tucked behind his ears. Indian hippie.

"I wonder who thought it was a good idea to erect in the first place?"

"Eee-reeec-tion!" Peyton sings, raising his arms like the eagle.

"I wish someone would tear it down."

"It *is* a tourist attraction." Gar points out.

People like to stop and have their picture taken with the totem pole, the carved wood garishly painted, faces leering with cartoonish idiocy. There's a small gravel parking lot for cars. A stone's throw up the road is the old boarded up Star View Motel. At some point, someone decided to construct a deck and railing around the pole, but it has long since rotted away, only parts of the rickety wood remain, sticking out like teeth. Behind the landmark is a small field, with trees pressing in close. Teenagers Gar's age like to camp out amidst the gnarled roots, drink, and light bonfires. The acidity of the cedar kills off competition from under-growth, and fallen debris creates a soft, hollow soil.

Gar steps back, and a rusty nail punctures his shoe, and imbeds itself half an inch into the sole of his foot.

"Bloody hell!" Gar lifts his foot, and a piece of lumber comes with him. His friends laugh. "Place is a death trap!"

"Hope your tetanus shot is up-to-date!"

Gar hobbles away, his friends' laughter wafting after him with their smoke.

Later that afternoon, Gar returns to the totem pole. None of his friends are hanging around. He does a sweep of the trees; the place is deserted. Perfect. He finds a secluded spot in amongst the bush where he won't be disturbed. The land slopes upward from here, and he can see the carved faces maybe a thirty yards distance, hidden by the foliage from their knowing smiles. He doesn't want any witnesses.

The fire starts off small.

He builds a little log cabin and teepee side by side, each about a foot wide. Stuffs in balled-up lines of ink on crumpled newsprint, then layers sticks in increasing size. He snaps branches into smaller lengths over one knee, and when that doesn't work, positions one end raised on a stone, and stomps down to break it cleanly in the middle.

He wants to see which will burn faster, the log cabin, or the teepee.

He lights a strike-anywhere match on the same stone he used as an anchor point to snap branches, and then touches orange flame to bundled paper, here and there, around in a circle, so they catch from all sides. He watches with eagerness as the fire licks the edges of the paper, flaring green, and yellow, catching some of the smaller sticks, then the larger pieces of kindling, until finally the larger branches begin to burn, the warmth of the fire is matched by a growing warmth in his cheeks.

A familiar, welcome excitement fills him, a rush of euphoria, his breath comes faster and faster as if he is engaged in some activity more strenuous than simply observing. The growing heat is matched by a growing hardness in his jeans, and pleasant sensations wash through him. He loves this. Loves watching the fire grow, gathering momentum.

The log cabin caves in and topples, knocking over the teepee, creating one larger funeral pyre, the individual flames merging to create something larger and altogether more beautiful. He wants the fire to grow, bigger and louder, so the pleasant feelings will also continue to swell. Gar drags over larger and larger branches then stands back in awe as flames devour the timber. From the small seed of a matchhead touched to pieces of newsprint, he created this monster bonfire. The heat makes sweat bead on his forehead, but he won't step back, refuses to back down, only turning aside to feverishly gather more wood, more logs, more fuel.

The branches of a neighbouring tree are arching over the inferno; they blacken and burn, two feet above the tips of the flame, the pyramidal shape creating a focal point of greatest heat, as the smoke rises and curls, spinning centrifugal, sparks pop and fly in all directions as the wind blows, feeding a steady supply of oxygen. The conflagration seems to breathe, inhaling and exhaling as it sucks in more air and the flames burn with greater and greater intensity, producing a steady sound, almost like a growl.

Gar moans. It's so good. So good. He is close. So close. His eyes water from the smoke so he closes them as he listens to the fire snap and roar, feeling heat on his face, his arms, his chest, singeing his bangs. But he doesn't care. His eyelids flutter, catching glimpses of the curling orange flames, and this only inflames him more, carrying him away.

"Ywaacgh!" Gar yelps as a sharp pain interrupts his climax. His pant-leg is on fire! He leaps back from the blaze, slapping at the folded cuff of his jeans. *Oof!* He falls backwards over a log, and lands flat on his back.

From this new perspective, he sees that the nearby tree with over-arching branches is now engulfed, like a massive piece of kindling. His scalp prickles with sweat. Maybe he let the fire get too big? He couldn't just pee on it. It was much too much, too big for that to help now.

He scrambles back and watches the poor tree go up like a living torch, orgasm now overcome by the cosmic power. But something about the sight squares his shoulders, makes him feel the potential for strength in his muscles. This was *his* fire. The calf where his pant leg caught fire throbs like a reminder, alongside his sore foot from the rusty nail he stepped on earlier in the day, and he looks around to make sure he's still alone. There is always something to detract from or ruin a near-perfect moment.

Oh shit it's spreading.

Another tree has caught on fire. His forehead is slicked with sweat; he takes a step back from the blaze. The heat is intense. He can't believe how fast it's moving, like a living thing. Catching a third tree on fire, and the next, and the next—and Gar knows for sure that he screwed up. He created something entirely too big and beautiful for him to own—it's developed a life of its own, apart from him, and he has to let it chart its own course.

Gar retreats further and further from the inferno, finding a hilltop from which to watch the firestorm brew. This isn't just a bonfire anymore; it's now a mini forest-fire. He hears sirens in the distance. The volunteer fire-fighters over in Cheapaye. His fingers twitch. It's his fault. The waste. Using up their valuable resources. He wonders if Duncan answered the call when a report of the fire came in?

The sirens get closer and closer, coming to smother the ardour of his flames. From his position on the ridge, he can see the fire expand and contract, change directions and turn as the wind whips the flames into a fury, first one direction, and then the next, like some massive, lumbering beast, unsure which victim it should pounce on next. Too many targets to choose.

Rez Indians gather to watch, standing on the road, black forms silhouetted by waning orange light. The blood-red sunset matching the smaller fire here on earth. It seems to burn with greater intensity against the contrast of the coming night.

Gar chokes and coughs as the smoke shifts toward him, but he isn't willing to abandon his perch, the perfect vantage from which to view his creation. The fire reaches the clearing around the totem pole; the dry grass bursts into flame and races like a cresting wave towards the rotting remains of the railing. It gobbles up the old lumber, left out for so many years, soft as driftwood. The deck is on fire. The post rising amidst the flames like a mast. The leering faces take on a sinister cast in the cherry glow, like heretics at the stake.

The community members who've gathered to gawk suddenly seem to realize that the totem is at risk. They quickly get organized and take action; forming a daisy chain, they pass pail after pail of water, hand over hand, to douse the flames and save the monument, but each toss only disappears into sheets of steam—it's no use. The fire has gained too much momentum; burns too hot.

Fire fighters arrive and the volunteers with their buckets step back. The totem pole itself is on fire. Water flows in an arc from their hoses, but they might as well be peeing on it, it is just as effective. Hickory flames consume scowling, insane smiles, carved teeth gritted in pain, open wide in ecstasy, the eagle atop seems to rise, wings outstretched like the arms of the crucified Christ, a phoenix amidst the fury, rising from the ashes to become something new, something old, something it once was again—but then it too is swallowed, the whole structure shudders, shimmers, and then topples. The people gathered shriek, gasp, cry out.

It's too late.

Landmark destroyed, the fire seems sated, slowly dwindling as firemen dampen coals with their hoses. Volunteers are joined by more of a crowd who turn up to watch the unsuccessful combat with the fire; they mill about, and mutter slanderous accusations.

"How did this happen?"

"Who is responsible?"

"Good-old anti-Indigenous racism."

"Is it intentional?"

"Despicable!"

Gar is surprised by the vehemence of people's attachment to the road-side attraction, the sentimentality and sudden nostalgia for something that had been left to rot, it was unmaintained for years, the lead paint chipping and flaking, the old wood fading to grey. Suddenly the post assumed an importance and prominence that it never had before—it became something special, and unique to their community. Now that it was gone, everyone loved the memorial.

As it draws darker and the allure dims, the crowd disperses, voices drifting up to where Gar sits listening, watching the remaining embers glow, curtains of steam rising from the smoking ashes.

It had been a thrilling sight, but as with any high, Gar is now left with the low, left alone in the darkness, atop the desolate ridge, lit only by the stars.

It is said that Kitchi Manitou took the four essential elements: earth, wind, fire, water—and blew into them using a megis shell. From this union of breath, people were created. So we all have a little fire in our bellies, a fire in our heart, and if that ever goes out, we'd be hollow, puppets without strings. Humans can't live without food, or water, or air. Neither can we live without that spark, without that fire.

"Who would do this?" Cadence's lips corkscrew.

"It's just awful meanness I say." Peyton is seated on a log, hoodie up, hands in the pockets of his jeans, hunched in like he's cold.

"I hope they find the guy that did this and spit roast him." Zeke takes a swig and extends a flask towards Gar. "Ishkodewaaboo?"

"Gaawiin." Gar shakes his head, and Zeke passes the firewater back to Peyton. "I thought you guys hated the totem pole?" Gar's shoulders suddenly feel tense, like there's a WWII internment camp target painted on his back, and a laser pointer lining up a sightline down the scope.

"Oh the thing was front-face-ugly but that doesn't mean we wanted it gone." Cadence wears black makeup today, like she's drawn inspiration from *The Crow*.

"It had its charm." Zeke eyes the place where the pole should've been. "I mean, yeah it made absolutely no sense, but it's been here forever, practically an institution, a pillar of the community. Gave the place a bit of a character."

"Oh, yeah. I guess." Gar's cheeks burn, and he hopes his guilt isn't too obvious. The target now feels like a boulder, weighing on him. Crushing. "I never thought about it that way." A ladybug lands on his forearm, its legs tickle like the blink of eyelashes against skin. He raises his wrist to examine the insect, hard red shell dotted with black markings, tips of its folded wings protruding from beneath protective carapace.

Ladybug ladybug fly away home
your house is in fire
and your children are alone…

Gar chants the opening lines of the sing song nursery rhyme he learned as a child. He can't remember anyone teaching him the words—maybe they are a part of the ether, accessible to anyone of a certain age—though someone must have taught him. Urban legend has it, that if you sing the song just right, and the ladybug flies away, your wish will come true.

Ladybug ladybug
fly away
and bring me some luck some other day…

Finishing the rhyme, Gar purses his lips and blows gently on the insect, the way he would on the tiniest of embers in a bird's nest of straw. The ladybug lifts its glossy shell to unfold the translucent wings hidden underneath, and takes flight, beating the air in a blur, escaping the breath which disturbed it.

"What did you wish for?" Cadence asks. Gar looks away from the ladybug's flight path back to his friends. Peyton, Zeke, and Cadence are staring at him.

It was an accident really. He didn't mean for it to happen, it just got out of control. And it was a god-awful landmark anyway, tacky and horribly anachronistic. He doesn't know why people are so attached to the damned thing—totem poles certainly aren't an Anishinaabek thing—wrong tribe, wrong nation, wrong side of the bloody continent!

"Don't you wish you knew," Gar answers mysteriously.

Gar feels a tickling on his neck as Thera attempts to climb onto his head. Gar holds out his hand and the arachnid crawls onto his palm. He has to create more land as the tarantula walks, pillowing one hand in front of the other like he is pulling on a rope. Spider treadmill. The bristles on Thera's feet tickle as she walks. Usually she likes to sit on his shoulder like a parrot, but today she seems unusually active.

"Garion—dinner's ready!" Valene shouts from upstairs. His mother outright refuses to enter his room since he'd gotten the pet.

"Come on Thera, I'll have to get you a hamster wheel, burn off some of those excess calories." He lifts the spider and places her gently back into the aquarium retrofit as an arachnid habitat, dirt instead of water. The glass cuts a cross-section through her lair, and he watches as she climbs into her burrow. Thera has lined her home with silk, it glitters like silver under the black light.

"Coming!" Gar yells.

Gar is nine years old. It is his first time.

He steals a bottle of lighter fluid from the garage. And a pack of matches. A bunch of crumpled flyers that have come in the mail—actually everything that has come in the mail—flyers, bills in envelopes with their rectangular windows of cellophane, a rolled up newspaper, a Sears catalogue—everything that is crammed into the mail-box and hasn't been checked in a while. Hikes far enough into the woods behind his house so he won't be seen.

There is a rubber ball of excitement bouncing around inside him. It rises into his throat like a lake. He piles sticks, and a few stray branches. Squirts butane on the assembled materials, drags a match across the striker strip. Sparks fly. There's a flare. A burst of sulfur. He watches the wavering flame for a moment before throwing it on his pyre.

He feels a heady, overpowering rush; he's so light-headed he thinks he might pass out. A release of built up tension, like a coiled spring. It is a relief to have this weight finally lifted. He feels lighter, and weak as he watches the mail burn. He feels carried away by the flames, as if he is rising, rising, rising, higher and higher, curling up with the smoke and ash, up to the heavens like the twists of tobacco that are burnt as offerings, and said to carry prayers to the dead, the afterlife, the creator, or all of creation. He is up so high in the air, far away from himself, outside of his own body. He can see himself down on the ground, kneeling, brow-ridge and cheek bones, pants pooled around his ankles.

Waves of relief pour through him, and his body shakes, he is trembling, but he only notes this abstractly, distantly; he is too far away for it to matter, pleasure or pain, he is so far away from everything, hypnotized Dark Crystal podling, his essence slowly being sapped as he stares into the raging, red inferno.

Too soon the fire burns down, he settles back down into his body. Gar pulls up his pants, cheeks burning. Looks around to make sure no one has seen. Oh good. Exhales. He is alone. He pees on the ashes, a curtain of smoke rising as the last of the flames go out, and coals sizzle in complaint. Zips up the zipper on his jeans.

Gar's Stepfather Duncan is a volunteer firefighter. There are few actual firefighters on staff as paid public employees, given the relative rarity of house fires, and the rural setting—outside the provincial jurisdiction of forest fires. So Duncan works over the summer for the Parks Department in a similar capacity of Forest Management.

Yeah, yeah. One could probably make a federal case about the fact that Gar is kind of a pyro, and his stepdad is a firefighter—as a sort of rebellion against your parents kill-your-father and fuck-your-mother Oedipus-Rex-Freudian kind of thing—but Gar knows his fixation stems from long before his mother re-married. Back when it had just been Gar and his mom, and his dad had left. Maybe even before this. Before his mom and dad split up. Or maybe it was like what Lady GaGa said about the Gays, and he was born this way?

A moth trying to orient itself by the light of stars but distracted by flames.

Gar has been attracted to fire for as long as he can remember. His earliest memories. He and his dad—his real dad, not his stepdad Duncan—used to have campfires in the backyard. They'd sit around for hours telling stories. His dad drank Rusty until his words slurred. In the morning, the green and amber of beer bottles would be mixed with the ashes, signaling that the fire had burned hot enough, for long enough, to melt glass. Little rivers of molten lava, so different from the state they had been in the night before. Cool enough to handle and pick up. His dad asleep on the couch, having undergone his own transformation.

It is said that in the Anishinaabe way of seeing things, the future is predictable. Or at least, some portion of it is foreseeable enough to know what might happen. These are called fires. The 5th fire, the 6th fire, the 7th fire, the 8th fire. There is some debate as to which time of prophecy we are living; are we still in the 5th fire? Or the 7th? Each fire is a prophecy, each fire is a prophet, and each fire is an epoch. In the 8th fire there are two paths, one that leads to destruction, and one that leads to the creation of a new world. But maybe even in destruction there is hope, the way a forest fire clears ground for the birth of a new generation.

Standing at the edge of the forest, at the edge of a farmers-field, there is an old tumbled down house—not much larger than a shed really. Maybe someone's old hunting cabin left to ruin.

Gar collects kindling. Takes his time shredding birch bark for tinder. Piles up smaller sticks in a bundle, graduating to larger branches. Gar is deliberate with each step, like each motion is an act of devotion, a small part of a larger spell, and each ingredient must be arranged just so. He savours each element of the process, goes slow. Ceremony. Ritual. He doesn't want to rush this.

Once he has a good armload or three piled where there had once been a door, he is ready. He feels his cheeks flush with heat. He needs this. It's been too long. He's had to wait weeks while the furor surrounding the totem pole fire died down, and for gossip to land on subjects more ripe for speculation. It had been too risky to try sooner. He didn't want to attract attention, or for suspicion to land on him. He dared not take the chance of being found out. Duncan complained that the barest whisp of a campfire or BBQ was enough to set off a barrage of phone calls to the fire department. All false alarms. But as the weeks passed, and people began to go on with their lives, the totem pole fire became a thing of the past.

He is far enough away now that even a large fire shouldn't draw too much attention. Greysen Neyananoosic's farmhouse is nearest, but it's still a fair distance and hidden by the slope of the land. Many farmers burn unwanted refuse, leaves, flammable yard waste. His smoke shouldn't draw too much attention. If he is careful. He doesn't want a repeat of last time, but he's waited as long as he can.

Gar makes a sceptre, wrapping the head in an old sock and dousing it in kerosene like it's an Olympic torch, and he's the master of ceremonies. Gar lights the torch. Turning it like a marshmallow over the flames of a lighter. The fabric catches with a whoosh. Burning blue and green and then yellow. Translucent.

He stands in front of the brushwood he collected, and the tumbled down house. His breathing comes quick and heavy, as if he's been running, but there's a weight on his chest, his rib cage can't expand to its full capacity. His face burns hot, the tendons in his neck thrum as he lowers the improvised torch. The kindling catches, and after a few moments, the smaller sticks burn, graduating to the larger branches. Gar steps back to admire his handiwork once he is convinced the fledgling fire can manage on its own without any more help from him. It shouldn't need any the way he's laid everything out.

The fire is soon climbing up the edge of the door frame, and across the lintel beam like a ring of fire—he can step through it if he wants too—and he does, want to. His breath comes ragged as he watches the fire progress. Devouring the walls, devouring the rafters, devouring the skeletal architecture, lighting up the shadows inside, he can see all the corners. There are no places to hide. The dancing light is so beautiful, he wants to touch it, he wants to be inside it, he wants to burn too, he wants to join the flames, he wants to be beautiful too.

He wants badly to step inside—desperately—but manages to squash the urge. He stays still with effort. The worn shingles let off wisps of smoke that have been sealed inside by the tarpaper, forced to billow from the windows and door. But the peak is soon aflame. The flames are almost invisible, they shimmer with black-top-heat in the afternoon sunlight. Mirage distortion.

Gar feels a bit shaky too. He is shivering despite the heat. The wind picks up, feeding the fire, fanning it to a fever pitch as the entire structure is engulfed. He feels feverish, his forehead slick. Burning house effigy. The blaze rises a good fifteen feet, if not higher, keeling east towards the lake and the Neyananoosic's cottage—the direction the wind is blowing. Gar moans. It's so good. It's so good. Don't stop. Don't stop. Keep going. Keep going. Sweat drips down his temple, down his back, underneath his clothes. But he refuses to step back, even at the risk of having the entire arrangement topple on him as the foundation is eaten away. In fact, Gar can't move. He is transfixed. The flames are engrossing. Beautiful. Perfect.

Waves of sensation wash through him as the pleasure centers in his brain light up, as if he's been plugged in and zapped with electricity, like he's the patient in that childhood board game Operation and everything is tingling, buzzing. His cells vibrating.

A flare arches sideways with the gale, curving down almost to the ground before lashing upward like a whip, like a Seussian drawing, bent backward into an S. The wood is dry with age, and it burns with greater intensity than Gar anticipated. He loves this fervor. A small jet of flame seems to take a short leap, and hop away, suspended, independent from the main conflagration, it lands a short distance away.

In Greysen Neyananoosic's field.

Gar blinks. He didn't know fire could do that. Throw itself. Upon impact the jet splits into a dozen parts with tiny little cartoon running legs, radiant lines running out from the center. Oh. Shit. The little devils attack the field with gusto.

What is Greysen growing?

Something, dry and yellowed. Gar didn't pay much attention to the field. Until it started burning. He scrambles, trying to stamp out the flames, but the wind scatters the hellraisers in all directions like a corn-maze, little fires everywhere. Too many for him to put out. Behind him, he hears the cabin collapse in on itself, a hollow crunch and exhalation of sparks, but he's too distracted to pay it any mind. Greysen's field is burning. Following the slope of the land, up and across his entire crop. It's eating everything like some crazy wiindigo monster.

Oh man. Oh man. This is so awesome! Bad. Bad. Bad.

He didn't mean to burn down Greysen's crop. All he meant to do was burn down the old cabin. No one cares about it. He didn't know the wind would pick up. It isn't his fault. Gar hears the wail of sirens. Fire trucks approaching, the volunteer firemen, and Gar knows that it's time for him to go. He takes one last look Neyananoosic's burning fields, and the smoking heap that had once been the dilapidated cabin, suffocating now that it has lost the structure that allows air to circulate. Gar does his best to memorize the scene, and retreats. Trying to put as much distance between himself and the scene of destruction.

Nokomis eyes him as he trudges in through the kitchen: disheveled, covered in smudges of ash, reeking of wood-smoke. Delilah says nothing. A shimmer of emerald sequins, purple eyeshadow, and menthol cigarettes.

"Aanii," Gar mutters a greeting, and goes straight to his room. It isn't until later, when she hears of the fire, that he gets in trouble. His stepfather Duncan had been one of the firefighters to answer the call.

"I know you had something to do with that fire." Delilah's jowls shake. "Sneaking in here like a piece of toast."

"You won't tell Duncan, will you?" Gar's eyes find the corners of the room.

Delilah exhales shakily. "This is serious Garion. You could be charged. They could put you in jail. You're my grandson and I have to protect you. I won't tell your stepfather—goodness knows what he would think."

"Thank you Noko—"

"If!" Delilah raises her finger. "If you to go over to the 'Noosics and apologize. You could have burnt Greysen's house down! You're lucky the fire department put it out."

Gar nods, examining the pattern on the laminate floors. But breathing easier. Delilah is letting him off the hook—she's not going to tell. His mom is always working, and Duncan would not be happy to find out Gar set the fire—even if it was an accident.

"I'm worried about you." Delilah frowns, and he feels nausea rake through his gut. He feels like he might puke. He'd put that worry there, adding more creases to all the cares and worries which added their lines. He knew her life hadn't always been easy. He is shit. Scum.

Delilah drives him to Greysen's farm. "Why must White people name everything after Indians? Cherokee. Winnebago. Apache." Delilah complains on the way over, a rant he's heard many times, though he knows she loves the old van. "Why don't we start naming things after White people—Irish, English, Ukrainian."

As they roll up the long driveway, Delilah whistles.

"Eehng-gay!" The entire house is surrounded by the burnt stalks of whatever had been growing in the field. Gar wonders if she is regretting her agreement to keep it a secret. "What am I going to do with you?"

Baseball-cap-in-hand, Gar knocks. Standing on the front step, looking back over his shoulder at his grandmother. Delilah waits in her rusted Winnebago. Window down.

Greysen's adopted daughter answers the door. Eadie Neyananoosic. Blonde haired and blue-eyed. Her younger nephew Sion peaks out at him from the dim interior.

"What do you want?" Eadie crosses her arms. She wears a stone around her neck, sharpened to a point like an arrowhead.

"Is Greysen home?" Gar's eyes focus on the obsidian, watching the way the light reflects off the puckered edge. Eadie wraps her fingers around the polished stone.

"Daaaad!" Eadie yells over her shoulder. Sion retreats back inside somewhere and away from view. "There's some kid here to see you!" Then she too disappears into the house, leaving the door open. He waits for Greysen to appear.

Greysen lopes down the stairs from the second floor. His short-cropped hair is speckled with grey, his face bristles with white stubble like a shaved porcupine. Mid-forties maybe, not nearly as old as Delilah.

"Eh." Greysen frowns down at him. "Can I help you?"

Gar shuffles his feet, grasping for the right words to explain, to admit culpability, but also to express his sincere regret. He really *hadn't* meant to light the field on fire too, that had been unintentional. The fire though. It had been perfect.

Greysen looks out past Gar, sees Delilah smoking, windows rolled down in the Winnebago, ember glowing on inhale, raising and lowering the cigarette from her lips. He nods in greeting, then shifts his focus back to Gar. Gar hangs his head, not meeting his eyes.

"Boozhoo Mr. 'Noosic I'm sorry to bother you but my grandmother drove me out here so I could apologize for burning down your field I didn't mean too I was lighting a fire and it got out of control and I never meant to damage your crops I really am sorry." The story came out in one drawn-out sentence, with no pauses or breaks to take space to breathe, so his lungs were almost out of breath by the time he came to the last word, but he just wanted to get it all out at once, and not draw out the moment any longer than necessary.

Greysen stares at him, as if weighing him with his steely eyes, and stony expression. Gar waits, wishing he would say something. The moment stretches. And stretches. Greysen's eyes bore into him. Gar shuffles under that gaze, wants to be anywhere else but there. He looks away but keeps looking back to see if the man is still staring at him. He feels like an insect under that unwavering gaze. A magnifying glass that can see all his flaws. He feels like scum.

"That's very admirable of you, to own up to what you've done." Greysen's eyes still betray coldness. "There's been no major harm—I was leaving my fields fallow."

And Gar lets out his breath.

"But," Greysen adds, "you did damage some of my fencing. An apology isn't good enough. Your fooling around could have cost somebody their life."

If Gar thought his eyes had been cold before, they were now icebergs. Gar feels frozen in place. Held in place by their weight. And Gar knows Greysen is right. He messed up, messed up big time. He really is out of control. He really does deserve this judgement, he really does deserve this cold condemnation, this swift dispassionate sword of justice. All he can do is wait for that axe to fall and cut him down. He deserves it. He wants that axe to fall if only to get it over with and put him out of his misery.

Greysen scrubs his hand across his face. Exhales. "But jail is no place for a boy your age. Jail is no place for any of us. That's White man's justice."

"Sir?"

"Come back this weekend, and next, and the one after that. I'll put you to work, and you will repair the damage. You will work until you've repaired all the damage that you've caused." There is no question in his words, only statement.

"Yes, sir, Mr. Greysen."

Greysen's eyes soften. "You know you can't keep this a secret forever, people are going to find out sooner or later."

Gar turns away from the Neyananoosic's door, feeling eyes between his shoulder blades as he makes his way back to his grandmother's Winnebago, where Delilah sits in the driver's seat patiently smoking. "Greysen give you a good talking too, hey?" They drive away, his Nokomis's laughter filling the van. "Good."

Gar isn't too thrilled at having to work off his apology.

But it could be worse. Duncan and his mom could find out.

Gar arrives at their usual hangout. Peyton, Cadence, and Zeke are huddled under the trees near the blackened field where the totem pole once stood.

"Aniish na?"

Cadence looks at him with narrowed eyes, Zeke's eyes are wide, and Peyton's lip is curled. *Oh shit.*

"Wha-at?" Gar pitches his voice to indicate innocence, as if he doesn't already know, or at least suspect the reason. But hedging, just in case. Maybe some other thing has pissed them off?

"We know that it was you." Cadence cradles one elbow, arm held across her abdomen.

"What are you talking about?" *Fuck, guess not.*

Cadence rolls her eyes and throws her cigarette to the ground. "As if you don't already know—pyro. My brother told me you burnt down our field."

"Did you think we wouldn't find out?" Zeke gestures to the burnt field where the totem pole had once stood, like a giant firepit. "I mean, this is a small community. How many other arsonists could there be?"

"My uncle Oogie carved that totem pole!" Peyton spoke quietly. Arms held at his sides; his hands are shaking.

"What?"

"Really? Uncle Oogie carved that pole?" Cadence's voice is pitched.

"You're fuck-ing dead."

"Just wait. Hold on a minute. Just—come on man." Gar backs up, trying to reason with the other boy. Trying to douse his rage.

AAAARGHHH! Peyton screams as he charges. Fists clenched, head down. Peyton barrels into him, full steam ahead, knocks him to the ground. Peyton's blows are connecting. Gar raises his arms to shield his face, taking punches to the ribs, liver, kidneys instead. He can hear Cadence and Zeke shouting. It's all a smear. He's not sure what they are saying. Encouraging Peyton? Or trying to de-escalate the situation?

Gar manages to pull his knees forward, pops his feet up in line with Peyton's chest, and heaves with all his might, kicking out with both legs like a horse. Peyton is thrown off of him, landing a short distance away. Cadence kneels at Peyton's side. Zeke looks at Gar with an expression of pity. As if he is some kind of unidentifiable species of slug that he's never seen before.

Gar gets to his feet, bloody, bruised, ears ringing. Brushes ashes from his clothes and maintains a backward trajectory. When he's managed a few steps, he turns, shoulders hunched, and limps away as quickly as he can. Feeling like the target painted on his back has returned, and grown in size. It's now a neon flashing sign. *Guilty*.

"'Better run you damn hippie!" Cadence shouts after him. *Hippy?*

"Punkin' instigator!" Peyton shouts after him. *Instigator?*

"Hippie?" He hears Zeke questioning Cadence.

"Instigator?" He hears Cadence questioning Peyton.

"You should know, you know, how they always like to burn things down."

"From the song, you know? Firestarter."

"Ohhh." The sound of Zeke's laughter follows him as Gar makes his retreat.

It is said that *once upon a time*, abading iizan, Wanaboozhoo stole fire from Old Man Thunderbird. He took on the form of a cuddly rabbit, and was invited inside where it was warm and dry. Once the old man fell asleep, Wanaboozhoo stuck his cotton tail into the hearth, lit himself on fire, and ran out of the lodge, carrying the flames all the way back to his grandmother to light her kindling. And it is this fire from which all fire spread.

Mommy is gone. Gone South for work and left him with Aunty Bliss. He plays on the old train tracks, balancing precariously on the metal lines, trying not to fall. Bliss is nearby, sleeping. She is always sleeping, even in the middle of the day. Garion lifts one eyelid to see the whites of her eye, pupil rolled up in the back of her skull, her breath coming shallow and even. The bottle of Rusty beside her, empty, still clutched securely in one hand. She is out cold.

He goes back to playing on the train tracks, balancing precariously on the metal lines, one step in front of the other like Harry Houdini, stunt man, tight-rope walker, hundred-of-feet up, Niagara Falls, the Grand Canyon. He loses his balance and falls sideways onto the wooden rungs. *Oof!* The air rushes out of him. His elbow hits the pulverized stones between the wooden rungs, bright orange flair of pain. He sucks in breath. He doesn't cry. What's the point? Bliss won't wake up and comfort him. He looks at the elbow, skin rubbed raw, blood trickling down his forearm. He'll have a nice scab to pick at in the coming days, and weeks. He likes picking at the dried blood, ripping off the protective seal before the skin has a chance to heal, so a new scab will form, and the process can start all over again. Hurts now, fun later.

He hums to himself. Arms outstretched like an aeroplane for balance as he walks the rails, further and further away from Aunty. This is a dis-used section of track, a *spur* which the forest swallowed years ago. He probably won't get a chance to see a choo-choo since the rails don't lead anywhere. The busy lines run to the north and south, this middle track dead-ending short of Ghost Lake. Dragonflies zip this way and that, bees buzz by, the sun is bright, the day is heating up, and those loud insects—cicada—are also humming loudly to themselves in the trees.

After a few hours Garion gets bored. And hungry. He's tired of eating the sour berries that grow along the track. He isn't sure what they are, but they don't seem to be poisonous.

He shakes Aunty's shoulder. Bliss sits up, clutching her head, hair disarranged, red lipstick smudged, eyeliner streaked. A smudge of dirt on her cheek. "What time is it?" she frowns at the empty bottle.

Garion takes her hand, and they walk back toward the dead end. There had been a terrible accident here once. A train derailment. The old steam-engine could still be found out there, lost a few hundred feet into the trees where it finally came to a rest, four hundred thousand pounds of broken, hulking mass. The crash must have been cataclysmic. Sparks flying. Brakes screeching. Metal on metal. Unable to slow the monster. Now just a rusting bramble.

They walk the remaining length of the spur. Trees edge closer and closer to the tracks, until the canopy closes over above their heads. They are inside the forest. The iron rails hidden under logs and fallen leaves; plants grow up from between the wooden ties.

They make their way back to Grandfather's cabin.

Bliss is passed out again. She is asleep in the hammock outside, even though it's nighttime now, and it still gets cold at night even in the summer. Grandfather is away too, gone into town for some fishing tackle, so Garion is alone. He wants to make a fire. The way he's seen grown-ups make fire. He pads out into the main room, the soles of his Thunder Cats jammies making soft whispers on the floorboards. Lion-O's face glows in the dark on his shirt.

He crumples up newspaper, the Sterling Standard, black ink from the letters staining his hands. Soot streaks the well-used fireplace. He goes outside to get firewood, stacked up logs split into halved and quartered sections, carrying one log at a time to stack in the hearth. He opens the tin with the matchsticks inside, the lid is on hinges, red-tipped strike-anywheres. He scrapes a red tipped match against the mantle and holds the wavering flame to the newsprint, watching words ignite, burning green and orange. The small flames catch the sticks alight, then the larger lengths of timber. He smiles, pushes his shoulders back, puffing out his chest, stands up tall. He's a big boy now. He can start fires all by himself.

The fire burns with vigor, making a rushing sound almost like it is growling as it sucks all the oxygen from the room and sends flames swirling, spinning up the chimney with the sparks and ash and smoke. Snapping and popping as the logs sizzle and the moisture burbles at the sides of the log to escape. He peeks out at his aunt but she's still asleep.

Something makes a thump behind him. He turns back to see that a log has rolled out of the fireplace, it sits on the carpet, burning, still on fire, and something snaps with a loud *pop* within the flames and he flinches. A coal jumps out, thrown out of the fireplace. The burning log and the hot coal now rest on the rug, smouldering. He stands frozen as the fire emerges from the confines of the hearth, crawling out of the chimney like some sort of living thing, growing larger and hungrier the more it consumes.

Garion runs to his bedroom and hides under the blanket the way he does when he has a nightmare, as if the blanket can repel anything. Protect him like a suit of armour. He can hear the hungry thing in the next room, groaning. He curls in a tight ball to make himself as small as possible, and rocks back and forth, and back and forth. He wishes it would go away.

"I didn't mean to, I didn't mean to" he says, aloud. "It was an accident. I'm sorry. So sorry. Please don't be mad. Please don't be mad." The tears sting his eyes, and the room fills with smoke. He chokes, it's hard to breathe.

The monster is roaring now, eyes glowing red under the crack of the bedroom door, the white paint on the wall bubbles and curls, the smoke is black, coiling up around the ceiling. Flames burst through the door with a *clunk* like a fist punching through. Wetness saturates his jammies. He's wet the bed like a baby. The door is on fire, the jets of flame taller than any man, flattening out where they hit the ceiling. And he is coughing, his whole body is wracking with coughs, wracking with sobs, his eyes blur with tears, burning from the clouds of smoke, he can't see anymore, the smoke is too dense, like a dark fog.

--*Bang*--

His grandfather's boot kicks in what's left of the door, it slams open on its frame, smacking into the opposite wall. Shoomsey holds a rag to his mouth, his long grey beard is singed, his eyes squint against the glare and run with tears. He spots Garion on the bed and scoops him up in his arms along with the blanket. They rush back into the main room, which is both living room and kitchen. Everything is on fire, the walls are made of flames, they shimmer like curtains of light. Intensely bright, intensely hot, though the blanket protects Garion from much of the heat, he is *burning*. The pain is intense. Garion screams as they run through the room of fire, dodge furniture, charging toward the open front door, which appears like a doorway to darkness surrounded by a halo of writhing flames. They barrel out into the cool night, and manage to stumble a few feet before Shoomsey collapses to the ground. Shoomsey is breathing so heavily, Garion is worried he might die. Maybe he breathed in too much of the black smoke? They are both wheezing, coughing, gasping.

The entire cabin is on fire. The flames reach up and up and up, singeing the limbs of the nearby trees. Aunty Bliss rushes to them, sobbing, hugging Garion fiercely. "I'm so glad you're alive. You're okay now, you're okay, everything is going to be fine."

"I didn't mean to, I didn't mean to," he says again, like a prayer. "It was an accident. I'm sorry. So sorry…" But then he's crying too hard to speak.

"Shush now." Aunty touches his face, holding his face in her hands. "Everything is okay. You're going to be fine. Everything will be okay." And then she stands back, tears running down her cheeks as grandfather's cabin goes up in flames, smoke rising up to the sky-world like a twist of tobacco smoke. The cabin seems so small now compared to the stars. Though there are no prayers. No thanks. No prayers of thanksgiving, only tears.

"You're alive, and that's all that matters," Aunty says. "Your mother won't kill me." Garion watches the flames, reflected as a twin pyre dancing in his eyes.

HYDRANGEAS

A child died here.

Aanzheyaawin stops at the roadside, gravel plinking away from her boots. There are three wooden crosses staked in the ground, plush toys looped around one vertical crossbeam like garishly crucified teddy bears, their smiles set by context in rictus-grin. Someone has put down tobacco, and a synthetic wreath of flowers. Someone takes the time to care for the small shrine. To replace the mementos with new ones as they moulder. What happened? A car accident? A drunk driver? Were they speeding? Had they hit a slick patch?

"Elk," Aanzheyaawin's twin sister says, reading her mind again. A few flower petals stick to Augus's hair, tangled up in her long tresses. Where had those come from? Their birthday had come and gone last week. It would have been their eighteenth birthday if Augus was still alive.

"Quit that!" Aanzheyaawin waves her hand as if shooing away a mosquito, "I hate it when you go poking around in my head."

"I'm not poking around." Her sister says placidly—which is another thing that irritates her—Augus seems beyond the moodiness so endemic to her in life. Death has changed her.

"The barriers are gone. Your thoughts are as easy to read as the weather. If I look, I see."

"Don't look then," Aanzheyaawin says. And then to keep her talking and to change the subject, or return to the present subject. "It was a moose?"

"Bull elk."

"How do you know?" she asks, then answers the question herself: "oh right… the barriers." Elk aren't as common in the area, though they are making a comeback after their reintroduction some years ago.

Augus grabs Aanzheyaawin's head, and for once she feels like a solid presence instead of a holographic image. Augus's hands are ice-cold, pain flares through Aanzheyaawin's brain, a bright burst of red, sunlight seen through closed eyelids. A flood of information pours into her head like an entire movie with the reel sped-up. It is intense, and it hurts.

—headlights on dotted lines of the road. Streak of an animal with a full rack of antlers. Slamming on the brakes. The car swerves. Screech of tires. Antlers smash through the windshield. Glass kernels in all directions. Car horn blares incessantly like a train. Horns skewer Mushkeg in the driver seat, pinning her the way an entomologist would pin a bug to a balsa-wood board—the metaphor is not Aanzheyaawin's—the dying woman is studying to become an entomologist. For a moment, she sees Mushkeg doing just that, pinning a particularly beautiful bug with an iridized metallic carapace to a balsa-wood board. Antlers puncture her chest. Her neck. Her left eye. Her kidneys. Blood geysers from her body.

Sadie, the passenger, escapes the horns, though she won't walk away from the crash—the car hits the ditch, flips a few times and wraps itself around a tree, creating a concave in the frame of the car, her body gives way, and the trunk takes up the space where her body had been, displacing it to the sides, or crushing the parts that don't displace fast enough.

And baby Jayden. Jayden is in the back seat. The young parents are on a tight budget. Sadie and Wolf hadn't planned on starting a family but are nonetheless delighted. For a moment Aanzheyaawin sees them in a store, they are purchasing a safety seat second-hand, not realizing the product has been re-called—during a certain percentage of high-speed collisions, the locking mechanism that secures the seat can fail, and in this case, it does.

Aanzheyaawin opens her eyes slowly, as if waking up with a hangover, the light slices her eyeballs like razor blades. For a moment she wavers thinking she will lose consciousness, but finds herself kneeling in front of the crosses, grit grinding itself into her bare knees. She's skinned one of them quite badly. Stone rug-burn. She'll have a scab, like a twelve-year-old tomboy version of herself.

Wipes her nose with a knuckle. Hunh. Nosebleed.

"Geez, give me some warning next time, will ya?"

That's why there are three crosses. One for the child, one for the woman driving, and one for the young mother in the passenger's seat. A necklace is laced around one cross-brace, silver engagement ring dangling from the chain. An Mp3 player is draped around the other, ear buds plugged-in to the port. The father had lost his child and the mother of his child in one night.

A shadow threatens to engulf Aanzheyaawin in a wave of grief. She wonders how Wolf manages to withstand the loss; she wonders what kind of music Mushkeg listened to. She reaches out to touch the player and has to resist the impulse to flip through the display screen.

She pictures her sister Augus alive, staying up late to binge-watch some boring romantic-tragedy set in the 18th century, wearing fuzzy pajamas, bowl of popcorn in her lap. Aanzheyaawin can't sit through the program for more than five minutes. She sees Augus sitting bent over at the kitchen table, long hair falling down in a veil, sunlight streaming in, clutching a cup of green tea, studying for an exam, *on the weekend*, on a beautiful day, while Aanzheyaawin is headed outdoors to feel the light and fresh air on her skin. Augus has always been so dedicated. They might have shared the exact same DNA, and look identical, but they are very different people.

"Take it," her sister says. "Mushkeg wants you to have it."

"Does she?" Aanzheyaawin looks around to see if she can spot the presence of still more ghosts—ghosts she can't see—but ghosts which Augus can, apparently, commune with. Do ghosts usually talk to each other? The afterlife is still a mystery.

Figuring she isn't going to get any better permission, Aanzheyaawin delicately removes the music player, silently thanking the dead woman. She clips the small device to her pocket, threads the wires up through her shirt, and inserts the earbuds in her ears. To her surprise, the display screen flares to life when she presses the "home" button, and the battery-bar shows that it still has half a charge. Better than leaving it out for the rain to destroy.

And, she still has a long walk ahead.

She puts the device on shuffle rather than flipping through the music library, but it still feels like an invasion of privacy, or some form of puerile, ghoulish curiosity. She recognizes that she has this curiosity, but resists it. At least when it is on shuffle, every song will be a surprise. *Smells Like Teen Spirit. Mouthful of Cavities. Bobby McGee. What I Got.* Aanzheyaawin is beginning to notice a pattern—all artists that died tragic, premature deaths. Was some unseen hand guiding the supposedly random song selection?

A bit morbid, but the music suits her. Makes every step heavier, and lighter. Sadness weighs her down, but the music lifts her up. The more she listens, the more she feels she would have liked Mushkeg, though it's too late for all that now. She hopes the family won't mind—is she no better than a grave robber? No use explaining that she had permission to take the device, that it was gifted to her through the voice of her dead sister.

Aanzheyaawin keeps walking along the side of the road, gravel crunching under the toes of her boots. Feeling both lighter and heavier. Spruce rise up around her on either side of the road like tall sentinels tracking her progress. No one else can see Augus, so she tries not to talk to the ghost in public. If anyone is watching, they think she is talking to herself. Unhinged by the death of her sister. Mostly they let her be. She sees their frowns; their lips pursed together in pity. They speak, too gently. And maybe they are right? Maybe she is unhinged? Do crazy people always know they are crazy? She is skeptical enough to acknowledge that madness is a more likely explanation than the existence of ghosts, no matter how real they seem.

A car approaches. Aanzheyaawin adjusts her bra, hangs a thumb over the road.

The car passes.

No dice.

Hitchhiking is dangerous, but Aanzheyaawin is confident in her ability to flirt her way out of most situations. What straight guy can resist a pretty girl batting their eye lashes? And if that doesn't work, she can defend herself. She has a right to protect herself. If some dick-weed tries to pull some shit, she will make him regret it.

No way is she going to freeze up in a confrontation. Aanzheyaawin is the wrong girl to fuck with. It's possible these thoughts are bravado—she might not be so brave when push comes to shove and the shoving starts—but she wants to be tough. And she dresses the part; lip ring, low-cut tank, tight black cut-off jeans, jean jacket, combat boots.

She walks with a determined stride, crunching down gravel towards Ghost Lake. Maybe the same stretch of road her sister disappeared from one year ago, while hitchhiking home from Sterling, never to be heard from or seen again.

At least not alive.

Augus's ghost appeared seven days after her disappearance and, real or imagined, this convinced Aanzheyaawin there was no hope of finding her sister alive. She has been hitchhiking alone everywhere ever since, for the better part of a year. She often wears short skirts, and low-cut blouses. The clothes and what they reveal are the lure—but this pretty girl has claws: glazier-points crazy-glued to the underside of her black-lacquered finger-nails, a can of pepper-spray, a switch-blade, a stun-gun, a butterfly knife, and the OTF (Out-The-Front) spring-loaded telescopic joker-knives built into the soles of her combat boots. You can find anything on the internet. And her jewelry provides more than decoration: the cold stainless steel of a razorblade around her neck is actually sharp as fuck. What she's doing is dangerous, but she isn't unprepared. She feels like *James Bond*... or an Anishinaabe *Buffy the Vampire Slayer*.

The police don't really care. They barely bothered looking for Augus—no body, no crime—just another missing Indian, just another missing or murdered Indigenous woman. God knows, there are enough of them—what is one more? Laissez-faire. Open season.

No one would look for her. No one would care.

Aanzheyaawin knows for certain Augus didn't run away to live on the streets of Sterling or the Twin Cities. Augus would never pick up and leave like that, not without some warning, not without telling Aanzheyaawin first.

And Aanzheyaawin can't let the murder go unpunished. Since the ghost showed up, she has no doubt this is what happened. Her sister was murdered. She wishes Augus could give her some answers, but Augus isn't able to answer even the most simple questions surrounding her disappearance. And Aanzheyaawin, more than Augus, is the one who can't let go. The living haunting the dead.

It isn't called *Ghost* Lake for nothing.

The sun sits high in the sky, hours before full dark. Sweat trickles down her back, making her curse her Gothic fashion sense. She sticks out her thumb and tries to hail the occasional car that flies by sending up a cloud of dust—but so far... no dice. The sun beats down. She takes off her jacket and carries it, unable to stand the weight of it on her shoulders. She hates to have her arms encumbered, but still finds it preferable; she can no longer swing her arms freely, but at least the breeze dries the sweat before it has a chance to bead.

And besides—she isn't really alone. She has her sister for company.

A pickup truck drives by sending up a cloud of road dust. The hick in the driver seat slows down long enough to leer at her out the window, but for some reason doesn't bother to stop and give her a ride, despite the universally understood symbol of thumbs-up. "Fucking pervert!" she shouts at the tailgate of the receding pickup.

"Did you fucking see that guy?" she says to her sister.

Augus doesn't answer… she often stays quiet.

Augus's voice comes out in a rasp when she tries to talk, probably owing to the manner in which she died. Aanzheyaawin's guess is *strangulation*, though her vocal cords could have been cut too. That would explain the blood. Augus still wears the white shift she'd been wearing. Clean and recently pressed, except for the slashes of crimson that never turn that brown shade of dried blood—they stay as fresh as the day she died. A few flower petals stick here and there to the smears.

Augus is semi-transparent—translucent really—like certain species of jellyfish. Aanzheyaawin can see right through her form to the passing scenery beyond—grazing cattle, and mounds of farm-stones, probably piled up when the first amichigoozi began farming here years ago—before treaty even. *Settlers*. Augus' bare feet float above the roadway. When she walks, her feet don't touch the ground, they hover two inches above the gravel. She is out of synch with this world, walking half in this world, and half in some other, unseen world.

Still, her sister manages to get enough traction to keep pace. Aanzheyaawin supposes the dead don't have to worry about working up a sweat, or things like hot and cold. Or much of anything at all really. The worst has already happened. Augus is dead.

So Aanzheyaawin keeps walking. And walking. And walking.

She raises her arm, holding out a thumb to a passing motorist, expecting to be ignored by yet another vehicle. She barely turns to look at the SUV as it slides by, having given up hope of catching a ride. Not really believing this car will stop, while so many others have driven by.

But she's wrong.

The SUV slows and pulls over onto the shoulder. There isn't much 'side of the road' to pull onto out here. Just bush. But the guy manages to unblock most of the lane, not that there's much traffic to worry about. Some yahoos like to drive way faster than they should, just 'cause they're out in the country and there aren't many cops around. That doesn't mean they should drive like maniacs.

Looking down into her purse, she tests the stun-gun, it glows with an electric blue sizzle. Smiling, Aanzheyaawin jogs forward, already anticipating the air conditioning blasting full on her face and the scenery gliding by outside the window at a less plodding rate. When she reaches the SUV the side door slides open.

"Hop in." The driver nods toward the door. Mid-to-late thirties. Indian. Shaggy salt-and-pepper mop of hair that doesn't look like it's been combed recently, but held in check by a bandana like Cheech or Chong. She forgets which one is which. One eye is discoloured like her grandfather's glaucoma—but this guy doesn't look like a stoner—the other eye holds her gaze with intensity—despite the dopey smile.

"Going as far as Tyner's Creek?"

He nods, and she hops into the car thinking *beggars can't be choosers*. Augus follows with a waft of floral scent. The sliding door closes with pneumatic smoothness, hydraulics slowing it down so the door can't be slammed shut, no matter how much force you use. What if you want to slam the door? she wonders.

You would be foiled by technology when you want to storm off in anger.

The man hasn't offered her the front seat, and when she climbs in, she can see it is already occupied. A box has been strapped in with the seat belt, so it won't go flying if he has to come to a sudden stop. The box is closed so she can't tell what's inside, but Aanzheyaawin is happy to sit in the back. It gives her more personal space, and there is less chance the guy can 'cop a feel' if he is so inclined.

"I'm Aanzheyaawin. Are you from around here?" She tries to catch his eye in the rear-view mirror. He turns the key in the ignition and pulls back onto the road, stones flung up by the tread of the wheels behind as they accelerate.

"Fanon," the man reaches back to shake her hand, keeping one hand on the wheel. The vehicle is still in motion. "I come out to visit my Auntie Ogers."

"Aanhh, is that Edna?" Aanzheyaawin feels the knot of tension in her shoulders loosen now that she is able to place this guy within the sphere of her social galaxy, the local web of who is related to who, and by how much, and how distantly.

"Yeah. You know her?" Fanon's glaucoma-filled eye seems to swirl with interior galaxies, his hand keeps straying to the box in the passenger seat, stroking it like he is petting a dog.

"Yeah, of course," she laughs. "Everyone knows Edna Ogers." What she doesn't say is that the woman is a crackpot. Edna Ogers is a recluse who lives out in the swamp, some sort of crazy cat lady. But beyond the run-of-the-mill gossip, Aanzheyaawin knows little about the woman.

The air-conditioning is on full blast. She leans back in her seat, enjoying the cool air, watching the landscape slide by outside her window. Mentally counting the steps she won't have to take to cover that distance. Fanon looks back at her in the rear-view as he drives, one milky eye staring off kilter. His teeth are sharp, especially the fang teeth, like a wolf or coyote.

Her sister Augus has grown quiet, or rather, she is speaking, but without sound. Her lips move urgently on mute. Aanzheyaawin has seen this before and she has a theory. It is like there are rules. Augus is dead, and therefore, is not capable of unduly influencing the outcome of certain events, to intercede, or to pass on certain information—Aanzheyaawin doesn't know whether she is being prevented by some mysterious rules of the universe, or whether she is simply unable to get her message across.

Is she trying to warn her of something? Is she trying to say something about the shrine? Aanzheyaawin scans the trees ahead for the appearance of an elk streaking across the road to freedom and their certain death, a new set of crosses left to decorate the roadside where they crash and burn.

"What's your poison?" Fanon interrupts her thoughts of collision and fiery death.

"Hunh?" Aanzheyaawin grunts.

"Your headphones." In the rear-view he points with a quick protrusion of the lips. "What are you listening to?"

Aanzheyaawin forgot she has her earbuds plugged in, set at such a low volume the strains of the stringed instruments are barely audible, background noise, hardly registering in her conscious awareness. She has to concentrate for a moment to distinguish the artist.

"Dandelow." An old noise-grunge band that is still played on 64.5 SRS sometimes, another roadside catastrophe that ended in flames. Before the car crash, they had been local celebrities for achieving a modicum of success.

"I didn't know anyone still listens to those songs..."

"It's not mine." Aanzheyaawin holds up the small device. "A friend gave this to me." The lead-singer's vocals sob through the disjointed, off-key strains of the song.

"I knew him." Fanon's voice is deep and gravelly. "Jared. The lead singer. He had so much talent." The Dandelow song winds down, ending in a strangled sort of cry as the notes recede.

The road seems to connect them. What are the chances they all have so much in common? Jared self-destructed—or so this is the popular narrative—drugs, alcohol, and possible suicide—the rock-and-roll lifestyle of 'live-fast-and-die-young.' The Dandelow song appearing on the dead woman's MP3 player, herself a car-accident victim—maybe on the same stretch of the road where Jared crashed and burned? Maybe the same stretch of road where her sister went missing?

Fanon is talking again. Something about Jared, and the shows he used to attend, the house parties and living-room jam sessions. It's clear that before their dissolution, the band had been close to his heart. Fanon seems harmless enough, though Aanzheyaawin can't help putting him under the microscope. For all she knows Edna Ogers' nephew could have murdered her sister.

"You know, it's not safe for you to be hitchhiking," Fanon's words immediately get her guard up. Is he threatening her? She eyes Fanon again. What is in the box he keeps touching? Strapped in like a safety seat, his hand rests on top of the cardboard. "That's why I stopped to pick you up, you know. I know I'm not a sicko, so I'd rather be the one to give you a ride, because that way, at least, I know you'll arrive safely."

"Thanks—I guess." Aanzheyaawin is not convinced Fanon isn't a sicko. "Lots of teenagers from the rez hitchhike—it's in the middle of nowhere, it's the only way to get around if you don't have wheels." There are always stories of girls going missing, being raped, all kinds of things. "It's not like there's a bus. Can't afford a taxi every time I want to go into town." Sometimes you could wrangle a ride with friends or relatives with a working car. "Besides—everybody knows everyone around here."

"You know a young girl went missing here last year?" Fanon adjusts his rear-view. "They still haven't found her." And every muscle in her body goes tense. Aanzheyaawin has to fight the urge not to lash out in some way. To keep her voice level, to speak evenly.

"I know," Aanzheyaawin says. "I read about it in the paper." Which is true, she has read about her sister's disappearance in the paper. The article implies Augus ran away, that she was "troubled" like so many "high-risk youth these days," and that she might one day show up again, whole and unmolested.

"Maybe you should consider a different means of transportation," Fanon's star-filled eye meets hers in the rear-view mirror, his free hand strokes the cardboard box, like something precious.

There is a high-pitched keening sound. A tinnitus mosquito ringing in her ears. It slowly grows louder. She knows it's only in her mind, but it drowns out all other sounds. Fanon is still speaking, but she can't make out the words, all she can hear is the high-pitched keening. KEENING.

Aanzheyaawin can't stand it anymore. She *has* to know what's in the box.

When Fanon's eyes return to the road, Aanzheyaawin springs forward and pulls apart the inter-leaved flaps of cardboard.

Bones. The box is filled with bones.

She lurches back, gasping. She'd been prepared for the worst, but she'd been just as prepared to discover something mundane, and make a fool of herself for invading his privacy.

Augus's ghost is still speaking, still saying something, but her raspy voice is still on mute. No sound issues from her spectral throat. Whatever words of warning she sought to relate, it is already too late.

Aanzheyaawin throws open the side door. The vehicle is still moving. Fanon hits the brakes, and the SUV fishtails as they come to stop. Aanzheyaawin has her seat belt off, and she tumbles ungainly into the front passenger's seat with the bones. Aanzheyaawin does not reach for her knife, or one of her other weapons. She reaches for the door handle.

She is out of the vehicle and down the street in seconds, tears stream down her face as she runs down the road. Fanon stands leaning out of the driver's side of the vehicle, one elbow on the roof of his car as he shouts something after her, but her head is too filled with emotional static, chaos and noise. He is on mute now, just like her sister. She can't decipher the words. All she can see in her mind are the bones.

The bones of her sister.

Fanon watches her retreat but makes no move to chase her down. And after a few moments, he shrugs and gets back into the car. Gravel is thrown up from the wheel treads and leaves a cloud of dust in his wake. Aanzheyaawin keeps running, grateful that for whatever the reason, Fanon chose not to hunt her down.

She flags down the next car that comes down the road, waving her arms and blocking the road, not really giving the motorist a choice. Not really giving a shit what she looks like, with her tear-streaked face. This is an *emergency.*

The truck she flagged rolls down the driver's side window.

"What seems to be the problem, miss?" White. Middle-aged. Straw hat and denim. It is the same hick that drove by earlier ogling her. His brow is creased with concern.

"Please, I just need a ride home." She quickly explains what happened, she had been getting a ride from a stranger, and the driver freaked her out. She omits the fact she thinks he might be a murderer. Downplaying her fear.

"You better get in. I can take you to the police if you want to file a complaint."

"Oh, thank you, thank you," she says, coming around to the passenger's side and climbing up into the vehicle. Augus sits between them. Aanzheyaawin sniffs and wipes at her smeared eye-makeup in the vanity mirror as they drive. Black mascara bleeding like dark tears. The man does a three-point turn and heads in the opposite direction, back into town.

"...what a freak. The guy had a box of bones on his front seat."

"You know it's not safe to be out here hitchhiking by yourself." The man speaks gently, like a kindly father. "You never know what sorts of people you're going to run into." The truck doesn't have very good shocks, and they bump and hobble over potholes in the dirt road.

"Thanks for stopping to pick me up mister—?" Aanzhey draws out the hard "t" sound of the *terrr* in mister, framing the silence as a question. There is something familiar about the guy, like maybe she's seen him around town, the post office, the bank.

"—Menthol." He holds up a lit a cigarette, menthol flavoured wisp of smoke rising, and then takes a puff, red heater flaring. "Like the cigarette." The car's ashtray is overflowing with butts.

Aanzheyaawin watches the scenery slide by, tears sliding down her cheeks. She wipes them away. "Maybe I overreacted? But why else would he have those old bones?" It is odd that Fanon didn't chase after her if, in fact, she discovered human remains in a box strapped to the passenger's seat. And, if he was a murderer, would he have let her get away so easily?

"Ghost Lake is known for its unusual stratigraphic record—folks are always coming across fossils around here."

Menthol is right. She has no real proof that the remains in the box were human, let alone her sister's—they could be the remains of some prehistoric creature. Aanzheyaawin had reacted on pure emotion, instead of taking the time to stop and think, and consider the situation. And wasn't that what he shouted after her as she ran away? Something about the museum? Fanon might even work for that new museum they're opening up.

Her rescuer makes a turn, and she becomes aware that she has lost track of which route they are taking. Aanzheyaawin's hand goes to her side, the place where her purse should be, filled with weapons. The butterfly knife, the pepper spray, the 8.8M-volt taser. It isn't there. In her haste, she must have left it in Fanon's van, or shed it along the roadside somewhere.

"Missing something?" Menthol asks.

"It's nothing." Aanzheyaawin smiles.

They make another turn. She knows most of the country roads around here, but isn't sure where they are now. She grips the grab-bar beside her tightly, even though they aren't speeding.

"Where are we going?" She tries to keep her voice level.

"It's a short cut," he says. Aanzheyaawin tries to relax. There is no use jumping to conclusions—again. The man who rescued her doesn't make much small talk. His hands grip, un-grip, and re-grip the steering wheel as if to relieve some tension. The dirt roads get smaller, and less unfamiliar.

Has she jumped out of the frying pan and into the fire? Aanzheyaawin hugs her arms to her chest. Augus sits between Aanzheyaawin and her rescuer. Like a statue. Like she's been put on pause and mute.

Aanzheyaawin glances sidelong at her rescuer, absently playing with the razor blade she wears around her neck. The man is old, but not ancient, with a slight paunch to his belly, rather slovenly dressed, plaid work-shirt, jeans muddy around the cuffs of the pant-legs, work-boots with un-tied laces. He is unremarkable, and in this area, rather forgettable. There are probably a dozen or so men similarly dressed in a ten-mile radius to their immediate vicinity. No one would look at him twice.

"You can use the phone in the kitchen," Menthol says as they turn to bump down a long driveway, farmhouse set far back from the road. "This sort of thing shouldn't go unreported."

Aanzheyaawin says nothing, and tries to take stock of the situation. She still has the spring-loaded knives in her boots and weaponized jewelry—razor-blade necklace, and the barbs under her fingernails. Menthol parks sideways on the lawn in front of the porch, switches off the engine, hops out and walks around the vehicle to open her door. Aanzheyaawin slides out of the high truck, still fondling the razor at her neck, ready to yank hard on the chain to break the clasp, and slash at her potential attacker.

But all he does is hold the door open, and smile. Conciliatory.

She follows the man up to the porch, a tense ball of energy, holding her arms close to her body. She pauses at the bottom of the steps, not wanting to proceed further, but when the man looks back, she quickly steps-to to disguise her hesitance. She doesn't want to let on that she is suspicious. Doesn't want to give up whatever advantage she has in being prepared for malicious intent—if there is any malicious intent. She doesn't know for sure. Any more than she can be sure about Fanon and his box of bones.

"... my perennials are coming along nicely now, I just have to watch with all this heat that they don't get too dried out—" Menthol is talking, making small talk, maybe trying to put her at ease.

The second she enters the farmhouse, the man whirls around and smashes an open fist into her face. Knocks her on her ass, and leaves her dazed. The blow came so quick, and though she had been wary, the sudden violence still surprised her. He grabs her by the hair and drags her down the hallway. Aanzheyaawin cries out, hating how weak she sounds, hating how quickly and entirely she lost control of the situation, writhing and kicking as he drags her further into the house. She reaches up to grab his wrists, to take some of the pressure off of her scalp so hanks of her hair won't rip out. But that just makes it easier for him to pull her inside. She digs in the sharp glazier-points crazy glued to the underside of her nails, rakes them down his arms, clawing, but the barbs stick into the meat of his forearms and are quickly wrenched out, only good for one good scrape. He grunts, but ignores the rivulets of blood that flow.

His arms are like tree trunks. She doesn't know how she ever mistook this man for a dumpy-looking farmer. It is as if a mask has been dropped, the slight paunch to his belly and slouch to his shoulders are gone.

The hardwood floors of the hallway give way to the patterned linoleum of the kitchen, and then his knees are crushing her chest, one hand gripping her wrists and pinning them to the floor above her head, the other forearm choking her. The weight of him makes it difficult to breathe. She struggles to draw breath, squirms and bucks, but he has effectively immobilized her with a few deft movements.

The man smiles down at her, teeth gritted. He is enjoying the power he holds over her. Hurting her. Her pain and terror. She can see it in the gleam of his pale green eyes.

Augus has followed them into the kitchen and stands watching impassively as the drama plays out.

"Augus!" she croaks through her crushed windpipe, even though she knows her sister can't help. Can't intervene.

The man follows her gaze, then looks back down at her, head quirked to the side.

"So you knew her, did you?"

Aanzheyaawin isn't sure if he sees her sister's ghost, or whether he is simply responding to her plea. Aanzheyaawin's eyes widen. This is as much as a confession. This man—this is the man who took her sister away from her—this is the man who murdered Augus.

For a moment Aanzheyaawin can't see. Her vision goes red, like sunlight seen through closed eyelids, like her vision is again being eclipsed by the vision of a strange woman's death on the side of the road. Every muscle in her body screams, rushing with adrenaline, filling with impotent, stupid strength.

"My. Sister." Aanzheyaawin chokes out the words.

"How lucky." The man smiles again, his teeth discoloured, rotten, gap-toothed. His breath smells like menthol cigarettes, minty and pleasant. She wonders if this was one of the last things her sister sensed.

A plate flies off the counter and smashes on the floor. Shattering. It isn't much, but it is enough to distract the Menthol man. He pops up and twists his body to the left as he turns. The pressure lifts off her neck, and his weight re-distributes so that her legs now have a range of movement that wasn't possible a moment before. Aanzheyaawin takes a breath—thanks the manitous she kept up with her workout regimen over the past winter—and triggers the spring-loaded blades imbedded in the soles of her boots, she swings her feet up and forward until she feels her toes thud into the man's shoulders as both blades sink in.

His body goes rigid as he cries out, fingers curled, reaching back to the site of the injury. Knives puncture muscle and grind against bone, blade to shoulder blade. Aanzheyaawin finds that her arms are now free, though she is still pinned to the floor by the weight crushing her chest, and rather than let the fucker recover, she performs the same maneuver again, swinging her legs up and forward, the inch-long OTF knives telescoping into his back and scraping across bone. She only wishes they were longer.

Menthol screams. But rather than reach uselessly toward the injury, his thick hands find her neck and squeeze. The blades have already done their damage, entrance and exit. He leans forward, his face florid, spittle flying from his lips. *This is not good* Aanzheyaawin thinks as his hands tighten their grip and squeeze, and squeeze, and squeeze—he wants her dead. But the fact that both his fists are now clamped around her neck also means she has both her arms free. Aanzheyaawin grasps the razor at her neck, and pulls, ripping the steel from its clasp and breaking the chain. She brings the sharp edge up in a diagonal sweep across the bridge of his nose, splicing open the flesh like over-ripe fruit. Blood sprays across her face, and the two halves of the wound created by her upward slash hang down in grotesque flaps, white bone glistens in the opening like a pearl.

Menthol tightens his grip, and brown splotches appear at the edges of her vision, and she knows if those splotches coalesce, the darkness will envelop her, and that once the darkness takes hold, it will never let go. She brings the sharp-edge of the razor down in a diagonal sweep across his forehead, grazing one eye-lid and cheek, missing the soft egg-whites of his eyes recessed in the brow-ridges of his skull, but slicing open the meat and exposing shimmering fat—the sight alone sends a surge of exhilaration through her veins. She feels like celebrating. Doing a happy dance. She's injured him! But still, he doesn't let go. He doesn't let go. He doesn't let go. And she knows, no matter how badly she injures the man, no matter how ghastly his disfigurement, she will be dead, and he will still be alive.

If. He. Doesn't. Let. Go.

Slash. Slash. Slash. Slash. Slash.

In desperation, she brings the razor back and forth, slicing his face into ribbons, white bone gleaming amongst the red, stringy bits of skin hanging down from his skull like the stringy bits of vegetable matter inside a pumpkin. A spaghetti squash. The face above her a horror-movie skeleton. *Jason and the Argonauts. Iron Maiden. Return of the Living Dead Part II.*

Menthol no longer seems human. Maybe he never was, maybe he is some sort of monster in human form, and all she has done is reveal the horror that lies hidden beneath. How does he not pass out? Why is he not screaming in pain? How can he still be intent on murder with his face ripped off? It doesn't seem possible.

More dishes and plates fly off the shelf. Corning Ware. Stoneware. Crockery and glass. A butter dish. A metal tray. Then utensils—forks, spoons and knives—they all come clattering down, spilling chaotically from an upended drawer. The cupboards fly open and entire stacks of tableware come tumbling, smashing against the linoleum floor with a deafening crash.

Is the disturbance a result of their struggle? Or is Augus trying to help? It's possible the phenomenon is a manifestation of her own psychic trauma. Maybe Augus's ghost isn't real? Maybe it's all in her own head, a hallucination, imagining spiritual assistance where there is none. A crutch she has come to rely on to get her through a hard time. A crutch that has given her the strength to continue and that led her here. To this moment.

But what worked once as a distraction, does not work again.

The Menthol man ignores all distractions as he squeezes the life out of her, even when the toaster flies across the room and cracks him in the back of the skull, and shards of broken pottery rain down from more kitchenware. Even then, he continues to strangle her. How he can ignore the pain, she doesn't know. It doesn't seem humanly possible. As if he possesses more-than-human strength. Something supernatural. Like someone possessed. To continue to pursue the offensive, to seek to bring about her destruction with such implacable will, no matter what sort of resistance he encounters, no matter how much damage he assumes; he wants her dead.

Only moments have passed, but when you can't breathe, it feels like an eternity. Aanzheyaawin knows that sometimes it only takes seconds to choke someone out. She probably only has seconds left to make him loosen his grip. Changing tactics, she gives up on slashing the man's face, and goes for the tendons and veins standing out starkly in relief on his neck as he continues to strain. New flaps of skin appear, dangling like strips of paper-mâché from an effigy. Flour. Water. Newspaper. More blood rains down, splashing against her face, her eyes, her lips. The warmth leaks out of him to decorate her face.

Menthol brings his forehead down in a vicious headbutt. She sees a bright flash and feels her horizon-line tilt. Blood drips into her mouth, metallic like a rusty bobby-pin, her lips working uselessly like a fish, blood drips into her eyes making them sting, obscuring her vision.

But the new tactic works. The grip on her neck finally loosens. The hands are removed, and she gasps, drawing oxygen into her lungs to feed her veins and her starving brain, though she can't see—she is now blind—from blood filling the recesses of her eyes. Or maybe the brown clouds have coalesced? Maybe she passed out as he bucked and moaned on top of her?

She senses the man, sitting on his haunches, kneeling over her. And then for a moment, she sees herself, as if she is watching from one corner of the kitchen. All that is light, is dark, and all that is dark, is light, like an inverted photo negative, x-ray vision. Watching through her dead-sister's eyes? Lying broken and beaten on the tile-pattern of the linoleum floor, gasping for breath, covered in sweat and blood, Menthol kneeling next to her, his hands clutching at his own neck to prevent the blood from spurting from his body, applying pressure to staunch the flow.

Maybe she hit an artery? One can only hope. Aanzheyaawin wipes the blood from her face with the denim sleeve of her jacket, and can't help lamenting the mess this creates. She'd never be able to get out all the bloodstains. Strange. The thoughts that go through your mind in moments of crisis. But at least she can see again, see again with her own eyes.

Menthol man stares down at her, the orbs of his eyes seem to protrude unnaturally from his skull, his hands wrapped around his own throat, as if strangling himself. He stumbles to his feet, trips over her in his floppy boots, and begins digging around in the kitchen drawers. Aanzheyaawin sits up, drinking in the air greedily, breathing deeply like a deep-diving swimmer coming up for air, gasping, hyperventilating. Her neck is probably black with bruises where his hands gripped her throat.

What is Augus's murderer searching for? A knife, or maybe some other weapon? It isn't a bad idea—and Aanzheyaawin too, looks around for something to defend herself with. She still has the bloody razor blade clutched in her hand. Her fingers too, have been sliced open in the vicious assault, the blade cutting both ways, and no doubt she will need stitches. But the razor doesn't have much reach, and she doesn't want to get that close to her attacker again, not if she can help it. She still has the switchblades imbedded in the soles of her boots, and she is deeply thankful that she invested in them. She longs for the butterfly-knife in her purse, or the ballistic knife she saw advertised somewhere, now regretting she hadn't purchased that too—though it is illegal—all the weapons she carries are illegal. She could be law-abiding, or she could be dead. She could have tried to make do with a pocketknife, but where would that have left her when she was being pinned to the floor and strangled?

Aanzheyaawin staggers to her feet, leaning on the back of a kitchen chair. She picks up the chair, holding it front of her like a lion-tamer, hoping the man doesn't have a firearm. Menthol pulls out a roll of duct tape from the drawer, not a knife or a gun, and wraps the duct tape slowly around his neck. His movements are jerky and uncoordinated, like he is being controlled by the strings of a marionette.

He turns back to Aanzheyaawin with a rictus grin. As if he is pleased with the makeshift bandage. He smiles, even though his face is basically ground beef, bone gleaming through strips of mutilated flesh. How can he still smile like that? How can he still find amusement? The muscles in his cheek must be screaming in pain, forced to drag up the corners of his lips—that smile—that smile is insane.

He lurches forward, and Aanzheyaawin screams, brandishing the kitchen chair, making herself loud and large, like she's been taught to scare off black bears—though she doesn't think it will scare off this predator. He pauses, head tilted to the side, grin affixed to his face.

He has no weapons, but that doesn't mean he isn't dangerous. He is a killer, a murderer.

"Where's Augus?" She screams, her voice is hoarse.

Menthol takes a step towards her. Aanzheyaawin brings the chair down on the man's head, the wood shatters into splinters, like they are in a wrestling ring, and the chair is made of kindling. Wishing that it was made out metal.

His body buckles and absorbs the impact, but he doesn't go down. He looks at her, with that same gruesome smile ripping apart his face. She no longer has the chair to use as a shield. She turns and runs. Racing down the dark hallway, ripping open the screen door, and dashing down the front steps.

When she reaches the truck, she turns to look back to see if he is following her, but the entrance to the house is dark, the front door hangs open on its hinges. The truck's engine makes quiet *plinking* noises beside her as it cools. She looks at the long driveway, and knows that if she takes off on foot, he'll be able to chase her down in the truck. And even if she makes it out to the road, these country thoroughfares are so rarely trafficked, there is no guarantee she'll find safety in flagging down another vehicle, or making it to one of the neighbours' houses in time.

Augus touches her temple. Cold pain blooms inside her brain, a vision of a shovel, hanging suspended from a rusty nail. "In the barn."

Aanzheyaawin stands for a second waiting for the dizziness to pass, then takes-off down the side of the house, just as she hears the screen door slam, crushing flowers and ornamental plants under her boots. She peeks around the corner to see the sicko, his hands holding a rifle as he casts about for his quarry. There is a *machete* tucked under the belt at his waist. She has little chance fighting against a bullet.

At the side of the house there is a stand-alone garage, and further back a small shed and an old barn. She makes her way towards the wooden structures, gaps between the faded grey boards, snatching quick glances over her shoulder for signs of pursuit. She ducks into the dim interior of the barn and finds the shovel, exactly where Augus showed her where it would be, hanging from a rusty nail. She feels a lot safer with the wooden handle griped in her bloody fingers—the metal spade sharp, and serviceable.

"OLLY-OLLY-OXEN-FREE!" The murderer shouts as he ambles around the side of the house. "COME OUT COME OUT WHEREVER YOU ARE!"

Aanzheyaawin raises the shovel like a baseball bat, and stands with her back to the sliding door, waiting for her would-be-killer to come closer. Despite all the injury she has doled out, the man still seems insanely confident that he can dominate her.

"RED-ROVER, RED-ROVER I CALL ANZHAAY OVER!"

How the fuck does he know her name???

The second he steps foot into the dim interior of the barn, she swings the shovel, beaning him on the head with a clang, and he goes down like threshed wheat. His eyes are open, but she can tell he isn't dead, merely stunned.

"Where is my sister?"

She places the point of the shovel at the joint between kneecap and shin, then she hops on the shovel to add weight to the dig. She hears things inside the leg pop and shift, though the shovel is too dull to sever the leg.

The cry he lets out is mewling and so full of pain as to be pathetic. She doesn't care. Not after what he's done to her sister, and probably to other women too, and what he planned to do to her.

"Where. Is. My. Sister?" She places the point of the blade at the intersection of the left knee, between tibia and patella. "Tell me."

The man gasps, breathless. His eyes shift from side to side, as if searching for some escape, before focusing on something in the distance. Aanzheyaawin turns her head to follow his gaze. The hydrangeas in the front garden. Looks back at Menthol to make sure she's accurately judged the trajectory. Something clicks into place inside her brain—matted hair and flower petals stuck to blood on a white dress.

"She's under the hydrangeas?"

Menthol's irises wobble minutely as his pupils dilate and constrict. Radial striations of amber shrink and expand amidst the predominance of grey-green. She can read the answer in his eyes, as good as a poker tell. A slight floral scent wafts into the barn on the breeze, cooling the sweat on her brow. Confirmation.

Aanzheyaawin hops on the shoulders of the spade, driving the point of the steel though ligaments below the femur, feeling the kneecap pop and shift. The man moans in agony and then goes silent. Unconscious. He won't be walking again any time soon. The last injury was probably gratuitous, but she doesn't want the psycho limping after her with a machete if he comes to.

She grabs the rifle and the shovel and heads out to the hydrangeas. Next to the rose bushes in the front garden, a profusion of beautiful flowers. Clusters of pale petals in a gradation from blue to white and yellow, like a cluster of butterfly wings, opening and closing as they cling to the same branch, their wings tremble in the breeze. The man is quite the gardener she notices, now that she isn't in a blind panic.

Aanzheyaawin falls to her knees, in front of the hydrangeas. The shovel clanks to the ground at her side. Tears stream down her face. Augus stands nearby in her blood-stained white dress.

UNDER THE ICE

Zachaeus went under the ice last winter.

I try to identify the exact spot on the rippling waters where my brother fell through, but I can't find it. Even when I fix my eyes in one place, they go cross-eyed and un-focus. I don't even know if these are the right coordinates. I know the general area where it happened, but the exact spot where he stood when the ice gave way? That's as unclear as my sliding vision.

"Come on Zaude. Let's check out Marsh's beach." My cousin Zeke, trying to distract me. Almost as if he knows what I'm thinking. Maybe he does. It wouldn't be that hard to guess. I continue staring at the water, searching for the right spot on the shifting surface.

I have a flash of sensation, like a psychic vision, though it's probably only my over-active imagination, teasing out the unknowns, filling in the gaps where there are gaps in knowledge. How it *feels* to die like that.

Water, land, sky, trees. Choking darkness. I can't breathe! I can't breathe! Panic-thoughts of near-death survival. Then I'm back in the here and now. Bobbing rhythm of the lake, gentle waters, white fluffy clouds. My mind fills in cracks in the mortar:

driving wind and the ice-cold shock as frigid waters soak through the layers of clothes he'd worn that day.

I know his first thought before he plunges through the ice is probably not for himself—it is for his camera. His stupid fucking camera. A vintage 35mm single-lens reflex with some fancy viewfinder. All the bells and whistles. Telephoto lens. High shutter speed. And he dropped it.

I imagine the way it happened like this:

Zach takes off his gloves to get a better shot, his numb fingers quickly lose feeling. They'd been aching from the cold even before he removed the protective insulation—but he is an artist, artists must suffer for their calling. The lanyard that should have affixed the camera to his neck is torn. It is a school camera, and even though it is well maintained, students are rough on equipment. He borrowed it from the A/V room and had to sign a waiver.

Now he watches it skitter across the ice. He knows that he shouldn't take one step further out onto the ice—he's gone as far as it is safe. Actually, it isn't safe to be out on the ice at all, there's been a recent freeze and thaw, freeze and thaw—it hasn't been consistently cold enough, for long enough, for it to be truly safe. All snowmobilers know this—they watch the weather network as religiously as his great-auntie's sudden Alzheimer church-going.

"Zhangweshi came to me in a dream." Ziibiiwenh stares up at the ceiling, her face puckered with wrinkles. "She said I should be more spiritual."

It is a subject of interpretation. "Maybe Zhangweshi meant sweat lodge?" Aunty Zelda's face breaks in laughter. She has a fondness for purple.

"Do you ever wonder how it all started?" Zeke again, breaking through the cobweb of my thoughts. He's paddling lightly now, hasn't bothered to drop the outboard motor. Wearing his usual basketball shorts and jersey. Almost thirteen years old now. It's too nice to disturb the quiet of the day with engine noise.

"How what started?" I frown. He's got me.

"You know, the zed-naming."

On Ghost Lake our family is known as 'the Zeds' (or, alternatively, as 'the Zees,' depending on the level of Americanization). This is based on our tradition of naming children only by names that start with the letter Z. "I doubt there's any Z-names left," Zachaeus once said. "We've used them all up already!"

No one knows how the tradition began. I think it's rooted in the Ojibwe language, with the Z-names of our great-aunt's, Ziibiiwenh and Zhangweshi: Little River and Walks From The South. Great-grandmother's name, Zilpah, is a corruption of Ziibaa'a'ii-Zegaanakwad—Under Stormy Skies.

"I think it's a fluke." I look up at the blue sky, puffy white clouds, the ribs of an extinct species. "Some ancestor decided to name all their kids with zeds. There you go. Tradition."

"There must be something more too it. You know? A reason." Zeke is paddling with more energy, we're making headway. I track our progress by a distant point of land as we pass Drinker's point. No one wants to risk deviating from the practice of Z-naming—just in case. If nothing else, it does provide a sense of kinship.

"I think Zilpah knows, but she's not talking." Anyone with a Z-name in Ghost Lake is bound to face the inevitable question: *are you one of those Zeds?* We have the real estate cornered on Z-names, and most folks take this into account when naming their kids.

Zeke paddles. I lapse back into morbid thoughts.

Zach scrambles forward, reaching for the stupid digital camera. Crab-walking, distributing his weight, reaching, reaching.

The first responders hand my mother the camera. A silent answer to her unspoken question. I flip through the developed film, trying to be calm, the ache in my chest as tight as the pain he must have felt, the hypothermia clutching a fist around my heart. I feel nothing, I tell myself as I flip through the pictures. My heart is as cold as the ice and snow. My heart is as unfeeling as the water that clogged his throat. Forcing its way into his lungs with undeterrable pressure.

Imagining. He's still safe and warm. Imagining him as he was. Safe and warm. Before the open casket. Kissing his cheek. A cold clammy shock. The feel of his flesh against my lips. Breathe. Breathe. I must remember to breathe.

Shots of his friends. Goofy cross-eyes, and crowded hallways. Lockers receding to the distance in vanishing-point perspective. Shots of the lake. Skinny leafless trees shivering like knobby knees, clacking together, shivering in the wind. Ghost of after-image smears. The sun in opposite relief, all that is light, dark, all that is dark, light. Like old-school, in-camera, over-used music-video effects from the 1990s. The sun is a black hole. The snow-swept landscape is a void. The trees and few bits of shade, appear as pure light. Bleached of their colour. High-school art-class photography bullshit. It looks nice. Not nice enough to be worth dying over. Stupid bastard, I think as I flip through the glossy four-by-sixes. What an asshole. What a complete jerk. I am so angry with him for being so stupid.

It only took a moment of stupidity to end up dead.

One mistake. That's it. One mistake, and, universe: couldn't you just have looked the other way? I myself have fucked-up so many times, and yet, I'm still here. Like that time I drank a bottle of vodka and chased it with prescription pills. My heart is still beating. Why can't my brother be as lucky?

More photographs. Zachaeus smiling, shamelessly taking selfies of himself. Smug. Disarmingly charming. Horizon of frozen ice and sky. Blurry something-or-other on the ice. Something or other? Something small, or maybe it is just further away, further in the distance? Perspective is playing mind games with my 2D depth perception. What is that? Some bit of fluff on the lens? No, there it is again. And again. Bare those ears. He's taken off his toque for the selfie, arm extended, hair sticking up in a disarranged mess. Ears red from the bite of the cold wind—

unobstructed, whipping across the bare, frozen lake. But there. Over his shoulder, in the distance. There it is again. Is that a face?

I know human brains are geared for facial recognition—I heard it on the radio—about how babies learn to recognize faces, and distinguish one face from another. A large percentage of our brains are devoted to facial recognition. That's why you can see a face in the notches on a dresser drawer, or in the gaping windows of a burnt-out building, or in the static on television. If you stare for long enough, shapes begin to form, but they disappear the moment your focus snaps back to alertness—but no. It is clearly a face. But an odd face. Could it be some trick of photography, some mirage of exposure, or grain on the film? There are many reasonable explanations. It almost looks like a dog.

A dog with teeth. A *lot* of teeth. And what are *those*? Blur of movement, like the quick succession of blades from a fan, too quick for the shutter-speed to pick-up on. Are those wings? The smudge appears again and again in the last succession of photos. Am I imagining things? Is my mind playing tricks on me? Do I want so badly to make sense of my brother's death that my brain is inventing mysteries? I stand up, going into the kitchen to dig through the drawer to look for the magnifying glass Zilpah uses when she is reading the paper.

I adjust the desk lamp to provide more light—I don't have macular degeneration like my great-grandmother but the thing in the image is so blurry. As an additional measure I grab Zilpah's reading glasses, perch them on my nose like a librarian. The bifocals bring the photo into focus as much as the magnifying glass, especially when I hold my head at an angle.

Yes. There it is. Something. A something. A thing with teeth and wings. I can see the grin of its receding-fractal-teeth. Misshapen bulbous snout. *What the fuck?*

"Zaude?"

My shoulders tense, and I'm broken from my intense focus. Spooked by the sudden interruption. I look up at my mother Zoe, bifocals perched precariously on the tip of my nostrils.

"Why are you wearing your great-grandma's reading glasses?" Zoe wipes her red eyes, puffy from quietly crying in her room, and tries to smile.

"You have another child to look after," I overheard aunty Zelda tell my mom. "She's lost her brother. You can't wallow away in your self-pity. You need to be strong. For Zaude." So here she is, swamped in her own grief, but still trying.

"Zach's pictures." I splay my hands out across several of the photographs.

"He had so much talent." Zoe tears up again.

"Why did Zach die?" I try to distract her.

"I don't know." Zoe's voice is hollow. Her eyes stare out the window, cherry blossoms shiver in the breeze. Uncle Zeamus had been so convinced they'd be able to survive in this climate, south facing window with full 180-degree exposure to the sun. He was right, in fact they defied the odds and thrived, they hung on tenaciously, when by all rights they should have shriveled up, turned brown, and fallen off their stems a long time ago like all of the other flora. The stuff of summer.

"No, I mean *how* did he die?"

"What do you mean?" Zoe looks at me, new worry pinching her face like frost burn. "He drowned. Or if they pulled him out in time, it was the hypothermia killed him."

"Are you sure?" I asked. "What exactly did the coroner say?"

"Why are you asking these questions?" My mother's brow furrows, her posture changes, suddenly attentive. For the first time since they dragged her son's body from the lake, Zoe is actually *looking* at me. "Do you know something we don't?"

"No. No. It's just these pictures..."

"What about them?" Zoe steps forward and pulls on Zilpah's reading glasses. Her eyes huge behind the lenses. Face inches from the photograph I'd been inspecting. "What am I supposed to be looking at?"

"That." I put my finger on the blurry shape of teeth and wings on the ice.

"It kind of looks like a dog." Zoe's curls bounce with the shift of her voice.

"I know," I said. "But it doesn't really look like a dog. Not really."

"It's too blurry. I don't know how you can tell." Zoe's nose is two millimeters from the photograph. "It could be a wolf or a coyote?"

"It doesn't look like any coyote or wolf I've ever seen." I shuffle through the photographs and place the magnifying glass over the shape. "Look at this one. Look at those teeth!"

"So that's why he went out on the ice. He was trying to save the dog! It wandered onto the ice, and Zachaeus was trying to save it!?" My mother's mind whirling, constructing senseless hero-narratives.

"Did they say anything about any injuries?" I tuck a strand of hair behind my ear, so it doesn't obstruct my vision. "Bite marks maybe?"

My mother's breath comes in sob-rattled intakes, barely suppressed. "She said that other than his ear, there were some 'lacerations' but that those were also likely caused by the ice. She said that Zach was the only one on the ice. Nothing to indicate ... foul play... no reason to believe this was anything but an accident." Zoe is just repeating the same things we all know, that we've all been repeating to ourselves, and each other. Trying to make sense of the senseless.

"If it was a dog, what happened to it? Maybe Zachaeus managed to rescue it? Do you think it could still be wandering around the Reserve somewhere?" Zoe's voice is suddenly hopeful. Imagining skinny Rez dog wandering around snow-swept ground on skinny trembling legs like a new-born calf. I feel like garbage.

"We could always check the pound," I say, not wanting to dispel Zoe's fantasies, or expose my outlandish hypotheses. I wrack my brain trying to remember the name. The name. The name I've only heard in Nokomis' stories. Gah, I can't remember. I'll ask Zephyr… and if she doesn't know, I'll ask Zilpah.

"Where are you going?" Zoe is examining the photograph—but turns her attention to the voice on the other end of the telephone, dial tone finally making way for a connection. Her eyes are huge behind Zilpah's lenses. Glasses Bird from *Alice in Wonderland*. "Hello. Yes. Have you picked up any new dogs recently…?"

I walk down the hall to Zephyr's room. The floorboards creak. The *Days of Our Lives* soap opera blares from tiny television speakers and vibrates through the wood door as I pass great-grandmother's room. "I might be half deaf and half blind," Zilpah likes to say, "but it's better to be half of one and half of the other, than to be all of one, or all of the other. No point in sitting around pitying yourself. It's still better than the alternative." It's clear here—the alternative is death.

I suppose being a bit deaf and blind is better than being dead. In contrast to Zephyr and Zoe, Zilpah didn't have children until later in life—Zelda, Zephyr, Zeno, and Zozep—she is now quite elderly, though she still has her wits about her. Passing great-grandma's room, I continue down the hall to my grandmother's room. Rap on the door politely with my knuckles, Nokomis' voice emerges muffled from the depths.

"Bindiigen." *Come in.*

I turn the knob. The smell of sage and sweetgrass cloys to fabric; curtains, clothes, bedspread. Scent envelopes me in a warm hug. I feel welcomed by the medicines. Zephyr is playing Killer's Kreed on her game console, a realistic avatar dressed in full Renaissance garb walks down crowded Renaissance streets.

"Aaniish na?" *What's up?* Zephyr doesn't look up from the screen, her avatar now somehow on the rooftops overlooking the city of Venice. Zeph's dyed hair, freed from braids, flows well past her jawline, tucked expertly behind ears. The same colour as a flamingo, or the girl's toy-aisle at the Big Box store in town. I never really thought anything of it, until I realized not everyone's grandma changes the colour of their hair as often as the weather. Or has so many piercings, or so many tattoos, or wears clothes that could have passed for a Halloween costume on any day of the week.

Nokomis is a forty-something year-old grandmother and can only be described as "Goth." Zephyr got pregnant when she was thirteen, and my mom Zoe had both her kids young, at age fifteen and seventeen. So Zephyr became a grandmother at twenty-nine when I was born, and again at thirty-one with my younger brother Zach. I'm seventeen now, and I have no plan on continuing the tradition of early teenage pregnancy. Accidents happen, but I've had '*the talk*.' Repeatedly. I've been given condoms, oral dams, birth control and other forms of contraceptives from the moment I started to bleed.

"I'm not sexually active!" I pointed out.

"Yes, but when you decide you're ready, you'll be prepared," Nokomis told me. I've gotten '*the talk*' not only from my mother and grandmother, but also from my great-grandmother.

"Nokomis?" I peek around the doorframe.

"Yes, honey?" Zephyr doesn't look away from the screen where her 17th century armour-clad avatar leaps off of a tall building and swan-dives into a muddy canal.

"D'you remember that story you told me about those monsters?"

"The wiindigo?" Zephyr still wears her work scrubs, pale grey with a subtle skull-and-cross-bone motif, which is probably as far as she can push the dress code. When she's at work, all her piercings and jewellery are removed, but the hair colour stays the same, pulled back into two, neatly plaited braids.

"No, not that one."

"The Flying Skeleton? The Ooghouls?"

"Not them."

"Bgwaji-nini?"

"You said they're shadowy little people, with wings, like a butterfly."

"Memengwesiag?"

"Memengwesiag!" That's it! "Will you tell me the story again?"

"There are many stories about them. Sometimes they are seen as an omen. Good or bad. In the scarier stories, they're not only tricksters, they're deadly. They steal our people and bring them into the rock—like that canoe-carving of those two headless boys. You remember?"

"Eenyanh." *Yes*. I've seen the rock carving. It comes into focus in my mind, the two headless boys, the shape of the canoe—I feel as if it has some kind of greater significance.

"They were out fishing on the lake one day, near the rock bluffs at the water's edge, all those little alcoves, inlets and bays where the water follows the twists and turns of the rock-wall. No one really knows what happened to them *for sure*. Some say it's the memengwesiag who stole those boys. Captured their image and brought them into the crag-stone, not far inland. Decapitated them, stole their heads and canoe, and only left the bodies behind."

"What would they want with their skulls?"

"Your guess is as good as mine," Nokomis shrugs. "I've heard they like meat."

Maybe there's still hope. Zachaeus wasn't decapitated. His left ear had been shorn off. Sliced cleanly, presumably by a razor-shard of ice as he dropped through the fractured surface. They had taken nothing else. He hadn't been beheaded, but he still drowned. Or froze to death.

What would they want with his *ear*? I wonder. I know I am placing too much weight on Zephyr's story. But everyone grieves differently, and it gives me something to think about beside the gaping hole in my chest. A hollow ache that makes my breath come tight, as if I am the one who is drowning.

"Why don't you ask your aunt Zelda? Or your great-grandma Zilpah? They know more than I do." That's what everyone says when I try to ask about anything. They all say someone else knows more than they do.

I leave Zephyr with her assassin, swimming gamely in the muddy canal. I walk to Zilpah's room, and hesitate before knocking. LIKE SANDS THROUGH THE HOURGLASS SO ARE THE DAYS OF OUR LIVES. Through the door I hear the soap's intro again. Talking to Zilpah can be frustrating. English is not her first language. At one time she spoke solely another language—our language—Ojibwe or Anishinaabemowin, though it doesn't feel like mine. Like most families haunted by the legacy of the Indian Residential Schools, there has been a break in the transmission of knowledge. Though I know some words, I am far from fluent. My brother Zach was better at picking up on the language. And Zilpah is quite deaf—so speaking to great-grandmother has additional challenges.

I knock loudly so that great-grandmother will hear over the television with her poor hearing. She is always misplacing her hearing aide. Zilpah opens the door a crack so I can see one dark eye peering out, as if she expects Mormons or Jehovah's Witnesses—which is crazy, since grandma Zeph never allows them past the threshold. Like vultures, they sense Zilpah's advancing age, and hover around so they can fight over the soul that must be hidden somewhere inside.

"Hi, Nokomis." I speak slow, and clearly.

"OH, IT'S YOU!" Zilpah seems to shout. I remind myself that great-grandma isn't shouting, it's just hearing loss. "BINDIIGEN! BINDIIGEN! LET ME TURN THIS THING DOWN." She hustles over to the flat-screen and lowers the volume on a remote control with an incomprehensible number of buttons. Her ropey arms are wrinkled with loose skin.

"Aaniish na?" Zilpah is quieter now with the volume low. *How are you?*

"Nishkide'e, idash-nmno-bmaadiz," I say. *I'm sad, but doing alright.*

"Giin iinshe. Zachaeus apane gaa-mashkawindibe." *Poor thing. Your brother was always so headstrong.*

"Great-grandma, will you tell me about something?" I peer around at her cluttered room, old family photos on the wall, woodland style paintings, a small sitting area, a bed, bookshelves, a hand-woven rug, bundles of gathered medicines hung up to dry on a bedside lamp.

"Of course, what is it?"

"The memengwesiag. Will you tell me about them?"

"Ohh them! Those little people don't have any noses. And they have razor sharp teeth, strong enough to chew through a clothesline. Nimama used to complain about it—our camp backed up onto the river here, just as ours does—"

When lots were drawn up for the re-establishment of an on-reserve community, Zilpah was vocal about selecting the site where our family traditionally made camp. She is old enough to remember the place, and wanted it as our home even if it meant fewer services from the Band so far out from the subdivision and business area they plotted out.

"—they stole our clothes if Nimama left them out on the line too long...." Zilpah continues. "Little thieves. After the garden was plowed, they'd come out to eat the churned-up grubs, just like dragonflies. I saw them once when I was very little, but that might've been my imagination."

"What did they look like?" My eyes are drawn to the window, in the distance I see greenery at the end of our allotment where the land slopes. Beyond that is the river.

Zilpah squints into the middle distance. "They're hard to see—like a blur of movement out of the corner of your eye. They have wings like a butterfly. Memengwanh. That's where they get their name. Their wings inflate and deflate like lungs, and sound just like voices. Sometimes, at night, I heard them talking."

I imagine the clacking of chitin. I imagine the four overlapping wings of a monarch, branches blocking the setting sun, blood red receding to a dark brocade interrupted by a pinprick of stars. Startling colour, like the stripes on a yellow-jacket, or the orange of a pylon.

Great-grandma brushes at invisible lint on her bedspread. Star quilted. Dust swirls in the sunlight. "The hum of wings or voices. They have rough skin—some say because they were made out of tree-bark by Nanaboozhoo or one of his brothers. But I think they are creatures of rock. Camouflaged to blend in with the cliff walls. That's where they live. In those twists and turns of the bluffs overlooking the water."

Ok, so maybe dun-coloured like a moth? I imagine wings like a Rorschach inkblot, the mirror-image halves mimicking the eyes of a predator.

"Mewinzha… *a long time ago*, there were some Ghost Lake Indians on a hunting expedition, and they made camp close to the cliffs. They were slowly roasting moose meat over the fire like a rotisserie dinner. It smelled so good, those memengwesiag couldn't resist. They stole that wiiyaas. And the hungry 'Nishnaabek took chase. They hopped in their canoes and followed the creatures, who rode in their own little canoes made of rock—which were somehow able to float!"

"The 'Nishnaabek almost caught up with the creatures—but they disappeared into the cliff face bluffs—into the rock itself. Maybe their molecules vibrate at a different frequency, the solid rock is like open space—they can pass through it, like a doorway. The hungry Indians drew their bows as the memengwesiag entered, but the arrows rebounded—unable to pass through.

"That's why people say not to fish in those waters, or make camp too close to the bluffs. Memengwesiag don't like 'Nishnaabek eating their catch. It's a matter of respect, not to poach on their territory—or you risk provoking them."

Our house isn't far from the bluffs. I played there as a kid, trying to climb up the slimy, moss-covered surface, impossible without the aid of that old knotted rope, slipping back to splash screeching with laughter down into the water. Leaping to splash from the heights.

Zilpah's story makes the memengwesiag seem so alive. As if they are real, living beings, who sometimes play tricks, and steal things. It's almost enough to make me believe. Almost.

So now I'm here with my cousin Zeke. Out on the lake. In a boat, just like that carving of the two headless boys—but we still have our heads. I want to investigate the scene-of-the-crime—the place where the memengwesiag stole the moosemeat. I also wanted to see the place where my brother Zachaeus fell through the ice and drowned. But I didn't tell Zeke.

Unlike the two boys, our craft has an out-board motor, which we could use if we chose to. But I don't want to make too much noise, or create too many waves. It might spook the spirits if there are any lingering around. We stick with the paddles.

Cousin Zeke must think I'm crazy, but he's always up for an adventure. A breeze tousles his black hair and his paddle flashes energetically. He's a good kid, Zeke is. The sweat dries at my temples but trickles between my shoulder blades. I wish I hadn't worn a bra. Too hot. I wear my hair in a single braid, so it won't whip around in the air. Sunlight sparkles on the water, a mesmerizing shift of compartmentalized, ovoidal, many-faceted shapes, a kaleidoscopic effect of endless reflection—as if Gustav Klimt painted Claude Monet's *Water Lilies*. Zoe has prints.

When we reach the place great-grandmother described in her story, we scramble onto shore, and drag the boat up after us so the current won't steal our craft. The bluffs rise up to our left, but here the coast is scalable. We head inland through the bush, ducking under branches, and zig-zagging thorny patches.

"I think it's this way." Zeke indicates uphill with his lips.

"I think we're getting close," I say, even though I'm not sure.

The carved standing stone is near a place called the Burnt Grounds. We've both seen it, but that was years ago. What Ghost Lake kid hasn't played amongst the mysterious stones? A place we are warned against, but that only makes it more interesting.

By the time we reach the top of the rise, we're both breathing heavily. At least it's cooler under the trees. Then we step out of the tree-line into a clearing. Ground zero. It's called "burnt" because nothing will grow here. Not even a blade of grass. No one seems to know why—not even the old people.

"Do you think there's something toxic about the soil?" Zeke frowns. "Or something radioactive?" Maybe parents have good reason to keep us away from the place. I shake my head at our own recklessness in disobeying our elders. It's like the surface of the moon, or another planet. Various sized boulders lay around like rubble. Maybe there had once been some sort of stone structure here?

"It's even creepier than I remember." The strangeness of the place didn't bother me when I was younger. Maybe I've become less reckless?

Zeke is examining a standing stone. I join him, gravel crunching under my rubber boots. The slab rises overhead, a twelve-foot obelisk, but not so rectangular that it couldn't have been formed by natural processes. I run my hands over the surface, feel the indentations. The graven image is reddish brown. Maybe because of the iron content? And the iron is rusting, like a scab. It dribbles down in dried-blood rivulets. Almost as if it is bleeding. Some of the reddish-flecks flake away with the touch of my palm.

Rather than being carved *in relief*, the icon is *engraved*. An upwards-curving slash of a line like a flattened smile forms the shape of a canoe. The two headless figures are formless lumps. Who created this image, and why? Could it have been one of our ancestors? One of the Ghost Lake Anishinaabek from a previous century? Or the memengwesiag? Who steal and cause trouble, even if they are mostly regarded as harmless—except when they are stealing people. Or could it have been put here by someone or something else?

We take leave of the Burnt Grounds and return to our boat. Zeke is at the helm paddling as I push us out from the shallows. Rubber boots keeping my feet dry.

"Let's go along the bluffs." I steer with my paddle and Zeke shifts sides to cooperate, so the craft turns. "I've heard there's rock paintings there."

The bluffs start small, rising higher as Zeke and I go by. We pass the place where I used to play as a kid, pitching our bodies from the top of the cliff, to splash limbs akimbo into the leech-infested waters, screeching with delight and terror as we scrambled back up, pulling ourselves hand-over-hand up the old mammoth-sized knotted rope. It's been there for as long as I can remember. I wonder what kind soul placed it there, and where they acquired such a thick length of rope. It has weathered many winters, the erosion of the elements, and still seems sturdy as the day it was strung into place.

We continue on. There is no shore along this stretch, the cliff face descends into the waters of Ghost Lake, becoming impossible to scale from above or below, so it's only accessible by boat. Fishing is supposedly poor here, though if Zilpah's story is accurate, maybe the reputation arose as a cautionary measure?

—Whooooooo, whoooo. Whoooo, whoooooo—

There is an odd howl. Zeke and I look at each other. We freeze, allowing the boat to drift. Neither of us speak. I can see sweat beading on Zeke's brow. Lip curled. One eyebrow raised. Other eye squinted. The wind dies down and the sound recedes. We wait. The breeze picks up and ruffles Zeke's messy hair.

—Whooooooo, whoooo. Whoooo, whoooooo—

The sound comes again, like the sound the culvert under our driveway makes when the wind hits it just right. A haunting sound; like a train, or an owl. A sound filled with longing and loneliness. But maybe I'm projecting? Imbuing feelings into things that don't contain those qualities in of themselves. Still. It feels as if it does. Longing and loneliness.

—Whoooooooo, whoooo. Whoooo, whoooooo—

The rippled sound fills the air. Zeke's head swivels, as he tries to discover the source of the odd noise. "What's that sound?" He speaks quietly. Weweni. *Gently.*

"There must be some sort of formation in the rock." We hear the sound every time there is a gust of wind. "Come on let's get closer." I paddle to bring our boat alongside the stratified layers of rock rising up from the lake. We maneuver so our craft is parallel to the cliff, and I place my hands palm-flat against the stone. Damp moss and lichen.

"Paddle us forward but keep us even," I tell Zeke.

As he paddles, I feel the uneven surface of the cliff flat against the palm of my hands, grazing by as we slide forward, until my hands suddenly fall forward *through* the stone, and my arms appear to be imbedded in the solid rock. It takes a few moments for my eyes to adjust to this new visual paradox. The stone doubles back on itself, like drapery, and blends so seamlessly together, I can't detect where one rock face begins and where the other comes to an end, though my physical body can't be fooled by this optical illusion.

"Whooah!" Zeke sticks out an oar to explore the mirage, "I didn't even see this cavity. It's virtually invisible." The fold in the rock is wide enough for our small boat.

"Let's go in."

"Alright." Zeke shrugs.

Having the forward position in the bow, he paddles while I steer from the back, digging my paddle in the water on our right so the aft swings around as Zeke provides propulsion. And just like that we are surrounded on either side by bluffs, a narrow channel in the rock, rising up twenty feet on either side of us. The temperature drops dramatically in the shade, the sunlight seems so distant above us. We glide forward, and the way opens up into a small grotto, a small gravel shoreline, and the dark entrance to a cave. This is what must be causing the wind to howl as it passes across the opening.

"Far out, man." Zeke's habitual impression of hippie slang is without irony; he's always had a fondness for the trappings of a generation not his own. I blame his dad.

We drag our boat up onto the tiny sliver of pebble beach, and clamber out, hopefully far enough onto dry land that the current won't take our craft. There isn't much space for me and Zeke and the boat on the skimpy bit of shore before the rock rises up sharply again in a sheer cliff. We poke around the cave entrance, about an arm-span across, and stick our heads in, hearing that ghostly howl as the breeze follows the channel of rock. *Whoooooo, whooooooo, whooooo, whooooo.* My suspicions are confirmed.

"Well," I look at Zeke, "you wanna check it out?"

"It's kind of dark in there, Zaude."

"Give me your lighter." I dig through my backpack and pull out a small coffin-kerosene oil lamp. It's compact but provides a surprising amount of light. It's an antique. I bought it at a garage sale for fifteen bucks from that hermit-guy who lives up on the hill near the observatory.

Setting the lantern down on a rock at the entrance to the cave, I pump the tank a few times to make sure there is enough air pressure in the cavity of the fuel well, give a quarter turn on the valve to release kerosene into the globe, and light the mantle with a flick of Zeke's lighter. Once the flames die down the glowing mantle gives off a steady, pure-white light, free from the flickering of candlelight, or even electric voltage. Slight hiss of propane like a barbeque. Delicate silk mantle like the cocoon a spider weaves to trap its victims. There is nothing snared inside this web except distilled light. Difficult to look at without leaving after-image scars burnt onto the field of my vision when I look away.

I hand the coffin lantern to Zeke. "Lead the way!" And we pick our way carefully into the cave, staying to one side because a channel of water continues on into the darkness. After twenty paces or so the channel ends in a wider pool, though the cave continues on into darkness. We had *not* brought the proper gear for underground exploration—flashlights, helmets, maybe some food and medical supplies, and some sort of emergency rescue beacon—it isn't wise to venture far. Our cell phones won't work here; they didn't work half the time *above* ground given our distance to the closest radio tower. There's zero chance they'd work surrounded by solid rock.

I can't help but to compare our current situation to the one Zachaeus placed himself in the previous winter. Him out on the ice. Us exploring a mysterious cave that no one knows about, and that is virtually invisible even upon close inspection, when no one knows where to look if something were to happen. Yeah, not smart. About as smart as going out on the ice after a freeze and thaw.

And there are the inevitable questions. *Was he depressed? Did he get into a fight with someone at school? Or with a family member? Could he have been suicidal?* I know my brother wouldn't commit suicide—not to say that he wasn't capable of it. Given a terrible set of circumstances, anyone can be pushed to desperate actions—only I know he didn't.

The cave smells of moss, and dark growing fungus, and cold rock, clammy and moist. It doesn't smell unpleasant, but it's not pleasant either. Water dripping. Muted whistle of the entrance in the distance *whoooo-whooo whooo-whooo whooo-whooo* each time the breeze whips across the hollow in the stone. The sound becomes distorted the further we go into the cave, somehow jumbled and backwards by the acoustics of the space; *ooohw-ooohw, ooooohw-ooohw, ooooh-oooohw.* Oooohw instead of whooooo. Strange and disjointed. Almost musical.

Zeke raises the lantern and shadows seem to race away from us at lightspeed, but I know this is a logical fallacy, the shadows aren't quick, the shadows don't *move* anywhere. The shadows were here first. It is *light* which is the interloper, and can only ever arrive second—or last. Whichever way you want to look at it.

With every wave of his arm, Zeke throws shadows from the stalagmites and stalactites into a frenzy, curving and elongating and stretching themselves away from the lantern, topsy-turvy like a tilt-a-whirl. I have difficulty tracking how far into the cavern we've come. The space opens up into a larger cavern, with multiple passages leading in different directions. More than one way to go. I look up, wondering how many tons of rock are above us. I know we aren't very far from the opening, but the weight overhead feels oppressive.

A flutter of wings beat the air, and I imagine the delicate wings of a freakishly sized moth. Then I see a furry-bodied creature backlit against Zeke's lantern, and I scream. I can't help it. I'm freaking out, and in the process upsetting more of the animals, who take to the air in the enclosed space, clicking and chattering in high pitched voices, and displaying tiny, vicious teeth. Like smiling monkeys with leathery wings.

"Chill, cousin." Zeke spreads his arms wide. Shadows swirl like a merry-go-round. "They're just bats!" Realizing this is true I take a few deep breaths to steady myself. Just bats. Just bats. These aren't nightmarish fairy creatures or leprechauns. Maybe bats are what inspire stories of small people with butterfly wings? Over time, even a small change in the telling makes a big difference. Like a game of telephone, errors can snowball.

My scream echoes and re-echoes through the chamber and into the network of tunnels. It seems to go on forever, bouncing and rebounding in ghostly mockery, like a smaller and smaller mirror of my voice, opposite and equal in reverse as the design on the sides of a moth's wings. Maybe the vibrations from my terror will multiply and cause the eruption of a volcano on the other side of the world? Or trigger an earthquake under the ocean that will then trigger a tsunami? My thoughts spiral down with my cry. The echo does reveal one thing though, it shows just how deep these caverns go.

Once I've calmed down, I look around at the rock formations. Stalagmites and stalactites form over hundreds or even thousands of years, one droplet at a time, with infinitesimal deposits of minerals—some are as long and thin as a knitting needle. Others are round and fat, or form large conical-shaped columns all the way to the ceiling. They glisten in the darkness like stone icicles. The many-fanged jaw of some monstrous beast. And we are willingly walking into it.

I examine one of the spikes, razor sharp and delicate, pitted where water acidity has eaten into the softer deposits. Something catches my eye. A glint of something reflective maybe, flashing for a moment as the lantern light glances off the object at the right angle. I make my way over to a rounded stalagmite and wave Zeke over.

"Shine the light over here," I whisper. I don't want to cause more echoes, imagining the flutter of a moth's wing, and tsunamis in the south pacific. I can almost imagine that I hear the flutter of wings beating the air as the sound of my whispers are recycled by the acoustics of the space. *Over. Shine. Here. The. Light. Here. The. Light. Shine. Over. Light. The. Shine. Here. Over. The. Over. Light. Shine. Here. Light. Hero verrr Liiiight*. Echo and re-echo of my words, overlapping and drowning each other out in a uniformity of consonants.

"That's weird," Zeke says. *Weird. That's. Weird. Weird. That's. Weird. Weird. That's. Weird. Ear. Ear. Ear. Ear. Ear. Ear. Ear. Ear. Ear. Eeeeeeaaaaarrrrrrrr.*

"Sssssshhhh!" I hold my hands to my ears. *Ssshhaaah. Ssshhhhaaah. Ssshhhaaah. Shush. Shush. Shush. Shush. Shhhhuuuuuurrrrrrrrrrrggghhh*. The sibilant sounds somehow end in a long drawn out growl.

—Definitely, that is weird—

Like seeing your movements in a mirror differ from your own movements, echo and re-echo suddenly seem divorced, taking on merely an incidental connection, rather than an indexical relationship, one with an independent life of its own.

Zeke adjusts the barn-doors on the lantern so light falls onto the object which caught my eye, the source of the reflective flash. It is a knife. Not just any knife. I recognize this knife. It is Zach's knife.

I recognize the fleur-de-lis design on the handle. The loopholes for fingers mould to the shape of your hand like something organic. He wore it, strapped to his hip in a leather sheath on his belt. A birch-bark harvesting knife. A hunting knife. An opening-a-can-of-beans-when-we-couldn't-find-the-can-opener-knife. An all-purpose knife. I would recognize it anywhere. It can't be confused with one off the shelf, not with those fleur-de-lis marks. Zach chiseled them into the pommel himself.

I pick it up. Let out my breath. Hadn't been aware I was holding it, until I let it out. Zach's knife. This is Zach's knife! But how had it gotten here? Breathe. Breathe. I have to keep reminding myself to breathe.

"Are you all right?" Zeke whispers. He whispers so quietly the acoustics of the space are unable to pick up his words, amplify or rebound them back in a distorted multiplicity of voices.

"This is Zach's knife," I say, not bothering to whisper. My lips are moving on autopilot, absent of any intonation or inflection. *This. Zach's. Is. Knife. Zack's. Knife. Knife. Zach's. Knife. Is. This. Zzzzzaaaaacccccchhhhhhh.*

—OMG. That was freaky—

Me and Zeke share a look, his eyes are probably as wide as my own.

PLOP

There is a wet *shplocking* sound, like a suction cup. We both turn toward the source. Glistening, ruddy in the angled fall of bisecting light. The cartilage jiggles slightly from the recent impact of landing, from wherever it's fallen from. Or been tossed.

A folded bit of flesh, rounded, curling in, and around, and back on itself in progressively deeper wells. There are stringy pieces attached that must be skin. It rests in a small pool of blood that looks almost black. The blood looks fresh.

Zeke grabs the coffin lantern in one hand and grabs my arm in the other. The rest is a blur. I know I'm crying as we scramble back the way we came. Retracing our steps, as carefully as we can towards the opening of the cavern. Running through a dark cave with uneven footing would not be a wise move. I take the knife, but we leave the ear.

I don't know if I learned anything from our little expedition. But I think the memengwesiag are real. Spirits are real. And occasionally something happens to remind you of that fact. If you burn yourself on a lantern, you're more likely to show it proper respect in the future. Even if you don't understand how it works.

… And Zach. I might as well blame a lynx for eating a rabbit, or a storm for drowning a sailor, or any other force of nature. I could just as well blame the cold for killing him—or the lake water for drowning him. It's not about blame.

Some people say that the memengwesiag are benevolent spirits. Some say they are malevolent; but maybe the truth is they are neither good nor bad. Maybe, like a force of nature—like thunderstorms, or lightning—they don't care about the plants they water, the life they give. Or the life they take. Nature isn't cruel, nature is kind—the kind of kindness you hate. Because death is a necessary part of life.

Necessary implies that there is some grand design, and things are the way they are for some particular intrinsic reason, some fundamental purpose or arrangement of the parts to the whole, when the fact of the matter is that things happen, or are the way they are, for no particular reason at all. There is no blind clockmaker who set the universe in motion, and the universe is not a clock with an interlocking arrangement of the parts all working together—no, things are messier than that. The universe is just a clump of stuff happening for no particular reason, because if stuff is happening, it has got to happen in one way or another.

Keep your distance, show your respect; be mindful of the dangers. Even if you don't believe they exist. Especially if you don't believe they exist. There are dangerous animals and things and forces. Not all of them are benevolent or look kindly on human intervention. Certainly Zach had been doing something foolish, and dangerous, to be out on the ice, at that time of year.

If anything beneficial came out of this whole mess, it is that I got a new dog. Mum returned from the animal rescue with a miniature, roan-coloured Bull Terrier. Zoe fell in love with the beast. She is convinced that this is the dog her son "rescued" out on the ice. She is now convinced that her son died rescuing the poor animal, and that her son is a hero. It is her way of making sense of a senseless world. It makes about as much sense as anything else.

I don't know if this is the same animal that I saw in Zach's photographs, but it is at least weird-enough-looking for it to be possible that it's the same animal that appears on the ice. It showed up at the shelter at around the right time, shivering and suffering from the cold; it had no collar or sign of previous ownership. We don't name him right away. We only refer to him as "Zach's dog." We'll have to come up with a good Z-name soon.

I still don't know what happened to my brother. Maybe it's just a bit of fluff on the lens. Or maybe he simply *pissed them off*. Maybe the memengwesiag didn't like him taking pictures. Or maybe they were hungry.

I might as well be angry with a storm. A lynx for eating a rabbit. The ice for his hypothermia. The water for infiltrating his lungs. This world is not without danger. Zach just happened to fall for one of its pitfalls. I still search the rocks on the shore near the bluffs, looking for his bleeding image carved into the stone. Or maybe just the shape of his ear. Maybe they will also display it there, like a collection of trophies for the lives that they have taken.

COYOTE

He is lost.

Lost. Lost. Lost.

How did it happen?

Fanon knows the land like the back of his hand—hell, he knows it as well as his own dick. Or at least thought he did. Maybe it is the sin of pride? The sin of over-confidence? The sin of taking for granted his ability to navigate and find his way out in the bush. But Fanon doesn't think he is overconfident, doesn't think he places more trust in his own abilities than they warrant—he is good—it isn't bravado to acknowledge this, is it?

Besides, Nshoomis says there is no such thing as sin, or damnation, or hell. "Those are all foreign concepts, they don't exist in Ojibwe."

But still, somehow. It has happened. Sin or no sin, he is lost.

It is late October. They're out hunting, fishing, checking the trap-lines. The trip is planned as a two-week expedition, camping at various sites, to share traditional skills and knowledge. The party consists of Owen and Oogie Neyananoosic, Charlie Mushkeg, Valene, some of the Zeds; Zoe and her brother Zeamus, their old uncle Zeno. Fanon—and his Mshoomis who leads the party, Giizis Dibikiziwinan. Giizis is getting on in years, though he's still in hardy condition.

"This trip isn't only about learning from your elders." Zeno raises his arms at the start of their excursion, expounding like the Ancient Greek philosopher after whom he's presumably been named. "It is also about learning from the land, and learning about survival."

"Some of these Elders are long-winded." Fanon elbows Zeamus in the ribs.

As one of the oshkaabeywis, a *helper*, at twenty-six years old, Fanon is older than the other youth, who are still kids really. He's probably closest in age to Zoe and Zeamus who are still years younger. Teenagers.

Owen, Oogie, Zeno, and Giizis are the knowledge keepers.

"We encourage you all to show independence." Giizis eyeballs the assembled youths, burdened under the weight of backpacks, pup tents, and other camping gear. "This is to build confidence and gain a sense of your own abilities."

Fanon takes the message to heart, and plans a solo trip at the end of their first week out.

"I think I'll go on a little day-trip," he tells Giizis and Zeno at the morning campfire. "Check on our trapline." Brews himself a cup of strong black coffee. It's still early, the others are still sleeping. Sunlight filters through evergreens, and it's actually clear for once.

"Try and be back before dark." Giizis stirs sweetener into his coffee. "And stop wearing cologne! You smell like bear-bait."

"Might as well marinate yourself." The corners of Zeno's eyes crinkle, and he yawns.

Fanon sniffs an arm pit, smelling himself.

He decides to set out on foot, rather than taking the dogsled. He leaves a trail of footprints in the fresh snow behind him. It crunches satisfyingly under his boots as he walks. Heading north and west towards the high-ground where the trees give way to more open terrain, rock and hills, and scattered tree-stands, the edges of which they've been skirting on their trek. He'll check on the traps they've left along the way, and return later in the day, burdened with the weight of their catch.

A few light flakes drift down. Nothing to worry about. The sky has been leaden for the past few days, and nothing has come of it.

He is wrong though.

By mid-afternoon, he reaches the highland, and the few flakes that were coming down, have become a blizzard—and he didn't bring snowshoes. The few inches that came down in the morning are now up to his knees—and getting deeper. He trudges through it like molasses. The pantlegs of his jeans are wet. His body heat melts the snow and it drips into his boots. He's feet are wet. Not good. The muscles in his legs burn with exertion. It is getting harder and harder to walk. Every step is more troublesome than the last. He considers turning back. But he's come so far. Maybe he's better off finding somewhere to make camp for the night?

Darkness comes so early now; it will be getting dark by 6:30 pm, and it will be full dark by 7 pm. Fanon wishes he brought more food. He only brought a sandwich, and the tough slog through the snow is sapping his energy—he can already feel his stomach grumbling in complaint. Every trap he checks is empty, otherwise he'd have a ready-made meal.

Fanon decides to keep trudging until he finds a trap with something he can cook, then he'll stop for the night and make camp. Light a fire. Head back in the morning after the storm. It won't be hard for his Mshoomis to guess what happened. His grandfather won't worry—Giizis knows Fanon has the skills he needs to survive on his own for more than a night or two.

He'll be fine.

The blizzard continues to get worse though, until Fanon can't see anything more than a foot or two in any direction. Sleet lashes at his eyes so he has to squint against the gale. He can feel his beard and eyelashes become encrusted with ice crystals.

Old man winter glitter beard. He won't be able to find any traps in this weather. And he certainly can't find his way back in this weather either. He'll have to hunker down somewhere and wait for the storm to pass.

The grey light of day is beginning to bleed from the sky. He needs to find somewhere promising as a shelter. The sooner the better. When he sees the shapes of boulders rising in the distance through a break in the sleet, and a small stand of trees, Fanon makes his way towards the darker shapes against the white-on-white. Ground and sky are almost inseparable, one from the other. It's disorienting, not being able to tell which way is which.

When he reaches the boulders, he finds some shelter between the hollow of two rocks. It'll do. He collects enough branches to light a small fire in the protection afforded by the windbreak. The temperature drops. He passes a long, cold night, not being able to get much sleep, lest his fire gutter and go out, leaving him in the cold and dark without any light or warmth. The wind still finds its way to the flames, feeds the fuel too much oxygen, making the wood burn too quick. The fire needs to be constantly fed. In the morning, there is a slight lightening to the sky, which slowly gives way to the greyness of dawn, and then to the greyness of day, but the storm doesn't let up. The blizzard howls strong as ever, the sleet whips every stand of trees and outcropping of rock with equal violence.

If he can make his way back to the tree-line, there will be more protection from the driving snow. It's best to head back. Fanon pees on the small fire—not that it's likely to spread. Trudges through the blizzard again, in the direction—he's almost certain—is the way he came the day before, but his tracks in the snow are long gone. Even moments after they're made, his steps fill in with new snowfall and are quickly smoothed out by the gale. When he looks back, he can't see where he's been, almost as if he dropped out of the sky, or as if he's a ghost. No footprints. He can't use the tracks like breadcrumbs.

The sky is white. The ground is white. The only thing that lets Fanon know he's still walking on the earth is the solidity of the ground beneath his feet. And even that isn't very solid; he sinks up to his knees with every step. He passes the occasional stand of trees, and small outcroppings of rock, which are nothing more than indistinct shadows. By mid-day he is already exhausted from his efforts and—even worse—he is lost.

Even with the deep snow that makes every step a battle, he should have made it to the tree-line by now. Even with the hail that pelts him, he should have made it to the tree-line by now. Vicious beads of ice blast any bits of exposed flesh—it will look as if he's got a sunburn, but the burn won't be from the sun, it will be from the wind. Somehow, he got turned around in the seamless white, sky and land and land and sky. White on white on white. He can't be hard on himself. Not even Owen, or Zeno or his old grandpa Giizis predicted this snowstorm—they would have warned him if they'd known.

And isn't that peculiar? With their combined experience, shouldn't they have predicted the coming storm? It's hard to believe they didn't know the snow was coming. They knew, and they didn't warn him. Maybe they thought he could handle it? Maybe they thought he had the necessary survival skills, so they weren't worried—they knew where he was if he truly got into trouble. They could come find him. A test of his mettle. Or maybe he was overthinking things? Maybe the storm had simply caught them all off guard—no matter how much experience you have—nature doesn't always co-operate, sometimes she throws a blizzard or two out of left field. No one can predict the future accurately 100% of the time—not even Elders.

Fanon trudges through the snow, *pushing* his legs through the snow like a plow. It's now so deep he can't lift his feet out of the deep snow in order to plunge them back in. It makes the going even slower. And the snow is heavy, his thigh muscles and calves ache, his toes are numb icicles. He hopes he doesn't have frostbite. And he is hungry, and he is tired, and he is weak. His brain is beginning to fog. He can feel it happening. It's becoming increasingly difficult to formulate a plan, to make a decision. Should he keep walking? Is he even walking in the right direction? Should he give up and rest for a while? Or make camp for another night?

No, Fanon decides. He is running low on energy, so he needs to keep walking while he still has the ability, and sitting still will simply sap the strength from his limbs, even with a fire burning. He needs to reach the tree-line.

Fanon prays to his manitous; Grandfather Sun, and Grandmother Moon, Mother Earth, the wind and the snow even—and Kitchi Manitou, the creator—he prays that he is walking in the right direction. The longer he walks the more energy he expends, and still the snowstorm doesn't let up. The light bleeds from the sky and he knows darkness is approaching again for a second night, and that he will soon have to find shelter, and build a fire, and keep the fire going or he will freeze to death.

So that's what he does. He finds a stand of trees, a depression in the earth, and hunkers down for another night, in the protection afforded by the roots of a fallen tree. He throws a few branches over top in a quick lean-to, and soon has a cozy shelter constructed with small fire burning merrily in a pit. And though the snow still falls, and the wind still howls, he is relatively safe and warm though exhausted, and hungry, and weak. There is nothing he can do until morning. So he prepares a large pile of wood to fuel the fire, so he won't have to get up multiple times during the night, and tries to get some rest. This time he actually manages to get some sleep; he is so exhausted, he can't stave it off. Though he has to relight the fire twice during the night, waking up from the cold to find the fire has burned down to ash.

In the morning—a thin, grey lightening to the sky—his fire has burned down again to a few blackened sticks. He is cold and his limbs are stiff, though he knows he mustn't stay in place. He has to keep moving. He has to keep moving while he still has the energy. He has to keep moving.

Fanon trudges through the white on white. The howling wind and the pelting sleet lashing at his eyes, blinding him. And still he walks. And walks. And walks. And knows he is lost. He must have become disoriented, and walked in a wrong direction, or else he's been walking in circles, for he should have retraced his steps, four times over by now, or been back at his starting point, for the number of steps he's taken, working twice as hard, pushing his legs through the weight of the snow.

Towards mid-day, Fanon knows he's in trouble. He can barely put one foot in front of the other anymore. He feels weakness in his muscles, in his veins, in his wrists, at his throat, at his ankles and in his heart. He is so screwed. He might as well give up. And he is tired. So tired. The snow now seems soft and fluffy. Inviting. Like a down-filled comforter. King bed. White goose-feathers. And in the distance.

He hears Coyotes.

Awoooooooh. Awoooonnnh. Woooh.

Howling.

They have a higher register than the howl of wolves. Long mournful notes like a train, and short sharp caws less drawn out. Whirring. Crying. Crowing. Bird barks. A spooky whistling concerto. How far away? He wonders? How many miles? How many kilometers? Fanon knows they are probably farther away than they sound. Much farther. Though they sound close. Like they are just over the next ridge. But it's so quiet. Sound can travel far out here on the highlands. But it's difficult to judge, the way the little valleys and bowls direct and redirect echoes. And the snow acts like a blanket, muffling. They could be quite near, or they could be quite far. Fanon's guess is that they are still several kilometers away, at least.

He continues walking. Trudging. Plowing through the sleet and snow. With the sound of coyotes. Yipping and calling to each other. Like they are talking to each other. And that's exactly what it sounds like. Like they are talking to each other. Calling back and forth. They sound like voices. Human voices.

Maybe the valleys and rock walls are playing tricks? Maybe they aren't coyotes? Maybe they are human after all? Voices distorted and stretched out to sound like coyotes? Those aren't coyotes! Or if there were coyotes earlier, what he hears now is definitely the sound of people, laughing and talking, though their voices are stretched and distorted by distance—they are human. He is certain of it now. But what are they doing out here? Has he stumbled so far off course? Are they hikers? Or campers? Or has he come across some sort of field party?

Fanon changes course, heading toward the sound of distant revelry. He hopes he isn't making a mistake by deviating from the route he chose, but it hasn't panned out so far. So what the hell. He knows based on his position, and the layout of the land, where their camp *should* be, so he heads in that direction. But he could be wrong. He's definitely lost his way once already. And it sure sounds like people. He can almost make out the occasional word. It sounds like a good party. Whoever it is, they sound like they're having a gay old time. The closer he gets, the more distinct the voices become.

He ascends a small rise. Ahead he can see the glow of a fire burning, obscured by a thick cluster of trees, branches and the shapes of people sitting around a fire are thrown into silhouette. Talking, laughing, drinking and eating. They don't seem to be troubled by the cold weather. They seem to be enjoying themselves.

He's saved!

Fanon makes his way through the tangle of trees, and into a small clearing where a group of mostly young people hang about. Drinking. Talking. Laughing.

"You're welcome to join the party." An older man stands upon seeing him. He'd been sitting on a rock near the fire. His face is flushed with drink, or the heat of the flames. The man gestures welcomingly to the circle of jovial, rosy faces, and the light of their fire.

"Oh, thank the manitous." Fanon falls to his knees. "I've been walking for so damn long. I thought my ass was going to freeze off."

"And well it might have." The older man comes forward, hands clasped before him. "You're lucky to have found our get-together. Nobody disturbs us out here." And the man throws his head back and laughs. Cackles really. Odd little dude. Kind of scrawny. His dark grizzled beard is streaked with white. Fanon doesn't know why this is so funny, but he is grateful for the warmth cast by the fire. He wonders if they are nudists or swingers or into some other kind of kink that they need to come all the way out here just to get their kicks.

Someone thrusts a bottle into his hands. Firewater. And before long, he's warm, and he has a satisfying buzz going on after only a few swigs. He hasn't eaten much in the last couple days. He is introduced all around, and is introduced to each in turn, though he is so light-headed and delirious with relief, he has trouble keeping track of everyone's name. If they are telling him, it seems to be going in one ear and out the other. Maybe too many to remember. Everyone is in such high spirits, laughing and joking and teasing each other.

Fanon isn't immune to their taunts.

"So got lost did you?"

"I think I almost died." And for some reason, this is suddenly utterly hilarious, they are all howling with laughter, the whole circle of faces crack open to show their teeth, and Fanon is howling right along with them. He is laughing so hard his stomach muscles hurt, he is laughing so hard tears form at the corner of his eyes, and he is laughing so hard he is gasping to draw in breath between bouts of hilarity.

They pull at his goatee and laugh at the streak of white at his temple. "Kind of young to be *going grey* already aren't you?" More laughter. More cackling. Fanon is howling with laughter. What is so G-D-damned funny? Fanon really has no idea. Is he high? Is he simply delirious from starvation and exhaustion? He doesn't know, and he doesn't care, he's having too much G-D fun to care.

"Everyone in our family has it," Fanon tries to explain between fits of laughter. "The patch of grey. It's genetic."

It must be the lack of calories. The alcohol has gone straight to his head. And all the stress from his journey is being released, endorphins spinning, all the muscles in his legs relax like warm jelly. Then there is the tantalizing smell of roasting meat, and a shank is shoved into his face. He is ravenous and doesn't hesitate to tear off chunks of flesh with his teeth. It is slightly charred on the outside and under-cooked on the inside, but it's the most delicious thing Fanon has ever tasted, and he isn't going to complain. It is food, and he is STARVING.

The merriment continues late into the night, they dance and twirl and sing all though the snowstorm which continues to gust outside the thicket. They are well stocked with food, and drink, and supplies. There are smiles all around. A delightful group of people. A pretty young girl has clearly taken a shine to him. The girl sits next to him, touching his arm as he talks and drinks. The woman has the most interesting shade of brown eyes, almost amber-yellow. So slanted they could have been oriental. Another young woman, with silver eyes—though no less captivating—sits on his right, and the two women tease and joke and compete for his attention. Not in a jealous way, instead they are playful and good-natured in their rivalry. Mischievous even. The way they share looks, and laugh at him when he asks, "What's so funny?" But they won't tell him. Maybe their interest in him is due to the fact that he is a newcomer to their group? He gets the sense they all know each other really well.

He is fresh meat.

Who knew that his near-death due to exposure would lead him to such an unlikely party? At some point during the night, the young women—whom are both close to him in age—lead him a short distance away from the fire and offer to share a sleeping bag. "It will be warmer if we share." The girl with the amber-coloured eyes smiles. "It is a very cold night." The woman with silver eyes has a matching grin.

Fanon smiles back, and they climb into the blankets. The two women are beautiful. Their long hair is so soft and sleek, like silk flowing down their backs. Their eyes are like honey and moonlight, large and captivating. Hungry even. They smell of wood-smoke from the fire, and the softness of summer. They are gentle, but insistent, and neither one seems to mind sharing more than his warmth. In fact, they seem thrilled. Uninhibited. He's never met women like this. Afterwards they hold each other in a pile. And Fanon is grateful for their warmth. It is a very cold night. He falls asleep in their arms, happy and content.

Fanon feels a light touch on one of his eyelashes. A rock is poking into his ribs. He shifts uncomfortably but doesn't want to withdraw entirely from the drowsy state of unconsciousness. He's enjoying his sleep. But the ground is hard. And he needs to pee. He's cold. The fire must have burned down.

He cracks an eyelid. Sunlight blurring through his lashes. So the sun has already risen. He opens them, sees the sky through the branches above. The sky is blue and clear of clouds. It's stopped snowing! The storm has passed. Finally. And then he remembers. *The party. The beer, the food—the women!* That's when he comes fully awake, realizing how cold he is. And alone. Where are the women who kept him company through the night? He sits up. Looks around the clearing. Everybody is gone.

And what's more, there is no sign of a party.

No empty beer bottles. No cigarette butts. No ashes where there should have been a cold fire pit, with a few embers still smoldering—no, there is nothing! No impressions in the ground where bodies slept, no footprints in the snow, or trail indicating the direction in which the people retreated as they made their way through the deep snow.

Correction—there are no human footprints. There are plenty of other footprints. Paw-prints. Paw-prints are everywhere in the snow. A swirl of paw-prints like a whirlwind in all directions, dissipating and concentrating in frequency as they change in distance and proximity from where he'd slept in the snow. He sits at their centre, the centre of the storm of paw-prints littering the snow. Surrounding him in a slowly expanding concentric circle, like a galaxy of rotating stars.

Coyote paw-prints. He recognizes the marks. They aren't so uncommon that he couldn't recognize these tracks. And he is a decent tracker. This isn't his first hunting trip. He knows what a coyote print looks like. Four claws. Four large round toes, closer together than a dog's. And a rounded triangular palm.

And. They. Are. Everywhere.

Lying on the ground a short distance from him is what remains of the carcass of a deer. The sightless eyes stare at him. Glistening milky white. Ribs curve like the concave in a stringed instrument, flesh stripped from the bone. The deer has been unwrapped, torn apart like a flower. The snow is drenched in carnage. Red on white and red on white. And closer to hand, the shank of one leg, the hoof and some fur still attached. It's been gnawed on. The shank of the leg retains the impression of teeth. Human teeth. Fanon raises his hand to his mouth, and his hand comes away bloody where it dripped down his chin and congealed. The front of his jacket is stained. He remembers the steaming, delicious flavour of the meat, and realizes it couldn't have been cooked. There is no indication of a campfire.

No beer bottles. No cigarette buts. No sleeping bags.

Just the coyote prints everywhere, surrounding him in a galaxy radiating outward from his centre. *And oh god!* The thought struck him. *What he'd done with those women?* Did that happen too? Or was it all a dream? Was his mind concocting lies to protect his psyche from the horrors he was forced to endure in order to survive?

Fanon stumbles to his feet. Staggers from the thicket of trees and takes his bearings. From where he stands, he can see the tree-line. He'd been a stone's-throw from the relative safety of the forest. Who knows how many hours he'd spent, wandering, mere yards from reaching his goal? But the blizzard had hidden everything, with visibility next to zero. He was lucky to have survived. He was lucky he hadn't wandered in the wrong direction entirely. He should have hunkered down, and waited for the storm to pass, instead of expending all his energy in futile efforts, and becoming swallowed in delirium. Hindsight is 20/20.

Fanon walks, descending from the highlands, making his way back to the camp where he knows his grandfather Giizis and the others will be waiting for his return, if they had not already set out searching for him. Someone would have been left at the camp, just in case he came back, while everyone was out searching for him.

He tries not to think on other things. Tries not to think of the party that he thought he'd crashed. Tries not to think of the people he'd met. Tries not to think of the night that didn't happen. Tries not to think of people that don't exist. It's all so confusing. Had they saved him? Fanon is certain, that if he hadn't stumbled upon that "party"—he would be dead. He wouldn't have survived the storm. Overcome by exhaustion and hypothermia.

When he gets back to camp, his grandfather Giizis leaps from his seat by the fire, and rushes to greet him. Wraps him in a large blanket, pushes a flask of Rusty into his hands to warm him. Owen and Zeno are out searching for him, and Giizis stayed behind with the other youths to hold down the fort in case he returned. They gather around him with a million questions, happy to see him alive.

Everyone knows how dangerous it can be out on the land during rough weather. They weren't sure if he would make it. Not even the most experienced hunters and trappers are immune to making mistakes, or getting caught out in a storm. Shit happens, and sometimes people died. But Fanon is lucky.

"I hope you realize that." Giizis's face is a mass of wrinkles.

In the distance, a coyote howls. And Fanon feels his face flush with heat.

What has he done? What has he done?

But, at least, he's still alive.

LIGHTNING STRIKE TWICE

They say lightning doesn't strike in the winter, but what they really mean, is that it is actually just a rare occurrence. I've seen it twice in my life, once when me and my brother were out ice-fishing with our dad Argyle. Holed up in an ice shack, fishing poles hanging over a hole in the ice three feet thick. Me and Zachaeus got bored and went out to play on the ice, sliding across the slick surface in our winter boots…

"Zaude?" Zachaeus asks. "Why don't the fish freeze solid?" Stupid kid. Almost three years younger than me, he is basically a baby. Red mittens threaded through the arms of his snowsuit so they can't get lost.

"It's not frozen all the way down, otherwise there'd be no point in ice-fishing duuunhh!"

"Well aren't they cold down there?" One knee planted, eye squinted shut, peering as if he can see through the thick layers of ice. We'd had to shovel the snow to reveal the slippery patch. Grey-green and smooth.

"Who?" I ask.

"The fiiish!"

"Nooo because they're cold-blooded. Sheesh don't you ever watch the nature channel?"

"Car-tooons!" Zachaeus says, then sings the theme song from some idiotic television program, spinning in a circle, but the lyrics come out all mangled because he sticks his tongue out to catch the snowflakes coming down. I shrug and join him, raise my arms and spin, trying to catch the snowflakes on my tongue.

"Witches dance between the raindrops!" I sing my own silly tune. It makes it a lot easier to dance between raindrops when they're frozen, but the flakes seem to shy away from my tongue, no matter how far I stick it out.

Zachaeus slips, his jaw smashes onto the ice, and his teeth chomp down with the additional strength from the weight of his skull.

"AANNNNHHWW" Zachaeus half scream-moans.

I stop spinning, but the horizon keeps lurching like I'm on a boat, I think I'm going to heave while I wait for the skyline to right itself. Zach is on his knees, his face slick with snot and tears, mittens dangling, pink fingers curled and waffling helpless in mid-air.

His mouth hangs open and blood is spraying out, it runs down the synthetic material of his coat in dark streaks, splatters across the ice, red droplets on blue-tinged ice.

"Oh fuck!" I know I'm not allowed to swear, but I also know some situations call for cursing.

"What's going on out there?" Argyle's voice emerges from the little wooden cabin, "You're scaring away all the fish!"

I dash to my brother's side, skidding to a halt where he kneels. The blood pools alarmingly, dramatic in contrast. I scan the ice, and am relieved not to see his severed tongue laying like an earthworm sliced in half. It isn't true. The two parts can't live independently. Even if they have five hearts, both halves die.

His tongue is still in there, even if it's damaged. Zachaeus's brown eyes are wide, trembling, and filling with tears as they land on the sight of his own blood. Red on white. I can see his chest rising as the breath rattles in past the mucus and blood, see him gearing up for a truly ear-piercing wail.

That's when the *thunderbirds* come, rolling in on wave after wave of thunder. I'm not sure what to call them—thunder*snow*-birds?—rolling in with the swirling snowflakes, and the storm-front of thick clouds that blanket the clap of overlapping sound so it somehow seems more intimate. The shock of something so loud in an enclosed space. For a second, I swear I can actually see them, though that's probably just my imagination. Animikiig. Shooting forked lighting from their eyes. Multiple zig-zag streaks burn neon pink into my corneas. I can definitely hear them, as if the rumbling is a result of concussions of air from the beat of their colossal wings.

The wail—which has been threatening to burst from the dam of Zachaeus' throat—stalls—he exhales instead, a rattle that gurgles blood as he stares wide-eyed at the uroboros clouds around us, a new, greater alarm overriding the urgency of his pain.

He is right. The proximity of lightning is a greater danger than a bitten tongue—despite the blood, I doubt Zach severed any major arteries, he's not going to bleed to death before he reaches medical attention. Our grandmother is a nurse after all, so I know the tongue is one of the fastest healing parts of the human body.

"Wha-eh-ell-is-aht?" His tongue hangs out of his mouth like a fat pink slug. Swollen to twice it's normal size. He'll probably talk with a lisp for months.

Another bolt of lightning rips through the sky, a strange purple-blue that leaves an after-image of yellow-orange burnt on the back of my eyelids. Close. The lightning is way too close. Like golfing in the rain. Electricity and conductive metal in a wide-open space. Sports and thunderstorms don't mix.

Our dad, Argyle, comes barreling out of the ice shack like a bat, just as cobalt stabs through the air. The winter day is suddenly blindingly bright, backwards like an x-ray. Argyle stands for a moment dazed by the flash of quicksilver. Shakes his head. Blinks as he takes in the blood on the snow, and rushes over to us. He kneels on Zachaeus's other side, making eye contact with me for a moment.

You're OK? His warm brown eyes seem to ask.

Yes, I'm fine. I try to telegraph back.

Dad grabs Zachaeus's jaw for a moment to inspect the damage—non-life-threatening—and in moments he has us both bundled up onto the snowmobile and careening at top speed across the frozen surface of the lake, away from the advancing storm, and to the relative safety of the shore.

The rumbling of the Thunderbirds disappear behind us.

The second time I saw lightning in the winter...

I'm driving home from school. Zachaeus is a few years dead, slipped beneath the ice on a photography mission, dead of hypothermia or drowned. It still feels like yesterday.

I stop to buy gas, grab a cup of coffee.

"A pack of Menthols please." Middle-aged White dude in line in front of me. Overalls, and a straw hat. Bet he dresses like that all year round. Eye the snow-flake icon on the television screen above the cash. Scrolling 24 hr. news station. Wait for my turn to pay. An early fall storm. The weather stations haven't been calling for a snowstorm. This is news to me.

Menthol guy smiles kindly at me as he passes, pale green eyes twinkling with warmth. I give him a tight-lipped smile. Take my purchases up to the counter. Pay, and dash back out to the car. A few flakes are already coming down. Darn. I haven't put my winter tires on yet.

Back on the road, it starts to rain—ice pellets. Could be lake-effect snow? The freezing rain turns to hail, then the hail turns to fat flakes, and I'm inside a giant snow-globe. It's pretty. But dangerous. There's next to zero visibility. I'm driving at a snail's pace. Thirty kilometres an hour. Then twenty. Then ten. The speed of a slow jog. And then a complete stop.

I pull over at what I hope is the side of the road, hazard lights blinking madly in the gloom. It is only 4 o'clock in the afternoon, it might as well be full-dark. The sun has already begun sinking earlier each day, but there should've still been several hours of light left.

I've pulled over on a hill, which is just as well since I doubt my summer tires will have enough grip on the road to make it up the steep incline. I hop out of the car and light a cigarette. A whirlwind blows my hair around my face in a crazy tangle, and I hold my far-to-thin jacket tightly around myself. The buttons have long since torn off and been lost. I like the jean jacket. It had been Zach's actually, purchased several sizes too large by Aunty Zelda one year. "He'll grow into it."

He never wore it. It hung in his closet for months before I could bring myself to claim it, to overcome the ghoulishness of taking something that had once belonged to my dead brother.

There is the glare of red brake lights as another car careens past, going far too fast for the weather, slowing as it passes, *kchhrrrr* from the whirl of tires skidding for traction on the slick roads as the idiot gives the engine more gas. Tourists. The car behind slams on his brakes, also travelling much too fast. Visibility is pea-soup, and the roads are icy, which means the stopping distance is basically nonexistent. I let out a short yelp as idiot driver behind smashes into idiot driver in front with the percussive *thudd* of fiberglass crunching together, accordion collapse of crumple-cushioning technology, and the driver in front loses control as he spins out in a circle, flipping over into the ditch, and rolls a few times before the vehicle finally comes to a rest.

Oh shit.

The driver isn't wearing his seat belt. He lays half-in, and half out of the driver's side window. Dead or alive? I can't tell. Unconscious for sure. His arm hangs limp, his head lolls to the side, there is a trickle of blood from one corner of his lips. I can't gauge what degree of injuries he's sustained.

Popping the trunk, I mutter a quick prayer to the manitous and grab the flares Zoe insisted on putting into a milk-crate along with a bunch of other emergency supplies on the day I started driving on my own. I count a hundred paces further back on the road to set up the flares and prevent further collisions from other idiot drivers driving too fast on slick roads without salt or winter-tires.

I don't smell gasoline; it should be safe. With a twist I remove the cap, rub the end of the flare against the striking surface and hold the shell as far away from myself as I can, the end erupts in a firework of sparks. I set the flare on the ground, and repeat the process a few yards away. A fountain of embers. Pretty.

The flares burn a pink-orange as the other driver and passengers come out from their vehicle, blinking like badgers emerging from their den into the light of day, dazed from the collision. Snow swirls around them and they hug themselves for warmth in the cold air without the protection of jackets.

Then I go to check on the other driver. The one who I'm not sure if he is alive or dead or comatose. Lolling half-in and half-out of his vehicle. Rag doll. It doesn't look like a comfortable position for his ribs. I carefully pick my way through the snow and sleet—my shoe-tread moccasins are not really up for the task. Brain-tanned moosehide, rabbit fur-trim, purple and lime-green chevron beadwork on the vamps. Bling.

I look up to check on the man, as I scout the layout of the ground. No hint of movement. Not a good sign. When I get close enough to touch the man, for it is a man, I hold two fingers to his throat to feel for a pulse. Count the seconds as they pass. His face and neck are smooth, recently clean shaven. I can smell the minty-cedar smell of his after-shave, though he already has the beginnings of a five o'clock shadow. Short dark hair, and an olive complexion, very international, he could pass for almost anything. White collar shirt, no wedding ring, a chunky gold wristwatch. The second hand has stopped spinning. No Pulse.

I'm not a medical doctor. But grandma Zeph is a nurse, and I know there are other ways to check vital signs. But as far as I can tell, the man is as dead. There is no rise and fall of his chest. No breath. I should begin chest compressions. CPR. Try to force some oxygen into his lungs and into his blood stream for his oxygen-starved brain.

And that's when the thunderbirds come, swooping down on waves of thunder.

CRAAAACK

I yelp as the bolt of lightning rips through the sky. A zap of static electricity runs down my arm. The electric clap localized by the insulating fall of snow. Quick flash stabbing down, scintillating like sunlight on water, zig-zagging like one of those toy-drawing gizmos that are impossible to control, one knob controlling the vertical axis and the other controlling the horizontal axis, neither working well enough in collaboration to get a diagonal; a line so bright it day-blinds me for a moment, burns into my mind, a curling advance of a tree-root growth captured time-lapse slow, a connect-the-dots crawl. To catch lighting at this speed, I would require a hell of lot more feet of film than I have left in my Bolex resting on the back seat of my car. A car accident isn't really the time or place to be pulling out your camera. Though I wish I had it with me. I have the urge to reach back to look for it, even though I'm not sitting in my driver's seat now. I do have my 35mm still-frame hanging around my neck from a leather cord. Zach's camera. The one with the `Property of Sterling High School` stamped on the side. I carry it with me everywhere. I forget sometimes that I'm wearing it. Sometimes it's in my hand, and I don't even remember taking it out of the leather case. As it is now. I wonder if I've captured anything?

I stand staring around me like the other badgers, blinking and waiting for my vision to come back to me. Thunder rolls like the bad special effects in a movie, but LOUD and VISCERAL. I can feel the percussion vibrating through my body as a physical force. If I was completely deaf I would still 'hear' the roll of the thunder as a sensation. That's how loud it is. Like standing in front of the speaker at a rock concert.

When the rumble subsides and the zig-zag after-image clears, I can see that the badgers have done the smart thing and returned to their car, the glow of smart-phones suffocated, cradled to their ears as they call for help.

I swear there had been no pulse. No sign of breath, no rise and fall of his chest. He'd been perfectly still. Perfectly dead. Then there was the bolt of lightning ripping through the sky—my momentary blindness. But as my vision clears, I see the dead man sitting up in the driver-seat, scrubbing at his face with one hand. He seems more faded somehow. Grey sprinkled through his dark hair. Salt and pepper. Three-days growth of stubble on his beard. I hadn't seen any movement. I hadn't felt a pulse.

"Wha-what happened?" he looks up at me bleary-eyed. Dark brown warmth. Stunningly handsome.

Like the eff I know.

Did my touch re-animate him? Were we electrocuted? I don't *feel* electrocuted. Like any rural kid, I've grabbed my share of electrified cow-fences, daring others to lick or pee on them, taking turns to see who can hold on for the longest—five seconds, ten, fifteen. And once, I'd plugged in the toaster and ended up flat on my ass. Frizzled hair and smelling like ham.

I do feel strange though. Woozy.

"It's alright, sir. You've been in an accident. Everything is going to be okay." I speak slowly. Are my words slurred? Am I even telling the truth? "Help is on the way."

STURGEON

Kylie stares into the coca-cola waters of the lake. Anything submerged is given a rusty tinge, her un-tanned toes turn red in the shallows at the shore's edge. If she scooped out a sample of the lake, the glass would be amber, filled with swirling suspended solids. She is baby-sitting her younger sister. Only three years difference between them, but sometimes Kylie feels like her sister's keeper.

Cadence is wearing her bright blue bathing suit, and wading out into the shallows, she takes one more step, and drops off a deep ledge hidden in the water. Where'd she go?

"Cadence?" Kylie waits, but Cadence doesn't come back up for air.

Shit. Shit. Shit.

Kylie runs out, lifting her knees high to get her feet above the waterline as she splashes into the lake and then dives, keeping her eyes open under the water. There is a gradation of colour radiating outwards, yellow-to-orange, red-to-brown, brown-to-black. Anything further than a few feet away is lost in the dimness. The deeper she dives, the murkier the water becomes. It's like being blind. She has to feel her way around with her hands. Her lungs burn, she can hear her heart pounding in her ears like a drum, her eyes sting with the strain of seeing. Her brain creates insane starburst flashes of false light.

Where is she? Where is she?

Kylie feels her fingers tangle in the strands of her sister's hair, and she pulls, dragging Cadence back up to light and life. Cadence takes huge breath of air as they surface, spluttering and gasping. Cadence is fine. Just disoriented by the sudden unexpected drop into deeper water.

Phew.

Anyone who has ever spent time on the lake has felt this panic. Being a good swimmer isn't good enough. Accidents happen. Kylie can't recount the litany of deaths, the number of stories she heard growing up, of relatives and community members who drowned, or fell through the ice and never came back. She is only thirteen and even she knew people who lost their lives through misfortune, carelessness, or just bad luck.

The lake is beautiful, but like all bodies of water, it is also dangerous. This one, more so than others. No matter how many precautions you take.

"Out on the water, the weather changes fast." Eamon threads an embroidery needle through a hooped piece of fabric, stitching an intricate floral design into the cloth. "One minute there are blue skies, and the next..."

"BAAM!" Eamon slaps palms to accentuate his point. "Angry purple thunderheads, forks of lightning stabbing down." He looks up, wiggles his fingers, then splays them like a rapper. "That's the thunderbirds and michi-bizhew, always fighting." His grey eyes shine like sapphires out of his brown face, his grey hair pulled back in two evenly parted braids.

There is a CRACK of lightning, and a ROLL of thunder like the soundtrack to a movie, perfectly timed. Beings from out of Anishinaabe legends with life, and physical form. Both their shoulders give a jolt. Kylie's grandfather gathers his embroidery stuff and heads down the hallway for his room. Eamon is leery of thunderstorms. He hides in his room burning twists of tobacco whenever there's a storm.

Kylie kind of likes them. They are exciting, and loud, and the flickers of light arcing across the sky over Cope's bay is spectacular to see. She goes to sit on the screened-off front deck to watch the storm progress. Thunder makes the irises in the front garden tremble and rattles the windows in their frames. Flashes of light like knitting needles thrust through bundles of purple yarn. There is no use hiding, Kylie thinks. Lightning can strike you dead anywhere.

Their lake, *Ghost Lake*, or Jiibay Zaaga'igan in Ojibwe, is located in a remote area. Thirty-five minutes to the town of Cheapaye, and another hour or two to Sterling. Poplars grow on the shore among the spruce, like skeletons in all that green. They're used for tanning hides. Maybe that's what accounts for the colour of the water?

"I think the lake has always been this colour." Eadie sits on their dock, blue cut-off jeans. Painting her toenails a shade of cream that matches her platinum hair.

"I dunno—I heard something happened to change it." Peyton has his jeans rolled up; his feet hang off the edge of the dock.

"Like what?" Kylie is laying on her stomach, her arms dangle over the edge, the reflection of her long dark hair rises up from the surface to meet the place where her long dark hair hangs down to meet the water.

"There's that iron-ore mine." Ripples circle out from Peyton's feet. Ovoid refractions on the surface, glittering sparkles of light.

"Yeah, but that's miles *downstream* of the outflow." Eadie lifts a foot awkwardly attempting to blow on her own toenails. Kylie giggles.

"It doesn't matter," Peyton scissors his feet, splashing. Eadie winces. "The waterways are all connected." Everyone has their own theories.

Recently there'd been grumbling in the community. A mining company discovered a rich vein of valuable minerals running under the lake, like marbled cheese.

"What are they going to do, drain the lake?" Edna Ogers asks rhetorically, at the last Annual General Meeting. The AGM is held at The Orchard, a conference space in Sterling. Edna Ogers does not really believe what she said was possible.

But the mood changes when Charlie Mushkeg stands up. Tattoos. Leather fringe. Moses beard. "They drained High Ground Lake during WWII and diverted Magma River. And iron ore is a sight bit *less* valuable than silver or copper. I'd say we *are* in danger of losing our lake."

Thanks to the construction of a museum, the community has been returning to their lands after the catastrophe of a flood many years ago. No one wants a repeat of history. Kylie wishes those mining jerks would buzz off and leave their lake alone. Too bad GPS keeps them from getting lost among the shifting islands, like some of the early explorers.

"Some lakes just have darker water," Cadence pipes up. "There's a lot of different factors, even the mineral composition of the surrounding rock." Kylie's know-it-all sister always has her nose stuck in a book, glasses perch on the bridge of her nose. She reads enough to know something about everything, and she isn't shy about sharing her knowledge. Greysen, their dad, calls her "Brainy Smurf" although they are both too young to have grown up watching that old cartoon. Sometimes it's on TV in French.

Which Smurf is she? Kylie wonders. *Maybe Grumpy? Or is that one of the Seven Dwarfs?* Oh, well. Whichever Smurf she is, it isn't Brainy Smurf; or Know-it-all Smurf either. Kylie would put herself in the running for *Clumsy Smurf.*

Kylie has never been frightened of the lake.

Floating around on an orange plastic dinghy close to shore that afternoon, she has a wooden paddle within easy reach. Comic books, sunlight, blue sky. She is more than happy to float, and read. Read and float. Squares blocked out in an organized pattern, thought bubble text, rhythmic lapping of waves as she bathes in the warmth of the sun like some sort of tropical lizard. Giant sunglasses like a movie star. Getting lost in the story-line as she drifts.

She glances up occasionally to make sure she hasn't drifted too far from shore. Fifty yards, sixty, it's still shallow enough to touch bottom on her tippy toes. One hand dangles over the edge of the dinghy, fingertips drawing trails in the water's surface. She turns her attention back to the black and white squares. A Shinigami soap opera. Japanese manga. Right to left. Dialogue and action. Faster paced than the novels Cadence likes to read.

The wind picks up, rattling her pages. Irritating. Ruffling her hair. The gentle waves have become a bit choppy. Bouncing her around. Less comfortable to read. A shadow darkens the page, and Kylie looks up, for the first time noticing the dark clouds. Thunderheads on the horizon. Those tall piled-up kind. Flattened out like an anvil. Not those fluffy animal shape kinds. These ones are dense with rain, the clouds look ready to drop. And they are approaching *fast*. The plants along the shore seem greener somehow, somehow *more* lush, even though they haven't yet had a drop to drink. Like they are opening their pores for the coming storm. The thunder growls like trumpets announcing the storm.

Shit! Where is the paddle? It's gone! She'd brought one with her. Where did it go? Did it drift away? She doesn't see it anywhere. And the orange dinghy has drifted, a current pulling them out into deeper waters outside Cope's bay. She didn't wear a life jacket either, not intending to go further than a few yards from shore. She wishes she had one now.

Kylie plunges her arms into the cool water and paddles. Cupping her fingers like flippers to get more traction. Slapping at the water to fight the current. The clouds approach, swiftly overtaking her. A cold drizzle falls. Oh no! The books! They're going to get ruined! She feels her eyes glaze with tears. It's ok, it's ok. She can always buy more. She needs to get to shore before it starts to rain any harder. She watches the shore to measure her progress. Is she gaining any ground? It's hard to tell, the current has pulled her out so far from the bay.

After a few minutes, the drizzle turns into rain. Soon the rain will turn into a downpour, the sky will crack open and drench everything. Like thousands of buckets waiting to be up-ended, there is a looming, hesitant sort-of expectancy.

An electric sort of patience.

She slaps harder at the water, despite her precious manga. They're getting wet! Waterlogged, puffing out like fish as the pages absorb moisture. She looks up to gauge the shoreline again. It seems as if she is still being swept further from her starting point. The current is winning. That's a lot more important than worrying about some stupid books.

The waves are becoming increasingly chaotic. A large wave drenches her. She worries the dinghy will sink if it takes on too much water, but she needs to lean forward, squishing the edges of the boat down so she can reach the water to paddle. Which also makes the dinghy take on more water each time a wave comes to drench her. But the further the boat goes out into the deeper waters, the less chance she will have of making it back to shore.

She realizes how dangerous her situation has become. She isn't crying for the danger to her books, now she is now crying for the danger she has placed herself in. She is frantic, clawing at the water, dragging the dinghy against the current as best she can. The rain has thoroughly soaked her. She's lost her movie-star sunglasses. Probably stolen by one of the waves. Her hair hangs wet and heavy from her scalp. Strands of it stick to her forehead, itchy, but she can't be bothered to swipe the hair out of the way. She's too focused on paddling. Get to shore. Get to shore. She needs to get to shore.

She looks up again to gauge the progress she's made. It doesn't seem as if she's made any. Maybe a few yards closer? Hopeful thinking. At best she might have reached a stale-mate with the current. They cancel each other out. Neither one winning. Though her arms are tired. She can't keep up this frantic pace forever. The waves though, they aren't getting tired at all. All they need to do is wait and they'll win. Hopeless. It's hopeless.

If she let the current take her, where will she end up? In the deepest part of the lake, and during a massive thunderstorm, her boat would take on too much water and sink. Or the waves would upend her, tip over the little boat. She'd drown. Is it too far for her to swim from here? She gauges the distance. And the progress she's made against the land. The ridges of the tree-line on the shore like a saw-blade. She thinks she's winning. Barely. But still making some headway. Best to keep paddling, keep fighting the current. It's probably not safe to risk it. Trying to swim from here. Better to have the flotation of the inflated plastic. Though the rubber seems to be losing of its firmness. It feels less-inflated than it was before. Like maybe the air is leaking out. It isn't as floaty as it was. She seems to be sitting heavier in the craft. Lower. And her weight makes a heavier impression in the soft plastic. When she leans over the edge of the boat to cup her hands in the water again, the ridge of the boat feels much softer, providing less resistance, less support against her weight, and it almost tips her into the lake. Leaning against that edge flattens it down, so the gunwale is almost at the level of the lake, making the boat take on more water. But there's not much she can do about that. She needs to lean down on that ridge and flatten the edge so she can reach the water to paddle.

Her boat takes on more and more water. But she's making progress. She's certain of it. She's getting a bit closer to Cope's bay. But the inflated plastic is getting so soft and mushy, it's lost so much air, she's barely staying afloat with all the water it's taken on. Kylie has to stop paddling to bail out some of the water or it'll sink. She cups her hands together, tossing handful after handful of the lake out of the craft and back into the body of water. Once she's tossed enough of the water out of the boat so that she thinks it won't sink, she goes back to paddling, she leans over with her chest against the gunwale, compressing the lip of the boat with her weight so she can reach the waterline. Imagines her hands like little motors. Like little webbed duck feet pawing at the lake.

There is an odd swirling of the waters, it lifts up her tiny dinghy as if a great beast is surfacing underneath, coming up for a breath of air. *Does it have something to do with the storm?* She wonders. *What could it be?* Some sturgeon can grow to be as large as a grown man, sometimes even larger. There are also stories nshoomis Eamon tells, of a creature that once lived in the lake. *Maybe it is still alive?* She never believed these stories, but this isn't normal. This isn't the storm, or her panic. This is something unusual.

Her boat goes up, and *stays* up for a few seconds. It is a sudden up-swell that lifts her plastic bubble of boat-shaped neon-orange plastic, and for a moment it feels as if she is air-borne, there is a blur of movement, there is a lurching, nausea-inducing sense of motion, rain lashes at her face and hair, and then she is slowly, almost gently lowered, until the dinghy is once again being jostled about by the water. It is unlike the crest of any wave she's ever experienced. It is as if a submarine briefly surfaced directly underneath her boat, carried her some distance as it equalized its air pressure, and then descended.

She might be stupid for getting caught in a dinghy with no lifejacket. But she *knows* this lake. Spends every summer swimming, pulling off black leeches with fishing line, sawing their wriggling bodies in half and scraping bloody sucker mouths from her wounded flesh. Spends every winter freezing in ice fishing shacks and skidooing along the shore to check on her grandfather's traps. But this? This is something out of the ordinary. It only lasts a few moments, and amidst her panic, it could easily be brushed off as something brought about by the storm, or chalked up to her imagination.

Is she closer to shore now? Or is she imagining things? Whatever caused the disturbance in the water, had come and gone quickly. She is again at the mercy of the currents. Currents pulling her into the deep waters of the lake. She still isn't out of danger. Regular waves, and regular panic overrides her confusion and out-of-the-ordinary fear.

She has to fight the current. Get to shore before the full force of the storm fills her dinghy faster than her cupped hands can bail out the chilly lake water. Her fingers are numb. She wouldn't be surprised if her lips were tinged blue. She can hardly believe how quickly the weather turned; how different the storm is compared to the hot summer day she'd been enjoying. The warmth of the sun replaced with the cold wind and rain plastering her white shirt to her body. Her hair, normally lank and dark to her shoulders, sticks wetly to her neck and cheeks. She would feel self-conscious if anyone was around to witness her wet t-shirt contest. She hadn't been planning on getting wet. She didn't even wear a swimsuit!

It is another rule broken: never go out on the lake if you're not prepared to get wet.

And she knows better than to get complacent. She heard enough stories of people going missing; their bodies never recovered. Any lecture she'd be given, she would nod and agree with. *Stupid. Stupid!* She knew better. Her father always taught her to be cautious when it comes to water safety. To always wear a life jacket when she was on the water. She will listen better in the future, she promises herself. *Just get me to shore first*, she prays. Then she will happily endure the lecture that she deserves.

She keeps paddling, keeping an eye on landmarks on the distant shore to track her progress, but she's getting tired. She's losing strength. And still she doesn't seem to be getting much closer. She's still having the same problems. All she accomplishes by setting course for their cabin is stasis, preventing the current from taking her any further out onto the lake, but getting no closer to her destination. She can't fight the current forever. It's a losing proposition. The muscles in her arms burn with exertion, but she has to keep paddling. But the more she paddles, the weaker her arms become, and the smaller the cabin appears.

This isn't working! She needs to change tactics. Abandoning her sights on Cope's bay and their distant speck of a dock, she settles for making for the closest point of land. It may not be close to the cabin, but at least it is dry land. With excruciating slowness she makes progress, running parallel to the shore now, being pulled further from the bay, and their cabin, but at least making head-way in getting closer to land. She can walk once she makes it to the shore. Less chance of drowning on dry land, even if she does have to walk through a downpour. She is already drenched.

When she judges that she's close enough to shore, Kylie flops over the edge of the dinghy and holds her breath, prepared to plunge fully immersed into the water, but hoping it is shallow enough for her to touch bottom. She lets out her breath when her toes touch the muddy bottom, chin raised to keep her lips above water. Ridiculously she hears the theme song from *Jaws* playing in her head—dum-dum, dum-dum, dum-dum, dum-dum-dum-dum-dum-dum. The last thing she needs to worry about are sharks. This is a *freshwater* lake. But she can't help looking around for a shark's fin, or a giant sturgeon, or whatever it was that lifted her boat out of the water. *Electric eels! Octopus! Giant-squid!* This line of thought isn't helping.

The crest of each wave comes up to her scalp, so she gives a little hop to keep her head above water. Keeping one hand latched onto a plastic cleat for tying off the boat. Between waves she walks, dragging the dingy behind her. There is more traction on the muddy lake bottom than her cupped hands can manage. Luckily she managed to paddle close enough to the shore to reach the shallows.

Walking on tip-toes. The waves seem to be getting bigger and bigger, whipped up by the winds and the storm. She holds her chin up, and keeps a tight hold of the sagging dinghy, unwilling to let go of the flotation device. Her teeth chatter uncontrollably in her jaw. She is chilled to the bone.

She stumbles over the rocky bottom closer to the shore. Bashes one of her shins so hard on a rock hidden in the shallows she has to stop for a moment, sucks in breath through her teeth, ragged, rattling seethe of air in and out from her chest. It. Hurts. So. Much. She can barely see; it blocks out all other sensation. Pain. Pain. Pain. All she wants to do is curl up in a ball, waiting for the pain to recede, but she can't, the waves still crash into the back of her thighs, threatening to topple her over if she doesn't maintain her footing. She's going to have a nasty bruise. Once the pain subsides enough to keep going, she clambers over the rocks. Slippery with moss and seaweed. Dangerously slick. Has to put a hand down to steady herself. She's so close. All she wants to do is get to the shore.

She steps on a sharp rock that pokes into the sole of her bare foot.

"Ow! Ow! Ow! OW!" At least it isn't as painful as her banged-up shin, at least she can vocalize this time. She treads carefully. Still it's impossible to avoid every sharp rock.

Finally she's made it to the shore! Kylie steps gingerly over the stones on the beach. She is shivering with cold, and weak from her exertions, but she hardly cares. She's made it! She wants to sob and kiss the ground like a sailor lost at sea. She still has a long, long walk back to the cabin on their bay, but at least she is safe from drowning. Bruised shins and bleeding heels she gladly welcomes over the alternative—being stuck out on the lake in a dinghy during a freaking thunderstorm!

She knows she got off easy. It could've gone worse. Much worse. It almost had been worse. She wants to stop and rest, but more than anything just wants to get back home. Rain pelts her as she makes her way along the shore. Thorns from bushes growing along the shore claw at her clothes and scratch her arms. Draw blood like cat scratches. Burrs catch and tangle in her hair. Her long hair catches on a branch, and she doesn't stop in time, so her head is pulled back, and a hank of hair is wrenched out from her scalp.

Hsss!

Keeps going.

Stubs her toes on a protruding root.

"Anh! Anh! Anh!" She whimpers as she stumbles forward, she has to keep going to maintain her balance. Limping softly over the pebbles under her feet. Kylie throws her hands down, lips jutting out. Imitating her brothers, the way they act when she's seen them fighting. "Skoden!" She shouts the word like a swear word, feels her left eyebrow twitch, right eye squinted shut. "Stoodis!"

Why does everything have to be so hard?

Nettles from fallen tree limbs stab the soles of her bare feet. She has to push aside branches overhanging the water's edge that block her path. Dragging the stupid orange dingy behind her through the downpour. The sky cracks open, and lightning zigzags across the sky, no longer rumbling in threat, but deafening with every bolt. There is barely enough time to count off the one-misses in Mississippi between each flash and bang, action and reaction. Mississippi is an Ojibwe word. Misi-ziibii. The lightning is not very far away. Not very far away at all.

She no longer feels the same fascination she had watching storms over the lake from the safety of the screened-in porch. All she feels now is a cautious exhaustion. Wishing she was back home. Safe and dry. What is the point of escaping a near-death encounter, only to get struck by lightning?

Feet battered and bruised, Kylie finally trudges up the slope towards the cabin, and forces her tired legs up the stairs to the screened-off porch, screened off to keep the mosquitos at bay, then pushes open the screen-door into the kitchen, a double layer of protection against blood-sucking beasts. She leaves a dripping trail as she crosses the linoleum, realizes she is still clutching the deflated orange-plastic dinghy. Releases her grip an lets it fall to the floor.

Like something the cat dragged in. Now she knows what the expression means, because this is what she feels like. Like one of

Atilla's many "gifts" left lying on the stairs. Eviscerated mice, and half-eaten voles. As if anyone wants to eat his leftovers.

"Dinner will be ready soon," Her dad pulls a pot out of the oven and sets it on top of the stove to cool. The TV is on in the den, and she can hear Cadence laughing over the sounds of some stupid program.

No one has even noticed that she was gone. Her father doesn't look up from the pot he is stirring. Cadence doesn't look away from the TV. No one notices her. *Didn't they* know *the danger she'd been in! Didn't they know she could have been killed!*

She makes a point of stomping down the hall to her bedroom. Maybe she hasn't been gone for as long as she thought, but the whole ordeal felt like an eternity.

Kylie takes a long shower, letting the hot water redden her clammy skin, the sound of rain pounding against the skylight matches the scalding water pounding against her skin. She dries off, twists the towel around her hair, and wraps herself in a cushy bathrobe. Ties the robe around herself, and goes down for dinner.

They have a long monastery style table with wooden benches to fit their big family. Kylie's older sister Eadie and their brothers are all over visiting at Uncle Owen's in Cheapaye, so the table seems bigger with just Cadence, Greysen, and Eamon.

When Kylie mentions the extra-ordinary occurrence—no one believes her.

"I saw something strange." Kylie pokes at her mashed potatoes with a fork. "Whatever it was, it was *big*. Like a whale." She neglects to mention the part where she allowed herself to be drawn out onto the lake in an orange plastic dingy, without a lifejacket, and in the middle of a thunderstorm. Her father trusts her. She doesn't want to ruin that if she doesn't have to. She will just have to live up to that trust better in the future.

"You're such a drama-queen." Cadence rolls her eyes. "Nothing that big lives in the lake."

"But I did! I saw something!"

"I'm sure you did honey," Greysen murmurs, his narrow-lensed reading glasses are perched on the end of his nose as he looks over some papers.

"The Loch Ness monster?" Cadence teases. What a twerp.

"The whole dinghy lifted up out of the water!"

"There are stories of creatures in the lake… but every lake has those stories." Greysen sets his papers aside. It's true, her nshoomis loves telling these stories, as if they are actual real live beings. "Maybe it was a sturgeon?"

"Sturgeon can grow to be quite large—up to twelve feet!" Cadence's face is lit from a below as she reads something off the internet. "And they can live to be a hundred years old, and they've been around since the Triassic age, so they're basically dinosaurs."

"When I was your age, I saw some strange things," nshoomis Eamon laughs, flashing his even-teethed smile, "Could be your spirit animal come calling. Most folks have to fast for days first. You're lucky."

"Baah! You old bearwalker," Greysen takes off his reading glasses and folds them into the pocket of his shirt. "It was probably an up-swell of methane gas. There used to be a timber mill on the other side of the lake around the turn of the century—Cottilon Heathe & Company. Used to float lumber across the water. Some sunk to the bottom and got buried in the mud."

Her father's right—a rotten log is a more rational explanation. *Bearwalker* though. Kylie's heard the rumours about her grandfather too, but it's just gossip. People around here have nothing else to do except spread lies. A bearwalker is a medicine person who can transform into an animal—whether spiritually or literally. It can be an insult, depending on how it's said.

"It's the Christians who turned our medicine-power into a bad word," her nshoomis once told her. "It isn't. But some people see the devil everywhere they look."

Eamon doesn't look all that bear-like to her. He's rather frail and old. Plaid shirt, jeans, he sits with crossed legs, worn fur-trim moccasins on his feet. His over-sized glasses make his eyes look unnaturally huge. Like a magnifying glass. More owl-like than bear. But hey, no one said what animal you had to transform into, just 'cause you're a bearwalker didn't mean you necessarily needed to transform into a bear—maybe an owl is his animal of choice?

After supper, Kylie crawls directly into bed even though it's early. Her limbs ache. She listens to the storm as she drifts off. The thunder still sounds close, but she feels so much safer from the warmth of her bed.

As she sinks into sleep it's as if she is sinking down into the lake. She dreams about what it would be like to be a dead log rotting in the mud at the bottom of the lake, weightless, careless, strangely at peace. Then she's in the body of a prehistoric monster, undisturbed by the fury of the storm which continues to rage far above. The water doesn't feel cold, because it's the same temperature as the blood in her veins. Her body is large, with a dark hollowness, and she can change direction easily. A gliding sense of freedom. And the ancient sort of patience of something that has been alive for longer than humans have been a species.

She is the monster in the deep.

Dawson and Mackenzie put down anchor at a shallow, crescent shaped atoll, the boat rocking and bobbing in rhythm with the choppy waves. The sky is overcast, and a slight drizzle comes down, making their work a bit more miserable, though they both wear raincoats.

Mackenzie pulls out his kit, and takes samples of the lake-water in small vials to be sent to the lab for analysis. Dawson sets up the portable drilling equipment to take a core sample, a narrow sliver that will show the stratified layers of rock under the lake-bed, going back in time, the deeper they drill, like the cross-section of a tree. Each layer of sediment represents the passing of an era and will provide more data to complete the picture of the geological formations under the lake. With each new location they drill, they gather more dots to place on the map, and more dots to connect between locations: a picture is beginning to emerge of how deep the arteries of precious metals run, and where they are closest to the surface of the earth.

The swirl of a creature's body, grey-green scales, are for a moment visible as the water cascades around it, rises for a moment out of the water before subsiding back into the depths.

"Whoah!" Mackenzie yelps. "Did you see that??"

"Sturgeon," Dawson grunts, dismissive. "Ugly prehistoric fish."

They go back to work for a few minutes. Something thumps into the metal of their boat and sets it to rocking precariously. Both men struggle to keep their balance.

"What the hell was that?" Mackenzie shouts. They search the waters, half-expecting the sturgeon to reappear. They wait a few moments. Choppy water. Drizzle. They shrug at each other and go back to their work.

The sturgeon thumps against their boat again, harder this time, and again sets it to rocking. "Damn sturgeon!" Dawson curses, his equipment discarded and forgotten for the moment beside his green, knee-high rubber boots.

"Sturgeon my ass!" Mackenzie pulls on the cord to start the engine. It stutters then snarls to life.

The world tips over. There's an odd sensation of weightlessness, followed by a crash, and immersion into ice cold water. Mackenzie sees Dawson smash his skull onto the side of the boat on his way down. A spurt of blood arching through the air, and a thud-clunk sound of bone meeting metal.

Mackenzie surfaces, choppy waves jockeying all around him. The horizon angled crazily, the water frothing like a pot set to boil. "Dawson! Dawson!" Mackenzie screams.

Their boat has capsized, but is still afloat even upside down. Dawson is nowhere in sight. But then he sees a stain where Dawson must have gone under. Blood red dissipating into the brown water. Oh fuck! *He'll never be able to find the man in the murky lake, especially if he's unconscious.*

Flash of grey-green scales.

And then he's being dragged under, he barely has time to get a gulp of air, horrified when he realizes he's swallowed some of the bloody water, he can taste the metallic tinge of iron, the dark waters made even murkier by the addition of blood, obscuring his vision, he can't tell which way is up or down. He tries to swim up, but he's lost all sense of which way is up. He struggles madly, but gets nowhere. He doesn't know which way to swim!

There is a tightness, as if something is constricting him, and the deeper he is pulled, the heavier the pressure becomes, building and building, as the weight of the water above mounts overhead so he knows he is sinking. Somehow he is being pulled down, despite the air trapped in his lungs, which should have buoyed him up, he is being drawn down, down, down, his lungs burn with the need for new breath. Something presses in close, and he knows he isn't alone. But he can't see well in the murky depths.

Then. He doesn't see anything at all.

It happens in the early hours just after dawn. The last stars still fading from the sky.

Kylie's father Greysen nudges her awake. Kylie and Cadence silently dress, drowsy with the last dregs of sleep.

They launch their boat, and paddle away from the shore until the water is deep enough to lower the out-board engine. Greysen pulls on the cord, and the engine stutters before roaring to life, propelling them forward with a lurch, and shredding the sleep still clinging to their consciousness. Lapping sounds, creaking crickets, croaking frogs, loons calling to each other like song. CHAINSAW. The motor brazenly loud after the hushed quiet.

Their boat zig-zags through the smoke-on-the-water before her dad gets ahold of the rudder. The fog seems to part to let them pass, and they are enveloped in mist. Waves appear out of the whiteness a few feet in front of their boat, and disappear six feet in their wake. The moist air rushes past Kylie's face as they pick up speed, the occasional spray of cold droplets splash across her orange life-vest.

Attila, their black and grey dappled gaazhagence, is wrapped in his own life jacket, and sits at the prow, sniffing the air like a dog. He watches the terrain of waves as it slides by their boat, studying the surface with interest, tail twitching, the occasional spray of droplets drizzling him when they thumped into a particularly large crest. Attila is an odd cat. His fur is wet and flattened down, making him appear twice as scrawny. More fur, than cat. Attila actually likes water, and likes going fishing.

After fifteen minutes they pass Manitou Island, a ways out from Drinker's Point, that peninsula of land pointing to the island like a skeletal finger.

"Us Anishinaabek used to use the Michipicoten islands as graveyards." Greysen points out the islands in the distance. "Scaffold Island. Bone Island. Pine Island."

Under the surface of the lake, it might as well be another world, an alien landscape where beings breathe water instead of air, as opposite as wet from dry, life from death. Kylie imagines fish swimming in and out of this world, swimming from the living world to the afterworld and back again, coming and going as they please. The things that live a watery existence below the surface seem so separate from air and land, and yet they are part of it. It's still early. Her sluggish thoughts wander. Fish float through her brain, schools swim into her daydreams and back out into the lake.

Further out they arrive at their destination, a shallower area where the fish like to congregate on early mornings, doing whatever it is that fish do. Her father cuts the engine, and ringing silence rushes in to fill the absence, slowly replaced by the quiet murmur of waves slapping against the metal ribs of their craft.

"The islands move around on footings of peat and bog. They're not fixed to the lakebed." Greysen releases the chain to lower anchor. "It used to confuse mapmakers and lead explorers to their death, lost amidst the maze of shifting islands."

Kylie imagines the islands as pirate ships, gliding unmoored about the lake.

"Some are swallowing ground now. Muskeg. Swamp. When the dam was built, many of the islands were submerged, forming sandbars. It's a strange landscape under the water."

Kylie nods. She's seen tourists bottom-out at thirty kilometers per hour. A boat speeding across the lake suddenly became beached on a sand-bar. The contents, and people inside, carried forward by momentum. Ghost Lake has always been a dangerous place for the unwary.

Whether this sand bar was once an island, Kylie doesn't know, but it is a place where fish like to go. She hopes none of them nibble on any of her ancestor's bones, mummified when the burial grounds turned to bog, before being swallowed by the lake. Better to push these cannibal thoughts out of her mind, or she'll have trouble eating the fish. Not that it's very likely. The bones would probably have disintegrated by now. Or be washed up onto shore, and worn down like broken-bottle beach glass, but ivory-yellowed and opaque. Slowly ground down to glittering grains of white sand.

Rationally, it's possible some fish once had the opportunity to nibble on decomposing bodies, but *these* fish, the ones that are alive now, could only be the descendants of fish that had once had that opportunity. For some reason, Kylie doesn't find this train of thought any more comforting. Imagining zombie-fish developing a taste for human flesh. She gives her head a shake, dispelling the ridiculous thoughts. Fishing is a part of their way of life. Fishing is who they are, not just what they do. It's a part of them.

The sky is starting to glow with the approach of day, and the first rays of light carve through the fog, shriveling back like burnt plastic shying away from the touch of flame.

It's an hour after casting their first line in that *it* happens. Kylie is staring into the lake, hypnotized by the constant shift of shadows and light. Her dad is standing at the prow with his back to her, facing out to deeper waters, and her sister Cadence sits in the middle facing starboard, eyes glued to the pages of a book, gripping the handle of her fishing rod mechanically while squinting in the dim light.

Kylie has the aft, line disappearing into her own reflection, shimmering at some disturbance below the surface. *Maybe she got a bite*? But no, there is no accompanying tug on the rod. Not even a nibble. The water roils and bubbles, and then starts to lift as something large rises from the water. A flash of grey-green scales two inches below the surface. Their boat rises, lifted by an up-swell, then falls gently. The boat rocks ever so slightly at the disturbance.

Kylie yelps and turns, her eyes wide. "Did you see—"

"Settle down there," her father grumbles without turning his head, his knees bend to maintain his balance with the motion of the boat. "Gunna frighten away all the fish."

Cadence doesn't look up from her book, engrossed in the characters, plot, and sensations of the story. "I didn't do it!" Cadence whines, "It was Kylie!"

They hadn't seen!

The flash of grey scales. The rise and fall of the *entire boat* as some portion of something immense rose slightly above the surface, displacing two inches of water above the level of the lake, then leaving the waters roiling as it sank back into the depths.

But they hadn't seen anything!

—Yyeeeaaonnnhhwww—

Attila stares into the depths, flash of pink tongue as he licks his lips in anticipation, his tail thrashes violently, this way and that, and a yowling sound emerges from the back of his throat as he studies the surface of the lake.

At least Attila had seen it!

"Shush!" Her father says. "We might as well go and try over at Cedar Creek. You girls horsing around has scared away all the fish." They should have had a bite by now; this is usually a well-populated area. But they haven't yet had so much as a nibble.

Kylie agrees. They probably *aren't* going to find any fish here. Something else has already scared away all the fish.

The engine noise cuts through the last of the early morning fog like a blade, and they streak across the silver-surface of the lake—to try their luck elsewhere.

The creature rises up out of the lake, allowing one eye to break through to the skyworld above, just an inch or two above the dividing line between the worlds, just enough so it can see the retreating floater. It can see the girl's puffy orange life-jacket, her eyes on the spot they vacated moments before, a small four-legged creature with claws sits at her side, green eyes watching with a predatory fascination. Tail twitching with tension. Brave little thing looks like it wants to leap into water and give chase. Bravo.

Their wake grows in a wider and wider V the further away the girl goes. Soon, the floater and its occupants are nothing but a small dot on the horizon. The creature sinks down into the world below the sky, and the dark water masks its presence. Though invisible, nothing can stay completely hidden, the slightest hint of movement travels through the medium of the world in waves, the school of fish making a quick departure, the drifting weeds anchored to the lake-bottom below, each nearby living being, and those farther away, give away their presence, like distant vibrating, pulsations of light, teasing the sensitive tendrils of its fins. It can stretch out its senses to feel, and to listen, to hear every part of the lake. If it wants to. Instead, it drifts for a while with the current, drawn out into the deepest parts of the lake, before allowing itself to sink into the depth where few animals live, and where it can rest undisturbed.

BUSH BABY

"Can I come with you Nshoomis?" Issa asks.

"You know that you can't Noozhis," Tolton already has his hand on the brass door handle, but he can't bring himself to turn it. When his granddaughter gets like this, it makes it hard to leave. Knife twist to the heart.

"I know," Issa scans the room. Rustic floorboards. Worn leather couch. Colourful hand-knit afghan. The kitchen and living room is one giant open concept, from before open concept was a thing. "I know that."

"What would you like to read?" Tolton asks. "I'll stop at the library in town." This is his way of softening reality, bringing home stories of people and places and adventures from all over the world. The way he used to bring home chocolate. These stories are as bittersweet. Issa is limited to their cabin in the woods, and the immediate environs. She is never permitted to stray very far. She feels a bit like a Fairy Tale princess locked in a tower. *Rapunzel let down your hair*. But she is not a prisoner, except of circumstance. No one knows of her existence. Even if she knows she is real, and alive, and breathing. She may as well not exist. For all that it matters in the minds of everyone else, she does not. She is real to no one.

No one, that is, except for her grandfather. Tolton Chadybadis. Long grey hair. Fringe jacket, floral beadwork. Face like worn leather. Issa usually sticks to white dresses. She sews them by hand herself, store-bought clothes just never fit.

Tolton steps outside, closing the door behind him. And there is Edna Ogers sitting with legs crossed on the bottom step of his front porch. Her white hair is disarranged, but she somehow makes it look wind-swept and artful. Faded skinny jeans. Jean jacket. Silver feather ear-rings. Crooked smile. The dogs hadn't even kicked up an alarm!

"Boozhoo."

"Edna." Tolton nods. "You know I don't like visitors."

"No man is an island."

"John Donne."

"Hanh?" Edna scrunches one eye.

"The poem—" *Paah*, Tolton exhales. "Never mind."

"I see you've done a little decorating." Edna eyes the wards, bits of sinew stretched across willow, CDs and shards of reflective glass dangle from the nearby trees.

"Something to discourage the brave-hearted." Ghost Lake Indians have probably all heard stories of how unfriendly he can be, and he plays into this. Encouraging rumours of witchcraft. Bad Medicine. Caution.

"As if the hike up that cliff isn't enough of a disincentive."

"Honestly Edna—you live in the middle of the swamp, if there is one place on reserve that is less accessible than my home, it would be yours." He doesn't step down; he paces the front porch instead.

"It's where I live, yes. But *I'm* not a hermit. I have visitors." She's laces her fingers together over her right knee, leans back, arms propping her upright like a tent.

"You mean customers."

"You make it sound so unseemly. Yes. There's always a demand for good luck charms, dream catchers, love spells, and abortions. Those never go out of style." Her eyes sparkle with flecks of light, as if galaxies are caught within.

"Bush medicine."

"At least I'm still practicing. Yes. Who trusts those White doctors?"

"I have everything I need here. I'm fine." Tolton had been trained in western medicine.

"We are a communal people."

"So much for those traditional values of non-interference." Tolton pats at his pockets, as if searching for something he misplaced.

"I'm not interfering. There are three kilometres between us and I am your closest neighbour. What if I fall in the bath? Who am I going to call?"

"I don't have a phone Edna."

"Neither do I."

Tolton sighs. Edna seems completely at her ease and isn't making any move to leave, she is looking out over the trees and the view beyond, Ghost Lake visible in the distance. She inhales and exhales deeply through her nostrils.

"The air feels fresher up here, don't you think?"

"What do you want Edna?"

"Sharing the wealth" Edna indicates with her lips. There's a brown cooler on the top step. "My nephew's catch. More than we can eat. And I get sick of dried fish." This too, is part of traditional values of generosity. You never know when one good turn is going to come in handy. One good turn deserves another. Reciprocity.

"Miigwetch Edna. I really appreciate that." And he does—Issa really enjoys the fish. "But I was just on my way into Cheapaye." Tolton takes one step down from the porch.

"I thought you were off-grid?"

"Mostly, but not one-hundred percent. There are still some things that are better to buy in a store."

"Like what?"

"Most people send their grandkids on this mission of neighbourliness." Tolton nudges the brown cooler with the toe of one boot. He's used to having gifts dropped off on his front porch. You ignore your neighbours' welfare at your own peril, should you ever have need to call upon their aid in the future. Most people don't knock, thanks to his carefully cultivated reputation. "Why didn't you send your nephew?"

"Because he wouldn't knock," Edna says over her shoulder, her hair swaying just below her shoulders. Earrings catching the light, flecks of silver that match her eyes. "I'll find my own way down."

Bryan and Ryan appear, tails wagging. They sniff and lick the newcomer. Edna pauses to scratch Ryan behind one ear and continues on her way. Strange woman.

"Some guard dogs you are." Tolton opens the front door so Bryan and Ryan can squeeze through, kicks the cooler in through the door after them.

Tolton often returns the favour. They two can only eat so much. Though Issa does have a healthy appetite. It's better to share than to let food spoil. Fur from the animals he caught. Bead and quillwork Issa creates. These too, they gifted. Tolton is a recluse—but he's not insane. He merely values his solitude. And strongly discourages over-friendliness.

And this is what Issa likes to do best. To bead, and quill, and knit blankets for babies. There is not a baby that has been born in the last five years in a twenty-five kilometre radius, who has not received the gift of a baby blanket knitted by Issa. Of course, they don't know that it is Issa who does the knitting. They assume Tolton himself possesses these skills of craftsmanship. And this is true—for he was the one to teach her—but she has long since surpassed his skill. Outstripping his talents by leaps and strides from constant practice.

This is not the life Tolton would have chosen for Issa—if he had a choice. That he makes this choice is for her sake. To keep her safe.

Issa stays inside, crouched down low to stay out of sight. In case the woman looked in the window. Listening. She has good hearing. And Issa is grateful. Her grandfather loves her so much, he loves her so much that he lives his life in exile, living as a hermit in this cabin—he does this for her. And she knows how much Tolton sacrifices, how much her grandfather has given up in order to keep her safe. But still, she chafes under his care, she chafes under his watchful eye. His cautious nature. They are far away from the closest inhabitants. And he's always so careful. Sometimes she just wants to escape, to run away and say, "screw the consequences!" But Issa knows she will never do this. Tolton has sacrificed so much. So, so much. All to keep her safe.

Sometimes Issa wonders why he bothers. Is she really worth all this trouble? This fuss and secrecy? All the lies. Hiding from people and society. His own family, and friends, and relatives? His own people?

"Something fantastical," Issa says. "Or something from the Science Fiction section. Nothing real. Nothing of this world. I don't want anything that will remind me of everything outside that door."

"Something by David Eddings then?" Tolton asks. "Or Robert Jordan?"

"George R.R. Martin?" Issa pitches her voices into a slightly higher register to indicate the question. Or as high a register as her voice could go anyway.

"Kind of bloody isn't it?" Tolton scrunches up his face.

"The kind of mood I'm in," Issa shows her teeth.

The mood lightens, Tolton smiles at her, and turns the brass door-knob, letting in a stream of golden early-morning sunlight. They might be hermits, but they still need to stock up on supplies now and then. They aren't completely off the grid. At least, not yet. Tolton is always talking about ways of becoming more independent; solar panels, satellite TV. Though they do have a generator. And the internet! She would go crazy without a computer. Their flat screen can stream anything available on the world-wide-web. What need does Issa have for the world, when it is already at her fingertips?

Issa waits until Tolton has been gone for fifteen minutes, before she peeks out the curtains to make sure he's gone. He always leaves his truck parked out at the access road, some several kilometres distance; a good long hike along a rough trail. Their cabin is located at the top of a steep ridge, and surrounded on three sides by swamp—it's pretty inaccessible by anything that isn't on two, or sometimes four legs—and possibly a helicopter—not even an ATV can manage the trek. The terrain is too rough. This is intentional. There isn't much point in being a hermit if you live in town.

With Tolton gone, Issa decides to take a walk. She needs to get away from the cabin for a while. Besides. There is no one around for miles and miles. Tolton likes for her to wait for sunset to go for a walk, or nasty weather—when there is less chance anyone will be around. And never during hunting season. And never near any of the areas where other people are known to sometimes frequent. On days like today, she isn't permitted to go beyond sight of the house. Sometimes she feels like a child under Tolton's watchful eye, with his constant over-protectiveness.

Shoulders hunched, Issa opens the door a crack and peeks outside.

It is a beautiful sunny day. The birds are singing. The forest is alive with sound. Buzzing and humming with life. And there is no sign of Tolton to worry her with his concerns. Feeling daring, Issa ducks her head under the door-frame, steps outside, and takes the steps two-at-a-time, feeling her boots crunching over gravel.

Bryan and Ryan, her two dogs, follow closely at her heels as she sets out towards Jiibay Zaaga'igan. *Ghost Lake.* Though the lake is a popular place—it is a big lake, and her chances of running into anyone are still minimal. There are boats, and hikers, and swimming holes, and people. Not a lot of people, true, but on a day like today, they are bound to be around, especially out at the lake. Despite her height, Issa is good at staying hidden, blending in, and melting into the bush.

There have been a few close calls. No matter how careful they are. No matter how cautious. There have still been a few… unfortunate encounters. On these occasions she got to see first-hand why it is so important for her to stay inside. To remain hidden from the world. She doesn't like to dwell on these thoughts. Wide eyes peering through splayed hands. Lips pulling back from teeth. Contorted Faces. And the screams. The screams—

She shakes herself. It's a beautiful day. And Issa intends to enjoy it.

And for once, Issa *wants* to feel reckless. And hiking down the trail to the lake, Issa feels this recklessness keenly, the air brushing against her skin, the breeze rustling her long black hair. It almost feels as if she is naked, though she is modestly covered in her standard white dress. Good sturdy hiking boots. The heat soon has her sweating, even though her route is downhill. The way back will be three times as difficult.

But she is in good health, and strong, and luxuriating in the extravagance of being out and about on such a glorious day. No raincoat needed. The leaves all rustling in the canopy, branches clacking, buttery-soft sunlight given a greenish tinge as it passes through the leaves overhead.

Large rocks have tumbled down the slope to form small caves. And to her right a small chasm has formed, narrow and deadly in the dark. But Issa knows this hill-top, and the surroundings topography like shape of her own hips; she's spent almost her entire life here; fourteen years and counting since Tolton adopted her at four years old, and she barely remembers what life had been like before—doesn't want to remember—and she doesn't spend all that much time studying her own hips. The breeze shifts, the leaves rustle. She hears a faint groaning-mewling sound, like that of an animal in pain.

—Eeennnhhhaannnhhh—

Issa stops to listen. Nothing. Her dogs stop too, quirking their heads to the side—emulating her. Listening. Shaking her head, she chalks it up to her imagination. The way, sometimes, late at night, when she is working on a beading project, making two tiny little moccasins for a new-born, and over-tired, she imagines hearing things, voices or thumping sounds; or how sometimes, in the middle of the night she wakes, and in the darkness, in absence of any other visual stimulation she sees flashes of light as her mind invents imagery to fill the lack. The mind isn't designed to process nothing for very long. Gaawiin gego. *Nothing.*

She starts walking, but then stops again.

—Haeaoooeerrgh—

She's certain she heard something. For real this time. That wasn't her imagination. Her dogs heard it too; they sniff the air, clearly scenting something. They have a better sense of smell. She freezes like a rabbit sensing danger, nose twitching as it strains to catch some scent on the air. She remains completely still, as if the slightest of movements might draw the eye of an airborne predator. Flood of adrenaline, her thigh muscles twitch, jittering with signals denied. Fight or flight response. Her eyes scan the trees, roving for any sign of a threat. Danger. Suddenly feeling naked to be out in the open, in the daylight. And without the assistance of her grandfather. Either to invent a cover story, or distract the interlopers while she makes a quick getaway—as they had done on such occasions, other close-calls and near-misses. Like asteroids flying by on a collision-course with the earth, an impact could prove disastrous, as it had for the dinosaurs.

This time she is on her own.

—Hreeeeeeeunhhh—

The moaning sound again. What is it? She doesn't see anyone around. She doesn't see anything. She creeps closer to the sound, trying to keep her steps light. It seems to be coming from the crevice. She stoops and kneels, crawls forward on her hands and knees, military style. Peeks over the edge. Her dogs on either side of her, miming her actions like caricatures. They take direction from her. Images of old movies fill her head—the Lion, the Tin-Man, and the Scare-Crow taking a gander at their enemies over the top of a ridge.

Ow-wee-oh, yowh-wuh. Ow-wee-oh—

In the crevice below her is a young man.

His hair is a mess, blood has dripped down from a goose-egg on his forehead and dried in a drip-pattern down his face. His chin is swollen and scraped, he wears a back-pack that looks to have been wedged uncomfortably underneath him, and his leg is twisted at an impossible angle, like it has somehow become wedged under a boulder. Clearly the young man tripped, or tumbled down the embankment, picking up bumps and bruises along the way, before arriving in a mangled heap at the bottom. Leg broken. Issa can see part of the bone protruding from the stretched bag of his skin. She can see the white of the bone glistening in the dimness. His eyelids flutter, half closed, listless. Either from exhaustion, disorientation, or despair. Maybe he has already given himself up for a dead man. Who knows how long he's been down there? In that crevice, screaming and crying for help with no one close enough to hear.

The area is quite remote.

"Heeeeey!" His eyes fly open. He must have caught a glimpse of her and her dogs peeking over the edge. She ducks back quickly, her breaths coming fast. *He saw!*

"Hey! Hey. You up there. Help me! Come back! I know you're there. I saw you. Help. I need help! Get me out of here! Heeey! Heeeelp meee! Heey!"

Issa crab-walks back from the edge before she stands up, trying to get farther away from his line of sight. But having seen her—hope seems to have given the young man newfound energy, though his voice already sounds raw. Even a few paces away his cries are not all that loud. The acoustics of the fissure seem to be working against him. No wonder no one had heard him—even if he hadn't been out in the middle of nowhere—even a few steps away from a well-travelled path he might have gone unnoticed.

Problem solved.

All he could have caught was a glimpse. Maybe all he saw was her long black hair, dangling over the edge in a cascade. All she has to do is wait. He'd soon run out of energy. People can only live so long without food or water. And she is certain no one else is likely to find him. He won't be able to tell anyone he's seen her! All she has to do is walk away and pretend she never found him.

She turns around and walks back the way she came.

The young man behind her keeps screaming. "Heeey! Come back! I know you're there! I saw you! Come baaack! Please! Get me out of here! Where are you going? Heeeelp!"

Ryan and Bryan stay near the breach, listening.

Se-hay'. *Fuck.*

Issa stops. She can't leave him. She can't leave him and pretend she never saw him. She can't leave him out here to die. And besides—if he'd told someone where he was hiking—search teams would come. A rescue party would be formed to look for him, or to recover the body. They wouldn't stop until they found him—dead or alive—or it would be weeks before they gave up and things settled down. Weeks of unwanted scrutiny.

Tolton wouldn't like a dead body being found so near to their home. Tolton wouldn't like so many strangers being around. And Tolton wouldn't like search and rescue teams scouring his property. He owns several hectares next to the abutment beside the reserve. The rest of the land hereabouts is either reserve land, or owned by that wiindigo family—and they never come poking around.

Issa changes course, and hikes downhill. She follows the slope of the land to where the crevice begins, where it is only a small furrow in the ground. Then she follows the narrow corridor of rock, waist-high until it rises high above her—thirty yards or more. If he fell down from that height, the young man is lucky to be alive. Certainly no cell phone would get reception down here.

At certain points the cliff walls narrow, and she has to turn side-ways to fit through. At another point, the way becomes impassable with tumbled-down rocks. She climbs over the obstruction, her dogs yipping and whining behind her. They are unhappy to be left on their own.

In the distance she can hear the young man screaming, his voice echoes and re-echoes off the rock walls, and she wishes he would just give it a rest for a moment—though his voice becomes quieter as he grows hoarse, it is no less filled with desperation. For a brief moment she pictures smashing his head in with a rock, just to silence him, but quickly pushes the thought aside. She'd seen Tolton put an injured robin out of its misery once. One mangled wing folded back on itself, blood and feathers, flapping uselessly. There was no way it could survive.

She climbs over another barrier of tumbled-down rocks.

"I saw you! I saw you!" The boy screams, his eyes focused on the sliver of light from above. "Come back! You can't just leave me down here! You have to help me! Heeeeelp! Heeelp! Someone! Please! Help meeee! Heeelp—"

The young man cuts off abruptly when he sees her. She is standing only a few yards from him now—down in the hole with him, instead of up at the top of the gap. His face goes pale, his mouth hangs open, his hands shake. He tries to back up, to crawl away, but his leg is trapped. Pinning him in place. Mouse in a trap.

"Don't hurt me. Oh please. God." His eyes show off the white sclera around his irises, light brown with flecks of green and gold glitter in the light—somehow a patch of sunlight has managed to make its way through the canopy high above, and filter down to this subterranean-level like a spot-light. But he is shivering despite being bathed in warmth. No doubt this brightness has also ruined his night-vision in the dimness. "What are you?"

"I'm just tall" Issa says. "It's a genetic thing. Chill out." The lie rolls off her lips and seems to calm him, though she knows he doesn't believe her. He seems more frightened now, than when he thought he was a dead man—fallen down a fissure in the earth—where no one would ever find him. That fate is more natural, easier to comprehend, than this—whatever *this* is. He isn't certain. Maybe he just banged his head real hard? Maybe he is hallucinating? Maybe he is already dead? Dead and dreaming?

Issa knows how she appears. As she must seem to him. In form and feature, she is nothing more than a young woman herself. Though tall and big, proportionate to her height. Far taller than most human women ever grew to be. As tall as the tallest female basketball players; Malgorzata Dydek, Uljana Semjonova, and Gitika Srivastava. And other tall women like Sandy Allen, who is a Guinness Book of World Records holder. She read about these women on the Internet. Women with whom she shares the trait of height, though her stature is not some fluke of genetics, or the result of some medical condition—she is in perfect health.

She doesn't know how long she can expect to live, but if she were human she couldn't expect to live long given her size. Like Andre the Giant, people of her stature just don't tend to live all that long. It's too hard on the heart. But she is of average size for her kind. And according to Tolton, the Misaabe are long-lived, longer than humans anyway. It's hard to know for sure. There are so few left. There's no one with first-hand knowledge. Only glimmers she can glean from second-hand histories. Old stories. Legends.

Though Issa is female—she is not a woman.

She is Misaabe, a *Giantess*.

"Misaabe are considered lucky," Tolton always tells her. "They lived alongside the Anishinaabek. Appreciated for their strength, and skill in labour—warriors, and hunters, and builders. They weren't feared or derided—they were respected members of our nations—with rights and responsibilities the same as any other member of our communities—but with their own traditions and customs. You aren't a monster, Issa—there just aren't many of your kind left in the world. At one time, there were more, but now there are only very few."

"What if I'm the last one?" Issa asks. "The last of the Misaabe?"

"You aren't," Tolton said. "I'm sure of it. Miikinakominis... *Turtle Island*—Is a big place."

"What if I left? I could pretend to be human."

"You'd never be able to live a normal life. If people found out about you—it's not the kind of life you would want to live."

"What is normal?" Issa spreads her arms to take in the cozy, furnished walls of their cabin. One of her two dogs, the rottweiler Ryan, tilts his head and whines sympathetically. The bulldog Bryan continues dozing. "Is this normal? Is this life of hiding normal? We could tell people I have a medical condition—we could say I have a tumor in my pituitary gland like Yao Defen!"

"The medical community would examine you. They'd take blood samples, genetic testing—they'd find out you aren't human, you'd be a lab rat—they'd never let you go." Tolton holds her gaze so she can see his concern. "That's not the kind of life I want for you."

Issa nods. She understands, though she doesn't have to like it. And she agrees with him. But she still can't help venting her frustrations now and then. She learned enough of the world from newspapers, books, the radio, and the Internet—enough to know that it would be a very bad thing if the world ever found out about her existence, or if scientists ever got their hands on her.

She isn't human, and Tolton is correct to fear that the same rights to life and liberty might not be applied to her, any more than they are to other sentient creatures, let alone his fellow human beings. Many would react with fear and hate, as they do with anything that is different, or other.

She would never be safe again.

And again Issa considers simply bashing the young man's head in with a rock, but quickly pushes the thought aside. Doing such a thing would only confirm her worst fears—that she is truly a monster.

Ryan the Rottweiler and Bryan the Bulldog have found their way past the tumbled down rocks, and come snuffling up to the young man, tails wagging, sniffing him with interest. Bryan licks his face, and the young man lifts his chin, so the dog can't lick his mouth.

"What's your name?" Issa asks. She searches his features—is he one of the Ghost Lake Anishinaabek? Or is he a tourist?

"P-P-Peyton." He stutters. "Peyton Neyananoosic."

A band member then. So many had married-out. But what is he doing here? The Ojibwe know better than to come poking around here. Although, along with the Burnt Grounds and the house of the Wiindigo's Daughter, she supposes there are a lot of places that are off-limits.

"Don't you know you're not supposed to come up here?"

"I, l-l-like hiking," the Neyananoosic boy says. "I-I thought I'd have a better view from the top of the ridge. I c-c-couldn't get through the swamp. S-s-so c-came around from the south-east..."

"That must hurt," Issa's hand hovers over the shard of bone protruding from Peyton's shin. His pupils are widely dilated from adrenaline, he squints against the glare to make out the details of her face—his pupils contract as his eyes shift focus.

"It's just kind of numb," he says, "I can't feel it anymore."

"You're probably in shock," Issa crouches to bring herself closer to his level. "My name's Issa."

"Are you going to k-kill me?"

"I thought about it." Issa purses her lips. Tries to keep the depth of her voice within the human range. The lower octaves—like the double rows of her teeth—give her away as something other than human. Issa knows she isn't evil, but Peyton doesn't know that. And she's seen enough horror movies to know her speaking voice can sound demonic. If she keeps her voice high—it can pass for normal. "But I don't think there's much point.

You're a dead man anyway if I just walk away. There's no need to murder you? Now is there?"

"You're not going to eat me?"

She laughs—hating the way it sounds, hearing the low and high registers in chorus, and probably showing off the double row of her teeth, one line of dentition inside the other. Supernumerary, Tolton called them, or hyperdontia. "I'm not a wiindigo."

"What are you?" Peyton's Adam's apple bobs up and down as he dry-spit swallows from dehydration.

"I told you," Issa says, knowing how hollow the lie sounds. "I'm just tall."

"W-what are you going to do?" Peyton asks.

"Hold on. This is going to hurt." Issa puts two hands on either side of the boulder where Peyton's foot is wedged, the size of three or four bowling balls—and lifts—it looks like a basketball in her hands. She sets it down gently on the earth beside him, next to his head.

"Huunh. Heeeunh. Huunh. Heeeeunh." Peyton takes sharp intakes of breath. He groans in and out as he manages the new pain. His leg strained, his foot flopping free. It isn't half as numb as he thought. Not at all. He passes out, darkness swallows the pain.

Issa kneels, and scoops him up like a rag doll, like she is carrying a child in her arms. She stands up carefully to maintain her balance—she doesn't want to drop the unfortunate Anishinaabe—and then she makes her way back out through the canyon, the way she'd come. It is probably better that he lost consciousness, at certain points, the passage is quite narrow, and it is impossible not to jostle his injured leg. At one point, Issa is forced to lift him high over her head so they can both fit through at the same time, as she is unable to carry him through side-ways single file. Not enough leverage. But holding him under the arm-pits and lifting him straight up so that his legs dangle in front of her, she is able to squeeze them both through. Just barely. Had he been awake, it would've been a painful experience.

She hopes she isn't doing more damage. Unconscious, he seems so fragile and easy to break. Like a marionette made of sticks. She makes her way out of the furrow, then starts the ascent, carrying him piggyback, his head and arms draped over her shoulders and neck. Her hands support him under his thighs, so when she leans forward, most of the weight is on her back. This way if she trips on the upward-slope, she is more likely to fall face first, he'll have a softer landing, instead of crushing the burden under her own weight.

Ryan and Bryan lead the way, tongues lolling happily as they back-track, turning their heads and waiting for her to catch up. Issa climbs the front steps and opens the door, awkwardly manoeuvring them through the doorframe. She lays Peyton on the couch, tries to position him comfortably, raises the injured leg on a pillow, and covers him with a blanket. Cleans dried blood from his face with a damp cloth. He moans in his sleep, but doesn't wake up. She waits for Tolton to come back. Tolton will know what to do.

The light is failing by the time Tolton returns home. For once the dogs alert Issa to his arrival before she detects his presence. She'd nodded off in the lazy-boy and didn't hear him until he was already standing in the doorway, silhouetted by the setting sun like a halo, his grim expression in shadow. She sees the tightness of his brow, and the thin line of his lips as he takes in the sight of the Anishinaabe boy sleeping on the sofa. Leg raised, injury on full display.

"I found him on the ridge," she whispers. "He fell into a crevice. I couldn't just leave him there."

"No. Of course not," Tolton finally says, closing the door behind him and blocking off the light from the setting sun. "Has he seen you? Or was he unconscious the whole time?"

Issa looks at the uneven floorboards. "He was awake when I found him."

Tolton lets out his breath in a rush, as if he's been holding it.

"He's seen you then?"

"I told him I'm just tall."

Tolton laughs. Crow's-feet crinkle at the corner of his eyes. Tolton isn't really old enough to be her grandfather, but he is aging into the role—and it's the closest way of describing their kinship. She is his granddaughter in every sense that matters.

Peyton stirs and mumbles in his sleep. Tolton shakes his shoulder and holds a glass of water to his lips. He must be thirsty, because the moment the mug touches his lips, he grabs the cup on either side with his hands and upends it, draining it down in under seven seconds, his Adam's apple bobbing. In his haste, the excess flows around his lips and down his chin, dampening the front of his shirt.

"Here. I'll get you another," Tolton takes the mug and refills it. "I'm Tolton."

"Mr. Chadybadis. I know. Grandad has me drop off fish. I only ever leave it at the front door though." Peyton turns his head to see Issa watching from the lazy-boy. He flinches. "I thought I just dreamed you."

"Powerful dreams," Tolton pulls a first aid kit down from the shelf, and readies the tools he will need to treat the injuries; needle and thread, tweezers, plyers, scissors, medical tape, gauze, tensor bandages, alcohol, cotton swabs… lucky for Peyton, they are well stocked with common drugs and medical supplies. It's a long ways away to any kind of treatment facility. Though Issa has never been treated. Not for anything. "You're lucky Issa found you. Not a lot of folks around here."

"I know," Peyton turns his face into the couch. "My grandad says not to bother you. Just to drop off the fish and go. Not to hang around. That you don't like visitors."

"Your grandad is right." Tolton frowns at the boy. "Are you allergic to hydromorphone or other opioid narcotics?"

"Not that I know of." Peyton shrugs.

"Good." Tolton holds out three pills in the palm of his hand. "Take this. You're going to need it."

"What is it?" Peyton asks, but takes the pills and swallows them before he hears the answer—he must be in a lot of pain.

"Two are painkillers. I don't have intravenous drugs like propofol, those will have to do. The other is a blood-thinner." Tolton takes the empty glass. "It'll take a few minutes for the drugs kick in. We need to re-set the bone. It looks like a clean break. An open and displaced compound fracture."

"Shouldn't you take me to the hospital?" Peyton tries to push himself up into more of an upright position. Winces, and falls back.

Tolton shakes his head.

"Tolton is a doctor," Issa tells him. "You're in safe hands."

"Not unless you want to be air-vac'd." Tolton laces his fingers together, thumb sticking up like a steeple. "Might do more damage. Better off if we re-set the bone and splint your leg before we try moving you."

"How long before the pain-killers kick in?" Peyton's lips are pulled back from his teeth in a grin. He takes quick, shallow breaths.

"It shouldn't take long," Tolton says. "But first…we need to talk about Issa."

While they'd been talking, Peyton avoided looking at Issa, as if by not acknowledging her presence, he could ignore her existence. For some reason, this was making Issa antsy; she wanted to get up and start pacing. But standing up to her full height would certainly draw attention, so she struggled to sit still. Finally, she'd gotten to meet another human being, someone other than her grandfather; she'd rescued him from certain death, and still he couldn't even bring himself to look at her.

Something tight in her chest aches. She feels like a monster.

Peyton turns his head but doesn't meet her eyes. His nostrils flare. He's afraid of her, Issa realizes. And that suddenly seems far worse than being ignored. She loses it. She can't help it, her eyes fill with tears, her nose gets all snotty and the tears slide down her cheeks. She's started bawling. The tightness in her chest has moved, it's in her throat now, and her eyes, and a whole-body despair swallows her. She tries to keep her keening down to a minimum, not wanting to hear the double-octave sound of her own sobs. She is such a freak. No wonder Tolton hid her away all these years. She is a monster.

Peyton raises his eyes, and finally looks at her.

"What's wrong? Peyton asks. "Why is she crying?"

"I think she's just overwhelmed," Tolton put one had on Peyton's shoulder. "She doesn't get to meet many strangers."

"*I'm a monster*!" Issa wails, crying louder, and covering her face with her hands as sobs wrack her body.

"Listen," Tolton crouches in front of Peyton to bring himself to eye-level. "You can't tell anybody about this. You can't tell anybody about Issa. People won't understand. And it wouldn't be safe for us here anymore. We'd have to leave."

"I won't tell anybody," Peyton says, then laughs. He's feeling a bit lighter as the pain recedes. "Besides—what would I say? I've met a *Giant*? No one would believe me!"

Issa pulls herself together and wipes tears from her face. She wants to hide in her room like a child and have a good sulk. Not that sulking would help change the situation any. Crying doesn't change anything.

"You saved me," Peyton says, looking her in the eyes now. Brown eyes flecked with green and amber. "I'd be dead if Issa didn't save me. I won't say anything. I promise. It costs me nothing to keep your secret. I've got nothing to gain by spilling the beans."

"Good. I'm glad you understand." Tolton pats his shoulder.

"It's time to set that tibia. Issa, I'm going to need your help for this. I want you to hold Peyton down. This is going to hurt."

Issa finishes wiping her eyes, and comes over to Peyton. She kneels on the floor behind the couch, reaching over the back so Tolton will have unobstructed access to his patient. She puts one hand on Peyton's shoulder, and her other hand on his thigh. He won't be able to do much moving around with Issa's weight anchoring him—no matter how much he writhes. She'll hold him steady.

"I'll do this quick, like a band-aid." Tolton places one hand on Peyton's shin below the fracture, and the other above the bone protruding below the knee. "Ready?"

Before Peyton can answer, Tolton pulls, first drawing the shards back into a horizontal position and flattening the tent of skin, then adjusting the two halves of the break, feeling with his fingers to make sure the parts are in alignment.

Heeaaunh!

Peyton gasps.

Issa holds him down as Peyton jerks and writhes—screaming—but he might as well have been strapped down with iron bands. Issa holds him stationary while Tolton works. Obviously the painkillers aren't strong enough to mask the pain.

Peyton lies panting heavily, sweat beads on his forehead as the waves of agony radiate outwards, lessening by degrees as the seconds pass, progressing forward in time from the source of action.

Tolton waits a few moments for him to recover.

"This next part won't hurt as much." He quickly and efficiently cleans the wound where the shard of bone tore through skin, stitches and bandages the wound, places a plank of wood padded with gauze along the re-set bone—a re-purposed spatula—and wraps both the plank and his shin with medical tape and tensor bandages.

"You're going to need an X-ray to make sure the bone is set right. We don't want your leg healing wrong. And there is a risk of infection because of the wound."

"Don't I need a cast?" Peyton lifts his head from the pillow.

"X-rays first," Tolton says. "There's minimal soft tissue damage—good given the type of fracture. You may still require surgery. Six months recovery. You'll also need crutches." Peyton nods, and closes his eyes. Resting now that the pain has faded somewhat, he can wallow in the haze of the painkillers.

Tolton and Issa share a look, and Tolton shrugs. Shit happens.

"Greysen?" Tolton holds the receiver of an old rotary dial to his ear—he'd lied to Edna about not having a phone. "You'll be happy to know I have your boy up here, my dogs found him. Managed to throw himself into a ravine..."

The next morning, they heft Peyton carefully into Issa's arms. And again she carries him like a child as they carefully make their descent from the ridge. Picking their way slowly so as not to jostle the injury. Once they have Peyton bundled into the truck, he lifts a hand in goodbye. "Thanks." Tolton shuts the door.

Issa watches as they drive away, bouncing down the access road towards the rest of the reserve, and the paved roads that lead to Cheapaye, and further on down to Sterling. Peyton raises his hand in a wave. Issa winces as she watched the truck traverse the pot-holes in the rough road. Even though Tolton drives slow, the truck doesn't have very good shocks. Issa waves back, then turns to disappear back into the shadows of the forest. It isn't safe for her to linger out in the open for long, by the road where anyone can drive by and gawk at her.

Shoulders slumped, Issa makes her way back up the trail to their house. She's certain Peyton will keep her secret. And for some reason that too, makes her sad. She recognizes that what she is feeling is disappointment. She almost wishes that Peyton would tell, they'd be all over the news, and their reclusive life would be busted wide open. But she knows that this is for the best. She's better off in hiding.

Over the next few months, Issa returns to her usual routines and occupations, reading and watching TV, scrolling endless cat memes, sewing moccasins and blankets for newborn babies. And when it rains, going for long walks in the woods, Bryan and Ryan following closely at her heels. The rain doesn't bother them either. At least she has the dogs for company. They don't care if she isn't human. They don't care that she's Misaabe. A monster. They love her just the same.

The weather cools. The trees burst with ochre and drop their leaves. The first snow fall comes and goes. The first blizzard comes and stays. The lake freezes over. The lake thaws. And freezes over again. The snow melts, and trees bud. The thunderers come to douse the world in rain. Issa heads out on one of her long meandering walks in the rain.

She is just stepping down the front steps when she notices the dogs sniffing the air. Their ears perk up. She sort of zoned out and didn't pick up on whatever it is they are sensing. "What is it Rye? What it is Brye?"

Peyton walks into the clearing that surrounds their house. Issa jerks back. He wears a transparent blue raincoat over top of his clothes, with the hood drawn up to protect himself from the rain. Her eyes dart around looking for danger. She wants to dash back into the house and hide, but then she remembers that he already knows what she is. He already knows her secret, and true to his word, he's kept those secrets to himself.

"What are you doing here?" Issa's shoulders hunch.

"I never got to properly thank you." Peyton pulls up the pant-leg on his jeans to show off his calf, and a long, wicked scar. "And look! It's all healed now. I walked all the way up here—no crutches!"

"I was just taking the dogs out for a walk." Bryan and Ryan circle Peyton excitedly, leaping, spinning in place.

"I would've come sooner." Peyton smiles. "But my leg wasn't up for the climb." Peyton holds up a basket full of all kinds of goodies—jams and soaps and candles in an arrangement. "Grandad sent me up with gifts. To thank you for saving my life."

"You're not afraid of me anymore?" Issa asks. Bryan and Ryan sniff Peyton, their tails wag enthusiastically as they greet the newcomer.

"Of course not. I would've died if you hadn't rescued me! Although—" Peyton kneels to pat Ryan. "I would have expected a Giant to be more hairy."

"I'm not Bigfoot!" Issa says as they start out on her walk. Ryan and Bryan keep pace as they enter the forest. Issa makes a point of keeping her strides short, so Peyton won't have to sprint to keep up. He walks with a slight limp.

"You're not Bigfoot?"

"No. I told you. I'm just tall." Issa laughs.

"Yeah. Tall for a Giant!" Peyton teases.

"Misaabe," Issa says. "That's what I am. Misaabe."

"Is that why you like dogs?"

"You've heard that too? That Misaabe had them first."

"—and gave them to Anishinaabek as a gift. At least you don't eat them!"

"Who would eat a dog?" Issa makes a face.

"Edna Ogers out by the swamp—says they're traditional."

"They are not!" Issa exclaims. "That can't be true."

"She's more of a cat person."

They walk along the ridge, a light rain falls, but neither of them notice. Too wrapped up in their banter to pay it any mind. Bryan and Ryan trot along beside them, happy to be outside even if they get wet.

HUNTERS' GREEN

What is that?

Crap. Cadence needs a new pair of glasses.

She's picking her way along the shore. She wears strappy sandals, overall-shorts and a light pink blouse with ruffles at the shoulders. She doesn't like her fat thighs showing, but at least the air feels cool. Her back is sweating underneath the straps. And besides, it's not like there's anyone around spying on her. This stretch of lake is pretty quiet.

She's mostly looking at the ground. She likes to look for fossils. Objects that wash up onto shore. One time she even found an arrowhead. Ghost Lake is known for its geology. That's why they're building the museum. If she keeps an eye out, she usually finds something of interest. Kylie thinks she's a total geek, which is *true*. But Cadence is the youngest, so everyone has to be nice to her, or so Kylie says. She's got it easy.

So far she's only found seashells, beach glass, rocks, sticks, driftwood, feathers.

Cadence looks up.

Dark shape in the bend of the lake. An arc describing a portion of the curve of a circle. 3.14… PI. Her favourite number.

Kylie just shook her head when Cadence happened to mention it once.

"Your such a weirdo. Of course you'd like a weirdo number too."

Thirty yards away. Is it a man? Some hunter tricked-out in camo-gear? Her recently-cut bangs scrape her eyelids, she tries to push the strands behinds her ears, but they aren't long enough and fan back into place. Awkward length. She can't wait until it grows out. Never let Sion cut her hair. Ever again.

Cadence doesn't see any fluorescent. Hunters always wear a certain amount of neon. Pylon orange or lime green. A certain percentage of clothing or a minimum of square inches above the waist. Her glasses are too scratched, and greasy. Cadence has no doubt that she also needs a new prescription.

Is it a bear? A moose? A deer? A Lynx? A Cougar?

Cadence tilts the frame of her glasses so the light has to pass through more of the lens before it reaches her eyes, trying to make sense of what she is seeing. It's definitely some kind of animal. It doesn't look like a moose. It doesn't really look like any animal she's ever seen before. But then, it *is* far away. And her vision is blurry.

She squints. It is a bear. It must be a bear. A brown bear. Coming to have a drink down at the water. Bears are definitely around, but she doesn't see them often, they're reclusive and need a pretty wide swath of territory. They are few and far between—except around the dump. But it doesn't really look like a bear either.

Then it stands up.

Not like a bear stands up—a bear stands up on its hind legs stretching its neck to see over some tall grass. A bear looks rotund and cute like a living, life-sized—though dangerous—stuffed animal. And bears have pointed snouts like a dog's.

This animal *doesn't* look like that. And Cadence doesn't think bears stand up all that often anyway. They prefer to walk on all fours. This animal is standing up like a man. In profile, it doesn't have that long muzzle. So it isn't a bear. And it isn't a moose or any other animal she's ever seen. It looks more like some kind of *ape*. It is monkey-like. Almost human. Andookomeshiinh. With a pendulous swing of breasts. It is female.

Her scalp tingles. She feels a chill despite the warm weather. Why would Anishinaabe even have a word for monkey? Cadence tries to remember what the word means. Something about lice. Maybe it's a new word? Like the ones for *computer* and *television*. Mamaandaawaabik. Mazinaatesijigan. Words she learned in Ojibwe language class at the community centre. She and Eadie were going every other Thursday.

Cadence has heard of Marmosets, and Capuchins, and Howlers, and Muriquis. Species from Central and South America. Scientists never seem to want to admit that anything comes from here, so they say those animals rafted over from other parts of the world. If it's one of those monkeys though, it would still be pretty damn far from home. And even *if* a monkey somehow managed to escape from a Zoo, or it was someone's exotic pet—they are still too small to be the creature she sees now: roughly human-sized, standing at the edge of Ghost Lake.

New species are discovered all the time, in the depth of the ocean, in the Amazon rainforest, in the super-market even. Every day new species are found—and even more are probably lost—going extinct before they've even been described. It's at least possible that a primate could've gone undetected—though unlikely given this creature's size. Someone should have shot one by now. To avoid capture and classification for so long would require intelligence.

But have they? Have they escaped detection and classification? Anishinaabek have names for *monsters*—numsookan in fairy tales, and aadisookaan, the *sacred stories* of winter. Stories of misaabe, and wiindigo, memengwesiag, and paguk. Bwaji-nini. Bigfoot. The wild-men of the forest. Little people. Mermaids, lake monsters, and thunderbirds.

Her eyes are as unreliable as those grainy bigfoot hoaxes Cadence has seen on the internet. The sasquatch is always grainy, always out of focus, and the footage jerky, shot with a hand-held camera. Some doofus in a bigfoot costume is going to get shot some day, some hunter will think it's a bear, because the costume doesn't have any fluorescent colours. It's not safe to be gallivanting around the woods wearing fur!

Cadence doesn't believe any of those grainy videos are reliable, and no one will believe her either, because her eyes aren't reliable. She doesn't believe it herself. She wishes she brought her cell phone. She could've made her own grainy bigfoot video. Documentary evidence. But these shorts have oddly shallow pockets, and nothing fits inside them. Very impractical. She wishes she hadn't made fun of her sister so much that one time, a few summers ago, when Kylie saw the Loch Ness monster out on the lake.

This is kind of like that—no one will believe her.

Cadence tears her gaze away from the animal for long enough to look around. Trees. Lakeshore. Lake. She doesn't see any cameras. No film crew. No red record button glowing in the undergrowth-of-the-woods-gloom. Only poplar trees and spruce. Shrubs and evergreens. A slight breeze ruffles the surface of the water creating finger-like ripples, lapping waves working the shoreline at her feet. Fluffy white clouds in the sky. It is a beautiful, clear day. Not the sort of day one would expect to see monsters or apparitions.

But there it is.

A dark shape standing at the edge of the lake, where the lake curves around, and there is a small sandy area where she and her siblings like to swim. Her brothers Sion and Severn, and Peyton. Her sisters Eadie, and Kylie. There are less rocks and less reeds and less leeches along this stretch of shore. It's a place where they lounge in the sun, soaking up the rays in swim-shorts. A towel. A paper-back novel. Shades and sunscreen. Maybe a bar of eco-friendly soap for a bath *Jiibay*-style.

The animal stands for a long moment at the edge of the lake. Is it looking at the water? Looking at the curve of the shore? Looking at her? It is too far away for her to see its eyes, or where it's looking. Maybe it's some sort of optical illusion? A mirage? Some trick of the light, reflecting off the surface of the water? A hallucination?

She pinches her arm. She's not dreaming. Should she hide? It suddenly occurs to her how odd this moment is. She can't move. She is unable to shift her weight, unable to look away, and now unable to even breathe. Even the rise and fall of her chest feels like too much movement, the beating of her heart is loud in her ears. Like gunshots thudding away in the peace-and-quite of the day.

Thump-thump, thump-thump, thump-thump.

Like a dead give-away of her presence.

But then the creature turns and lopes away. Walking smoothly into the brush and trees, walking quickly on two legs; an odd sort of gait. It is soon shrouded from view. Visible in brief snatches. Gone. Not gone. Gone. Not gone, then gone from sight. Out there somewhere. There is a lot of woods out here. A lot of forest. A lot of wilderness.

Cadence has never felt uncomfortable in the bush. She spent every summer growing up, coming out to the Lake. Hiking for kilometers to get out to their camp, before the roads were bult, before they moved out here full time. Greysen—her father, took her out hunting, let Cadence carry the rifle. Let her shoot. Sitting in their tree-blind for a week in November, waiting for a deer to walk by. Afterwards, she helped cut up the carcass.

They wore the hunks of meat like a vest, weighting themselves down like pack-horses to carry it home. There are photos of her smiling, wearing those meat parcels—reddish purple, slick reflective sheen, veins of yellow-white fat, marbled like cheese, marbled like cords of precious metal running through layers of the earth. Slabs of raw meat, no different from picking up ground-beef from the store, holding bags of groceries.

Smiling, because she shot her first deer, smiling because she knew that they'd be eating well for weeks, and that they'd have lots to share with their neighbours, friends, and relatives. And that old hermit on the hill. She'd felt so proud.

In all that time in the bush, she never felt scared.

Not once. Until now.

She's thirteen. Not a kid anymore. Too little to be scared of monsters. But monsters aren't real. And this, whatever this was—felt pretty real. The sight of the 'sasquatch' is burned into her mind, ingrained in fluorescent lights. Lit up like Victoria Day. The Fourth of July in the States. It isn't something Cadence can easily forget, or gloss over. Or un-remember having seen. Black-lit glowing in her brain.

As soon as the creature is out of sight, Cadence turns. She turns and runs. And she isn't even ashamed to admit it. Cadence has seen a lot of wild animals, but never anything she's been unable to identify. Could it have been a being from the spirit-world? Come to offer guidance or insight? Like a helper? Or is it a warning? Or just some animal? Some undocumented species of ape, roaming the forests in scientific obscurity? She doesn't know. And she doesn't want to get close enough to find out, so she runs, back the way she came, and away from the direction in which she saw the creature walking.

Branches and brambles slash at her face, her eyes, her arms. She makes her way as quickly and quietly as she can manage, hoping that she isn't being careless.

"Sound like an elephant" her shoomis complained once when they'd gone out hunting. "Like a rhinoceros."

Jejiibadakiinh. Ojaanzhingwedeyshkanaad.

Zoo animals from other places also have names to describe them.

Since there are words for animals from other continents, it isn't so unusual that there'd also be a word for a monkey. But there are also other words. Words like misaabe. *Giant*. Bgwaji-nini. *Wild-man*. And there are stories. There are always stories.

A friend of a friend who swore they saw a bigfoot. No one ever really believes these stories. Not really. They're just something to tell kids around the campfire. Like the stories of pa'iins. *The little people*. Or paagak. *The flying skeleton*. They aren't real.

When Cadence reaches the edge of their camp, she stops to catch her breath, breathing heavily beside their dock. Did she imagine the whole thing? Did she really see what she thinks she saw? Now, away from the place on the lake, the curve of the lake where she'd seen the monster, she doubts herself. Doubts that she's seen anything. Maybe it was only a bear. Or a moose.

Maybe it's time she got a new pair of glasses. Shkiinzhigokaajiganan.

VALEDICTION AT THE STAR VIEW MOTEL

"What did you say about my sister?"

"Your sist—?" is all Charlene manages to say before Eadie's fist connects with the girl's eye. Charlene's head snaps back with the force of the blow, and she reels and doubles over, palm cupped to the site of the injury. Charlene won't make that mistake again.

Charlene hasn't even spilled her drink though—Eadie will give her that—left hand held above her head to keep the brown beer bottle level, just-suppressed sobs hidden beneath her heavy breathing.

Eadie is one of the White kids. White-as-white-can-be with her pale blonde hair lighter than strawberry, now neon-pink to match the stud in her lip. But she'd also been adopted by the Neyananoosics. More than one White kid has realized their mistake when she drew attention to their racist bullshit.

Case in point: Charlene.

A few minutes earlier, Charlene started in. "Look at that chick over there," she indicated with a lift of her chin. "I bet she's screwed half the town by now." Sitting on a log on the other side of the fire was Eadie's younger step-sister Cadence, and some punk who was clearly keen on her. Charlene obviously didn't realize Cadence and Eadie are sisters.

There was some hooting and hollering from the guys around the fire at the potential cat-fight, but the confrontation was over quickly, with Charlene now holding her beer bottle to her eye to keep the swelling down, her boyfriend Jordie comforting her as she whines, "how was I supposed to know they're sisters!?"

"I told you to watch what you say around here. This isn't Sterling…" Eadie hears Jordie say as he leads his girlfriend to the edge of the ring of light. To the opposite side of the bonfire. As far away as they can get from Eadie, without actually leaving the flickering, popping radius cast by the flames. "Eadie talks with her fists."

After the brief outburst of violence, the laughter and chatter of the party resumes, rising and falling in waves from the various groups congregated around the fire.

This sort of misunderstanding happens more often since she returned home the year before last. At sixteen, Eadie left foster care and came back to Ghost Lake. By then, many people had forgotten her. But the Neyananoosics never forgot. They raised Eadie before her biological mother died, before Children's Aid swooped in to take her. The whole system is wrong, preferring that she live with messed-up people of her own race instead of a caring family who loves her.

Eadie hadn't really felt like going to the bonfire, even though it's a Friday night, but she knew Cadence planned on being there. She wanted to keep an eye on her. So Eadie went too. Separately, though, to give Cadence space.

On the way to the party, Eadie stopped at the Star View Motel, looking up at the unlit sign, the logo of a tree-line silhouette backlit by the night sky. It belonged to her Uncle Oogie, before his life spiralled out of control. Before he hit the alcohol and drugs pretty hard, before he ended up in jail. Eadie had been too young to know what sent him off the rails. She thinks he's still alive somewhere. Maybe. Maybe not. Maybe he's dead. There is an ache in her chest, squeezing, the way she imagines a mild heart-attack would feel.

They aren't blood-related, but Eadie remembers one time when Oogie took her and her siblings out for ice cream at the Cream Queen on Violin Road in Sterling. She remembers his gap-toothed smile, too. He was always smiling. Even though it made him look like a pumpkin.

Eadie and her siblings stayed up all night to watch the Leonid meteor shower.

"It only happens once every thirty-three years, you know?" Oogie says, his eyes glittering like stars.

The telescope is set up at the edge of the parking lot. They roast marshmallows, the glow of their campfire contained within the rusted metal O-ring of a tire. The only source of light pollution. In the background is the static and pop of the baby monitor in case Eadie's sisters wake up in the night. Kylie and Cadence, being younger, have already been put to bed, so it's just Eadie and her brothers, Peyton, Sion, and Severn. Bundled up in their winter clothes, earmuffs, and scarves, with mugs of steaming hot chocolate from a thermos, and the rhythm of Oogie's voice as he tells stories about the constellations. The Wintermaker and the Underwater Panther. The Sweat-Lodge. Moose, Crane, Loon, and Fisher. The Road of All Souls, and Hole in the Day.

"A meteoroid is part of an asteroid or comet. It's called a meteor if it burns up as it enters the Earth's atmosphere, and a meteorite if it actually hits the ground." Oogie knows everything there ever was to know about the sky.

An observatory was built north of Ghost Lake, probably owing to the uncommon lack of light pollution and the clarity of the night skies. Maybe that's what triggered Oogie's love of astronomy.

One by one, Eadie's brothers slowly drop off to sleep as exhaustion overcomes excitement. Eadie's eyelids feel heavy, too, though she struggles to stay awake, to see every last streak of light as they speed across the sky.

"Do you see that?" Oogie's voice is hushed. Eadie's eyelids pop open in time to see a meteor blaze across the sky, so bright it blocks out the light of the other stars, creating its own halo of day, so close it seems to hit the ground just over the next rise. She knows it must've been an optical illusion because she would have felt the thud of impact if it hit the ground.

"A meteorite!" Eadie turns to her brothers, but they are fast asleep in their fold-up chairs.

"Anang." Uncle Oogie smiles his pumpkin-faced smile, his eyes sparkle, and his cheeks are ruddy with the cold. Eadie shares the smile; co-conspirators. The only ones to witness the magic moment. Anang. Star.

She falls asleep not long after, the brightest of meteors illuminating her dreams.

She feels a distant lightness as Oogie carries her to bed. She knows that he must have carried each of her siblings, one by one, to their beds, too. They'd been up way past their bedtimes.

...But that was many years ago.

Eadie stands in Oogie's old Star View Motel, looking up at a hole in the roof where the rain has got in. Ironic, now, that stars are actually visible from inside. Though the windows are boarded up, teenagers have pried apart the plywood so they can squeeze through. Stepping through the window frame, she feels the glass grind beneath her combat boots. The occasional party or hook-up takes place here. The occasional transient sleeping in an old motel bed. Most of the rooms are undamaged, though the building as a whole is in bad shape—especially here, where a sapling grows in the middle of the room, bathed in a beam of moonlight. Nature is slowly reclaiming its rightful place. Water stains and algae mould crawl up the peeling walls.

Was that shooting star really a meteorite? Or did it burn up in the atmosphere, before it ever had the chance to hit the ground? Every time she goes for a hike, Eadie wonders about it. If one day she might find it.

The party is in the forest, a short walk from the motel, out past the old Anishinaabek version of a totem pole surrounded by disintegrating railing with rusty nails. Far enough away from the road that the noise and light won't attract attention. There isn't all that much to do in Ghost Lake or the nearby town of Cheapaye. The name is a perversion of an Ojibwa word—Jiibay, the same name as the lake.

Jiibay means ghost.

Eadie has never seen one. But there are lots of stories.

The motel isn't haunted as far as Eadie knows, though it stirs up memories. A dusty sadness sifts down in the still air, her thoughts as sad as the old Star View. She picks her way through the rubble of broken beer bottles, human excrement, and smashed furniture, and finally outside to the fresh air. She steps away from the crumbled-down motel and towards the party.

It's that ugly tail-end of winter, when all the snow is mostly melted, revealing all the hidden garbage underneath, but it's still cold; Eadie's breath is visible with every exhale. When she gets to the bonfire, she hangs back, watching the revelry. Kids from Ghost Lake and kids from Cheapaye. Mostly Indians. But some White kids, too. Clumps of teenagers sitting on felled log benches. The fire pit has been dug deep, and you can't stand too close for the heat.

There is Garion, wearing black and steadily feeding the fire, dragging entire branches out of the bush. The fire dances in the twin pupil of his eyes, like mirrors reflecting his soul. A natural born fire-starter. Eadie wonders if he's ever received fire-keeper teachings. The bonfire is too large to jump across, though that doesn't stop kids from trying and getting their asses burnt.

It's a stupid game. Entertaining, but stupid.

That's when Charlene sidles up to her, probably thinking Eadie's another White girl she can bond with over White-girl things and oh-so-casual us-and-them racism. No matter that Charlene's boyfriend Jordie is an Indian.

Mushkeg is at that field party, too, in a leather fringe jacket, matching fringe purse, bright red lipstick, and high-heels. Native high-fashionista. Rez-chic. Man, is Mushkeg ever beautiful. Forties hair-do like a World War II nurse, hair piled up on top of her head in waves. Eadie notices Mushkeg smiling at her from across the flames, watching through a bird-cage veil as the scuffle with Charlene plays out. Is it approval at how Eadie handles herself? Derisiveness? Amusement?

Eadie learned in art class that the eye goes to the point of highest contrast. Maybe that's what Mushkeg is, and why Eadie's eyes go to her. A point of higher contrast.

Eadie's own fashion sense tends more towards grunge/punk-rock than high-fashion-anything. It's a lot easier to dump a new shade of Kool-Aid in her hair each week than it is to pile it up into something that elaborate.

"Hey chick-itaaa kwe!" Mushkeg makes her way over, flask held high, hips swaying in a way Eadie can only think of as a runway model sashay. How can she walk in those heels? "I like your style."

Eadie doesn't get the sense that Mush is referring to her wardrobe. Faded jean jacket sloppily stitched with patches from various bands. Ripped green cargo pants. Boots she'd gotten from an army surplus store.

"Thanks." Eadie feels her cheeks flush.

"You're plucky, just like Tinker Bell." Mush takes a sip from the metal flask, her face puckers. "Good shit."

Eadie waggles her fingers. "I will curdle your milk and make your livestock siick." Mushkeg giggles, much to Eadie's relief. It's a lame joke. Humour can fall flat. Make things awkward.

"Tink isn't a witch," Mushkeg says, one eye scrunched up. "She's a fairy."

Eadie snorts. "What does that make you? Peter Pan?"

"Tiger Lily, of course. Fuck Peter Pan." Mushkeg flicks her head, as if to use the motion to toss hair out of her eyes. But her hair is pinned up, so it stays immobile. The interlaced web of the fishnet-veil makes her look glamorous, like some sort of film noir star.

"I always wanted to be one of the lost boys." Mushkeg raises her eyes to the sky, maybe searching for that second-star-to-the-right, past the glare of the bonfire and the brightness of the moon. "I never want to grow up."

"Who does?" Eadie takes one last puff on her cigarette, and then crushes it out on the log they're sitting on. She needs to quit. Maybe next week.

Mushkeg holds her flask out, eyebrow raised. Eadie takes a swig—it's Rusty. Eadie hadn't figured the girl for a whiskey drinker. It has a slight sweetness that burns on the way down.

Mushkeg nods. "Wish fulfillment, I guess."

Eadie often has the same thought. Press the right buttons, light up those pleasure centers of the brain, and you'd get the correct results. Carve up the brain into its component parts and people aren't all that complicated. Eadie had her fair share of social workers trying to analyze her. Figure out why she "acts out." That psycho-babble is easy to pick up.

"The unconscious repression of desire?" Eadie's eyes follow the curving path of sparks.

"Repressed? Who said I'm repressed?" Mushkeg's voice pitches high. "Fuck Freud. And his damned cigar." She takes a haul on her cigarette, red lips melodramatically pursed around the filter.

"I always thought Peter Pan was gay." Higher and higher the sparks rise, until they disappear into the stars.

"Because of the tights?" Mushkeg has a shrill laugh, and Eadie can't tell at first if it's real or if she's just pretending. She decides no one would pretend to have such an ugly laugh.

Eadie launches into it. "What was so horrible about Victorian England, that Pan had to retreat into a fantasy world of make-believe? One where he would never have to grow up, or face his latent homosexuality."

"That's so twisted!" Mushkeg cackles. Eadie feels a warm glow spread through her ribs that has nothing to do with the Rusty, pleased that her rant is being met with amusement.

It emboldens her to go on.

Eadie leans in and drops her voice to a deeper, wispier register. "Wendy, Tiger Lily, Tink—even the bloody mermaids—they all want him baaad. But Pan? He only has eyes for his lost boys."

"Well I'm not repressed!" Mushkeg sits with her back straight, shoulders pushed back in defiance, eyes flashing about the clearing. The heat creeps up Eadie's neck and into her cheeks. She's up in the clouds, tingling. Eadie doesn't want to get her hopes up if she's misreading the signs. But, screw it! No pain, no gain. If she doesn't take risks and play the game, there'll be no way she'll ever have a chance of winning. Right?

Or losing. But she quickly pushes that thought aside.

She eyes her sister Cadence, laughing amongst her circle of friends, the rangy boy still fawning over her. She trusts Cadence enough not to get knocked up, anyway.

"Come on." Eadie grabs Mushkeg's hand and pulls her to her feet. But the flask is raised mid-drink, so Mushkeg splutters and chokes, laughing.

"Hey! That's good shit. Yer making me waste it!"

Charlene is enfolded in the shelter of Jordie's arms, Eadie can feel her tracking them as they leave the circle of light cast by the bonfire. Eadie doesn't care what that townie thinks. She is probably going to spread nasty lies about her. Eadie knows the type, and is happy she'd hit her as hard as she had. The fight was over before it started, but Eadie will probably still have to deal with some fallout.

They pause on the wooden footbridge spanning Tyner's Creek.

"Some kid died here. You know?"

"I know." Eadie nods. Everyone has heard the story. An urban legend, really. It's said the spirit of a small child walks the shore's edge, haunting the river where he'd been murdered. 'Tyner' is an Anglicization of the original 'Tynuck.' Whether the story is real or not, the origins of the name is likely pre-colonial.

This close to the source of the spring, the water is pure and clean, unadulterated by the dilution of runoff and the various tributaries, before it joins with the larger body of Ghost Lake. The source for the stream is actually subterranean, so it's a popular place for people to come and collect fresh spring water.

Mushkeg and Eadie peer over the railing, watching the water rush by below, bubbles and froth floating on the surface of the churning river.

"Hcccuuaaacchk, chhhkkkkaaaccht."

Mushkeg stands on tip-toes, her high heels perched on the railing as she horks a loogie over the side. They watch as the ball of spittle, phlegm, and snot separates, and spins about by its center of mass, connected by an extending translucent strand before landing on the surface of the water, just another bit of froth carried away on the swiftly moving surface. It is mesmerizing.

"That was very attractive."

"I do try," Mushkeg curtseys.

They make their way through the trees and across the barren parking lot of the Star View, walking across chewed up asphalt and the lines of faded yellow paint, and over to one of the motel's rooms.

"How do you have a key?" Mushkeg raises an eyebrow as Eadie flips through her key ring. She fits the correct one into the lock, and feels the vibration as the dead bolt shuffles aside.

"My uncle Oogie gave it to me. A long time ago. Back when he was still running the motel—just in case I ever needed a place to stay."

"Oh, right. I keep forgetting you're a 'Noosic."

"You and everybody else," Eadie mutters as the door swings open and the stale air trapped inside wafts out. It's musty, but the roof hasn't caved in here so there's no mould or mildew, just the drab brown carpets, grey coverlet, peach walls, and green drapes. Eadie tries the light switch, but of course it doesn't work. The power had been shut off long ago, so she opens the curtains to let in natural light from the moon, metal loops sliding across the metal rung with a shfff. At least it's relatively warm away from the windchill.

"Is your dad ever going to do anything with this old place?

"I think he's still hoping Oogie will come back one day."

"Sad."

"This is the honeymoon suite." Eadie swipes her arms to the left and right to clear a path through the cobwebs. "It's the only room with a chimney."

"You know you're never further away than three feet from a spider."

"Uounhh," Eadie shudders. "That's not true!"

"Well, in most natural environments. They occupy almost every ecological niche. Want to know how many pounds of bugs people eat in their lifetime, just from the ones that fall into our food?"

"Okay," Eadie holds up her hand. "Let me stop you there."

"—estimated, like, one or two pounds! Per year!"

Mushkeg kneels before the interlocking stone of the hearth, holding a butane lighter to some crumpled napkins that still have the ruby impression of her lips. Within moments, the old dry logs in the fireplace are lit, and the flames throw a cheerful glow that quickly spread to the rest of the room.

"How'd you do that?" Eadie asks.

"Do what?" Mushkeg rolls back on her heels. The stiletto-spiked boots are the kind Elvira would wear. Mushkeg certainly has the boobs for it. Elvira boobs.

"Get the fire going so fast. Like some sort of wizard."

"Magic." Mushkeg's face scrunches up in a smile.

"I don't believe in magic." The stillness of the motel infects Eadie's voice with its melancholy silence.

"Everybody's got some kind of magic." Mushkeg plunks down on the mattress, her boobs bouncing with the bed-springs. "Even if they don't know it."

"Wait, what's your magic?"

"I thought you said you don't believe in magic?" Mush smiles, eyes sparkling, a hint of purple eye-shadow amongst the coal. I'm not going to tell you unless you tell me you believe. "Every time you say that, a fairy dies."

"Oh, come on!" Eadie rolls her eyes and flops onto the bed. "Tell me."

"Have you ever read Charlotte's Web?"

Eadie frowns. "Yeah. And the movie—the cartoon."

"Well, that's my magic. That's what I can do."

"You can talk to spiders!?" Eadie's lip curls, the backing on the pink stud scrapes against her teeth. When she is nervous, she can't keep her tongue from feeling around the crevices of the piercing. A nervous tic.

"Nooo! Well—maybe." She looks down at the patterned carpeting on the floor. Shrugs. "They talk to me. Same thing."

Eadie props herself up on one elbow. "Can you get them to write letters in a spider web?"

"I don't know," Mushkeg tilts her head. "I've never tried."

"So you're more like Templeton."

"Templeton was the rat!"

"It's either that or the pig."

"Fern! I'm the girl! Fern! Obviously."

"Goof!" Eadie hits Mush with a motel pillow. Mush squeals, picks up a pillow.

"Errr, not so hard you dweeb!"

"Hoser."

"Khcnunh khcnunh khcnunh." Eadie makes oinking sounds. "Templeton! Wilbur!"

"I yield! I yield!"

Eadie holds the pillow above her head, poised for another blow. Mush's hair is disarranged, make-up smudged, eyes squinted shut. Eadie drops the pillow, performs a reverse push-up to bring her face close to Mushkeg's. And kisses her. Mushkeg's eyes fly open in surprise for a moment before her lips melt into the kiss, and her eyelids flicker shut again.

Eadie pulls back after a minute like a swimmer surfacing for air.

Mush's dark eyes filled her vision, reflecting the light from the moon—it's close to being full, though it's hard to tell, sometimes.

Feathers from the down-filled pillows drifted around them like they're inside a giant, shook-up, snow-globe. A fox in a henhouse. Chicken slaughterhouse. Pillow factory that exploded. Silver-blue spotlight of the moon.

"It's a full moon," Mush says.

"How can you tell?"

"We're in sync, me and her. Like werewolves."

Eadie raises her head and howls, and Mushkeg joins her. They are werewolves now, they are changing, metamorphosing, their clothes rip as their limbs elongate, shredded in the sudden urgency to get at the meat of each other's bodies, as if they really are wolves, instead of just pretending.

Mush lies back, naked on the floral-patterned bedspread, her hands reach toward Eadie, drawing her down. The air is cool on their bare flesh, but Eadie doesn't care. They'll make their own heat. Eadie leans down into the kiss, and in a flash Mushkeg raises herself up on her side and flips Edie over, so Eadie is now looking up into Mush's eyes. Sparkling. Her hair has escaped the elaborate system of loops and whorls which kept it imprisoned. Now it falls down in waves. Framing her face. A dark Botticelli.

Then Mush's lips are on hers again. And the room slowly grows warmer with their heat, and from the heat of the flames in the hearth.

"So what's my magic, then?" Eadie asks.

"I don't know." Mushkeg's eyes slide around the room, finding the darker shadows. "You probably just haven't found it yet. Some people never do. Blame it on bad luck, the weather, some external factor, never recognizing it." Her red lips pucker. Like a pixie. If Eadie is Tink—which pixie is Mush?

"Spiders creep me out."

"No! They're artists! They weave the most beautiful patterns. And they keep your dreams safe—where do you think us Ojibways got the idea for the dream-catcher?"

"Did the spiders tell you that?" Eadie tickles the other girl's ribs with a stray pinion feather. Mush arms herself, and things quickly devolve into a squirming, laughter-and-scream-filled tickle fight. Eadie wonders why she is she being so silly. Eadie is a punk-rocker. She kicks butt. She doesn't giggle. But something about Mush makes her feel like being silly.

They fall asleep, tangled in the sheets and in each other's arms, the heat of the fire slowly dwindling, with only the heat of their bodies to keep each other warm.

When Eadie wakes up, the room is cold, the fire has burned down to ash, and Mushkeg is gone. Bright sunlight illuminates the windows with a warm yellow glow, misty where it refracts through the gauzy material of the curtain.

What does it mean that Mush left without saying anything? What does it mean that Mush took off while Eadie was still asleep? Without waking her up, or saying goodbye, or letting her know that she was leaving? Is Mushkeg upset? Is she feeling guilty or ashamed? Does she regret hooking up with another chick?

Eadie stretches and yawns, looking around for her shirt. There's no use panicking. Mushkeg might've left for any number of reasons. To get home before dark so her parents don't discover she's been out all night. To avoid awkward morning conversations. Maybe she had somewhere to be early, and she needed to get ready. Maybe she just didn't want to wake Eadie up. She'd been sleeping so peacefully.

In the dim bathroom, Eadie turns on the taps to scrub her face, but of course the water doesn't work. It'd been shut off where the pipes enter the building to keep the pipes from freezing and exploding during the winter. Damn.

Eadie looks up at her face in the mirror, then lets her features blur as she shifts focus to what has been drawn, in blood-red lipstick, the colour of fire engines and flames, inside a heart.

XOXOXOXO, the ten digits of a cell phone number, signed 'Mushk' with a long trailing "k." For a moment they are together in the mirror, Mushkeg and Eadie, floating inside the thick red outline of a heart.

Eadie smiles, losing some of the tension in her shoulders now that she knows Mushkeg didn't simply ditch her like the Queen song, loving and leaving her. Feeling floaty, she drifts out to tidy the room.

To make it look as if no one has been here.

Eadie goes to draw the curtains, to close the Star View parking lot from view. That's when she sees the delicate tracery of lines, only visible because of the intensity of the morning sunlight, so finely woven, the strands would go unnoticed in any other kind of light. A web of lines, radiating outward like the central arms of a spiral galaxy. So thin, the silk dances in the slight exhalation of her breath.

A spider's web.

And amongst the delicate tracery of lines, a word written in spider's silk.

A word. Blurring, as her eyes fill with tears.

Anang. Star.

TYNER'S CREEK

Oose-Tynuck splashes through the shallows at the creek's edge, the water sparkles in the sunlight, minnows run from his bare feet, pink toes gripping the rock and sand, water so ice cold it hurts his bones. That ache slides up his calves and makes them sing. The fount of the little stream is subterranean, which means it comes out of a cave under the ground where it stays cold all year round, even when it's the height of summer. The closer you are to the springs, the colder the water becomes. Could've been frozen solid if it wasn't in constant motion.

He scrambles up the small embankment on the other side—the short stride of his legs makes it difficult to clamber back onto solid ground, but he manages it, just barely. It isn't a very big river, barely a stream. A brook really. Too small to have a name. But Tynuck is still growing, and he knows that one day he will be big enough to step across this brook without even trying. His birch-bark bucket full, he struggles not to spill any of the fresh water he's collected.

He's gotten mud all over his leggings, but the sun will bake it dry, turn the mud to dust and then it'll flake off with his every movement. The water sloshes over the top of the mkaak as he walks, the birch-bark *bucket* sewn together and sealed with bear fat and pitch so it's waterproof. It doesn't leak, but it's still tricky not to spill any. The water is heavy. When it's flowing out of the rock, burbling nicely and sparkling in the light, it doesn't look heavy. But as soon as he scoops out a portion it seems to pick up a lot of weight.

The sun is hot on his face, and sweat beads, even though he's only made it a short span in the direction back to camp. A drop of salty water trickles off his forehead and drips into the bucket. Ripples in the sheen distort his reflection.

Eww, gross Tynuck thinks, *this water is for cooking!*

Oh well. He pictures the radiant smile that will surely be on his mother's face when he returns with his cargo. Sun bathing her in a corona of light, back lit so the frizzy split ends of her hair catch in the light like spider webs. Aate will appreciate his efforts to fetch the water. She will be proud of him. He is seven winters old now, and he wants to prove that he's old enough to collect water. She's never allowed him to do so on his own before.

He wishes there were somewhere closer for them to gather water, but this area of land is high in elevation and dry, lacking in streams, ponds, or rivers—with only a few marshy areas where the water is stagnant and not fit to drink. The springs are the closest source of freshwater on the plateau, Ghost Lake is too far. Tynuck doesn't mind. He is a big boy now, and his mother trusts him enough to go to the stream to gather water by himself.

He pauses to wipe the sweat from his forehead so more of it doesn't drip into the bucket before beginning the steep ascent. It's a very steep hill. He notices movement in the distance, and sees his omishoomeyan, his *stepfather* coming down the hill towards him. A cold fist grips Tynuck's heart. He wants to squirm back into the shallows like a snake, hide in the reeds and bulrushes. What does *he* want? Tynuck's face feels hot, not from the heat, but like a medicine bundle squeezed tight, forcing the contents into a tighter and tighter space until the bag rips open.

He almost drops the birch-bark mkaak, but manages to lower it gently to the ground without sloshing too much over the sides—though waves rock back and forth and continue to make the bucket dance.

Chaboy doesn't like him. Gshkaadiz. *Angry*. Chaboy is always angry with Tynuck.

No matter what he does, he can never do anything right.

"Why are you so stupid?" His stepfather towers over him. Then speaks in a soft, kindly voice when his mother comes back, "You're a good boy, Tynuck." Tynuck can see through the fake kindness. It is a lie. Chaboy is only kind to him for show. He turns nasty again the second they are left alone. His face is a mask. It changes so quickly no one else sees it. They are all fooled. Only Tynuck sees through the mask.

"Chaboy doesn't like me."

"Oose. Don't be silly," his mother says. "Your stepfather is a good man, a good provider. He wants to be your De-De. It will take some time getting used to. That's all."

But Tynuck knows this isn't true. Chaboy hates him. His eyes squint, crinkled around the edges, lips curl back from his teeth like a snarling dog, face twisted up. Lopsided. Like Oose is something that disgusts him. That is his true face.

"There you are." Chaboy comes close, teeth gritted in a smile. Chaboy actually seems happy to see him for once. Tynuck doesn't trust it, that smile. Fears it is some trick. His legs feel weak.

Chaboy grabs him by the shoulders and shakes him. Then shoves him down. *Oof!* The strength with which Tynuck hits the ground forces the air from his lungs. It doesn't take much. Chaboy is a grown man, and Tynuck is still only a boy.

Tynuck scrambles to his feet and turns to run, tears sting his face, making his vision blur. He runs towards the nameless creek, but Chaboy catches up with him in the shallows. Chaboy grabs his foot as Tynuck runs, making him fall, so he trips face-first with a splash, half of his body submerged in frogs' depth water. The sand and grit of the river-bottom imprint into the flesh on his palms. He kicks and struggles, but Chaboy is too strong. Tynuck's head is forced down. No deeper than a puddle, but bubbling like a kettle when he screams.

He can't breathe! He can't breathe.

KAAW! KAAW! KAAW! KAAW! KAAW!

The weight of Chaboy's hand on the back of Tynuck's head lets up for a moment as his stepfather turns to look at the crow, cawing like crazy up in the branches of a tree. Tynuck gasps, drawing in air frantically now that he's able to raise his face from the stream.

Chaboy is trying to kill him!

Tynuck doesn't want to lose this brief opportunity to escape, in case the attack resumes. He has to get away. He has to get away. Chaboy palms a river-stone, his body turns, and his arm extends as he aims for the noisy bird up in the tree. Tynuck crawls, scrambles to his feet, taking off towards the embankment, and towards the village. He doesn't look back to see if Chaboy has hit his mark.

Heavy hands wrench Tynuck back, and his legs go out from under him as momentum carries him forward. *Oof!* The back of his head bangs against the ground. Hard. He is staring at the sky again like an upended turtle, the wind knocked out of him. Chaboy's face swims into view above him, smiling, maskless, looking down at Tynuck upside down. There is a large rock in Chaboy's left hand. Tynuck raises his arms to protect himself as the rock descends towards him, growing larger as it fills the field of his vision. He turns his face away, every muscle in his body clamps tight, preparing for the blow.

The rock hits him. The world goes red. Then black. Blood flows.

Chaboy lobs the bloody stone into the creek, gathers the boy in his arms and carries the limp form a few yards away, places the body where the banks are steepest, and the shore littered with stones—much like the one he'd used to cave in the boy's skull.

He never liked the little shit. Always whining and crying to his mother, stealing all her affection from him. He had no intention of rearing another man's son. And as long as Aate had her dear little boy, she was uninterested in bearing more children. He wanted to father his own sons, strong sons, not to be tasked with her onaabeman's child. The child of her deceased *husband*, like a ghost trailing after.

The blood flows down over the rocks, co-mingling with the waters at the river's edge, where it slowly becomes diluted, curling away like a red ribbon of smoke. So much blood flows from his skull, it is shocking that so much blood can flow from such a small form. He's killed many things. All manner of fowl and game, he is a skilled hunter—elk, moose, deer, beaver, marten, porcupines, pheasants, duck, geese, loons. His family is never short of meat. This didn't feel any different from killing any other animal.

Except the blood is surprising.

The way it flows, as if the boy's heart still pumps, as if the blood still circles through his veins, branching out from his head in a series of red rivulets, the stream tinged brackish brown.

His mother places far too much confidence in the boy. He fell from the bank and hit his head on the rocks. An accident. Nothing more. A sad occurrence, but not exceptional. The land is a dangerous place.

In a nearby tree, that damned crow caws again, and Chaboy looks up at it. The sole witness to his crime. Aandeg tilts his head, looking down at Chaboy, and crows, a long cawing sound like a rattle. Chaboy rinses his hands in the water of the cold, cold stream, chilling his fingers to the bone. Then turns to collect the bucket, washing the ground where he hit the boy, spilling out the contents—the boy's hard work—to clean the blood and brain matter. The evidence washes away from the site where Oose-Tynuck died. Then Chaboy lays the birch-bark bucket at the top of the steep embankment.

The boy's body lies bleeding out into the creek below. The network of blood extending out from his head like horns, like the antlers of some beast. For a moment, the atmospheric pressure seems to shift, as if Chaboy dove into Ghost Lake, and the weight of the surrounding water is pressing in on him from all sides before lifting as he rose. For a moment, he feels stretched and distorted, before reality reasserts itself around him. It is odd the way the blood continues to flow, long after Tynuck's chest has ceased to rise and fall, rise and fall, his heart has surely stilled by now. But the flow is continuous, and if anything, seems to blossom and grow as he watches. Probably owing to the fact he's positioned the corpse head-first on a slope, so all the fluids drain downward. That's probably it. The flow of blood will slow once all the fluids have drained out.

He walks away, to finish his hunt, pleased. With that unpleasantness accomplished, he will now possess all of his Aate's affection, and she will now be more amenable to bearing his children. He will have sons of his own to raise.

After a successful hunt, Chaboy returns to camp a few hours before dark, carrying slabs of moose-meat on his back in a bundle of flesh, a young bull-calf tied together with intestines, the way people carry their children in a dikinaagan, a *cradle-board*. He passes first through the forest and then through the high-ground plateau, where the stands of trees cluster together like islands here and there on the more open areas of the plane.

By the time he arrives, their summer-camp is already in a disarray. No one is working or going about their various tasks and occupations. The boy's body has no doubt already been discovered. Aate was the one to send Tynuck to the creek bed to fetch water after all, so she would have known where to look when he didn't return.

Aate is sobbing, her head on the shoulder of wizened old Maingan, scrawny as tree-branch limbs.

Maingan squints at him.

"What's all this now?" Chaboy asks. Gruff.

"Where have you been?" Maingan frowns at him. Aate abandons Maingan's shoulder to throw her arms around Chaboy, her face is streaked with tears, the long strands of her dark hair sticking to the moisture on her cheeks.

"Bizaan. *Shh-shh-shh*. What's this?" he soothes Aate, and then turned to Maingan. "Hunting." Chaboy lowers the bundle of meat to the ground at Maingan's feet like an offering, tied tightly together with sinew and intestines. Maingan's eyes widen at the sight of the dead calf. Nostrils flaring. It's against proper decorum, disrespectful even, to hunt such young moose.

"He's deeeaaad," Aate wails. She speaks more, but her words are incoherent, too choked by her own despair.

"Who's dead?" Chaboy asks, looking towards Maingan. He lets some of his actual apprehension show on his face, to give his question legitimacy.

The lines on Maingan's face soften. "Oose Tynuck. He never returned. Aate sent one of the other boys to fetch him from the creek. He must have fallen from the bank. Hit his head. Tynuck's dead."

The low continuous keening from Aate is getting on his nerves. Chaboy pats Aate's dishevelled hair and holds the woman tight.

"Oh my dear. I'm so so sorry." He turns Aate away from the wizened old Medicine Man and leads her to their round-house, whispering comforting nonsense words in her ear. Following the unfortunate passing of Aate's late onaabeman, her *husband*, Chaboy had moved in shortly after the twelve moons of her mourning period elapsed, in order to help console her through that difficult winter.

Maingan stands his ground, watching them as they walk away, face creased with lines, as if there are more wrinkles etched onto his face than there had been yesterday.

Nosy old man.

When Chaboy emerges from his endaad, his *home*, the old man is waiting.

"I need to speak with you."

Chaboy nods his head soberly in assent. Of course, of course. These are terrible times, terrible times.

"I've instructed everyone to leave the boy where he lies for the time being."

"Why?" Chaboy asks, finally allowing some irritation to slip through in his voice. "We need to prepare. He deserves a proper funeral. It's cruel to make his spirit wait."

"I'm going to hold a shaking tent. Something about the boy's death doesn't feel right." The jowls on Maingan's neck jiggle as his head shakes. "I need to speak to the manitous."

And for the first time, Chaboy feels a twinge of real alarm. He doesn't want the old man talking to his *spirit guides*. Who knows what they will have to say? Not that he has much faith in Maingan's abilities—always predicting the weather—incorrectly. Stupid old man. Chaboy nods again, unable to come up with a suitable reason to delay the ceremony.

"I've already begun fasting." Maingan turns, and it's Chaboy who watches this time as the old man walks away.

Chaboy watches the construction of a small burial hut being built around the child's body to ward off predators, though this will not be the grave-site. Oose-Tynuck cannot be moved until after Maingan has finished fasting for three days, not until after the shaking tent ceremony. Funeral rites are being delayed, put on hold for this foolishness.

They have had to move the little house back from the edge of the stream, not once, not twice, but *three* times, as the level of the waters continue to rise, mysteriously, as there has been no rain. But since the source for the spring is subterranean, something else must be causing the flood. Swelling the small creek like winter snow melt, until the waters rise far above their normal bounds.

The little creek has become a river. Trout leap from the waters. New life congregates on the banks to drink, to grow. Tynuck's Creek is now teaming with all manner of animals and plants, fish, fauna, and fowl. This change has not gone unremarked.

Someone is stationed with the body at all times. A fire is lit. Family, friends and community members come to put down tobacco and say their prayers.

"It's strange." The old magician shakes his head.

The corners of Chaboy's mouth turn down as he overhears talk of others from the village:

"Isn't it marvellous?"

"It can't be a coincidence."

"The swelling of the stream. The child's death. They must somehow be connected."

"Maingan is correct in calling for a shaking tent. He is wise."

Standing on the embankment, the image of Tynuck comes to Chaboy's mind: skull caved in, the blood continuously flowing, branching out like a fine network of lightning arcing across the sky. Valleys filling between the peaks of the rock, interminably swelling the waters. Foolishness.

The boy would've bled out, and the flow would've stopped days ago. Chaboy is tempted to rip apart the little wigwam perched at the edge of the engorged stream to find out. But he knows this is folly. There is nothing to see. Unless he wants to look on the boy's corpse, surely beginning to rot by now in this heat.

On the third day of his fast, Maingan will perform the shaking tent. And then they can be finished with all this foolishness.

Far below, the tiny stream carves a silver ribbon through the forest. This is one of Euwen's favourite places in time to visit, back when the water is fresh and new, and the ice has retreated from the land. Wings extended, Euwen skims across the tops of the trees. Some of their leaves have already begun to turn as the light shifts, despite the continuing heat of the summer. He pulls his tail feathers forward and flaps his wings to bring his body into position as he comes to alight on the branch of a tree overlooking a small creek. Barely a rut in the ground really, though the slight tinkling of sound is soothing. The wind blows and attempts to ruffle his feathers, though they all remain in place, not a single feather goes astray.

Best thing in the world to be is a crow. Better than the two legged or four. Or the sleek-scaled fins of the things that live in the rivers and lakes. Though Euwen knows Nimosh, *Dog*, would disagree. Euwen wouldn't trade his wings for anything. Two legs, fins, or four. Two wings are better than four legs on any day of the year. If Nimosh had wings, then maybe he would agree. Maybe he would understand. The best thing in the world to be—is a *crow*.

Aandeg.

That's what Anishinaabek call him. Though he prefers to think of himself as Euwen. The king had named him. No one else ever thought to give him his own name before. He puffs out his chest and refolds his wings so they are nicely tucked. Euwen tilts his head, watches a two-legged Anishinaabe gathering water in a *birch-bark* pail. They are wasteful beings, always leaving food behind. Though rarely willing to share. Greedy two-legged beasts.

Euwen watches the two-legged child struggle across the small stream, carrying the bucket heavy with water now. Maybe the child will leave some scrap behind? Some morsel? Wasteful beings.

Euwen loves them.

This is why he often he visits the withered old man, who is king for a brood of roosting crows. But that's far in the future from here. Euwen is always willing to accept an easy meal. Though he knows most humans are not generous. Far from it. Euwen's beautiful blue-black plumage is mottled with a splatter of white where bleach, tossed maliciously from a jam-jar, had sprayed his feathers. Not all humans are so generous, or kind; some are out-right mean. And greedy. Greedy. Wasteful. How he loves them.

But he's learned to be cautious.

Another human appears on the hill. It walks towards the young one. Euwen doesn't recognize either. Friend or foe. Neither is the withered old man. The king. They are unlikely to feed him morsels of flesh, though they may leave scraps behind. Greedy. Greedy. Wasteful. It is worth waiting for a moment or two, to see what they will leave behind. His eyesight is keen. He feels sorry for the beasts below with their poor vision, blundering around in the dark, almost blind. And they have no feathers!

A commotion below.

The wiigwas gourd, with its captured spring water is rocking back and forth, sloshing, threatening to tip over. The grown man has knocked the young one to the ground. Is holding the boy's head, face down in the water.

KAAW! KAAW! KAAW! KAAW! Euwen calls out in alarm.

The man turns, stone in hand, and the boy scrambles to escape. Euwen tries to evade the projectile. It clips one wing. And by the time he has resettled on his perch, the boy is once more pinned by the weight of his attacker. The man raises a rock above its head. Mad beasts, always throwing the world into chaos. Disturbing the balance of the day with their violence. Dumb beasts.

KAAW! KAAW! Euwen calls out again.

But it is already too late. The young one is dead. Head smashed in with the rock, brain and bodily fluid leaking out onto the ground.

KAAW!

Upon hearing his call, the two-legged Anishinaabek again looks up at Euwen. Their eyes meet. Brown-black to red. Too much of the whites of the man's eyes showing. Eyes too large. Pupils dilated to gather in the light. *Darkness. Madness*, Euwen thinks. He is glad he isn't human. Irrational beasts.

Murder! Murder! Euwen calls. KAAW! KAAW!

He launches himself into the air, pushing off with all his might to get maximum lift-off from his perch, extending his hind limbs for propulsion, and then flapping away from the creek and the mad gleam in the human's eye.

Worst thing in the world to be is a human. Useless beasts. Their original instructions came from Wanabozhoo. No wonder. Such foolishness. Such a one as that, the Hare, with a forked head. It is *his* fault for making them. Anishinaabek. For-nothing-man. Such flawed beasts.

The best thing in the world to be is a crow. No matter what Nimosh says. Allowing himself to be *owned* by humans. What kind of creature does that!? Worse than Boozhence, that *Cat*.

To the King! To the King!

Euwen flaps his wings, heading to the withered old man who is the king of a murder of young male crows. They roost in a dead cherry tree. Far, far away from here. He will find refuge there, refuge from the mad eyes of the two-legged beast, and his bloody deed. Far away from this time. Far away from this place. Flying direct, the way only a crow can fly, if a crow only knows how. Across time as well as space. Not every crow can master this. Not like Euwen. The First Crow. Crow of Crows.

Euwen has been around for a long time, and he will be around for a lot longer. What is distance to a time-travelling crow? He can traverse great distances in space as easily as time. Why other beings feel obligated to live by so many rules, Euwen doesn't understand.

Euwen briefly considers pecking at the brain-matter of the dead boy, but dismisses the idea. The mad one would surely murder Euwen as well if he got too close. It will go to waste. The brains. Poor thing. He can always come back later for a taste.

To the king then! To the king!

If the king will listen, Euwen will tell the tale. The entire murder will know of this deed before the end of the day. He'll raise a ruckus, he will. A murder. The others will hear of this. His brothers. They always know to avoid the human beast, with the gleam of madness in his eyes. No friend to fowl. No friend to the crow.

The villagers gather around, watching the tent as Maingan, the djessakid, *seer,* begins banging on his drum, singing and calling out to his manitous, imploring their assistance. Chaboy hates to think of what secrets they have to tell—though he has never trusted such things. It still makes him shift his feet, unable to sit still while the ceremony commences. Maingan's high, ululating voice emerges from the tent, and rises to the stars which are just beginning to appear in the quickly darkening skies. Medicines are burning, and the smoke from those too drift out. Out and up to the sky.

The jiisakaan, the *shaking tent* is not large. It's a roundhouse just big enough for the old man to enter. Saplings of spruce and birch bent into a frame, and secured with more saplings of spruce and birch hoops, and layered with birch bark.

The opening is sealed, so that once Maingan entered, nothing of what happens within can be seen from the outside.

The ritual songs drag on. Chaboy yawns. The red light from the sunset has almost entirely fled. Shadows are long.

Various sounds are heard emerging from the tent as Maingan continues to sing and drum, sounds which could never emerge so perfectly from a human throat; and the small birch-bark enclosure begins to shake as the spirits enter, shaking, whether from spirits or from the fervour with which Maingan performs the ritual—first a growl, like that of a mountain lion, then a hooting sound like an owl, and finally a *cawing*. A cawing sound, exactly like that of a crow.

A fist grips his heart. Chaboy can hear the beat of his heart in his ears.

Lub-dub, lub-dub, lub-dub.

Thumping. Thumping.

Despite the raucous noises Maingan is making inside the tent, even Chaboy is getting caught up in the ceremony. The drumming comes faster and faster, like the tempo of his heartbeat in his ears, and Maingan's voice comes louder and louder and more urgent as the tent shakes as if blown back and forth by a strong wind, though the air is still, and the tent is filled with a cacophony; the cacophony as of a murder of crows.

KAAW! KAAW! KAAW! KAAW! KAAW! KAAW! KAAW! KAAW!

Dozens of them must be in there. Wings flapping, beating chaotically along with the drums, along with his heartbeat, and the djessakid's ululating cries. Finally, the tent comes to an abrupt stillness. Silence.

Maingan emerges from the shaking tent.

He looks directly at Chaboy. His eyes are red. He tilts his head to the side. And lets out one single rattling-caw, like no human voice can mimic, so perfectly as to be indistinguishable from the real thing. Exactly like the sound a crow would make.

INTERMEDIARIES

Clay Cutter, Dare Theremin, and Tyler Kendrars are bored.

"We could play video games?" Tyler says over the noise from the little pen-motor. "Or skidoo along the ridge?" The sewing needle rises and falls as it punctures Dare's flesh, the salvaged motor buzzing as it delivers blue ink into skin.

"Go fishing in one of your dad's ice-shacks?" Dare has his shirt off, face scrunched in a grimace. The needle skitters like a sewing machine. There isn't anywhere in town to get a tattoo, so they make-do by affixing a motor and a needle to a pen. They each have one or two of these home-made tattoos. Something to do to pass the time. Even if they turn out awful.

"Hike out to our fort in the woods?" Clay is lounging on a ratty old couch with a maroon floral pattern, his legs stick out off one end. And his blond hair sticks up in disarranged tufts. "Smoke that weed Theremin lifted from his uncle's stash?" They have a habit of using their last names to refer to each other.

"What kind of name is Theremin anyway?" Clay asked once.

"It's Russian." Dare's green eyes squint at Clay. "What kind of name is Cutter?"

"American. I think. Empire Loyalists." Clay forks fingers through his wheat-sheaf hair.

"I don't even know about Kendrars." Tyler shrugs.

There's never much to do except snowmobile, swim, build forts—fine for kids—but as they get older these occupations are losing some of their thrill. They are country boys, but there isn't much trouble to get into, far away from the lights of the big city of Sterling—which isn't even that big either—but it seems a lot more exciting than their town. Cheapaye is a blip on the map—barely deserving a dot on most maps. A general store, a gas station, a motel, a restaurant, a school or two, some houses—a few churches that have been competing for souls for close to a century. Mostly German and Swedish immigrants, the odd family of Ojibwe Indians.

If not for the road, the necessity for passerby to stop to eat, drink, rest, and buy gas—Cheapaye would most likely not exist. There is some tourism—hunters and fishers coming up from Sterling, or the Twin Cities. Cabins can be rented out in the bush, tour guides can be hired to show you the best places to shoot a moose, or deer—the best places to go fly-fishing on the Jiibay River. And in winter, ice-fishing shacks can be rented out on Ghost Lake.

"We could raid Cutter's liquor cabinet." Tyler looks up from the design he's drawing on one of Dare's shoulders. Bright blue eyes hopeful.

"Nah, Cutter's grandma got wise to us." Dare is sitting backwards on an old bench-press, armpits resting on the barbell so his arms are dangling, "Put on a combination lock." The muscles in his arms flex, his hands reach around the upright supports to grip each other.

"—but Cutter knows the combo." Tyler blows up with his lips to clear the sandy-brown hair hanging in front of his eyes.

It's Clay who first comes up with the idea:

"Let's take the ice-road out to Ghost Lake. I heard this story about an old Indian burial ground. This woman went out there and took all these pictures—and when she got the film developed—there were all these ghostly figures in the photos."

"That's just an urban legend," Tyler flips his head to throw the hair out of his eyes. "There isn't even a graveyard out there. I've been out to the lake hundreds of times and I've never seen any graves." Tyler's dad operates one of the campgrounds on the lake and rents out ice-shacks for tourists.

"There is one out on the Reserve somewhere." Clay pulls his legs in, so now his knees stick up.

"The Indians get all uppity when folks go tromping around their land." Dare winces as the needle goes in and out of his flesh with the ink-soaked needle. His reddish-brown rocker hair hangs from either side of his head. 70's new wave.

"So what?" Clay's knees butterfly restlessly. "It's not like we'd get caught. There's hardly anyone out there this time of year. We should go check it out."

"I dunno if that's such a great idea," Tyler wipes away blood welling up on Dare's shoulder blade so he can see the image.

"Why not? You sc-scared of the ghosts?" Clay mock-stutters.

"What's so great about a graveyard?" Tyler scrunches one cobalt eye.

"It isn't just any graveyard—it's an Indian burial ground." Clay wiggles his fingers.

"So?" Tyler pulls one blue latex glove tighter. "Haven't you seen any horror movies? Poltergeist? Pet Cemetery? The Amityville Horror?"

"How does it look?" Dare tries to look over his shoulder to see the progress that's been made on his back.

"It looks like shit," Tyler smiles, admiring his handiwork.

"How hard can it be to draw a skull?" Dare frowns, deep furrows in his brow. "You draw two eye cavities, a hole for the nose, and some grinning teeth."

"It looks great." Clay doesn't even look at the tattoo. "I say we check it out."

Dare hooks s thumb aver his shoulder. "Wait 'til Kendrars finishes my ink!?"

"Fine." Clay crouches to take a peek at Tyler's work. "It looks like shit, by the way."

"Better than your face." Dare palms Clay's face like a basketball and shoves him away.

"You wish you had this face." Clay poses superman, hands on hips, chin raised, face in profile. Sparse blonde fuzz of a 'stache; he thinks it makes him look deadly. Carny more-like.

"Boy you're ugly." Dare curls a lip.

Tyler pours Rusty whisky on the tattoo to disinfect it, takes a swig from the bottle for himself, applies white gauze, and then Saran Wrap with duct tape around the edges to protect the place on Dare's shoulder where he's drawn a death's head. "It'll take a few days to heal."

Dare gingerly puts his t-shirt back on. His face puckers. The additional weight puts pressure on his new tattoo. It hurts like a motherfucker.

"Don't be such a wuss." Clay flexes to show off a truly terrible tattoo of a wolf howling at the moon. "I didn't cry when I got this baby."

"There's no bones in your bicep, moron!"

"Oh, you'll be alright." Clay puts one arm around the shorter boy's shoulder in a comradely manner, knowing full well the weight of his arm put further pressure on the fresh tattoo, and probably hurt like a motherfucker.

"Dickweed!" Dare hisses, to much laughter from the other two boys. "You know, you guys really are assholes, you know that?" Which only results in more peals of laughter.

"Come on, let's go." Clay pulls on his heavy boots.

They all clomp out of the Kendrars' house, hop on their skidoos, and take off along one of innumerable trails through the forest, which will eventually take them out to Ghost Lake, and the ice-road, a seasonal route across the frozen surface. At one time it had been the only way out to the Reserve in the winter, before the Access Road was built, which weaves its way through multiple obstacles—swamps, rivers, and rocky outcroppings. A lot of local folks still use the ice-road to cross the lake, because it's a quicker, and a more direct-route than going around.

The shortest distance between two points is a straight line.

Dare leads the way in his orange helmet, bombing down the narrow paths at a break-neck speed that would have been reckless for anyone who didn't know the paths as well as they do. None of them are old enough to have a driver's license yet—and snowmobiles are a good means of travel for half of the year anyway. Clay and Tyler keep up the pace, knowing the paths just as well as Dare. Sometimes they take short cuts through the trees to cut corners, making in-roads through fresh powder. They whoop and cat-call to each other, even though they can't hear their insults over the sound of engine noise and wind whipping past their ears. It isn't that windy, but given their pace, the still air is a solid wall rushing past as they punch through.

The air is bright and cold, their breath streams like smoke with each exhale. Every twig and tendril is coated in frost from the night before, and it seems almost revolutionary that the world can change so drastically in such a short span of time, transforming everything into a magical wonderland. They speed through this landscape of ice and snow, and frozen trees—not really paying mind to its beauty. They've grown up in the bush, nature is familiar and un-noteworthy, so the change goes unremarked.

It's been cold enough, for long enough—far colder and for longer than required to make the ice-road safe—and the bright, clear day will make navigating the lake that much easier. The trees whip past as they barrel along the skidoo-paths, the wind drives into their cheeks like pins-and-needles, burning their faces to a rosy sheen. No matter how well they bundle up—it's impossible to cover every square-inch of exposed skin. When they reach the Jiibay River, which leads to the outflow of Ghost Lake, they skirt the edges, sticking to the thicker ice, avoiding those chasms where the ice hasn't fully crusted over towards the center. Flowing water is always less willing to freeze.

Everyone has heard stories of unwary skidoo-ers not paying attention to their surroundings, or venturing out onto thin ice. They know safety protocols, and they mostly follow them. No one wants to plunge five hundred pounds headfirst into an open pit of ice water. So they steer clear, only venturing onto the edges of the river where the ice is thickest. Or where there's already skidoo-tracks showing where it's safe to trek. They follow the course of the Jiibay River to its source, and then on out to the open, frozen surface of Ghost Lake.

They join up with the path of the ice-road, and follow that across the wide expanse, past the islands like ice-locked pirate ships, unable to shift on their mooring of peat and bog, the poplars and pines their solitary occupants standing sentinel on deck. The seasonal ice-road will take them past the Reserve, where they can veer off.

They weave in and out, chasing each other, seeing who can take the lead. Sunlight illuminates everything but provides little warmth, the blinding white snow acts like a mirror—reflecting the light upwards and out—to a sky free from any insulating clouds that could trap in the thermal heat. The sunniest days are often the coldest.

Clay leads the way in his red helmet as they swerve off the ice-road and towards the Indian reserve, making a new path though the tangle of trees on the north shore. For a while it's slow going as they forge through the woods, not wanting to slam into any fallen logs or other hollow pitfalls hidden under the snow. But eventually, they link up with a skidoo-trail so they follow that meandering path.

Most likely this excursion will turn out to be a pointless trek, but it's as good an excuse for an adventure as any. Better than sitting around Kendrar's basement. The skidoo tracks lead them past an area that is clearly still being used as a burial ground. Newer marble headstones and wooden crosses are mixed together with older structures made of wood, mausoleums standing on stilts, like little houses for the dead held up by scaffolding.

They remove helmets and abandon their skidoos, engines cooling like silenced chainsaws. A few crows caw to each other in the stark canopy overhead. Some of the trees hold human-shaped bundles, like Egyptian mummies wrapped in leather shrouds. Maybe it is the desiccated meat the birds are after, and the boys are intruding upon the meal. The trees creak, and it sounds like voices, as if they're complaining to each other of the burden they carry in their arms, or maybe it's the dead themselves that speak.

"Whoah," Tyler whispers. "This place is creepy." His sandy hair is matted down from wearing his blue helmet

"Of course it's creepy." Clay also keeps his voice hushed. "It's a graveyard, moron."

They spread out, picking their way through the cemetery, examining the older wooden structures, and avoiding the newer dead; those with names and dates inscribed on polished stone. The platforms only have the occasional pictograph or clan symbol carved into the lumber, but their age could be assessed by the level of disrepair. Some have clearly been maintained; others have long since fallen into ruin. A pile of boards like a collapsed barn. The path of a tornado. Many of the little houses hold pouches, bowls, dolls, and other trinkets and tchotchkes like decorations, or offerings for the departed.

Dare picks up a pipe, examining the elaborate starburst pattern carved into the saddle, and shank. The device is embellished with little suns, lines radiate outward from each sun, and cross lines radiating from neighbouring spheres, creating a pleasant texture under the loops and whorls of his fingertips.

"What are you doing?" Tyler hisses. His blue eyes ocean wide.

"It looks like a nice pipe." Dare pops the bit between his teeth and poses, hands on hips, like a long-haired Popeye the Sailor man. "We could smoke up with this."

"It belongs to a dead person." Tyler curls a lip.

"Yeah, so what?" Clay waves a hand. "It's not like it's any use to them."

"Yeah . . . but still." Tyler's lip twitches.

"Lighten up." Clay kneels next to a collapsed tomb, and examines what looks like a jawbone. His hair looks more yellow against the snow. His eyes are icebergs.

"*Kaanh.*" Tyler makes a disgusted sound. "You guys really are hopeless, you know that? That could be someone's grandma for all you know!"

Clay shrugs, picks up an object from the wreckage of the crumbling grave. It is a small, carved figurine.

"What is it?" Tyler's eyebrows draw together.

"Some kind of animal." Clay turns it around between his fingers.

"Looks like something somewhere between a bear and a wolf." Tyler stands looking over Clay's shoulder to inspect his find.

"Yeah. But bears don't have bushy tails." Clay isn't sure what kind of animal it's supposed to represent. It is too wide in and around the rump to be a wolf. It resembles the shape of a skunk or badger more than anything else, though the shape still isn't quite right to be either animal. There's a hole gouged out in the top of the animal's tail, and a wider, flat opening at the snout.

"Maybe it's meant to be some kind of whistle or flute?" Tyler leans forward, hands on his knees. Dare comes to huddle around Clay's find.

Clay puts his lips to the "mouth" of the strange beast, and mouth-to-mouth, he suddenly becomes aware that he is putting something that he had found on the ground, in a cemetery, and that looks to have been carved from some sort of bone—into his mouth—but when he blows into it, no sound comes out. "Hunh. No sound"

"Maybe it is like a didgeridoo?" Tyler mimes holding the long hollow tube of an Australian instrument. "You have to do it, just right, or no sound will come out."

"Or maybe it's like a dog whistle?" Clay is saying. "And the sound is outside the range of human hearing—"

"—or, maybe it just doesn't work right." Dare cuts him off. Pushes a curly lock of hair behind one ear.

"Just some stupid carving." Clay slips it into his coat pocket next to the jawbone for later inspection. He doesn't want Dare or Tyler to get their hands on it, and then conveniently forget who found it first.

Dare pulls out a lighter and a pouch of Heller hand-rolled. He sparks up the pipe, flame wavering in his green eyes, and the scent of tobacco smoke wafts over them as Dare walks the aisles of the dead. Tyler wanders further into the gloom of the trees, where more of the shroud-wrapped mummies hover, picking his way across the pitted ground.

"An arrow-head!" Tyler hears Clay exclaim excitedly in the distance. He turns his head to look in Clay's direction. *Oof!* There's a sudden drop, his legs crumple, and he falls forward. He puts his hands out to break his fall, but his ankle twists. He's stepped into a cavity where a coffin no doubt collapsed underground, leaving behind a depression. There's no marker for the grave, it must have long-since mouldered away.

Tyler sits for a moment cradling his ankle. His eyes are now level with a small mausoleum, like a hut on stilts. There's an ancient, faded toy rattle resting on a ledge under the over-hang of the peaked roof. He can make out a racing stripe of red paint, and some faded blue stars. He picks up the rattle and gives it a few shakes, listening to the sound of beads shifting around inside. Like waves lapping against the shore of Ghost Lake.

Tyler smiles. He collects old children's toys and noisemakers to use as supporting instruments—they're perfect on background tracks. Looping the sounds in his audio software to create distinctive beats. Tyler slips the rattle into his pocket, and slowly stands, testing his weight on the injured foot. Nothing broken. He heads over to check on the others and see the arrowhead Clay found.

As Tyler makes his way over, Dare stands over Clay who is crouched examining the weapon. The edges of the arrowhead are puckered like a serrated edge where another, denser stone was used to chip the more brittle stone into a razor-sharp point.

"You could use it to shave!" Dare is puffing away on the pipe like Sherlock Holmes.

"Cutter doesn't shave." Tyler smirks. He can't help taking a dig at Clay's confidence when he sees an opening. "He hasn't hit puberty yet!"

"Not unless I want to slice my face apart." Clay stands from his crouched position and puts the barb into the inside pocket of his leather jacket, next to his heart. "Come on. Let's get out of here. This place is starting to give me the creeps."

"Ooh, now look who's scared," Tyler sneers, and Dare snickers.

"It's *supposed* to be creepy; it's a burial ground. Besides, why do I want to hang out in a cemetery all day? There's plenty of time for that later—like when I'm dead."

They trudge silently back to the skidoo trail, snow crunching under their boots, the trees creak and groan in the wind. They mount their skidoos like 20th Century horses. Again, Clay leads the way in his red helmet, and Dare and Tyler follow. Orange, then blue. They make quicker progress now that they know the route, and where the hazards lie. A small stream, and a hollow where the snow hides a pit in the ground—it had become over-laid with branches and sticks that made the ground seem flat. Once past the perils and back out on the frozen lake, they zip across on the ice-road, back toward the outflow of the Jiibay, parting half-way through the trees to take separate routes homes.

They've all had enough adventure for one day. It isn't every day they visit an ancient Indian burial ground. And though they would never admit it, the place creeped them out, far more than any of them would admit.

Clay steers his skidoo off to one side of the path. Hops off the machine and sits at the base of a big old tree. Pulls off his chipped red helmet, which makes his yellow hair stick up in all directions. He smooths it out with one hand, but it only springs back into place. If he sits too long the snow will melt and his jeans will get wet.

He pulls out the piece of bone he retrieved from the Indian burial ground and examines it. Turning it over and in his fingers. It's lighter than he expects, small holes are worn into the bone like coal, a greater surface area inside than out. Like a bird's bones, hollowness for flight. Wearing it smooth by the work of his fingers, like a tumbled stone at the lake shore.

"That's my jaw-bone you've got there." A man's voice. Clay flinches. It makes him jump, like the sudden audio spur in a horror movie during the quiet part.

He looks up to see a man sitting on a sturdy, low-hanging branch. *Where the fuck did he come from?* And how long has he been sitting there? Was the man there the whole time? Or had the man somehow snuck up on him? Clay's back rests against the tree trunk, and the man would have somehow had to scale the other side so quietly and deftly that Clay wouldn't have noticed. Maybe the man was simply sitting so still, and silent, Clay overlooked his presence.

"F-Fuck off." Clay would have backed up, if the tree trunk wasn't bracing him.

The man hops down off his perch, landing smoothly. He wears black jeans, and a black shirt, his hair is pulled back into two long braids that fall past his shoulders, but as he walks towards Clay, his image flickers as if he is a hologram, or a television channel cutting in and out of reception—jumping back and forth between two channels, the present and a historical channel—for on the other channel, the man wears fringed buckskin pants, leather moccasins puckered around the seams, a roach comprised of stiff guard-hairs from a porcupine standing stiffly on top of his head, a leather vest decorated with elaborate quill-work, and bone-beads like an interlocking pattern of supernumerary ribs over top of his own.

The man kneels down with the practiced ease of a routine motion, shrugging off the bow worn carelessly over one shoulder, and in the same fluid motion raises his arm to reach back over his shoulder to retrieve a bolt from his quiver, he licks the fletched feather as he draws back the taught sinew to an anchor point along his jaw, quarrel nocked and ready to fly, the point of the arrow-head positioned two millimeters from the dead-center of Clay's forehead. The man performs this unexpected maneuver in a matter of seconds, and though the point never touches Clay's skin, he can feel the pent-up elasticity in the bowstring and a tension in the bull's-eye of his pineal gland, the third-eye. It reminds him of the sensation he sometimes has, when someone is looking at him but he can't identify the source—or when someone reads a newspaper over his shoulder. It is not a comfortable sensation. He has to struggle to remain perfectly still, and fight against the urge to rub his forehead, as if he could wipe away the grubby feeling, like a smudge of dirt, but Clay knows, if the man releases the draw—he will be dead.

Clay licks his lips, and tries to ignore the arrowhead so he can look past it to the man's face, eyes shifting focus from the puckered edges of the obsidian blade, he follows the shaft back to the feathered vane, the draw-string, and the tensed muscles holding back who-knows-how-many-pounds of stored force waiting to be let loose. Probably more than enough kinetic energy to drive the bolt right through his skull, into his brain, and out the back of his head. Pinning him to the tree behind him. The man is obviously an Indian. He's certainly gone to what would have to be great lengths, to dress in what seems to be a 100% historically accurate style of dress from over a century earlier. He is most definitely—probably—an Ojibwe. Maybe some of the Ghost Lake Indians got wind of their trespass, and this dude in the Indian get-up decided to go all vigilante on his ass?

But somehow this explanation doesn't make much sense to Clay. It's too far-fetched. And it doesn't explain the odd flickering. Did he only imagine it? Was it only a hallucination? Was it all in his head? That seems to be the only rational explanation.

"What do you want?" Clay swallows audibly. His voice comes out more stretched and reedy than he anticipates. "Who are you?"

The man sneers. "You aren't deserving enough to know my name—you can call me Aya'ah."

"Well listen, Aya'ah," Clay licks his lips again. "I don't know what you've heard, but whatever someone's told you—it isn't true. Okay? So why don't you just go ahead and put the bow-and-arrow down. Yes?"

"You have some things that don't belong to you," Aya'ah says. "And I want them back." Except, the only thing is, when Aya'ah says these words—his lips—they don't *move*. Clay is staring right at his face as the lips, which should have been forming the words, remain compressed in a thin line. It is as if the man is speaking directly into his mind, maybe through the vulnerable spot where the coiled pressure continues to bore into his forehead.

Clay sees Aya'ah squint against glare, his eyelashes filtering the light and increasing focus. Clay instantly realizes that Aya'ah is about to loose the bolt. Clay feels his eyes widen, there's no time for any other reaction, because Aya'ah releases the notched quarrel, his hand opens, palm-wide, there is a bright red explosion of pain, and Clay screams and screams and screams, he's rolling on the ground, he doesn't wonder how he can scream with an arrow punching through his skull at point-blank range, or wonder why there is anything at all—when realistically he shouldn't feel much of anything at all—at least not for very long, because he should be dead. But the flare of scalding pain subsides.

Clay cracks one eyelid open to the sound of laughter.

Aya'ah is doubled over, tears form at the corners of his eyes he is laughing so hard. "*Oh my, oh my, oh my, oh my*," he keeps saying, over and over again, before breaking into more peals of laughter. "You. Should. Have. Seen your face."

What. The Fuck. Clay thinks, *has he just been pranked?* Clay seems to have burst a blood vessel—because his chin, his lips, the front of his coat, and the snow around him are drenched in a spray of blood, which continues to drip, drip, drip, drip from the tip of his nose—maybe the shock of being convinced he was about to be shot in the head with an arrow at point blank-range caused some sort of hemorrhage, and a vein burst somewhere inside him? Certainly he hasn't been shot, because he is still alive—although the nosebleed is somewhat of a mystery—Clay isn't prone to nosebleeds, and this is a deluge. The snow around him looks as if there'd been a lot more damage done than a simple nosebleed, almost enough for him to imagine that he *has* been shot with an arrow, dramatic red against the stark white.

In his lap is the arrowhead he took from the Indian burial ground, the edges of the obsidian puckered from where the blade had been chipped out of surrounding rock. So similar to the one Aya'ah had pointed at his forehead only moments before. In fact, if he didn't know any better—he would guess it is the exact same one. The arrowhead had been in the inside pocket of his leather jacket, zipped up, and safely stowed next to his heart. He doesn't remember taking it out, or know how it somehow ended up in his lap. But there it is; the blue-black glass, glistening, catching the light, razor-sharp even after so many years.

When Clay looks back up, Aya'ah is gone. He is nowhere to be seen. And there are no footsteps in the snow other than his own. Clay is alone, with the sound of the man's receding laughter.

Dare Theremin lays on his bed, rocker hair fanned out across his pillow, a plush basketball in his hands. He throws the ball up into the air and catches it. He screwed an orange hoop of metal to the wall above his bed, so if he bounces the ball just right off the stucco ceiling, it bounces off the wall like a back-board and falls through the net, and back into his waiting hands.

Dare aims and throws. Misses.

But the soft toy bounces off the ceiling and he manages to catch it, so he can try again. He tosses the ball in the air a few times and catches it, just to calibrate the weight, and the amount of force needed to reach the basket, then aims and takes another shot. The ball bounces off the rim and goes flying across the room and out of reach. *Fuck.*

Dare sniffs. He smells something. Is something burning? What is that smell? It smells like cigarette smoke. He looks around for the source of the smell but can't find anything. He isn't allowed to smoke—let alone smoke inside the house. When he does smoke inside, he hangs his head out the window, or huddles under the vent in the adjoining bathroom next to his bedroom, blowing smoke towards the fan that will hopefully suck most of the smoke outside.

But he hasn't been smoking. Where is that smell coming from? His parents don't smoke. He sits up in bed, looks around. Old band posters on the wall. Led Zeppelin. Sonic Youth. The Velvet Underground. Pushes his hair back from one side in a wave. He doesn't see any haze from tobacco smoke hanging in the air—only the smell of it filling his nostrils. Woody, citrusy, pungent.

"Are you smoking up there?" His dad's voice rumbles through the floorboards. His room is directly above the living room.

THUMP. THUMP. THUMP.

"I told you not to smoke in the house!" His dad pounds on the ceiling with something—maybe a broom-handle, maybe his fists. The smoke alarm above the door goes off.

BEEP. BEEP. BEEP. BEEP. BEEP.

His room is suddenly filled with blue smoke. Where did all the smoke come from? Did he leave a cigarette burning somewhere and it somehow caught fire? He hears his dad's steps pounding up the stairs.

Thrump, thrump, thrump, thrump.

Dare jumps off the bed, opens a window, and turns on the fan in his adjoining bathroom. The door to his room pops open and tobacco smoke swirls in commotion from the currents of air.

Scowl. Red moustache. Veins.

His dad is not pleased.

And there is no point in even denying it. Even though he *hasn't* been smoking. The smoke is everywhere. He's been caught red-handed, though he can't explain it. He searches and searches his room. But can't identify the source of the smoke. An old cigarette but. A lighter. A tin of old hand-rolled Heller tobacco. These things he finds, but none show any sign of recent ignition. The old phrase crosses his mind. *Where there's smoke, there's fire.*

But where is the fire?

"Who-who are you?" Tyler asks the night.

It is so dark, it's hard to see. He's standing in the Indian burial ground again. He knows that because he can see the outline of the platforms and scaffolds, and the sheen from some of the newer headstones. It's so dark, there must be no moon, or else it is shrouded by clouds, masking even the light from the stars.

What is he doing here again?

Tyler isn't alone. There is someone else there with him in the darkness.

"My name? You want to know my name?" an old woman asks. He can't see her, but he can hear the age in her voice, rustling of a rattle-snake shedding its skin. "You aren't worthy of knowing my name. You may call me *Naphtha*, because when you die, I will be waiting, and I will make sure you burn."

There is relief to the darkness, because Naphtha's eyes *glow* like coals. Her face is a mask of sharp angles and deep shadows. Her pupils dance with the strangest colours—cobalt, violet, crimson, chartreuse—as if the northern lights were distilled to an intense flame. He's never seen a campfire with so many colours.

Naphtha's eyes blaze, light explodes outward to envelop her in a halo, leaving her eyes dual-coloured like a husky. One eye is filmy-blue as if from glaucoma, filled with stars like constellations in the night sky, the other eye is an opaque sphere. The multi-hued radiance only scorches her skin for an instant—it flickers and illuminates her features. Frizzled white hair sticks up in all directions.

Naphtha is the fuel source and the flame. Her hands extend like claws, and she launches herself toward him, technicolour jets spread like deformed wings—a phoenix in human form.

Her arms wrap around him. Tyler thrashes and struggles to get away. He isn't weak, he works out five days a week. But no matter how hard he pushes, Naphtha's arms are like iron bands that won't release him. He can't get away. So they burn together, like the corpses of two lovers embracing in the grave as their flesh dissolves and rots away. The flames burn red-hot and iridescent, trembling hypnotically.

He once accidentally placed the palm of his hand on the glowing coils of a stove element, letting out a shriek when his skin sizzled and stuck to the nichrome. He feels that now—that same searing pain, but much worse because it isn't only his hand that sears; his entire body is a torch. He can't see through the smoke, his nose is thick with the burning-sulphur smell of human hair, and human flesh—his flesh. Then he can't see anything. He can't see the light the wick of his body makes, or what shadows it casts. Maybe his eyeballs have melted and drip down his face like candle wax? All he can feel is pain. It has become everything. There is nothing else other than pain.

Tyler screams, thrashing in tangled, sweaty sheets. Breathing heavy like he's just run a marathon. No flames. No heat. And no homicidal woman like some sort of avenging X-man. It was just a dream. Just a dream. He is welcomed by the familiar sight of his basement bedroom; exposed pipes, ductwork, and beams overhead. Sallow morning light filters through the small rectangular windows set at ground level.

"What's all that racket down there?" His mother's voice comes muffled from upstairs. "It's time for you to get ready for school. Stop fooling around!"

What kind of name is Naphtha? What a strange dream!

But like all dreams, this one too, begins to fade as his breathing returns to normal, the sweat dries, and he goes about the business of getting ready for the day. Strange dream, or no strange dream.

Tyler Kendrars meets Dare and Clay on the path to school. They trudge lethargically to their Monday morning classes, snow crunching beneath their boots.

"Cutter, can I have a puff?" Dare holds out his hand, two fingers extended. They always share smokes when one of them is out.

"I'm not smoking, retard." Clay pretends to inhale a non-existent cigarette, then exhales a stream of his breath only visible because of the cold air. Clay and Tyler laugh like hyenas. "I ran out last night."

"Oh," Dare says. "I thought I smelled smoke." His long hair is squished under an orange toque but flares out at the sides.

—Wooonhh. Woooonh. Wooooonh. Woooonh.—

A gale sweeps through the trees and sets branches to clacking; a drainage ditch somewhere gives off a haunting howl. And distantly, distantly—Tyler tilts his head—he thinks he hears the distinct sound of a baby crying. Wailing off in the trees somewhere.

"Do you hear something?" Tyler stops walking. The others pause and look back.

"You mean like a snarling sound?" Clay wears his cool leather jacket, but it doesn't look very warm. Drumsticks in his back pocket. "I think I heard it too. It's probably just some animal out in the woods."

"No. Not snarling" Tyler squints his eyes, his hood is drawn up against the cold wind so his vision is framed by a faux-fur trim. "It sounds like a baby."

"Oh." Clay sounds disappointed his senses aren't being validated.

"It's just the wind ya' dumbasses," Dare says. And he and Clay laugh. Dare wears his usual army-green camo guitar case strapped upside down on his back.

"No. It's not the wind." Tyler scans the trees to either side of the path. "It's something else."

Dare and Clay shrug at each other. Tyler takes off into the trees, branches snapping as he barrels his way through the dense bush.

—Weeenhh. Weeeenh. Weeeeenh. Weeeenh—

The baby cries rhythmically, pausing only between breaths for the next wail. Tyler imagines it abandoned in the woods, left to die, or maybe somehow fallen off the back of a snowmobile or toboggan. The parents will be frantic when they discover their baby missing.

"Seriously you guys! You don't hear it?" Tyler calls to his to friends, who have continued walking. He only hears their snickers and lame jokes in response. *How could they* not *hear the baby?* It is in the distance somewhere, but still clearly audible. At least, to his ears.

—*Waaaanhh. Waaanhh. Waaaaaanh.*—

The baby cries. Louder now. It is unmistakably the sound of a baby crying. Tyler pictures the squalling, helpless thing, swaddled in blankets, pink arms flailing, mouth open wide, hands balled into tight little fists, face wrinkled in displeasure like a blood hound.

—*Weeeenh. Weeeenh. Weeeeenh.*—

Quieter now as the wind shifts this way and that, stealing the sound, stretching it, bringing it back to his ears. He listens, trying to pinpoint a location.

Over there!

He crashes through the bush, branches snapping and breaking as he barrels through, knees high, forearms raised to protect his face. But when he gets to the place where he could have sworn he heard the baby crying, he hears the baby clearly over there, over the next rise. Something about the way the wind blows is playing tricks with his ears, echoing through the trees. Maybe the baby is much farther away than it seems to be? Maybe the sound is being carried by the wind? But how far can the wind actually carry sound?

Tyler sloughs through brush, hip deep in snow in some places. He's crossing a small ravine when he takes a step and his right foot drops, plunges through a crust of ice and into a hidden creek buried under the snow.

—*Heeyeaanhh*—

Tyler gasps. Instant shock of ice-cold water.

Oh man, soaker!

He lifts his foot and waters cascades from the shoe. His foot is frozen, the pantleg on his jeans is wet up to his knee. The denim instantly freezes crunchy on contact with the air, ice flakes off as he walks. *Damn that's cold.* Frostbite is a concern.

—Aaaaanhh. Aaaanhh. Aaaaaaanh.—

The baby cries. He looks up, branches obscure the grey sky. He needs to keep going. Tyler is more careful of where he steps. He doesn't want another soaker. He finds a fallen log and crosses the hidden creek. His shoe squelches with every step.

The bush is dense here. Branches scratch at his face and hands, slash at his eyes. Thorns hook through his coat. He's beginning to sweat under his winter clothes, despite the cold. The toes on his right foot are numb. They've stopped hurting, pinching from the cold. That's worrying. Like maybe the whole foot is an ice-cube. It feels solid, like a brick. Like his foot has become a statue. He should probably consider turning back, getting somewhere warm to defrost.

—Aaaaanhh. Aaaanhh. Aaaaaaanh.—

But he needs to keep going. He has to help the baby.

He hikes up a hill to reach the next decline. Deeper and deeper into the forest he is led, but no matter how close he seems to get to the baby's cries, whenever he arrives at the place where the baby should be, he hears the baby crying somewhere else. And he imagines one of his little brothers, lost somewhere in the snow, lost and alone. And he forces himself to go on. Though he is beginning to think that he is simply crazy. There is no baby, and the sound of the baby crying is all in his head. Clay and Dare hadn't heard the sound, or had at least mistaken it for the wind howling. Maybe that's all it is? Maybe it is the wind howling?

—Waaanhh. Waaanhh. Waaaaanh.—

The baby cries. It sounds real. Coming from the top of the next rise. He's certain of it.

He's panting heavily as he reaches the top of the steep incline, a large branch whacks him in the forehead, the pain is sharp and intense, for a moment he sees stars, and the sound of the baby crying goes dead silent. All he can hear is the whisper of a thousand pine needles as they scrape through the wind. Combing. Dead branches clack together like voices, the trees, all talking amongst themselves about the lone boy trudging frantically through the wilderness looking for something that isn't real.

He listens. No more cries. Gone, just as mysteriously as the sound arrived.

He feels hollow. Ragged. His muscles burn with the effort of the climb. His foot is cold and wet. The baby is dead. There is no baby. And his heart like the drop from a roller-coaster. He feels like he's just woken up from a dream, as if he's been locked into some kind of daze. Some sort of waking mania. There is no baby. He's certain of that now. What is he doing out here? He has no idea where he is. He realizes he has long ago lost track of his place in relation to the school, and the surrounding geography.

Where the hell is he? He is lost.

Shit. What should he do?

From his elevated position, he can see the same hilly terrain in all directions. Trees. Rocks. Snow. Sky. Clouds. No defining landmark or distinguishing feature by which to measure his placement. He's not sure which direction he should go in. He looks up at the sun, high in the sky now. He's not sure which way is North, South, East, West. Not that it would help much, since he still wouldn't know where he was or which directions to go in. A breeze blows, a few whisps of sleet sparkle in the sunlight. All is quiet. Peaceful even. No car sounds. No airplanes. No radio towers. Nothing. No sign of civilization. Vast wilderness. He's so screwed.

What should he do? Pick one direction at random? Eeny-meeny-miney-moe and start walking? Hope for the best? One-in-four odds he's picked the right way? Better than a lottery. Tyler's not sure he is willing to bet his life on it though. It wouldn't take long to die of exposure out here in the elements. Hypothermia, starvation, dehydration, potential injuries along the way, dangerous animals. Scavengers and predators.

He looks back down the steep incline he just scaled. Sees his own footsteps in the snow. *Ahh.* A flash goes off in his brain. The only sure way back, is to retrace the zig-zag route he's just traversed. He could travel in a more direct route if he knew where he was, but any direction he picks would be a guess, and might simply lead him further away and out into the forest. He chooses the safer option.

He hobbles down the hill, the entire foot numb now. No more pinching pain. Only numbness. He has a long trek back through the woods, following the path of his own footprints, much slower going on the way back, depleted of energy. He periodically stops to listen, but no more baby cries haunt him. Whatever it was, it's gone now. Maybe it was just the wind? He's not sure why he'd gotten so worked up. Just the wind.

It's third-quarter by the time Tyler reaches the high school. Everything aches. He is wet, cold, and exhausted. He limps through empty hallways, multicoloured flecks of granite, marble, quartz, and glass shine in the polished terrazzo floors. Institutional floors. Easy to keep clean. Everyone's in class. He makes his way to home-room.

Turns the brass knob on the door and walks to his seat, fifteen minutes late for the last class of the day, trailing a wet path of leaves and melted snow in his wake. He ignores all the looks from his teacher and classmates.

"What happened to you?" Clay whispers, as he trudges past Cutter's desk. But Tyler gives no answer. Says nothing of his excursion through the woods.

The Sterling Standard, January 12th
Grave Robbers Desecrate Ancient Indian Burial Ground

Racism is being blamed for the recent vandalism of a cemetery that took place last week on the Ghost Lake First Nation. Headstones and burial platforms were knocked over and defaced, with the word 'squaw' and other epithets scrawled across tombstones.

Family members and loved ones have reported that certain sacred items and ceremonial objects were missing or stolen, possibly taken by the same perpetrators or by relic hunters.

The incident is being investigated by the RCMP as a possible Hate Crime, as it seems likely the desecration was racially motivated.

Fair Action, a local organization dubbing itself an "equal rights group," has drawn suspicion, though there is no indication of their involvement. The group has been accused of hate crimes in the past – in particular the recent spate of arsons that took place on reserve, which damaged a beloved heritage site.

The Sterling mayor, the chief of Ghost Lake, as well as other local officials have all released statements condemning these acts.

"These crimes are unacceptable," Mayor Meriquin said, "and are by no means representative of the cooperation and respect between our communities."

The furnace kicks on and Tyler Kendrars' ink drawings flutter in the artificial breeze where they've been tacked to the supporting beams. Potential tattoo designs, old and new, cover exposed pipes, duct-work, and pink fiber-glass insulation.

"Oh shit, look at this!" Tyler waits while Clay and Dare scan the news article.

"We didn't do this!" Dare flicks the newsprint with his knuckles.

"*I* know that." Tyler takes few steps, turns, retraces his steps, turns. His socked feet create zaps of static against the area rug covering the concrete floors. "But *this* must have happened shortly after we were there. This paper is dated January twelfth and we were there, what—on the fifth? Do you know what this means?"

"If someone remembers seeing us at the Indian burial ground…" Dare sits on the orange couch, slowly working the logic of his thoughts out loud. "…or even saw us crossing the lake out to the Reserve, they could connect us to this vandalism—people will think we're the ones who did this!"

"But we didn't!" Clay sits up straighter in the bean bag chair he's sprawled in, drumsticks stilled where he'd been playing the air. "All we did was look for ghosts."

"YOU took that arrowhead." Dare points at the blonde-haired boy. "I SAW you."

"Oh slag off!" Clay says. "I didn't take anything. I've seen YOU smoking that *pipe*. That doesn't belong to you either!"

"Yeah, but we didn't go around kicking over gravestones." Dare spreads his hands open, "All we did was look around!"

"It won't matter if someone finds out we went there." Tyler drops down heavily onto the padded leather of the bench press. "We'll still be blamed."

"Maybe we should return the stuff we took." Dare's picked up his acoustic guitar, and his fingers pick absently at the frets.

"No. That's the last thing we should do." Tyler rubs the back of his head. "Someone might see us. What reason do a bunch of White kids have to go out to an Indian burial ground? Especially after *this!* That will just make us look guilty."

"Well, maybe we should each go alone—or at night—separately." Dare's 70's rocker-hair swings as he looks back and forth between the other two… "It won't draw as much attention."

"Fawck." Clay stares at the floor. And they all nod in agreement. None of them like the idea of going back to the graveyard alone and at night. But it's better than getting nailed for vandalism—something they didn't even do—or worse, getting caught for grave-robbing, which they *are* guilty of.

Tyler looks at his friends. "We should probably wait a few days, for things to settle down. The place is likely to be busy with visitors now, checking on their relatives."

They are all quite now, staring sullenly as they think about what they need to do.

It is snowing the day Clay skidoos across the ice-road out to the Indian Reserve. During the day. He'd be fucked if he was going to go visit a creepy-as-fuck graveyard in the middle of the night. That would probably be more suspicious than simply stopping by on the pretense of checking out the vandalism. The heavy snowfall hides everything in a blanket of white, and visibility is poor. No one is likely to see where he's going, and he knows the way well enough not to worry about getting lost. The snow falls in large, fat flakes, landing delicately on top of the four inches of soft snow that have already fallen overnight, muffling sound like insulation.

His boots crunch through the snow making squeaky sounds like Styrofoam as he makes his way through the trees to where the clearing opens up, and the underbrush was cleared long ago to make way for the platforms and scaffolding erected to hold the dead. Headstones, some old, some new, are interspersed with the wooden constructions, which clearly show signs of repair after being knocked over. *Who could be so callous?* Clay wonders. Who is that filled with hate, they could go so far as to kick over a grave? Or scrawl graffiti across a tombstone?

Who could be so callous as to rob the dead? Another, smaller voice asks. For that is exactly what *they* had done. Though Clay never frames it to himself like that—as grave robbery. They had just been adventure-seeking. Had heard the rumours of ghosts and goblins and the idea of an Indian burial ground captured their imagination. And isn't that the premise for countless horror movies?

The silence is eerie. The snow falls like a curtain drawn across the world, blankets of white absorbing every sound like cotton balls. Even the crunch of the snow under his boots seems muffled. Like any sound would be too loud for this place, as if the burial grounds are in mourning for the desecration that occurred here. Clay feels his cheeks burn. How could he have contributed in any way towards that sadness? In the hush, he makes his way towards the scaffolding where he'd found the arrowhead, the jawbone, and the carved figurine.

At first, he thinks it is his imagination. He hears someone crying. Quiet sobbing under the dampening effect of snow. Clay looks around to see the source of the sound but doesn't see anyone anywhere. Maybe it's another ghost? Or a person—this is a graveyard after all. People tend to cry in graveyards.

Clay changes course and follows the sound towards its source, winding his way through the wooden platforms towards the section with the newly dead, marked by polished marble head-stones and simple wooden crosses. The burial grounds had only recently been reclaimed for the interment of the dead, and there were comparatively few new gravestones compared to the older graves. A mix of old and new, Christian and non-Christian, pagans and those who followed the old religions. There seemed to be a gap of a hundred years or so, where the dead must have been laid to rest elsewhere, in the graveyards of the towns and cities after many of the Indians fled, or were dragged away, or displaced from their homes. He didn't know the history of the Ghost Lake Indians that well, but he knew enough to know that they had gotten a pretty raw deal.

A girl in white snow-pants, a pale-blue coat, and a pink toque is kneeling in the snow at the foot of one of the more recent graves. Sobbing. The headstone is a light grey, polished granite, with the name MUSHKEG written across it in deeply incised letters. The word 'SQUAW' had been scrawled diagonally across the marker with red paint. Where the woman's blond hair escaped from the confines of her toque, Clay can see that it had been died blue at the tips. As if those too had frozen.

The girl reaches out with red mittens and brushes off the snow that accumulated on top of the headstone. Clay's stomach turns, he feels queasy. It's as if he just kicked a cat or a dog or done something terrible. He needs to puke. Clay knows that he didn't deface the headstone by scrawling the word across the grave, but somehow he still feels guilty; after all, hadn't he done something just as disrespectful—maybe even worse—by taking things that didn't rightfully belong to him, objects that had been placed with deceased loved ones, objects which surely must have some great significance to the departed or to those they left behind? He'd even taken a jawbone, like some ghoulish Indiana Jones relic hunter.

It's true that Aya'ah didn't seem to mind, he'd used it as an opportunity to play a practical joke—what did he need his jawbone for? But still. It bothers Clay that he ever thought it was okay to steal from the dead. With the sound of the girl's tears, nausea crashes down on him. Clay doubles over, and retches. His straw hair feathering down in front of his face. The snow cold under his fingers.

Eadie looks up. Is that a dog barking? When she heard about the vandalism, she needed to come and see what the jerks had done—needed to come and see if her love's grave had been defaced. Even though Mushkeg is gone. The marker is just a monument for her earthly remains—nothing more.

Disturbed by the sound of a dog barking, Eadie quickly wipes her tears. She thought she'd been alone. Maybe someone was walking their dog? But when she turns, she sees a boy, on all fours, gagging, puking up his lunch onto the snow. What the heck?

Eadie stands and makes her way over to the young man. "Are you okay?" She sniffles and bends her knees to crouch slightly. Her long coat doesn't let her bend easily. Tries to pretend she wasn't crying a moment before. She is fine. Everything is okay. It is okay.

"I'm fine," the kid says, breathing heavy, then retches some more. His hair sticks out in all directions and flares out in front of his face, but she can still see the pale blue colour of his eyes through the baby-chick strands.

"Yeah, you seem fine," Eadie says. The boy finishes barfing and then gets to his feet, wiping his mouth and hands with a gob of snow.

Eadie straightens. "What are you doing out here? I mean… who are you visiting?"

The boy's nostrils flare for a moment.

"Aya'ah." He waves toward the older tombs. "How 'bout you?"

"Aya'ah? I don't know them—just a… a friend—when I, when I heard about the vandalism, I wanted to come see for myself. I don't know how anyone could do such an awful thing—how can people be so heartless?"

Clay's stomach feels dizzy, but he manages to suppress the urge to throw up again.

"I don't know." Clay looks down at his puke melting splattered holes through the snow.

"You know what that means? Don't you?" She tries to catch his eyes.

"What?" Clay takes a step back from the girl.

"Aya'ah. *So-and-so*. What you say when you've forgot someone's name."

"It's the only name he gave me." Clay pats his hands together, and for some reason this answer seems to satisfy the girl. "Who was she?" He asks, looking past her and nodding towards Mushkeg's gravestone.

"I've gotta go," Eadie steps around the boy, and heads back to the path that leads up and out toward the access road.

"Wait!"

Eadie stops, half-turned. "What is it?"

"I'm sorry," he says, not knowing why he is apologizing, or what he is apologizing for. Puking? Or for intruding on her moment of grief? Maybe both.

Eadie nods, turns, and continues walking away. She leaves a trail of footsteps through the cover of trees. Large snowflakes continue to fall.

Clay trudges back through the graveyard, searching for Aya'ah's tomb. He locates it quickly this time, a mostly-collapsed grave platform. He places the bone underneath two pieces of fallen timber, in roughly the place he remembers finding it.

"Sorry, dude. Didn't mean to disturb you."

Clay hopes returning the jaw will save him from being the butt of further practical jokes. He touches the lump in his jacket pocket. Wonders. Should he return the other things he took too? *Naah*, Aya'ah only mentioned his jaw. That should be enough to appease the man's ghost. He half-expects Aya'ah to re-appear, but the graveyard is as silent as… well—the grave.

Task accomplished, Clay shuffles back to his skidoo and away from the oppressive silence. Happy to be free from the burden of Aya'ah's jawbone. His steps fall easier, and his shoulders feel light. He's done the right thing.

Dare Theremin brings the head of the axe down in an arc, driving the iron wedge into the wood and splitting it into two pieces on the first try. Stacking another log on top of a wider log he's using as a base, he lines up his axe-head to make sure his aim is on target, raises up the gavel with his right arm, throwing it up into the air, and letting the weight of the anvil do much of the work of splitting the wood, rather than using his own strength. He still has a lot of logs to split, and muscling the swing is a waste of energy, and throws his aim off balance anyway.

Aim. Raise. Drop. Split. Align the next log.

Aim. Raise, Drop. Split. Align.

Repeat.

Ninety times, or two-hundred times, or three-hundred times. However many times it takes until all the logs have been split into more manageable pieces for burning. If you're muscling it too much, your arms will let you know—they'll be sore before you make your way through half of the cord of stacked logs. Proper form is important. Each time, he makes sure to line up the sharp edge with the center of the concentric rings of growth, the side-ways cross-section of the log, with his arms fully extended—it's better to check his aim, than to miss, and have to raise the heavy splinth up any more times than necessary. And missing and hitting the ground sends shockwaves up his arms and into his shoulders, when they are already absorbing enough vibrations. It's something better to avoid.

So each time he puts a new log in place, he takes aim then raises the axe. Sometimes the log wobbles and doesn't want to stand straight, making his task harder. But the challenge of splitting each log perfectly is its own sort of game. Its own sort of zen problem-to-overcome, satisfaction-upon-completion, endorphins-reward system.

Dare has soon worked himself into the rhythm of the task, and despite the cold, the hard work staves off any discomfort, his breath streams in the frigid air. His hair is tied back so it stays out of his way while he works. He is soon feeling too warm. He takes off his army jacket, wearing only his red plaid. Soon even that feels too hot, and he strips down to his white tank. Not that there's anyone to show off his killer new skull tattoo too.

From out of the corner of his eye, Dare catches sight of something in the darkened entryway to the small woodshed. Some shape. He does a double-take, at first dismissing his eyes, then taking a second look to confirm that he really is seeing what he thought he saw. The silhouette of a woman, standing outlined against the dim interior of the shed. The smell of fresh tobacco is strong, filling his nostrils; sweet, woody, resinous. How did he not notice it before? Maybe he was so engrossed in chopping wood, it hadn't registered? At least not consciously.

The woman leans against the door-jam, arms folded across her chest. Her shoulders are widened by shoulder-pads and puffs of lace, and her narrow waist flares out at the hips like a wasp or a hornet. She wears an old-fashioned dress, of the type Dare's only seen on TV in historical dramas, or in the museum. It isn't the sort of thing people wear anymore. Her face is in shadow. How long has she been standing there watching him? The thought makes him shuffle his feet, tamping down the already packed-down snow where he's been working.

He lets the axe-head fall to the ground, still holding loosely onto the grip.

"Hello?" Dare's head waffles, trying to get a better look into the shadows. "Can I help you?"

The woman steps back into the dark shed. A fall of light slants in at just the right angle so her features emerge from the gloom. Interrupted by slatted boards like venetian blinds. Very film-noir. Her face is angular and heart shaped. Pretty. Her skin is smooth, though the crow's feet around her eyes reveal age, as does the streak of white in her long, black hair. Her eyes are as dark as the night sky, glittering. Expression unreadable.

"My name is Bagonegiizhig. I believe that you have something that belongs to me." She bites her upper lip. Her voice is soft. The smell of tobacco smoke is overpowering. Dare looks around, but doesn't see any smoke, or see a possible source.

"Hunh?"

"I think you know what I'm talking about."

"The pipe?" Theremin swallows, his mouth suddenly dry. All his hackles are up, as if his brain has antennae and the feelers are all shivering from whatever they're picking up. His scalp tingles, adrenaline surges like a tide, the veins in his neck feel tight.

The woman nods.

That simple acknowledgment confirms all of his fear, suspicion, and wild speculation. The scent that has been haunting him for days now, ever since he lifted that pipe from the graveyard. Dare is certain of it. She is a ghost. A dead woman. What other explanation could there be?

"What's so special about this pipe?" he manages to croak, his windpipe feels too narrow, his legs feel weak. The throat of the axe slips from his loose fingers and lands hollowly on the packed-down snow. He hopes he won't fall over too. His heart is thumping in his chest, pounding in his ears, harder than when he'd actually been working hard, rather than simply struggling to remain standing.

The ghost woman tilts her head in thought.

"It's not really. It is an ordinary pipe, though I've had it in my possession for quite some time—since my first trip abroad. The king of France, Louis Dieudonné the XIV gave it to me as a parting gift."

As Bagonegiizhig speaks, she steps forward so smoothly, Dare barely registers her movement, coming ever closer, slowly, slowly—as if her feet, hidden under her long skirts, make no contact with the ground.

"Fouquet—Dieudonne's Superintendent of Finances—allowed his greed to over-extend his reach. He set himself up in the chateau Vaux-le-Vicompte, and what is worse, began fortifying Belle Ile. And I can smell greed in all of its many forms—"

The light slanting in through the boards of the shed shifts down the landscape of her face, tracing the curves and concaves.

"—When I left Paris, the poor ajidamoons was in the dungeons. Colbert's greed overshadowed that of Fouquet. Though Dieudonné did not listen to me, he was pleased by this outcome. I secured the Sun King's favour for the Anishinaabek, when the Wemtigoosh held more power in Miikinakominis than the Zhaaganaashag. The tobacco market brought in extensive revenue for their Monarchy, Louis the XIVth levied taxes of thirty sols on every pound of semaa..."

Bagonegiizhig is closer now, close enough for him to smell the cloying scent of her perfume; earth, citrus, and tar. No not perfume. Tobacco. Fresh tobacco. And under that. Something else. Metallic. Copper. She circles him. Dare can't move. He feels like one of those squirrels that freeze when they sense the eyes of a predator. Hoping that if they just stay still, they might escape detection. Even though it's far too late for that. He still can move.

"...snuff was in fashion among the aristocracy, and Dieudonné saw the potential for greater control of this market. He viewed me as a symbol of both New France, and this influx of wealth. You may have noticed the sun-medallions on the shank?"

As she speaks, Dare realizes that he can actually feel the embossed texture of the medallions under the whorls of his fingertips. He looks down, and realizes the pipe with the sun motifs is in his right hand—though he doesn't remember removing it from the jacket pocket where he'd stored it. And the woman named Bah-go-nah-gee-zhick is stroking the pipe with her skeletal fingers. So thin the joints seem over-large. Skin stretched over bones.

"—It is just a trinket, really. I guess you could say I have a sentimental attachment—not because Louis gave it to me—kaa!"

She scoffs, a sound deep in the back of her throat like a growl. "—But because I carried it with me for so, so many years."

"I'm s-s-sorry," Theremin says, spellbound, trying to follow this outpouring of memories, names, histories, most of which he does not understand, he only knows that this woman—if she is a woman—is very old, or lived a long, long time ago. He still doesn't fully accept this ghost-theory. But if she *is* so old, how can she still be alive? How is she standing here, speaking of events which took place *centuries* before he had been born? None of it made any sense.

"I'm sorry," Theremin says again and dry swallows. He wishes he hadn't let the axe fall through his fingers, he wishes he was still holding the handle, realizing how close the Ojibwe woman has come to him. Not that he was thinking of using the axe as a *weapon*, but it would give him a sense of security.

"And I'm *hun-gree*." A small smile plays itself over her lips. She traces an index finger in a line down his chest. Exposed flesh and the thin material of his white tank.

"Do you know what a wiindigo is gwiizence?"

"Yes." Theremin has heard the stories—everyone has heard the stories of the wiindigo up here. Like bigfoot, or the Ogopogo—they aren't really real. They are just stories. He isn't sure what *gwiiz-ence* means, but he isn't about to ask. Can't be bothered to muster the courage for an inconsequential question. "It's like a cannibal, I think."

Dare Theremin trembles. He can only remember being this scared once before in his life, when he accidentally stumbled across a mountain lion and her cubs out in the woods. On spotting the wild animals, he froze to the spot, immediately making eye contact with the mother, glowing amber and green, as alien and predatory as any monster in a horror movie, a mere dozen feet away, and he knew that if she felt threatened, she would protect her young—and that he was an intruder. That time, he'd wet himself. Too scared to move. Too scared to breathe even. Not knowing the right thing to do in the situation. He probably would've run away if he hadn't been rooted to the spot, unable to move in a fearful paralysis. He'd felt the expanding wetness saturate his jeans, urine flowing down one pantleg, and trickling out a cuff. And the large cat finally looked away, as if in disdain, and led her babies away.

Leaving him with his face burning, and his jeans wet, but alive and unmolested.

And that's how he feels now; too scared to move. As if he's stumbled upon a wild animal. He doesn't know why the woman frightens him so much—but there is something unsettling about her movements. Slow and careful the way old people move—but despite the streaks of white in her black hair, she doesn't look that old. Or slow and careful, like a predator preparing to strike.

"Not exactly shkiniigish." Bagonegiizhig strokes Dare's smooth chin with the back of her boney fingers. Her fingers are cold. "I'd need to be *human* in the first place, in order for me to be a cannibal."

Bagonegiizhig smiles again, and if anything, her teeth seem sharper than they were before. Her smile has altogether too many teeth. "You—you would merely confirm what I already know—I am a hunter. Through and through."

"Wh-what do you mean?"

"My father wiindigo is a creature of Spirit, my mother was human. And I require a body in order to feed—without that…" She shrugs, a rise of one shoulder, tilt of the head. "…I'm not much more than a ghost."

Bagonegiizhig reaches up and grabs him on either side of the head. Her hands are ice. She covers his ears, holding his head immobile so that he can't turn his head to look away. He closes his eyes. He doesn't want to look her in the eye.

The wiindigo woman says: "I'm patient, I can wait." Her voice is sing-song, feminine, gentle. He finds himself wanting to comply, even though he knows it is probably NOT a good idea. But Dare also knows he can't keep his eyes closed forever. He'll have to open them eventually, sooner or later. He considers struggling, putting up a fight, but something in his gut screams at him that would be even an even WORSE idea. No use putting off the inevitable. He takes a breath, mentally braces himself, and opens his eyes.

She is waiting. Her hands hold his head straight ahead like vise-grips, so he is looking directly into her eyes. Two deep, dark wells of infinity. He feels like a deer caught in the glare of headlights. The train is coming closer, and closer, and there is nothing he can do to get off the tracks. He can't even look away. That option is no longer available. He is being drawn in, or maybe she is being pulled out? He isn't sure which. It is a strange sensation—he is being stretched—long and thin. His face, his eyes, his brains, his blood, his lungs, his heart, his kidneys, all his organs and skin and body parts are being tugged, tugged, tugged, like fish caught on a line. He is a thousand strands of falling spaghetti.

Then he is hungry.

Very, very, very, hungry.

Hungrier than he has ever been in his entire life, hungrier than he ever imagined it was even possible to be. This is abject starvation before the weakness and delirium sets in. Starvation before the last burst of speed and strength gives out, when there is only one last burst of speed and strength left, and a desperate drive for survival—to capture a meal, to win some kind of sustenance, no matter what it cost, no matter if it burned up the last reserves of energy, and left nothing to look forward to except death—it doesn't matter, because if this last burst of speed and strength isn't successful—then death won't be long in the waiting. Death has wings.

Then they are eating. The time in between missing. He sees it again like sped-up film, with frames cut out from the movie, touching only on the highlights, then slowing down for the action. The forest floor flying under his feet with what seems like impossible speed as he runs and runs and runs, the undergrowth is like a field of swaying grass, and he can see every blade, somehow avoiding every tree-root, swamp, thorn and bramble, there is the quick flash of movement in the trees, something with horns, antlers. There is a chase. Then the animal is struggling underneath the grip of their teeth as it kicks and bucks in death throes, never giving up that effort to survive.

And Dare knows this feeling—intimately. The same desperation consumes them both as they follow the beat of the beast's heart down into the darkness. When the animal has finally lost enough strength, they begin to eat, tearing through the thick hide of the elk, rending the flesh with bare hands, bringing handfuls of steaming meat to their lips, biting into the mass, chewing and choking when they eat too fast, choking it down even as the animal twitches, shakes. He isn't even sure the animal is completely dead yet—which would be a horrible thought under normal circumstances, but the hunger which drives them, *them* because he is more than one; *they* are plural—him, her and it—all three at once, and *it* is a merciless hunger. They are hunger, and hunger has no mercy. Mercy isn't in their nature.

Kneeling on all fours, they put his face to the animal and began to eat, like a wolf gnawing at a downed kill, eating as steadily and methodically as possible so no one else can steal their share, except there are no other dogs to share with, because they took down this elk on their own. No pack necessary for them to hunt, and no mongrel would dare try to steal. Still, they ate quickly, and greedily. As if there are scavengers waiting to snatch their meal. Though no matter how much of the meat they consume, they are still hungry.

The blood coats his jaws and his face, his forehead, and his arms up to his elbows and then his shoulders as they dig his way further in. It must look as if he'd bathed in a bathtub full of blood. Everything is sticky. Even the hair on his head is moist and thick, drying in ragged tufts.

He smiles, blood coating teeth. Collected in the ridges.

It has been too long.

It has been too long.

When they are done eating, they stand up, lick their lips and worry at every morsel caught in the nooks and crannies of his teeth, leaving the empty husk of skin and bones—for that is all that is left of the shredded elk—everything else has been devoured. The coyotes can gnaw on the bones and fight tug-of-war over the hide.

Then they walk. Again Dare is amazed at how clear the night is, how precise their vision. From only the light of a sliver moon, the snow glows blue, and together, he can see the movement of every pine needle, every branch, as if it's high noon. The pillars of the tree trunks pass by like sentinels. They come to the shore of a clear, clean, cold, river—mostly locked in ice, but open water flows where the current is strongest, and where the rocks create rapids too boisterous to freeze over. There they undress. They slip out of his blood-sodden clothes, his jeans fall to their ankles revealing his nimble thighs, and a triangle of pubic hair at his pelvis, which for some reason strikes him as odd, though it is as familiar to them as the rest of their body.

They step out of the jeans, pull the shirt up and over his head, freeing their breasts and disarranging his hair. They wade in—letting the swirling waters envelope them, walking in up to the waist, then the nipples, their shoulders and neck, nose, eyes and teeth, until the water is well over his head, but still they don't float. Their feet remain in contact with the ground, despite the physics of buoyancy, and the raging current, which rushes past with strength, it should have pulled them off their feet and dragged them under the ice scabbing its way over the surface further downstream—entombing them forever.

But this doesn't happen. Instead the frigid water tears at their limbs, their long black hair, their breasts, and their fingers, blasting every grimy fleck of blood from their flesh. And it is cold, cold, cold, cold, cold—except it doesn't feel more cold than anything else—it feels like more of the same. Until the coldness inside matches the coldness without. And it is all a matter of sameness. Uniformity.

When they are raked clean, they wade back to the shore. Their feet freeze to the icy ground with every step. His toes stick like tongues pressed to cold iron. The suction-cup toes of a frog. And that's the last thing Dare remembers for a time. The darkness closes in on him. A gap in consciousness and memory, which he can only assume is sleep. Timeless, measureless, sleep.

When Theremin wakes up, he is in his own bed. Wrapped in blankets and shivering. His teeth clatter together as his jaw trembles rhythmically and uncontrollably, bone on bone. *Has the furnace stopped working again?* he wonders. *He is freezing!*

Then: *What a fucked-up dream. He'd been a woman!* With his very own set of small breasts! He remembered the way they felt, swaying in the raging current of the water under the surface of the icy river with their own separate buoyancy. At the time, it hadn't seemed strange, they had felt like a part of his own body—and what is more, they felt familiar to him. As did the long, dark hair that appeared snarled as the water forked and lashed, dragging it in the direction of the current, trying to pull the weight of it from his scalp. Tugging. Tugging. Tugging, as they raised their hands to the light above, and the unseen sky above the surface, some fourteen feet overhead—that division between water and sky forming a new ceiling, a new sky—and a sky beyond the sky. 'They' because they had been three together, like the Father, Son and the Holy Ghost? Wasn't that what they said in church?

Dare, Bagonegiizhig, and Hunger.

Then he remembered the elk. The blood. *Oh god. The blood.* And *the meat!* The raw, still steaming globs of meat he had gorged on, slaking his hunger with that gory meal. But the thought of the organs, glistening wetly in the light, now turned his stomach. He remembers eating the gleaming, dark liver. And the red, cartilaged chambers of the heart, the size of both his fists put together. Theremin turns over on his side and throws up into the wastebasket, his stomach twists like a dish-rag as he empties some of the contents in a bloody-red stream mixed with unidentifiable chunks. When he is done, he stays hunched over, waiting in case he has to throw-up some more, and wipes the side of his mouth with a sleeve, breathing heavily.

Holding his belly, he realizes how much it hurts.

He feels full. Too full. Like he sometimes did after eating giant meal during the holidays. But this feels worse. He never felt this badly after a meal—not ever. He lowers the blanket covering his midriff. His belly is distended and tight like a drum. Pregnant. Packed full of more meat than he's ever eaten in one sitting.

—Eeaaeeaaauuunnnhhh—

Dare groans and turns over. His eyes half-lidded in pain, he spots the lump of filthy clothes he wore the day before. His boots, and jeans, and white tank are crusted with a dark brown crustiness. Which could have been mud, but which he knows is not. It doesn't smell like mud. It smells like blood. A meaty copper smell.

It wasn't a dream. Or at least—it's more real than any dream he ever had in the past. Real enough to leave him sick, shivering, and bloated from glutting on raw elk-meat.

Dare's eyes land on the old pipe resting on his bedside table. *It's the pipe!* The pipe he took from the Indian burial ground. It belonged to that wiindigo woman with the streak of white in her long, dark hair. What did she say her name was? Bah-go-nah-gee-zhick. Bagonegiizhig. He remembers her icy hands holding the sides of his head steady, forcing him to look into her eyes, like two bottomless holes, and then he was falling, falling, falling, and then he was her. She was him. And they, they were hungry.

Dare groans. Can you die from eating too much meat? Does raw elk hold pathogens or viruses or bacteria which could make him more sick than he already feels? He can't imagine feeling worse than he already does. Flashbacks of the carnage flicker through his mind, like the stray bits of half-remembered song, wafting back to him with the scent of fresh tobacco; honey, ammonia, licorice. A song of ripping and rending and tearing.

Guttural strains. Lyrics of blood. A chorus of death and dying and feeding.

And through it all the pungent smell of tobacco, woven through the parts of the dream. And it is still haunting him. Lingering in the air. He can smell it as strong as ever filling his nostrils; wood-chips, vanilla, and formaldehyde. Dare eyeballs the pipe on the night-side table, like an innocuous little rattlesnake. Sun-burst medallions decorate the sides, the rough image of a face with lines like rays of light stabbing out.

Effing thing! Dare Theremin wishes he'd never laid eyes on the damned instrument. He can't wait to be rid of it. For a moment he pictures destroying it, crushing it under his boot heels or throwing it into the fire. But he can't be sure doing that would put an end to his ordeal—he thinks only one thing will put things right, and that is if he returns the cursed object. And he prays that he never encounters the ghost of the wiindigo woman named Bagonegiizhig, ever again.

Bagonegiizhig appears, stepping out of the shadows. It's evening now, the sun has gone down, but Church hasn't bothered to flick on the lights. Human-wiindigo hybrids have good night vision. The dark doesn't bother him. He prefers it usually. He's camped out in one corner of the kitchen where he's set up an easel for painting his oils, watercolours, ink washes. Shades of grey. It doesn't matter what colours he uses, they all look grey in this light.

His great-grandmother licks her lips with a pleased smile, and her eyes lack some of their usual predatory focus, as if she's just finished eating a stellar meal and is still relishing the memory. But it must be pretty rare for her to enjoy a meal these days—being dead and all. It should have been a physical impossibility. But as is often the case with his great-grandmother, what is impossible isn't less likely to be true. What has she been up to? Church wonders, then dismisses the thought. Sometimes—it's better if he doesn't know.

"Boozhoo aanikoobijigen." *Hello great-grandmother.*

"Aaniin noozhishenh." *Hello grandson,* Bagonegiizhig says with the same distracted smile. When she was alive, she always seemed so ancient to him. Now she seems ageless. Not old or young, but somehow both at once. Maybe because she's dead? She can take on the form of her youthful self, without giving up any of the knowledge she acquired with age.

"I've been talking to Aabitiba." Church raises his brush and sketches out the shape of his great-grandmother's dress, narrow at the waist, flaring out the hips, a long drapery of fabric. A laced-up bodice. Starvation-thin like a supermodel.

His words bring Bagonegiizhig out of her food fog, and she tilts her head narrowing her eyes for a moment before looking up at the exposed beams of the kitchen ceiling, white sclera of her eyes showing. She looks towards the attic, as if she can see through the tin roof, and through the eastern facing walls of the second floor, through the floorboards and into the attic high above. X-ray vision.

"So you have," she says, speaking in English. "It was bound to happen eventually. It's not called Ghost Lake for nothing you know." Though they aren't at Ghost Lake, they're at the house in Sterling. Can ghosts have Alzheimer's too?

"It's nice to meet you—?" Dare Theremin asks, inflecting the "you" so that makes it sound more like a question. Professor Chase abandoned him temporarily with the goth boy to go join another party of milling, and well-dressed attendees. A charity fund-raiser for the new Ghost Lake museum. "I didn't quite catch your name. Was it *Kurt*?"

The goth boy wears a grey suit, a purple paisley vest with brass buttons, and a red Norval Morrisseau neck-tie. His bangs are long, the dark hair grazes his heavy-lidded eyes. Lights shine through the ribs of a nearby T-rex skeleton and cast shadows across Church's face.

"It's Church. Church Bagonegiizhig." He doesn't stick out his hand to shake hands.

Dare feels his face go pale, as if someone slit his throat and all the blood is draining out.

Strange—Church had only seen this reaction in people who'd met Bagonegiizhig. "Ohhh. I didn't realize you had met my great-grandmother."

"How did you know?" Dare's tongue darts out like a lizard's to moisten his lips, but his mouth has gone dry, and his tongue feels like leather. His eyes dart to the sides, looking for some avenue of escape. Exit signs. Windows. The room is filled with dinosaurid fossils, black-suit-and ties. Women in dresses. A few dancers in flashy traditional regalia. Fringe and feathers.

"You recognized my last name. *Bagonegiizhig*—after my great-grandmother."

"Ah. Uh, yes." Theremin chokes, his eyes bugging out slightly. "I've had the—uh… fortune, to meet her."

"I see," Church says. But Dare is saved from the need of making further conversation with wiindigo-woman's great-grandson when Chase returns from the neighbouring circle of partygoers. She couldn't come back soon enough as far as Dare is concerned. And he can't get away from the older boy fast enough. There is something about Church's smile that reminds him of the woman who once came to him in a dream, hungry and smelling of tobacco.

"Louis the fourteenth!" Dare barks out, and Chase looks at him frowning.

"Sorry?" Church asks.

"Ask-ask your great-grandmother," Dare stutters. "The next time you see her. Ask her about Louis the fourteenth."

"Alright." Church smiles. Dare wishes he wouldn't.

Dare shudders as he and Chase move away, and he catches the barest whiff of that familiar, acrid scent, like smoky perfume. The memory alone is enough to make him gag every time he smells it on the street, or outside the front of a building.

If nothing else, Bagonegiizhig saved him from lung cancer. Dare can't stand the smell of tobacco.

Church is in the kitchen, sitting on the sofa set in one corner of the large room, next to the wall of bookshelves. His easel is set up in front of him, oil paints, paint thinner, linseed oil, charcoal. The kitchen has always been the center of their home, doubling as both living space, and food preparation site. He hasn't bothered to turn on the lights, and Marie's old TV is set to *off*. His mother has switched strategies. Like Inri, she's found other ways of distracting herself.

In the dim light, Bagonegiizhig appears next to the range stove, running one finger along the top of the hood-system, as if checking the stainless steel for an accumulation of dust. The appliances are new, as is the stone fireplace, and the new tin-roof Church installed to prevent leaking during rainstorms. These are among the first improvements Church made when he inherited the money Bagonegiizhig had left for him. *Lots* of it—a large sum held in trust until he came of age at eighteen. How long has she been standing there? Maybe she's been there the whole time, and it just took the right state of mind for him to notice?

"Louis the XIVth," Church says. "I've been told to ask you about him."

"Gichi-mewinzha." *That was a long time ago.* Bagonegiizhig remains in shadow. She is black-lace back-lit against the light coming in from the windows. The small jets of flame from the pilot lights are unable to dispel the gloom, so her features are in darkness. Silhouette of a narrow waist, flaring out to impossible hips. "Gaa-niibin ezhi 1663. Ingodwaak jibwaa Wemitigoozhiiwakiing bagidinamaw akiiing izhi-Zhaaganaashiiwakiing." *It was the summer of 1663. A hundred years before France ceded nearly all of its colonies to Britain.*

Bagonegiizhig crosses the room, heels clicking across the floor-boards. Stands in from of the hearth, one arm resting on the mantle. Church flips a page on the grainy watercolour-paper he's been working on. Sets to creating a new picture. Sets aside the pastels and picks up the charcoal to sketch the scene. Bagonegiizhig, standing in front of the fireplace, flames shimmering through lace. Exposed wood beams of the lofted ceiling projecting forward in linear space. He'll use the pastels once he's satisfied with the layout on the flat surface.

"A council of the Niswi-mishkodewin, the *Three Fires Confederacy*, was called at Bawating, Miishinimakinago, to address our struggles ahead. The Prophecy that scattered Anishinaabek into three, was coming true—the British and French were wreaking havoc amongst the nations, seeding discord and disease. A great hunger was growing..."

Bagonegiizhig crosses one arm across her abdomen, as if to contain the appetite growing there. "Growing for many winters, centuries—so much like our hunger—except this hunger threatened the whole world."

Church's eyes shift focus, back and forth between the shapes on the page, and the details in the distance. Floorboards. River-stones in the massive chimney. Mudroom door. Angle of his aanikoobijigan's cheekbone.

"It was decided that an Izhinizhawaagan, an *Emissary* should be sent to the monarchs in Europe—the Spanish, the French, the Dutch, the English; all those Nations who had a foothold in Miikinakominis—a speaker who could command the ear of the Great Fathers and Great Mothers across the Great-Salt-Sea." Bagonegiizhig leans back against the lintel, and for a moment, Church worries her dress might catch fire, but he reminds himself she is a ghost. Her dress can't catch fire.

"It was decided that I should be the one to retrace the steps of our migration, take passage aboard a Zhaagaanaashi ship with an envoy of ambassadors, and make the journey agamakiing, *overseas*, laden with fine furs and valuable gifts. Who could understand the storm that was to devour our nations, if not a wiindigo? None of the other ambassadors survived the crossing, except Harquebus."

"Our journey led us up the St Lawrence river, by canoe of course, and we saw first-hand the devastation to come. The shores of the great river barren; ravaged by war. A sign of the troubles to come—one of the first casualties of the fur-trade, the battle for territory, the foreign economic engines which stir the pot. Grinding people and nations into dust. We all wanted to secure trade with the Europeans, and those who controlled the St Lawrence River valley, also controlled this trade."

Bagonegiizhig pauses for a moment, silent as she looks back into her mind, back into the events of the distant past. The only sound is the soft scritch, scritch, scritch, of Church's charcoal on the page. Rendering Bagonegiizhig in shades of grey. He can always add colour later. Orange and hickory of the flames.

"My responsibility was three-fold—to establish a personal relationship with the Gchi-Ogimaa of the Wemitigoozhi and Zhaaganaashi, to curry favour for the concerns of the Anishinaabek, and if possible, to establish an alliance."

Church hates to interrupt his great-grandmother's narrative, but he can't help but ask: "Aaniin endas-biboonagiziyan!?" *How many winters have you survived*? According to the timeline in the story, this pushed Bagonegiizhig's age back farther than he thought possible—Church knows she is *old*—but not that old! If she'd been twenty in 1633, that would put her age at over 400 years old—if she had still been alive. He figures death put an end to counting though.

Bagonegiizhig tilts her head, lips pursed. "I am not *that* old. Time works differently for creatures of Spirit, even wiindigo like us—cursed with humanity. Spirit navigates under its own rules. Time speeds up, or slows down, according to need. Time flows backwards, forwards, folds-in-on-itself. All that has happened still exists. I wasn't born back 'den—but I was drawn there—same way you were once drawn, to a time and place of balance. It isn't a choice—it's necessity."

"An ambassador was needed, so I went. No matter I wasn't born yet—it's all perspective. It's enough for you to know that I was at Bawating for the Three Fires Council meeting in the summer of 1633. But death has changes things, as it does for all of us—eventually."

"Hey there champ," a voice says.

"Wha-what?" Clay cracks open a bleary eyelid, not wanting to be dragged to wakefulness from his deep sleep. In the blue-white light of the moon shining through his window, there is a face two inches away from his own. Their noses are almost touching! He feels a tickle in the whickers of his blonde-mustache.

"Aagh!" Clay lets out a short shriek and recoils from the too-close face, his heart suddenly kicks into fourth gear from a dead start, hammering in his chest like madly rotating pistons. "What the hell man! You scared the shit out of me!"

Aya'ah is silently chortling to himself, hand covering his mouth—clearly taking perverse joy in Clay's fear. "I know!" The dead man says. "That's what's so funny!" Forearm across his abs as if they are sore from laughing so hard. But how could they be sore if he isn't in his body? His hair hangs long and straight now, free from its braids.

"What are you doing here?" Clay hisses. "You're going to wake up my parents!"

Aya'ah tilts his head for a moment as if listening. "Asleep as a stone." Then looks back at Clay. "Thought you could get rid of me so easily did you?"

"Wha-what d-do want?" Clay stutters. "I already ah . . . re-returned your jaw."

Aya'ah waves his hand. "Maanooh. All's forgotten that's forgiven." Then wriggles his fingers like a caricature of a ghost, elbows raised, fringed leather of his coat dangling, shoulders hunched, he speaks in a drawn-out, low-register drawl: "I came here to waaarn you." As he speaks there is a distant growling which punctuates his words. Though Clay knows he is trying to be funny—those snarls kind of undercut the humour. A ghost pretending to be ghost.

Clay's eyes dart around the room, trying to identify the source of the strange noise, but like always he is unable to place it. It sounds like it might be coming from outside. Clay feels a growing dread, like coals simmering in the pit of his stomach. Bile threatens to rise up into his mouth, stomach acid burns the back of his throat. He swallows. "What the fuck is that?"

"Not everyone is happy," Aya'ah says, deadpan. "You didn't return everything."

"What are you talking about?" Clay's eyes dart around. But Aya'ah is already gone, as quickly as he appeared.

Clay tries to get back to sleep, but he sleeps only fitfully. He is haunted by that strange growling sound. Now that Aya'ah has pointed it out to him, he can't seem to tune it out the way he did before. His mind is focused on it. And the more he pays attention to it, the louder and more out-of-place it seems. Every time he comes close to consciousness, he can hear it. Like some beast prowling around outside his bedroom window, claws digging into his dreams.

He can hear the damn thing, even in his sleep.

Tyler Kendrars can't sleep.

His room is lit by a dull, greenish glow coming in through the basement windows. It is a clear, cold, cloudless night, the stars are showing off, and the northern lights are acting up. Coils of electric blue and jade shimmer in his room like the flashes from a television screen. Except his TV isn't on. The flicker forms a secondary phenomenon, a miniature version of the larger aurora outside. Curtains of light dance like a mind-bending cathedral.

It reminds Tyler of his nightmare—was it only the night before? The nightmare of the woman named Naphtha, her anger, and her fire—so much like the night sky with its pulsing ribbons and veins. Tyler knows the aurora is caused by charged particles, electrons and protons entering the atmosphere, the solar wind interacting with the Earth's magnetic field. But he also can't help believing that Naphtha has in some way caused this borealis, that she has something to do with this geomagnetic storm. It is his magnetic midnight, at the height of an eleven-year sunspot cycle. Naphtha is the magnetic centre, and her fury is the furnace of the sun.

But it isn't only the glow of the northern lights that keeps him awake. It is also the howling wind, rattling his windowpanes—and carrying with it the quiet sound of a baby. Crying. Crying. Crying. But by this time he knows it isn't real. There is no point in going out to slough through the mud and snow, searching for something that doesn't exist. It's only in his head.

A real baby would have froze to death by now. But even though he knows the baby isn't real, isn't lost out there in the woods somewhere—he still can't tune it out. He holds a pillow wrapped tightly around his head to muffle the sound.

But nothing seems to work. He can still hear the baby.

—Aaeenh. Aaeenh. Aaeenh.—

Wailing.

Tyler's mom opens his bedroom door, sees him lying on the bed with the pillow around his ears, and says, "Oh, you're going to bed already?" She looks at her watch, "It's only 9:30! At least you'll get a good start in the morning for once."

"Mom?"

"Yes honey?" She pauses as she turns from his door.

"Do you hear anything?"

She stands in the doorway for a moment, listening as a gust of wind blows outside, rattling the glass, whistling as it passes the opening of the chimney overhead.

—phwhoooh, phwhoooh, phwhoooh—

"Just the wind, honey," she says as she closes the door.

Tyler groans into his pillow. *I'm going crazy.*

—Weeenh. Weeenh. Weeeenh.—

The baby cries. Though he is the only one who can hear it.

He knows this has to have something to do with that dream—the woman with star-constellations and northern lights in her eyes. Naphtha. She tried to set him on fire. But he'd only been dreaming, and woke up screaming, untouched by the flames. Naphtha—she is so pissed. And he doesn't know why.

Tyler cracks one eye open, and sees the old, painted rattle on the nightstand table beside him. Red racing stripe. Faded blue stars. The toy he took from the Indian burial ground. He had come home, left it on the mantle, and promptly forgot about it. How did it end up on the night-side table? He doesn't remember moving it.

Of course! He finally connects the dots; he should've put two-and-two together by now. *I'm so dense. The baby!* No wonder Naphtha is so pissed. He'd taken her child's toy! He remembers the desperation that gripped him out in the woods, when he imagined that it was *his* baby brother that was missing, alone and lost, and it had pushed him to keep going, to keep searching, even when he thought it was hopeless.

Somehow, the child's spirit is tied to the toy; Tyler has the toy, and Naphtha wants her baby back. He pretty much stole her baby!

He needs to return that rattle.

He doesn't think he can stand another night listening to the ghost of a baby crying, or the nightmares Naphtha might send, if he was even able to fall asleep.

How long can you stay awake without going mad?

Tyler gets up. Pulls on long johns, jeans, socks, t-shirt, sweater, and his winter jacket with the faux-fur trim. He creeps up the back stairs, trying to avoid the places that creak. He steps gently through the laundry room so that the *swiff, swiff, swiff* of the rattle in his pocket doesn't make too much noise. It's still a school night after all, and he can't explain why he needs to leave the house at this time of night. Better if his mom still thinks he's asleep.

He closes the back door softly. Steps down the snow-covered stairs of the back porch. His breath streams in the air like smoke. If it was cloudy, it wouldn't have been so cold out, and the snow wouldn't have that same crunch. He heads towards the lean-to at the side of the garage where he keeps his skidoo. With each step, the rattle in his pocket makes a *swiff, swiff, swiff* in time with the *crunch, crunch, crunch* of the snow—like styrofoam under his boots. At least when the rattle sounds, he can't hear the baby crying—whether because it's drowned out, or because the rattle soothes the spirit into silence, Tyler isn't sure which. He is just glad he doesn't have to hear it anymore.

He straddles the skidoo. Goes through the practiced motions. Killswitch to running. Turnkey to on. Choke-pull for cold start. Pull-cord to start. He hopes the engine whine won't alert his mom. But it rarely has before.

Tyler makes his way along the skidoo path through the woods. Tall black spruce flank the path, back lit against the sky like an audio wave-form. Wildly vibrating bands of cobalt and crimson boil across the star-filled sky. What song would the horizon sing if he fed the treeline into a processor? Can't hear much over the whine of his skidoo.

Now he's glad it isn't overcast; that would have made the way tough going. But even without a moon he can see the tracks easily. Lit by the natural fireworks in the sky, the trail leads him out to frozen surface of Ghost Lake, and the ice-road. The folds of light look like drapes, fluttering in the cold, cold wind, freezing-him-to-the-bone beautiful.

Tyler has heard stories about the aurora—it is the dead, dancing in celebration on their journey to the afterlife; or walruses kicking human skulls in a spiritual game of kick-the-can, like the bowling giants he once believed caused thunder. One explanation is just as good as the other—it makes as much sense to him as magnetic midnight.

Somehow it seems fitting that his task should be lit by a borealis—returning a cursed object to the crypt where he found it—he imagined spirits dancing, lighting his way, just as they did the path of the dead.

Still he wonders. Why is this rattle so important? What power does it have over Naphtha or her child? Why aren't their spirits at rest, or dancing in the sky? It is a night for such questions.

He hopes returning the rattle will put things to right. A big part of him doesn't believe any of it is real—but he still needs to give back the pilfered instrument. The rest—the baby's cries, the dreams—are probably manifestations of guilt, like the ticking of Edgar Allen Poe's tell-tale heart. Tyler's heart doesn't tick. It makes a *swiff, swiff, swiff* sound in time to the *crunch, crunch, crunch* under his boots as he makes his way through the graveyard.

Oh shit. Which grave did he take the rattle from? They all look kind of the same. He goes from tomb to tomb, not sure which is the right one. He is sweating despite the cold. Would it be enough, if he simply left the plaything somewhere in the burial grounds? Would the spirits of the dead still haunt him?

Then his foot drops through a deadfall in the snow; he hears something *snap* and feels a sharp jolt of pain, he falls forward, his leg twists unnaturally, foot wedged in the hollow of a sunken grave. No doubt the same one he tripped in before. He sucks in cold air through his teeth, gritted against the pain, so cold it makes his fillings ache.

"*Fuck, fuck, fuck.*" He's really injured himself this time.

Tyler isn't sure if he's broken something, or just sprained an ankle. All he knows is that it hurts, hurts, hurts. But there is no way around it. He sucks in breath as he works through the pain, waiting for it to ease up, but disappointed when the throbbing continues, beating in time to his pulse.

Yep. He definitely damaged something.

On the plus side, his headlong tumble into the snow has brought him to eye level with the little house hovering on stilts above the snow, and the little ledge which is the rattle's original resting place.

He pulls the old rattle from his pocket. A bolt of fear stabs through him like a spear. The instrument is crushed. He must have landed on it in the fall. Part of the stitching is ripped open so beads spill out like blood. He holds the white, discoloured beads in his hands, not wanting to lose any part of the toy, hoping to keep the thing together, in one place, if not in one piece.

Hey! Tyler gasps. *These aren't beads. These are teeth!*

What he holds in his hand are the small, pointy, rounded teeth—the baby teeth of a child.

Tyler looks up, noticing the crowding of little houses on stilts, all congregated together. Each, he has no doubt, with their own teeth-filled rattles. If they survived long enough to grow teeth—he hates to think what else might be inside. Fingers? Toes? These smaller houses are clearly designed as the final resting place for children. Six or seven of them in a row. Some of the houses are so small they could only be meant for a newborn or still-born. How many babies did Naphtha lose? He has no doubt they are hers. He imagines a time before penicillin, or hospitals, and a new suite of diseases introduced by Europeans: small-pox, typhoid, cholera, measles—deadly invaders on a microbial scale for which there was no immunity, no treatment, and no cures.

So many dead children. So much loss. Tyler thinks he understands the woman better—the loss of children in life, and now in death too…

Did Naphtha sing? What songs would those have been? Goodbye songs, songs of memory and loss? Or songs to conjure the dead? He's glad he never got around to using the instrument to record an audio track. Once captured in digital software, how would he be able to return sound?

He shudders, imagining the rattle of shaking teeth following him around forever.

Tyler hopes returning the rattle will let her spirit rest.

Tyler reaches out and carefully places the instrument back on the ledge where he found it, letting the teeth pass through the palms of his hands like sand through an hourglass, back on the shelf with the toy where they belong. For the first time he notices the fine strands of dark hair decorating the pommel. Not ribbons. Hair, which likely also belongs to the child.

A mourning rattle.

Tyler wipes his eyes and tries to stand. Sharp stab of pain. He falls back to his knees. Nope. Nope. Nope.

His ankle isn't able to support his weight. *Crap.* He could hop? He decides to crawl. Snow crunches under his palms and under his knees. His mitts are soon soaked through. The knees on his jeans soak through. Chilly and wet down his calves. His hair hangs down in front of his face, scraping his eyes. He bumps his sore foot on a lump of snow.

"*Ow, ow, ow,*" he hisses.

His ankle screams in complaint every time he accidentally gives it a jolt. Through the graveyard, past the flash of newer headstones polished to a reflective sheen. Some plots have solar lights planted in the ground; they give off a foxfire glow.

He finally makes it back to his skidoo. He hops on one foot, and winces as he swings the injured ankle around to mount the machine. Magnetic midnight—and actual midnight—has passed, and light from the borealis is fading, so he is hard pressed to find his way by the light of the stars. Whine of the engine like a swarm of bees. The moon still hasn't made an appearance, but at least the snow reflects what light there is; a trembling shade of blue.

Once through the trees, he flies across the lake at a faster clip, but has to slow down again as he goes through the woods. Finally back home, he shuts off the engine to his skidoo, and he feels blessed to hear nothing except the wind rustling. No babies crying. No sonic static and pop of electrons colliding with the arctic atmosphere. Chilled and thoroughly exhausted, Tyler hasn't had enough sleep in days and days. He hobbles inside, down the stairs, and collapses onto his bed, panting with effort. He's too tired to even take off his clothes.

"Dibikiziwinan," he hears Naphtha whisper as he falls asleep, lips so close to his ear he can feel the brush of air from her words. "Dibikiziwinan. That's my name. Gashkii-dibik-ayaa. *Dark-as-night*. But you may call me Naphtha."

And then there is nothing but dreamless sleep.

Clay Cutter is sitting in detention after class. He is alone. The fluorescent lighting is starting to give him a headache. He rests his head on finger-tips, staring through the fall of blond hair that covers his eyes, watching the second hand twirl on the wall clock.

—Grrrrraaaaahhhhhhhrrrrrrllll—

Clay hears a distant growl. He's heard it before. In fact, he's been listening to it most of the day, and the night before. He is tired. He hasn't been able to get much sleep. It kept him awake. Deep grunting. Snuffling. Snarling. Like heavy rocks grinding against each other. The way he imagines a tyrannosaurus might sound.

Looking out his bedroom window he didn't see anything. Coyotes? Wolves? It didn't really sound like a coyote. At least not any coyote Clay ever heard. A wolf—maybe. But what would a wolf be doing hanging around? A rabid wolf then. One with rabies or neurological problems.

But it didn't sound like it is coming from outside. Not really. It sounded like it was coming from somewhere inside his bedroom. At first, he tried to identify a source for the sound. He searched. Under the bed. The small square hatch up to the attic in the closet. Nothing up there except pink fiberglass insulation. Under couch cushions even. Still the source of the odd sound remained a mystery.

—Hur, hurr, hurr, hrrrreeooghhh—

Chuffing. Demon warthog breathing. Some sort of large animal.

—Clunk—

Clay put his head on the desk with a hollow sound.

"*Fawk*," he wishes the noise would stop, whatever it is.

When he couldn't place the source, he tried to ignore it. But it didn't go away. It got slowly louder, and louder. He tries to pinpoint the exact moment he first became aware of the noise, but he can't. He swears it is the same sound he's been hearing for days. At first, it was barely loud enough to hear.

"Do you hear that?" He side-eyed Dare, sitting beside him in geography class earlier that day. His curly brown rocker hair tied back with a bandanna. He seemed a bit sickly, his skin a bit green even.

"Hunh? Hear what?" Dare sat stupidly, his eyes lidded. The rest of the class sat in their desks, looking forward as the teacher droned on. Distant rumble of a dragon. Horror monster roar. Hissing. Sasquatch vocalizations. No indication that anyone else heard anything. How was that even possible?

It is easier to dismiss with the background noise of the day, the clutter of heating systems turning on and off, the chatter of human voices, or the wind through the trees. But in moments like this, quiet moments when the furnace pumping heat through vents go silent, and the classes and hallways have quickly emptied after the last bell, it is impossible not to hear.

And what's more—it seems to be getting louder. Closer.

Clay wipes the tears that form at the corner of his eyes, straightens his back. He's not scared. It's fine. It's just his imagination. Maybe someone is playing a trick on him? Yeah that must be it. It must be some sort of trick. But how is that possible? How would anyone create the seemingly sourceless sound? He is just being a baby. He is too old to be afraid of this—whatever this is. There is probably some perfectly reasonable explanation.

Maybe a cat got stuck in the ducts? Clay eyeballs the fresh-air-return. Yeah. A cat. It doesn't sound like any cat Clay has ever heard before. A *dying* cat maybe? Too shrill. But it is the only realistic explanation. But that doesn't explain how he's been hearing it everywhere he goes, not just at school. There can't be a cat stuck in the ductwork everywhere he goes, at home, or when he's outside and there is no ductwork. There is no explanation for so many different locations. He looks towards the open classroom door. Wishes the teacher would come back, because at least then he wouldn't have to be alone.

—Grrraaaahhrrrraaaaahhhwhwr—

Jaguar. Werewolf. Vicious dog snarl.

Clay feels tears on his cheeks. He just wants it to stop.

"You have my Kekeenowin." A man's voice.

"Wha-what?" Clay raises his head from the desk.

Aya'ah is sitting on the teacher's desk. His long dark hair hangs straight and loose, free form their braids. He's in his full regalia, bone beads, feathers, buckskin, fringed leather.

"My gwiingwa'aage." Aya'ah points at Clay with a lift of his chin and an extension of his lips. What is he pointing at? Clays hand goes to the small figurine he wears around his neck like a necklace.

"I carved it after a powerful dream." Aya'ah's legs swing, dangling over the edge of the desk. "Gwiingwa'aage, *wolverine*, came to me, and revealed to me secret knowledge. The key to his bravery and strength, that I might also be strong and brave. I carved the statue to remind myself of the dream, and the lessons gwiingwa'aage taught me; and so his power would always protect me."

Clay feels the solid lump of the whistle under his shirt. How does Aya'ah know that he wears it?

"The wolverine stayed with me through life, though I didn't always know it. After I died, I was laid to rest with the object you now have in your possession. My gwiingwa'aage. My spirit-guide. MY protector." Aya'ah hops off the desk, the fringe on his buckskin dancing with the movement. Aya'ah walks slowly towards him, down the rows of desks, to where Clay sits at the back of the classroom.

"They are a gluttonous animal; did you know that?"

Clay rolls his eyes like marbles. He knows the hunter is probably just fucking with him. Trying to freak him out again. At least he hasn't drawn his bow-and-arrow this time.

"They are very opportunistic." Aya'ah draws out the word opportunistic: opp-pour-tune-iss-tic. "They will eat almost anything. But their preferred meal—their preferred meal is *meat*: rabbits, dead carcasses, even moose or caribou aren't too big for them to take down."

—grraawrrnnhhh, grraawrrnnhhh, grraawrrnnhhh, grraawrrnnhhh—

And here, Aya'ah pauses, and the horrible snarling grows louder, as if someone turned the volume up. Or as if it's in the hallway, or the ceiling above his head, exactly as if the creature is hiding in the ductwork. But that animalistic snarl, is definitely no house-cat.

"They can take on a bear or wolf easily. They aren't afraid of larger predators because of their fierceness and strength. They are not a quarry many animals underestimate, and do better to avoid."

"Why is it following me?" Clay searches the ceiling with his eyes.

"Because you called him to you." Aya'ah points at him again with a slight protrusion of his lips. "And it is upset, because it can't find me. Worried even. It misses me. Doesn't understand where I've gone, or where you came from. Without the whistle, gwiingwa'aage can't find me."

Aya'ah resumes walking down the aisles of empty desks towards him. "You have something that belongs to me."

"Here. T-take it." Clay holds out the carved figurine. He'd strung a loop of leather through the whistle so he could wear it like a necklace. "I don't want it anymore."

"I can't." Aya'ah comes to a stop just outside reach of the dangling wolverine. And Aya'ah smiles. "You know I'm doing you a favour, don't you? I could have just let the gwiingwa'aage find you."

And Clay feels the blood drain from his face. He doesn't want to know what would happen if the wolverine catches up with him. He's lucky the horror movies are all wrong, and Aya'ah isn't a vindictive spirit. "You must return it to the place you found it." The snarling comes louder, as if the animal is getting closer. Angrier.

"And if I were you," Aya'ah also looks toward the ceiling, "I'd do so sooner rather than later. Patience is not a trait wolverine are known for."

When Clay looks back down, Aya'ah is gone, and he is left staring at the empty space where the man had stood moments before. The snarling of the wolverine remains though, growling somewhere around the edges of his vision. But no matter which direction he looks, the animal is always just out of sight.

He spends the rest of his detention with the angry wolverine, his teacher returns and sets about marking papers, oblivious to the creature pacing the hallway, prowling the roof. Clay needs to get rid of the whistle. He wishes he'd never put the thing to his lips. He has no doubt the whistle works, even if he can't hear it. It isn't meant for his ears. Human ears.

He'll have to go back to the Indian burial ground again after all, even though that's the last place Clay wants to be.

Better than waiting around for the wolverine.

When Dare Theremin arrives at the Indian burial ground, he almost shits his pants.

He stops dead in his tracks, ankle deep in snow. It melts into his boots above the hemline. A light snow is falling delicately, large fat flakes that muffle sound. The sun is up there somewhere, hidden behind a uniformly leaden sky; there is no one source he can point to, the light seems to come from everywhere.

On the other side of the graveyard, twenty yards away, through the obstruction of trees and headstones, he sees a woman. She looks so much like the wiindigo from his dreams, he's certain it must be her. Bagonegiizhig.

Has she come back to take possession of his body and mind? Has she come back to ride him like a jockey, so they can hunt, rend, tear? Primal drives and hunger. Disturbingly, he feels himself getting hard. He looks down. There's a lurch in his guts, like a fish-hook tugging. He wants to be taken for a joy-ride. To feel the exhilaration of the hunt again. Then he remembers the initial gush of blood and fat filling his mouth, and his stomach rebels. He feels sick. Queasy. Like he might throw up.

Dare looks at the woman. Studies her face. Feels himself go slack. Though there is a strong resemblance—even down to the streak of white in her hair—this is a different person. Younger. More beautiful. Lithe. Like an achingly thin supermodel, though the fur coat adds bulk. And clearly, she is still alive. Not a ghost. At least Dare doesn't think she's a ghost.

Then she's joined by a man, who looks so similar to her, for a moment Dare thinks he's seeing double, but he quickly registers the difference of their gender. Her brother is clearly a guy, with stubble, an Adam's apple, and a squarer jaw, broader shoulders, and more upper-body mass, though his long hair is held back in a braid instead of worn free; he wears silver eye-shadow and diamond-shaped earrings that accentuate his femininity. They must be twins—and again Dare is wind-kicked by their resemblance to the woman from his dreams.

Bagonegiizhig.

His breath streams in the cold air like smoke.

He shouldn't be so surprised there are people here. He knew coming here during the day was a risk—but he wasn't willing to follow through on the plan of coming at night. Too creepy. Now that word has gotten out about the vandalism and theft, everyone from Ghost Lake is coming to check on their loved ones and their state of eternal rest. And he probably shouldn't be so surprised to find out Bagonegiizhig has living descendants—her grandchildren? Dare can't take his eyes off the pair.

The man with the braid notices Dare first.

He looks Dare in the eye.

And it's like there is no distance between them.

It's like looking into a well, impossible to tell how deep they go; and hungry. Dare recognizes this hunger. Hawk-like focus, blown out-pupils, narrow-rimmed irises.

The man frowns, recognizing his recognition, and turns to whisper something in his sister's ear. She is hunched over a grave.

When eye-contact is broken, Dare takes the opportunity to escape. He backpedals, not wanting to be drawn into an interaction with Bagonegiizhig's descendants, or have to make eye-contact again and be drawn into those bottomless pits. He trudges away into the trees, onto more trodden-on ground, where footsteps have already packed down the snow, further into the cemetery. He's soon shrouded from view by the trees and makes his way quickly to the place where he found the pipe. Whose headstone are the creepy twins visiting? He's curious, but not curious enough to want to get close enough to find out.

And the wiindigo twins aren't the only ones visiting the graveyard today. He can hear other voices, the rustling of clothes, branches, and other soft footfalls elsewhere throughout the site. That is only to be expected. Everywhere he looks, there are new floral arrangements, wreathes, placards, photographs, and other offerings—even a half-full bottle of Rusty, though he has zero desire to swipe it—even with the prospect of easy booze. He isn't even tempted. Headstones and crosses that were knocked over have been put to rights, and graffiti has been scrubbed clean from marble and granite.

An old woman appears like a ghost out of the snow, sitting on a low branch.

Dare gasps and drops his gloves. Hand to chest, his heart hammers in his ribcage, wants to jump into his throat, loud in his own ears. Goddamned, lady almost gave him a heart attack! Was she there the whole time? Or was she sitting so still, and quiet, that he didn't notice her until he was right in front of her?

Her white hair is held back from her face by a pale blue bandanna. Fur-trimmed mukluks and matching gauntlets. She wears a white fur coat that looks like it's made out of the hide from skinned cats. A dress over her jeans. The cloth had at one time been an intense colour, but is now faded from being washed too many times, though the lively pattern is still visible—if drab. No wonder she blends in with the snow. One of her eyes is slightly milky, as if from glaucoma—like his grandma had. Serene is the word that comes to mind—though she laughs when he gasps, wrinkles crinkling at the corner of her eyes.

"Oh! You scared me." Dare breathes heavily, trying to catch his breath, waiting for his heart rate to slow. "I thought you were a ghost!" This makes the woman laugh harder, showing off a gap in her teeth. The old bag is really getting a kick out of his discomfort. Was she trying to scare him half to death?

"Oh, there you are Aunty!" A younger woman brushes aside a branch as she emerges from some bushes. "We've been looking all over for you..." The newcomer pauses when she sees Dare, standing awkwardly below her Aunty. She too, has a streak of white in her brown hair, though thankfully the resemblance to Bagonegiizhig ends there. She wears a puffy white jacket, a pink toque, and a cream-coloured scarf made of some kind of natural-looking fiber; she's pretty and wears narrow glasses.

How many descendants had the wiindigo woman spawned? Dare knows descendants tend to multiply, like a pyramid scheme—his mom does genealogy. Maybe they only share a common ancestor? It must be a dominant gene, for so many to inherit the trait.

Would it be rude to walk away? Dare wants to return the stolen pipe, just get it over with already.

"Oh, hello. I didn't see you there." The younger woman frowns at him, then looks up at her aunt. "Who's your new friend Edna?"

"This is Dare. Dare Theremin." The old woman smiles at him, her face is creased with laugh lines, crow's feet, and marionette lines at the corner of her lips; all those wrinkles which those who laugh often accumulate over time from their habitual expressions. It gives her the illusion of kindness.

Dare's jaw works, but no sound comes out. How did the old lady know his name? He is certain he's never met Edna before. Though Ghost Lake and Cheapaye are small places—maybe she knows his parents or something?

"It's nice to meet you," The younger woman holds out her hand. She's wearing the sort of mittens that fold back with velcro to reveal cut-off fingertips of a glove underneath. "I'm Chase." This normality busts the strangeness of the moment, the primacy of polite social interaction demands he react, and frees him from his state of limbo.

"It's nice to meet you," Dare says, finding that he can now speak, the appropriate words come to him and he shakes Chase's hand.

"Who are you here to visit?" Chase asks. "I'm sort of new to the community, and I haven't really met many band members yet—I've heard stories about most of the families, but Theremin isn't a name I'm familiar with."

Again, Dare can't speak, though this time it isn't from inertia, or lack of capability—but because he isn't sure what to say. He knew coming here during the day was a risk. He wishes he wasn't such a god-damned chicken! Though coming here during the day didn't seem to be proving any less creepy.

Edna smiles at him, her face seems to glow with compassion. Dare shivers, not from the cold or the wet—but from her smug, upturned smile that seems to say, *I know what you did*, one eye squints at him speculatively, as if patiently waiting for his answer, and to see what lies he will come up with, or what excuses he'll make. Maybe he is imagining things, but Dare is convinced Edna will see through any lies he can come up with. He doesn't know where he gets this idea, but it's like a brainwave.

He decides to act on it. Dare knows Edna is just an old lady, squinting and smiling at him—she has no such power to read his mind—it is probably the Catholic guilt from what he's done, eating through his insides like acid, and he has to confess or it will burn through his body and hollow out his bones. Dare's family has never been particularly religious, though they are nominally Catholics. So maybe it isn't guilt?

But for whatever the reason, Dare speaks. The words bubble out of him, like a pot boiling over. A whistling kettle, with the fire put to his feet.

He can't seem to control himself. He tells the plain truth.

"I stole this pipe." Dare takes it out of his pocket, feeling the sun-medallions on the whorls of his thumb, "And I haven't been sleeping well since I took it. Then I heard about the vandalism—it wasn't me—we had nothing to do with that. But I still wanted to bring it back. Return it to where I got it from. It doesn't belong to me, and I never should have taken it. I'm sorry." Dare finishes, inhaling deeply and taking a breath.

Damn. Squealed like a kettle, but at least he managed not to rat out on his friends.

Chase covers her mouth with her hand. Edna keeps smiling at him. If anything, her smile seems to have grown.

"That was a brave thing for you to do." Edna speaks first, "To admit that you did something wrong, and that you are here to put things right. But things can't always be put to rights. Some wounds, you'll learn, can never be healed." Edna reaches down with one foot, one hand on Chase's shoulder for support, and climbs down from the branch she'd been sitting on. "Let's hope that this isn't one of those things."

"Whose resting place did you take that from?" Chase folds her lips under her teeth.

"I don't know." Dare flops his arms. "I mean, there was no headstone or anything—she said her name is Bah-go-nah-gee-zhick." He pronounces the name carefully, hoping he got the syllables correct.

Edna nods, her smile deepens. "That's good news. You're in luck!"

"I am?" Dare frowns. "Why?"

"Because!" Edna laughs. Her eyes glitter. There's something about her good cheer that isn't entirely sane. "You're still alive! If that one wanted you dead, you would have been done for already."

"Can you show us where this woman is buried Aunty?" Chase is frowning back and forth between Dare and the old lady, as if Edna's madness is his fault.

"Alright, follow me," Edna says as she pushes through the bush. Chase goes next, followed by Dare. At least he has a guide now. The trees open up and there are more graves and scaffolds, some with peaked roofs like little houses, others more like hammocks with the dead strung between the poles, the bodies wrapped in layers of hardened leather and birch-bark like some sort of Indian mummies, or like cocoons. What kind of creature would hatch from such a chrysalis? Dare shudders and tries to banish thoughts of metamorphosis. Horrible, horrible brain.

Why does his brain always want to go there? To the worst places imaginable. All those dark corners and impossibilities.

Edna leads the way through the platforms to a newer wooden structure. Skirt forcing her to take shorter steps. It can't be more than a dozen years old though it is built in the older scaffold-style. It's in better condition than the other, older mausoleums. The wood used to construct it is greener and there's no sign of it leaning or falling in; it stands firmly planted in the ground, undisturbed by elements or predators—if not grave robbers. Edna stops before the tomb, and Dare knows this is the right grave. He remembers it.

Dare pulls out the pipe again, feels the stippled sun medallions under his fingertips. It's a pleasant sensation. It really is a nice pipe. He pulls out a pouch of Heller hand-rolled, tamps down mossy tobacco into the bowl and draws a strike-anywhere across a nearby tombstone; there's a flare of heat and light as the phosphorous ignites. He circles the orange flame above the dried plant matter, puffs on the stem to get a good cherry going.

Chase watches; arms folded. Her cardigan looks too lightweight for the weather; it has straps that go around her hips like a terry-cloth robe to tie the sides together. She must be cold. She's still frowning at him, either because of his actions, or the whole theft situation, Dare's not sure which.

But this feels like the right thing to do.

When he knows the ember won't go out immediately, he places the pipe back where it belongs on the scaffold, smoke rising from the bowl, drifting across the cemetery—and carrying with it the scent that has haunted him since he'd taken the damn thing.

"I'm sorry, Bagonegiizhig." Dare pats a wooden beam of the structure, "I never should have disturbed your rest—I shouldn't have taken your pipe. I hope you can rest easier now."

Dare looks up from his prayer. He sees Bagonegiizhig's descendants standing on the other side of the grave.

"Inri. Marie." Edna greets them each with a nod of her head.

The creepy wiindigo twins. One male, one female, but their differences are overshadowed by their identical gaze; they watch him with a fixed intensity. Like mountain lions, eyeing him, assessing the quality of the way his meat might taste. A predators' gaze.

"Oh, I'm pretty sure she doesn't mind." The guy-twin smiles at Dare. "You'd be dead if it bothered her."

"You're the second person to tell me that." Dare's legs feel shaky.

And the man arches an eyebrow.

"Grandmother always did have a sense of humour." The girl-twin's voice is soft, dreamy, her gaze has gone unfocused, though she still looks at Dare in a way he finds disconcerting.

There are other families in the graveyard, visiting their dead. Dare can hear them in the distance, occasionally stopping by a nearby grave, but they all keep their distance, and none show any interest in the drama being played out here. Dare feels as if he's stumbled into some version of *The Village of the Damned*, with three of the players sporting that white streak in their hair.

The old woman—Aunty Edna—beams at him with a lopsided grin—radiating good-humour.

Chase presses a card into his hand. The card reads:

Chase Lausen, B.A, M.A, PhD

Doctor of Paleontology, Sterling University
Adjunct-Faculty Professor

On the back is listed her contact information, and office hours.

"You'll be old enough to be apply for post-secondary soon," Chase says as Dare stares down at the card. "Give me a call if you need a letter of recommendation." Chase turns to lead her Aunt away. Dare is left standing by Bagonegiizhig's tomb.

Chase looks back over her shoulder. "You probably wouldn't have gotten yourself into this mess, if you had no interest in archeology."

Dare is alone with the wiindigo's grandchildren now. Their gazes fixed on him like two predatory birds; they watch his every move with fascination. Is it sexual? Is it hunger? Are they assessing his body for physical characteristics? For how it might taste? Or are those desires one and the same? Maybe it's only his imagination, but Dare feels heat climbing up his face, unable to ignore the idea that they *want* him.

Jesus. Dare's never been stared at with such open lust before. He tries to look anywhere but at Inri and Marie. He doesn't want to give them the wrong idea. Even the slightest hint that he might be interested. God, he's *not* even. Interested. It's just… don't even go there, he instructs his brain. *Don't look directly at the sun, or you'll damage your eyes*. Isn't that what they say? Especially during an eclipse. Dare's unsure of where he should place his feet, or how he should hold his limbs.

"Dare," Dare says. "My name's Dare."

"Well, it's nice to meet you *Dare*." Inri slips an arm through Dare's, hooking his elbow to escort him. "My name is Inri. And this is my sister Marie." Marie nods but keeps her distance. And Dare can't help feeling that Inri has staked his claim, as if he is some found object which can simply be possessed.

They walk through the cemetery, Inri's arm casually looped through his. The snow falls gently in large fat flakes. It's pretty. Inri wears some sort of expensive cologne, which Dare has to admit, smells pretty good. Musk and bergamot. The fox fur from Inri's hood brushes softly against Dare's cheek.

Everything about Inri seems luxurious, his slow movements hiding coiled energy like a snake ready to strike.

Dare feels like he is caught in the crosshairs, on the wrong side of the barrel of a gun. He doesn't know how to resist, knowing that he is out-mustered, he's already lost the fight.

"I've always preferred my tobacco in menthol form," Inri says. "Pipes are so last century. But to each, their own."

Dare hasn't told them where he had parked his skidoo, but they wind their way through the burial grounds, invariably heading in that right direction. When they reach his snowmobile, Inri unlinks their arms, and Dare makes the mistake of making eye contact, again seeing that outright hunger, so much like Bagonegiizhig. Like he could easily be swallowed in those wells. It feels like he's falling. And Dare has to forcibly tear his gaze away.

Dare climbs onto the snowmobile, relieved they are letting him go. He turns the ignition, the engine whines to life, and Dare makes good his escape, before they change their minds. He can feel Inri and Marie watching him, their eyes on his back, tracking his progress as he recedes into the distance. Dare feels lighter now that the threat has passed, as if he's just narrowly escaped some danger. The anvil could have crushed his head, but he managed to slip out of the way at the last second.

Cold air rushes past his cheeks, cooling the heat.

Not *it*, and home free.

After detention, Clay rushes home and hops on his snowmobile. Attaches the strap on his orange helmet, snapping the clips tightly under his jaw. Revs the engine a few times and takes off toward the reserve, whipping down narrow paths through the trees. Sleet comes down in sheets. Sticks to his eyelashes. His blond moustache. He can't grow a beard yet, but if he could it would now be white. He ignores it and sets a fast pace. Hail plinks off the leather of his biker jacket.

Out on the ice-road that crosses the lake, the wind is stronger without the protection of the trees. Gusts push at him like a sail, trying to force him off the path, threatening to knock him off the skidoo. Wind needles his face and burns his cheeks. They feel like polished rubies. The cold finds a slice of exposed flesh at his hips where his low-slung pants sink below the shelter of his jacket, plunges down his crack. Damn it's cold. Colder than a witch's teat. No matter how many layers he wears, the cold always seems to find a way to catch his bones. Have to keep moving to generate heat. All he can do is duck down. Try to be aerodynamic.

It's shaping up to be a blizzard, but the machine is designed for snow and he isn't worried about fuel. He's already losing the light; darkness is approaching—he would be returning at night—not ideal conditions to visit the Indian burial ground, but he needs to get rid of the whistle. Fast. Clay swears he can hear the growl of the wolverine, even over the drone of the engine. Maybe it is getting close? Or maybe he is just being paranoid?

Back through the trees, the vehicle slogs its way through snowdrifts, old tracks obscured by new-fallen snow, rubber clacking over metal rollers like a tank. Nodules dig into the snow like teeth, pulling him ever forward. He has to pee, but he's afraid to stop. It feels like the wolverine is right behind him, that it's just over his shoulder, and if he stops for anything, it might just be the last thing he ever does. The beast will catch up to him. So instead he holds it in, his bladder filling. Uncomfortably full. But he has to keep going.

When at last he arrives at the graveyard, there isn't much light left in the sky, and it's even darker under the gloom of the trees. He cuts the engine, hops off the skidoo, undoes the straps under his jaw and pulls off his helmet, his hair sticks up in all directions. Sets the helmet on the seat. It's quiet now without the engine noise. Only the wind hissing through trees. The wolverine seems to have gone silent. Strange not to hear the monster's growls for once, it'd been a constant presence for so long. The absence is jarring.

Someone has gone around planting solar-powered-lights in front of their family plots, and the steady, blue-white orbs glow like unnatural beings in the darkness. It makes the cemetery seem haunted. And Clay barks out a laugh.

Lucky for him, there are no visitors to the cemetery because of the weather. There are clearly signs of more activity since the vandalism. He plows his way through the snow to Aya'ah's tumbled-down scaffolding, nothing but a mound of timber and mouldering bones, the shelter long since fallen in. In the glow of a solar-light, Clay can make out the markings of a symbol very much like the shape of the whistle—not quite skunk, not quite bear—technically a wolverine is a giant weasel. He pulls the whistle from where he wears it around his neck, holds it in front of his mouth, looking around at the skeletal branches of the trees above, takes a deep breath, and blows into it, his cheeks puffed out with the pressure—but no matter how hard he blows—no sound comes out. At least not any sound he can hear. But then again, it's not meant for him.

He hopes the creature will hear it.

Clay looked around the clearing, waiting for . . . waiting for something. He half expects to hear that persistent snarling and growling that has been trailing him for days and days, but the place is silent except for the faint sounds of the sleet falling like little beads bouncing off the surface of the snow. It is slightly more sheltered in the trees, and the wind doesn't blow as intensely here as it did rushing across the open expanse of the frozen lake.

Then, just when he's given up on anything happening; something happens.

A goddamned wolverine steps into the blue-glow of a solar-light, head raised like a komodo dragon, large white claws extended, beady eyes watching him malevolently. Much too big to be a skunk, but not quite large enough to be a small bear, the animal is larger than any wild animal he wants to take on in a fair fight, with no weapons, and only his bare hands for self-defense. The light of the garden-lamps makes it seem ghostly, but Clay can tell this is no ghost—this is an actual wild animal—a fucking wolverine!

Aya'ah appears beside him, standing next to his tumbled-down tomb. He is wearing his traditional clothes, shirtless, with only the bone-bead vest like supernumerary ribs, breechcloth and moccasins that are inadequate for the current weather, though he doesn't seem to mind the cold. The muscles on his biceps aren't even goose-fleshed. The dead probably don't care about things like hot and cold anymore, they're probably beyond all that now.

"You might want to return that now." Aya'ah doesn't take his gaze off of his spirit animal. "You know. Before gwiingwa'aage gets any closer."

Clay rips his eyes away from the animal, and offers Aya'ah the carved wolverine whistle. This time, Aya'ah is able to take it, and the second his fingers touch the instrument, wolverine's gaze shifts, from Clay to Aya'ah, as if only now seeing the man. Clay is happy to finally be rid of the cursed object.

The wolverine takes off running, faster than Clay would have believed possible for the creature to move—but move it did.

"Faawk!" Clay screams, raises one knee, his fore-arms caged around his mid-section and face in a defensive, flamingo-like posture.

But the gwiingwa'aage ignores him, as if it has forgotten his existence, it charges towards Aya'ah and his tumbled-down tomb. But they are standing so close to each other, it's hard for Clay to tell who the animal is really charging toward; it could be either one of them. And Aya'ah is a ghost. Clay doesn't have time to do anything except assume his defensive stance, before the wolverine is upon them. Clay watches through his eyelashes, one eye closed, the other squinted, he can't bear to watch, but he needs to see what's going to happen.

When it is several feet away, the wolverine gives a great leap, it flies through the air toward them, and Clay is certain he is doomed. A dead man. Clay feels the urine trickle down his pantleg. Pissing himself. Warmth from his bladder spreading across his groin.

But then through his eyelashes, he sees the creature disappear into Aya'ah's abdomen, it passes tight through him like a hologram, and vanishes as it enters his body. Jumping into Aya'ah like a doorway.

Clay slowly lowers his arms, relaxing his defensive posture. He can't quite believe that he's ok. He's ok. He's not dead. The animal hasn't attacked. It just wanted Aya'ah. It just wanted to go home. It never cared about him.

Aya'ah turns to Clay, one eyebrow raised. Aya'ah sees that Clay wet himself, and laughs. Barrel chested, full throated. Then he too fades, the same way the gwiingwa'aage dissolved. Leaving only the sound of his receding laughter. Laughing at him from beyond the grave. Clay is left alone, with the silent graves, and the sound of the sleet drifting down like sand from the branches above, and the trees creaking as they sway in the breeze.

Clay feels a bit shaky and weak. The goddamned wolverine charged directly at him! Scared the piss out of him. His inner thighs are now chilled, his urine-soaked jeans hardening, freezing solid in the cold air.

"Goddamnit! Aya'ah—" Clay yells at the dead man. "You did that on purpose! Scared the piss out of me."

"Gwiizence Neyananoosic," Aya'ah whispers, as if his lips are pressed closely to Clay's ear. "That was my name. Son of chief Point-of-Five-Hummingbird-Breadth's. Gwiizence Neyananoosic."

"Rest in peace Gwiizence." Clay rests a hand on a piece of tumbled-down timber. But this time, there is no answer except silence.

It's several days later when Clay finally remembers where he's heard the name "Neyananoosic" before. He saw it written across more than one headstone in the cemetery, but he also heard it at some time in a different context. It takes him time to work it out in his head. The Neyananoosics he knows are a local family of Ojibwe; many still live in the area. There's even one kid named Peyton he's certain goes to their school. But that isn't it either.

It's the girl. Eadie. The one he met sobbing in the cemetery. She's a Neyananoosic—adopted. She said that was her last name. Her half-brothers are Neyananoosics, and it's the only family she's ever known. He remembers her telling him all this. When he interrupted her, in her vulnerable moment, grieving for her lost loved one.

Clay still has the arrowhead Aya'ah gave him.

"Keep it. You can have it." Gwiizence smiled. "Or give it away. I'm sure you'll find something to do with it."

Turning the reflective, glass surface around in his hand, Clay thinks he knows exactly what he'd like to do with it.

One week earlier…

Clay puts his lips to the whistle, and blows, but he doesn't hear anything. But Itsy and Bitsy are going nuts! Which is great, since his mum's terrible yappy dogs are annoying, and it was time for some payback! Their little beady eyes almost pop out of their heads, they're barking so hard.

He has concluded that the whistle must be a wolverine, after googling various animals, otters, muskrat and lemurs, and learning that wolverines are in fact giant weasels, and known to be quite ferocious.

Clay blows into the whistle again and smiles. The Pomeranians go mad, spinning and barking and barring their teeth in an empty threatening gesture. Clay can't hear the sound the whistle makes, but clearly it is within the decibel range of Itsy and Bitsy.

"What's got Itsy and Bitsy so excited?" His mom's large hips sway into the room. Clay tucks the whistle away, hiding it in a pocket.

"Dunno." Clay shrugs. "They're always barking at something."

After school the next day, Clay hops up the steps to the front porch, taking them two at a time as he always does, but pausing when he comes across the red and pink carnage strewn across the steps, the yard, and the front porch.

Eww gross! He thinks. He almost stepped in it! *What is it?*

Some animal. Destroyed. Ripped into shreds. Tufts of ginger fur attached to limbs, a little drumstick of a leg, paws, teeth, parts of an ear. They don't live far from the woods, wild areas are all around them, but it isn't often he comes across shredded pieces of meat. Meat tends to get eaten. And this animal has been left, entrails and guts, strewn halfway across the yard. Whatever had done this wasn't hungry, it hadn't eaten the prey—it had simply torn them to bits. Like housecats that leave offerings on their doorstep, dead mice, birds, even a baby rabbit—and it is with dawning horror, that Clay comes to a realization, finally connecting the dismembered remains of the creature, with his mum's Pomeranians. Itsy and Bitsy.

A karma tsunami of guilt comes crushing him into the ground on the heels of denial. No. How could it be? He hates those dogs. Err maybe *hate* is the wrong word he corrects himself—but he did dislike those dogs—always yapping at the slightest thing. They are annoying as fuck. But they were also cute—adorable really—and companionable when you're in the right mood, when they aren't waking you up at six in the morning. Poor things.

What could have done this? Clay wonders. They'd been torn apart by something—some predator—maybe a coyote, or a fox, or a wolf, or a large bird of prey even? There are enough animals around, any one of them could have done this. But why not eat them? Why tear them apart and leave all the meat behind. It doesn't make sense.

It was only the other day he'd been torturing the little devils by blowing into that silent whistle, the high-pitched timbre outside the range of human hearing. But it had certainly driven Itsy and Bitsy mad; the thought still made him smile. Poor dogs. Shredded to bits like a baby in a blender. Oh, god! Why does his brain have to conjure such images in moments like these? Things are bad enough already.

Death by dismemberment.

And then another equally horrifying thought occurs to him. What if it had been a wolverine? Maybe the whistle does work! Could this be his fault? Could he actually have called the animal to him? He'd better stop blowing into the damn thing.

And he better clean up the mess, before his mom comes home and sees it. Itsy and Bitsy no longer seemed as terrible as he remembers. In death they've attained a kind of idealism. Soft fur and adorableness all rolled into one, their annoyingness forgiven.

The poor things!

MISSING JADE

A station-wagon with wood paneling approaches, and Aanzheyaawin holds her thumb out over the road. The car pulls over onto the gravel shoulder ahead, and she jogs forward. The man rolls down his window.

"Why are you carrying a shovel?" He squints up at her like a mole.

"I like gardening." Aanzhey shrugs.

She carries a small potted plant in her backpack, to justify the presence of the shovel. The flowers bounced around on their stalks with her every step. The shovel had belonged to Menthol, the serial killer that murdered her twin sister. He'd used that shovel to burry victims in his yard, an elaborately maintained garden, nature teased and sculpted and scraped and tamed into shape. The rough-hewn wood has the dark patina of age, worn down from years of use, and smoothest where his hands most often gripped the shaft. Once she laid hands on it, she hadn't been able to let go.

Besides, it's a serviceable weapon, the blade is *sharp*. But even with the shovel, she knows she doesn't strike a threatening posture. She is slightly built, lean and athletic, with long dark hair and enough curves to draw unsolicited catcalls since she was eleven. She wears combat boots, short black shorts, a black tank top that shows off the white straps of her bra, a metal spiked bracelet, a razor-blade necklace, black nail polish; the accoutrements of a goth aesthetic. Jewelry that doubles nicely as weapons.

Looks can be deceiving.

She also carries actual weapons: brass knuckles, throwing knives, a ballistic knife, pepper spray, and the spring-loaded switchblades imbedded in her boot-soles. She isn't going to want for lack of weapons in a face-to-face confrontation. She learned her lesson; never leave the house without weapons. Hell, she even has an Ojibwe style bow-and-arrow cut from poplars, custom-built by her cousin Fanon so it can be stashed in her backpack. Poplars have the same consistency as human bone. Something about the flex and give. Fanon likes to craft traditional flint knapping tools: arrowheads, tomahawks, spears. She isn't exactly sure how they are related, only that they are cousins of some sort. Easily half the families from her Rez are related to her in one way or another. If not by blood, then by marriage or shared history. They all came from the same place. Ghost Lake: known for its ghost stories and high incidences of twins. There is some place in Brazil and some place in Italy that are also known for twins. Maybe it's genetic, or maybe it's something in the water?

Her own twin sister is dead. Augus's translucent form follows Aanzhey wherever she goes, like a ghostly kite tethered to her by an umbilical cord. Though Augus has faded somewhat since her earthly remains were properly laid to rest in the Ghost Lake cemetery.

"Where are you headed?" The movement of the driver's mutton-chop sideburns does nothing to lessen his mole-like appearance.

"Glacier Falls."

Jade. Like the stone.

Aanzhey still remembers playing with her cousin Jade when they were kids.

Scratching hashtags in the dirt with sticks. Dusty Rez road. Nothing more than a logging jag cut through the spruce. Jade was smart even then, even though she was three years younger, she'd worked out a system to beat Aanzhey at X's and O's. Not once or twice. But every-god-damned-time. Jade smiled, dimples in her cheeks the size of saucepans. Aanzhey smiled back even though she'd just lost.

Earbuds in her ear, Aanzhey listens to songs quietly on shuffle. Never loud enough to distract her from sounds in her environment; cars passing, branches snapping, shoes on gravel. Tall spruce trees line the road in either direction, on both sides of the road. The peaks of the trees like crenellations of a castle against the blue blue blue of the sky. Never know when a person—or a bear—could come lumbering out of those woods. Best to be at her best, in case she needs to defend herself. Or run like mad.

Something warm and wet touches her fingers. She pulls her hand away as if burned, turning to see a black and white border collie, tail wagging, pink tongue hanging out in a pant as sweat drips. Where the hell did he come from?

Black body, black ears, white paws, white muzzle, white mane in a ring around his neck, white spot on his forehead connected to his white muzzle, the splotches of colour around his ears like dark circles bisecting his face.

She looks around for the dog's owner but doesn't see anyone in sight. She checks for a collar, but the dog is collar-less. "Where did you come from?" She crouches down. "Aren't you a pretty dog? Yes you are! Where'd you come from pretty dog? Hunh? Pretty pretty dog aren't you? Yes you *are* a pretty dog!"

The border collie spins in circles, absorbing the attention. A few sticks and branches are caught in the tangled matte of his fur—maybe he's gotten lost?

"What am I gunna do with you hunh? What am I gunna do?"

"Enough with the baby talk, geez," Augus says deadpan. The closest thing to a joke Aanzhey has heard her sister make since her death. Her ghostly form has slid forward, as if being pulled ahead by some invisible current.

A crow caws up in the evergreens, rolling rattle of his call like wheels rolling inside wheels, once the sound is set to spinning, momentum keeps the grind going.

The border collie bounds off, barking, pacing back and forth in front of the evergreens. "Caw. Caw. Caw. Caw." The crow flaps his wings, but maintains his perch, as if in annoyance, displaying a plumage splashed with white specks.

Strange bird. Strange dog.

The collie barks, spinning in place.

The crow lifts off from his branch and takes to the air, hovering for a moment, cawing down at the dog; the dog's tongue lolls out, corners of his mouth curved up as if wearing a perpetual smile. *Arf. Arf. Arf. Caw. Caw. Caw*. The canine and corvid face off, one four-legged and bound to the earth, and the other an air-born creature of the sky.

The crow swoops away and the collie takes off after it, barking, head tilted as he chases after the bird, leaping onto a tree-stump to get higher, launching himself into the air like a dolphin, trying to get closer.

"Haa! Haa! - Haa! Haa!" The crow calls down, exactly as if it is taunting the dog, laughing at him. Hovering just out of reach of the bounding body twisting in mid-air to land on all fours. The crow perches on the bough of a low-hanging birch, head tilted, watching the collie's antics. The dog finally settles down in the grass, panting, tongue lolling, watching the crow with some sort of lizard-brained fascination.

Aanzhey catches up to the pair, Augus leading the way, feeling a tugging on that invisible umbilical cord, whatever it was that ties them together in this world. As she gets closer, she is surprised that the bird doesn't fly away; instead it merely tilts its head to examine her silently, as Aanzhey stands looking up at the creature. Its eyes are a reddish brown, pupils dark and undilated, indistinguishable from any other crow if it wasn't for the unnatural splattering of white splotches across the noir; the feathers have an iridized metallic sheen.

And there is a small tag on one scale-armoured crow's foot. Maybe it'd been tagged as part of a scientific study? She reaches out and turns the tag over to read the inscription. EUWEN. Just the name spelled out in block letters.

"No wonder you're not scared. You're someone's *pet*."

Kaaw! The crow lets out a short little call, as if in denial. Kaa, gaawiin. *No*.

Something sparkles in the light, catching her eye. The crow is holding something in its beak. She's heard that crows liked to pilfer bits of bling. Euwen lowers his beak towards her. She holds out her hand to catch the small glittering thing in her palm. A purple sequin. It tugs at some familiarity deep within the cortices of her brain, but she can't quite track down the path of the memory.

The crow takes off, wings flapping, and the dog follows.

Aanzhey shakes her head. "Strange."

Gravel crunches under her boots as she follows the barking border collie led by the cawing crow, the ghost of her sister Augus trailing. A mad menagerie.

Location: Ghost Lake. Destination: Glacier Falls. Distance: 300km.

"Hey! You can't bring that dog in here."

Aanzhey looks back over her shoulder at the border collie. She is going to have to name the fucking thing if he keeps following her around. Nimosh? Too obvious. Bidoon maybe? *Fetch*.

"Oh, he's not mine." Aanzhey looks at the bald man. "Just some stray."

"Well he can't come in here." The bald man pushes the dog back with his foot and closes the chest-high gate. Aanzhey has come around back to a service entrance rather than using the front door. She is here for business.

Aanzhey shrugs. "I'm Jade's cousin. Is it okay if I look around? See if she left any personal items."

"Ohhh. Yes, of course." The bald man speaks in a softer voice, makes eye-contact. "She was a good kid; I hope she turns up." Real sincerity? Aanzhey wonders. It seems real, but she isn't a mind reader. She shoots a glance at her ghost sister, eyebrow raised. Augus gives a slight nod in agreement. That doesn't mean he still isn't on her list of suspects.

Aanzhey slips in through the gate. Hears Bidoon barking, and looks back to see a flash of black and white. The dog is jumping up and down to see over the fence. Straaange dog. She turns away and keeps walking.

AARF!

She looks back to see the dog leap, front paws catching purchase on the top of the fence, hind legs following, balanced precariously on the narrow ledge like a circus elephant, before leaping gracefully to the ground. The dog runs to her, tail wagging, tongue panting, corners of his mouth turned up in a smile.

"Fuck-ing dog!" Aanzhey reaches down to pat him, looking around to make sure the bald man isn't around. Could get them both kicked out. But he is nowhere in sight. It isn't a race day, but there are jockeys around the circular track and field, brushing down horses, riding horses, going over jumps—practicing, she assumes.

The racetrack is old. The stands are in disrepair, orange plastic seating, gaping holes in the armrests where ashtrays had once been built into the chairs, everything yellowed and nicotine stained, though smoking is now prohibited. Most of the building facing the track is glassed-in and overlooks the stands below. Inside she knows there are scattered tables ringed with coffee-stains. Flat-screens display horse names, and ranking, the different odds and bets that can be placed, and live-feed closed-circuit footage of the races—the only concessions towards modernity. A faded version of its former glory. Glacier Falls' one other claim to fame aside from the glacier itself and the waterfall, the racetrack is now a lukewarm attraction. Not the pearl it had once been. Mostly old men, with liver-spots and pickled livers occupy those tables, amber beer bottles clutched in their age-gnarled hands. They smoked cigars anyway, despite the no-smoking signs. It's an uphill battle to mend their ways.

Yes, the racetrack is a faded version of itself, just like the faded memories of previous decades, prior winnings, and accumulating debt. Still. The horse races are a place to go for a certain caliber of men like her father, and some of her uncles, and cousins. There are enough of the grizzled old fools to keep the place in business. She wonders how much longer it'll be enough, without some sort of gambling renaissance—she can see the signs of such change in the scattering of slot machines, a hint at possible future growth?

She spots the observatory post in the tower overlooking the field. A small wooden hut perched on top of a latticework of scaffolding. That's the place where Jade worked, so she makes her way toward it, Bidoon keeping pace happily at her heels.

"What's with the shovel?"

"This?" Aanzheyaawin holds up the large metal spade, "I like gardening." She squints up at the cute blond, a little man mounted on a large, roan-coloured horse, its coat glistening in the light. Round horse-eyes eyeing her warily, as if she represents a threat. Maybe the horse has better instincts than the man. Horsey intuition. Its nostrils flare.

"Easy, Shell." The mounted man pats the horse's neck, before answering her question. Blue-green eyes like a cruise-ship advertisement. "I saw her that day. Walking towards the tower, carrying her books—like usual."

Aanzheyaawin knows Jade wanted to get into law school, was already studying for the bar examination. Years away. Jade had ambition. Drive. Goals. She is the last one anyone worried about. Not like some of her other relatives that like to party and drink. Jade just liked to work hard, study. Kind of boring actually. Aanzheyaawin doesn't know where some girls get their backbone. As if they are cut whole from a different sort of cloth, a better, more pure material. But she knows that's bullshit. There is nothing wrong with wanting to chase boys and party. Hell, Aanzheyaawin was one of those girls until her twin sister disappeared. Augus had always been the more responsible one. More studious. She reminds her of Jade in that way.

"Did you notice anything unusual that day?" Aanzhey keeps her voice breathy as she looks up at the cute jockey, eyes wide, and runs a hand through her hair. "Maybe she acted different? Said something strange? Mentioned something to you in passing?"

"No. I'm sorry," the blond man says. He actually does seem truly sorry.

"He's lying," her sister says, and it feels like someone has doused Aanzhey in a bucket of ice-water. She tries not to react to the invisible voice of her twin as no one else can hear it. The quickest way to make yourself look crazy.

"Thanks *junior*." Aanzheyaawin leans forward to pat the horse's neck. "And Shelley too!" Gives the horse a nuzzle even though it blows its lips out in irritation.

—SHHHPUUUH.—

"What is he lying about?" Aanzhey murmurs quietly as she turns away.

"He's hiding something." Augus's voice is like barbed wire pulled through gravel. "A secret he doesn't want you to know."

Well that's certainly worth investigating.

Aanzheyaawin heads to the tower to scope out Jade's workplace. See if she can find any clues. She feels like a bad-ass Miss Marple with more weapons. She's never actually read much mystery, preferring fantasy or YA, anything with other fictional worlds, any world other than this one. Escapism. But is that such a crime? Oh well, if she has to play Harriet The Spy, Angela Lansbury's Jessica Fletcher, Nancy Drew—all of that shit—she'll do it. Sure, she can list the names, but she's watched more Quantum Leap than CSI.

Whatever. None of them look as good in a tight dress.

And it's not vanity to be aware of facts.

Gravel crunches under her boots; the shovel drags behind her rattling on the loose white-chipped rocks of the track. The border collie has taken off, leading the way, looking back once in a while to make sure she is still following, the petals of her potted flowers shiver with every step like the faltering tremors of a nearly spent earthquake. Her twin sister follows, tied to her like an unearthly helium balloon, walking slowly in her bloody dress, feet two inches above the ground, never touching akii, Mother *Earth*, out of sync with the world, only anchored to it by their spirits. Niizhodenyag, *two hearts*. Plural. Niizhoden. One *twin*. Singular.

Crunch-crunch-crunch of her combat boots, the rattle of Menthol's shovel. She makes her way to the tower overlooking the racetrack, the crow's nest from which the races are monitored. Euwen swoops ahead of her and the dog and alights on top of the tower, perching there, and letting out a long, slow rattle. Wheels inside of wheels.

She affixes the shovel into a strap on her backpack to free her hands, spits on her palms, and then climbs up the metal ladder of the tower, hand over hand, rung over rung. Retracing the positions of hand and foot Jade must've made. She's nearly certain it's only her imagination, but the tower almost seems to sway, shifting with the shift of her weight. She feels nauseous, like she might throw up. The thing is a death trap. It reminds her of an old roller-coaster. She'd never been too keen on roller-coasters. Maybe it's supposed to lean in the wind? Like multi-story office towers, designed to bend instead of break? The higher she climbs, the less she wants to look at the ground.

What was Jade's state of mind on the last day she came in to work? Had she been upset? Angry? Frightened? Climbing this rickety tower with a stack of books under one arm.

"Swiiinnh-swooohnw." Someone whistles from below.

Aanzhey turns, pausing a short way into her climb. The jockey is standing ten feet below her, golden beard catching the light, adorable blond fuzz. Breeches marking him as a horse-rider. Fucking. Pervert.

"Fuuck aufff."

Aanzheyaawin palms a throwing knife, ready to skewer one of his over-developed thighs. The jockey's eyes widen when he sees the flash of the blade.

"You don't mess around." His eyes aquamarine. Like cruise ship advertisements.

She'd fucked white men, but she would never date one. Aanzhey isn't shy about her body, her sexuality, or her promiscuity. And NO, that doesn't mean she deserves harm or shame. She has sovereignty over her body. Anything else is a declaration of war.

The throwing knife is about the size of a silver dollar, weighted to spin, flying end over end before hitting its mark.

"You gunna throw that at me?" The corner of his eyes crinkle in crow's feet when he smiles. Tempting.

"I haven't decided yet."

The border collie latches onto the jockey's pant-leg. "Your dog's got my leg!" Bidoon is tugging, tugging, tugging, and letting out a growl with each tug. *Hgrrr. Hgrrr. Hgrrr.*

"Oh, he's not my dog," Aanzhey says.

The man has thrown his hands up in neutrality, so she tucks the throwing knife back into the sheathe under one of her spiked bracelets.

"Come on! I saw you walking with him. Call off your dog."

"Some stray. Probably just wants a handout." Aanzhey turns from the jockey and the struggle for his pant-leg, steels herself against vertigo, and grips the next rung of the ladder leading up to the tower above.

Breathes in and out. She can do this.

Aanzheyaawin stands in the tower overlooking the horse-track. Sixty-seven feet of metal scaffolding—the safest place to be in a flood. Augus stayed on the ground, for some reason. Not wanting to climb? Maybe unable to climb? Or float?

The track and field are mostly empty. A few jockeys wipe down horses, adjust saddles, walk their steeds with harnesses in cool-down mode.

From up here Aanzhey can see the entire track laid out in a chalky "O" of crushed limestone. She can't see much of the town, even from up here, most of the buildings are too low, just the steeples of a Church and some roof peaks shrouded in the canopy of trees. The domed mushroom of the water tower, GLACIER FALLS spelled out in capital letters. The stands running alongside one parallel stretch of the track. A central announcer's cockpit from which the races are announced in the main building overlooks the stands and the field, a patchwork of glass. Loud-speakers sprout from tall posts at every corner of the "O." The starting gate at the far end of the field. Birds swoop, swirling, gliding. Occupying the same biome.

This is where Jade came every day after school for two years. Her cousin spent countless hours up here. Reading? Monitoring the races? Aanzhey isn't exactly sure what the job entailed, only that it left Jade with a lot of time on her own up here in this crow's nest. Bird's-eye view of the world. Calling out the winners? Jade wasn't the announcer, though there is a microphone, probably hooked up to the speaker system. Monitors and video equipment to record the races. Photo finish. A lot of money rode on those races.

Winners and losers.

Could Jade have got wrapped up in the gambling side of things?

She wonders what Jade thought of the view, this solitude, so high up from the world. Did she find it peaceful, far away from the lives of the people below? Was it an easy job? A place to get her schoolwork done while getting paid?

Aanzhey looks over the switchboard, an incomprehensible number of buttons and levers, an office chair on wheels. She plops herself down into the chair, feeling the wheels roll over the uneven linoleum. Someone stuck a Bugs Bunny sticker to the brown fake-wood ring-growth-patterned veneer of the desk. Elmer Fud clutches a shotgun to his chest. Hunting wabbits. Is that who she is looking for? Elmer Fud?

Aanzhey spins in a circle, trying to absorb every detail. A six-by-six space, she could probably almost touch either wall if she stretched out her arms. A desk, the switchboard, some hooks on the back of the door for employees to hang up their jackets, a narrow bookshelf against one wall. It smells musty, pressed-wood glue-chips, formaldehyde off-gassing. Whatever scents Jade left behind, the remnants are too faint, or overpowered by other smells. No hint of perfume, or the soap-smell of skin, shampoo.

She slides the office chair over to the narrow bookshelf, taking a look at the various titles, most of them related to the business of horse-racing to some degree or another. Some are about horses; others are about gambling if not horse-racing in particular. The place where the two pastimes intersect. Finding nothing of particular interest, she pushes off with her legs, intending to glide back over to the windows, but the wheels catch on an indentation where two pieces of linoleum meet up and curl; she's propelled herself with too-much force and momentum keeps her going. The chair flips over, she slams backwards, her head smacks against the floor, the whole tower seems to shake, although that might be her imagination, the wheels of the office chair make clacking noises as they continue to spin.

"Damnit!" Aanzhey lies stunned. Not ready to move yet for a moment, though she knows she hasn't seriously injured anything. Or is relatively confident that she hasn't. The floor isn't that hard.

She rolls onto her side, moving slowly. Her cheek sticks to the linoleum. Locks of hair across her face. Breath coming shallow. Her eyes focus, amongst the dust bunnies, paperclips, and crumpled bits of paper under the bookshelf; a rectangular slab. She reaches out, fingers pushing aside cobwebs and grit, finding purchase on the edges, and pulling out the cell phone that is hidden there. Intentionally? Or had it been dropped and lost?

Aanzhey sits up. Holds her breath, staring at her own face reflected back in the dark glass. A few pink and purple jeweled sequins are glued to the screen.

Jade's phone.

Aanzhey presses the home button, and the screen lights up.

The wallpaper is an image of the moon beneath the time display. The battery bar is at a critical yellow five percent. Not much juice left. The phone is locked. Aanzhey punches in the code—Jade had used the same password for everything for years. Clicks on the photo icons. Scrolls through her photo library. Nothing suspicious so far. Launches her social media app. Scrolls through her messaging software. Nothing. Nothing. Nothing. Email. Mostly junk. Digs through text messages. Her mom. Her brothers. Her friends. Most of the recent texts are from her family and friends wondering where she'd gone. At first angry, then concerned, and finally, desperate. PLEASE JUST COME HOME.

Someone named Wax.

She clicks on his name with her index finger. Scrolls through the texts, date and time stamped—date and time stamped from just before Jade went missing, Wax's messages appear left-justified in blue, and Jade's messages appeared right-justified in green. Aanzhey works her way backwards, from most recent to oldest—a flurry of angry text messages:

Don't be such a cunt

I think we should
break up

Working in reverse through the digital layers of archived words. Her thumb slides up on the touchscreen, sliding past blocks of more generic texts.

I'll meet you in the
tower

Want to meet after your
shift?

More words jumped out, catching her attention.

I love you.
I'm not seeing anyone else.
why do you have to be
such a jerk all the time?

I'll make sure of that.
If anyone else touches you,
I will kill you both. They
won't find your body.
Don't you ever cheat on me
You're a whore.

Skimming further back through the stratified layers of text messages:

You make me like this.
I'll make it up to you.
I promise.

don't hit me like that
ever again.

I'm sorry. I didn't mean it.

Scrolling further back. Further back. Words like dry leaves. Burrowing through arguments and declarations of love, like a yo-yo. A roller-coaster. This Wax guy was possessive, controlling, insecure, jealous. Aanzhey hates to think of her cousin drawn into a relationship with a man like that. A bird caught up in a manipulative cage of words. At times he plays the victim, "You don't really care about me!" At others he goes on the offensive, accusatory, demanding "Come here now or I'll never talk to you again." It rankles. But she's found Motive with a capital M.

Photos they texted to each other.

Pictures of body parts. Lacy underwear. Jade posing, her face angled down and away, shyly. *She is too young for sex!* Aanzhey's mind rebels, but knows this isn't the case. Aanzhey was fooling around at that age. Even younger. Jade *is* old enough. Almost seventeen. *He* is too old.

Pictures of a gold-bearded man, posing, flexing like Hulk Hogan. Closer to thirty, thirty-five maybe. Shirtless and showing of his muscles. Cock like a hammerhead shark. Modern art of seduction. Texts going back the good part of a year. Flirtatious. She knows that man, recognizes him from the pictures. Had just spoken to him, in fact.

The perverted jockey.

Today is race day.

Euwen is perched atop the turret like a crow-shaped gargoyle. Aanzhey can hear the damned thing cawing. That slow rolling caw. Like wheels inside of wheels set to spinning. Augus waits at the base of the ladder. Again, for some reason, unwilling or unable to make the climb. Maybe this is one of her "cannot intervene" moments?

Aanzhey pulls out the poplar bow Fanon made for her. A lightweight version, almost the length of her arms. With a protective sheathe so she can strap it to her backpack without being too conspicuous. She also carries turkey-fletched arrows, their heads wrapped in leather so they won't tear through the bag. She has a round birch case for the arrows but finds it too bulky.

Fanon is a good craftsman, and she trusts that the bow is well made. Besides, her target won't be that far—the horses run *around* the track. Her target will come to her. All she has to do is wait.

She hops up onto the desk, her combat boots making a thud. Stands to slide open a narrow window at the top of the glass. She has to duck her head slightly so it fits in under the ceiling. Tests the flex and give of the poplar and stringed sinew, feeling the weight of resistance, kinetic energy stored with the slightest retraction, ready to loose. Aanzhey aims the shaft of the arrow out through the open window.

She will have to account for the speed of her arrow, wind resistance, plus the speed of the horse. Rather than aiming for her target, since the target is moving, by the time her arrow gets to the target, it will have moved, she needs to aim not for where her target is, but for where it will be.

Qui Chang Kane shit. The Legend Continues.

God she'd watched so much TV as a kid.

Still, she is confident in her archery skills, even though this isn't the sort of practice she'd done with Fanon and his daughters.

Accomplished archers both. They'd aimed at straw figures with faces from pop-culture taped on, politicians and preachers.

Bouncing jockeys on even bouncier horses.

Scarecrows don't move.

Fuck it. If she misses, she misses.

She figures she'd only have one shot at this, there isn't really room for a second—assuming the first arrow is enough to interrupt the race. It probably won't go unnoticed.

A gunshot will start the race. Aanzhey will finish it.

On the track below, she picks out Shelley draped in a green tartan. Her mount, the whistling white boy, is petite like all the riders, with massive thighs from years of training with horses. Race day colours in every shade of the rainbow: reds, blues, yellows, orange, purple, pink. Rounded helmets to protect skulls, buts raised high in the air, shoulders and heads hunched low as they prepare for the crack of the starting pistol.

DOOOOOV.

There was an electric sounding pulse, indicating "on your marks," once.

DOOOOOV.

"On your marks," twice.

Followed by a CRAAACK! of the starting pistol, and they are off.

She follows the target with the point of her arrow, tracking his progress as he slips from second to third, and then third to fourth, but stays ahead of the fifth rider who lags behind. She remembers placing the point of her shovel to Menthol's knees, jumping with all of her weight, and driving the shoulders of the blade down through ligaments, gristle and bone, doing her best to separate the man limb from limb. No, she isn't going to blink. She wants that jockey. Fucking. Dead. She'll only feel relief that whatever he'd done to Jade, he won't be able to do to anyone else. He wouldn't be able to hurt anyone ever again if he's dead.

The crow swoops down, Aanzhey sees the splattered-bleach pattern of Euwen's feathers for a moment as it dives from its perch atop the tower, crossing the field of her vision, wings outspread, gaining speed like a swimmer swan-diving off a diving board before flattening out, wings parallel to the ground, flying parallel to the track, and parallel to the horse racers, easily keeping pace. And the damned dog has gotten onto the field again, and is now chasing after the damned crow, running parallel to the track, taking up position alongside Wax. What the hell is going on inside that little monster?

What is his damned fascination with that damned bird? What is with that bird? Maybe they are friends? Maybe he wants to fly like the crow? Take to the skies? Maybe he wants to see what the bird can see? Unaware of limitations like bodies and morphology and evolution. Dogs don't have wings.

The shadow of the crow slides across the dog, then slides across the jockey, taking the lead just ahead of her target.

Maybe it is just the *movement* that fascinates him. Border collies are bred as sheep dogs after all. Sheep herders. Maybe he is just a neurotic animal fixated with corralling anything on the move? Maybe he's trying to sheep-herd the crow? Coral it into stasis. Keep it from escaping, though it is a pen-less, untethered creature of the sky. She ignores the beasts and keeps her focus on the rider, keeps her breathing even, and keeps the tension on the stringed sinew, arrow notched. Ready.

But Wax has noticed the dog now too, and is splitting his focus, looking from the race to the dog and then back to the race in front of him. Is the dog racing him?

At the point at which Wax is closest to the tower, Aanzhey does her internal calculations, determining the speed of the rider, the speed of her arrow, wind resistance, and where her arrow should be when he reaches the point in the middle. Her focus narrows down to a point. That point in the future extending past the point of her arrow, the direction of time. Sinew pulled back to its furthest extension, she lets go, releasing the tension built up in the drawn bow. Too fast for the eye to see. One second feathers are brushing her cheekbone, in the next moment, rider meets bolt, and the fletching is perched atop the arrow now buried in the meat of the horse-rider. He doesn't fall off, though he kilters sideways, still folded, but losing his aerodynamic stance. The horse keeps running, not realizing their race is over, though the rider is lopsided, clutching the reigns, and the horse veers off track, slowing from the gallop, overtaken by the horse in last place.

Few people in the stands notice what has happened, they only know that the rider has faltered, their eyes glued to the horses still in the competition. Wax steers towards the baseball-style bullpen where stagehands grasp the reigns from the rudderless horse, and the jockey slides from the saddle, clutching at his thigh where a dark red stain has now drenched the khaki coloured fabric of his riding breeches, and from which the arrow is now imbedded. The stagehands catch the rider as he slides off and lowers him gently to the ground. No one seems to be looking around for a sniper.

It doesn't immediately occur to anyone that arrows don't simply appear from nowhere. But then again, why would they be expecting a sniper?

Fuck. She'd missed all the vital organs; the injury is not life threatening. Oh well. It's just as well that she hasn't killed him. If she gets caught, an assault charge is less serious than murder, or attempted murder. Dead men tell no tales, and she still wants to make him squeal. Make him literally spill his guts. This was a stupidly risky thing to do in the first place, and she knew that to begin with. But there is something about the poetic justice of using Jade's tower to help carry out the assassination. She stands by the confidence she had in her ability to hit the target, even a moving target. But she hadn't taken into account the crow, or the dog, and the way Wax kept shifting his weight, looking between the race and the racing dog.

She needs to get the hell out of there. *Now.*

Majaan. Majaan. Majaan.

She jams the bow back into her pack, slings the pack over her shoulder, hops down from the desk, and is out the door to the sky and half-way down the rungs of the ladder in less than a minute. No time for her fear of heights to slow her down, only room for the adrenaline which she kept tightly tamped down while aiming and shooting. She now lets it fly, lending strength to her muscles, and enough panic to overcome any terror of heights. The rickety scaffolding rings alarm bells. *Danger. Danger. Danger.* Well, those alarm bells are already ringing in her skull. *Oh fuck, oh fuck, oh fuck, oh fuck*—the running interior monologue of her thoughts.

She needs to get out of there. And the rungs are taking too long, hand over hand. She grips either side of the ladder, places the rubber insole of her boots on either side for balance, and slides down like a fireman's pole, two of them, rug-burn be damned, though it burns and rips off a layer of skin, the palms of her hands one giant blister. She hits the ground hard, boots to the dust, but hits the ground running, aches and pains be damned, things to worry about later should she somehow find herself outside a prison cell.

She dekes into the stands, the crowd now on its feet cheering or booing depending on which horse they'd bet on. She weaves through the people, making her way up into the glassed-in building, where she slows her pace down to a steady walk—no running—no panic—nothing to see here—whistling—she hasn't just shot someone in the thigh with an Ojibwe bow and arrow. No sirree. Out for a stroll at the races. A good day for gambling.

She'll collect her winnings later.

"Where's Jade?" Aanzhey holds the shaft of Menthol's shovel to Wax's throat.

It was easy to sneak up behind him, limping and leaning on his crutches. He didn't move very quickly. The white-domed mushroom of the water tower rises above them, GLACIER FALLS, written in large block letters.

Aanzhey isn't huge, but she is no weakling. Since her sister's death she's worked out religiously. Strength training. *And* she had the element of surprise. And even though the man is an athlete, he is a jockey. He isn't a huge guy either.

She slams Wax up against the tower, the back of his head hits hard, it makes a metallic gong, and his crutches clatter to the ground. Bidoon is yapping, excited about the commotion. And she hears distantly that crow cawing down, probably Euwen watching from somewhere above. Metal rungs of the water tower like stands. Bleachers. Her audience.

"Wh-what?" Wax's eyes roll back for a moment before righting themselves in his head. Aquamarine like a cruise-ship advertisement. "Not you again—" His eyes go wide as they shift focus to the crossbow protruding from her backpack. "What the fuck."

"Where's Jade?" Spit flies through her clenched teeth.

"Jade she's … she's gone"

"Gone where?" Aanzhey pulls him back and slams him against the wall again, like punctuation. "Tell me." Bidoon tugs at Wax's pant-leg, growling. Her sister hovers somewhere over her shoulder, watching impassively, unable to intervene.

"I don't know!"

"I found her phone. I saw all those text messages you sent. I know you killed her. Just tell me where she is."

"I would never …" His eyes shimmer with tears. "I love her."

"—then where is she?" Seeing the well of his eyes fill with tears, she actually wants to believe he is telling the truth.

"I don't know." His voice cracks.

She looks to her sister for confirmation.

"He's telling the truth," Augus rasps.

Wax *doesn't* know where Jade has gone.

"She's missing." His Adam's apple rises and falls as he swallows. His face blurs as her eyes fill with an answering wall of tears.

A crow calls from somewhere in the distance.

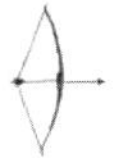

Her boots crunch on side-of-the-road gravel. Potted flowers sway next to Menthol's shovel. The border collie, Bidoon, looks back once in a while to make sure she's still following, pink tongue panting, corners of his mouth turned up in a smile. The ghost of her twin sister trails after her like a kite, connected to each other by an invisible umbilical cord.

Aanzhey doesn't know what happened to Jade. She isn't sure if she'll ever find out. Life isn't like TV. Mysteries where the murder is always solved, the missing returned, the guilty captured. Just because she found one murderer, doesn't mean she could repeat the feat. She doesn't know what happened to Jade. Or if she ever will.

Maybe one day she will find out.

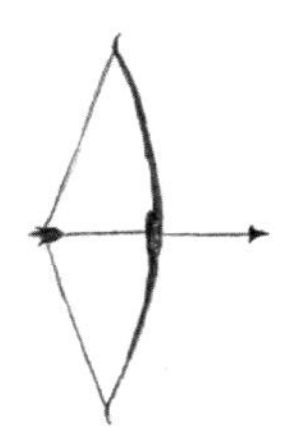

OFFERINGS

I watch as Zilpah sets the spirit plate precariously on the edge of the deck railing and beats the welcome mat with a wooden spoon to shake off dust and debris. The spirit plate contains a small sample of what we had for dinner that night, and a pinch of tobacco.

The branches of the willow tree sway gently in the breeze, drone of insects coming to life now that spring has finally sprung. Dragonflies zip by on iridescent wings, the metallic sheen of their bodies almost mechanical. Crickets creak. The sound of rushing water from the creek drifts from the back of our lot, high flow with the run-off from yesterday's thunderstorm.

"Why do you put that plate out every night?" I look up from *Tuck Everlasting,* the book I've been reading. I speak loudly so my great-grandmother can hear, Zilpah will now be going into her 80th winter, and she is a bit hard of hearing.

"For the manidook. The spirits. This is their land too. Better to have friends. Better not to make enemies. Mchi-manidoosh."

"Rats!" Zephyr exclaims. That's who she's feeding. Rats and squirrels, which are basically just rats with bigger tails." Zeph has her hair pinned up into two separate Bjork-like Princess-

Leia buns, her sleeves rolled up like the *We Can Do It!* feminist propaganda posters to reveal a constellation of ink swirling across her skin. Ojibwe florals and geometrics reminiscent of my mother's beadwork. But only a simple diamond stud in one nostril. She is dressing-down today. The spade flashes as she digs up the small herb garden she's taken to tending this last year. Basil. Rosemary. Sweetgrass. Sage. Grandmother Zephyr is proud of her status as a 43-year-old grandmother.

It's been over a year now since my brother Zachaeus drowned leaving us a household of women. My mother Zoe, my grandmother Zephyr, my great-grandmother Zilpah, and me: Zaude. I wonder abstractly if there is something unnatural or witchy about being a family of women, although I suppose Uncle Zeamus still counts and he visits often. I helped him build the deck last summer; the wood is still green. It has a nice shingled awning that provides shade, and it has quickly become our new favourite part of the house during the warm months.

I watch a ladybug with the red lacquer sheen of nail-polish and black polka-dots waddle across the green lumber beneath my lawn chair. Lady flaps her wings as if about to take to the air. I raise the old-school 35mm film camera that is almost permanently strapped around my neck—never know when you're going to stumble across that perfect, impossible shot—and you never will unless you're ready. Lady rises into the air, and oddly seems to hover in place just long enough for me to adjust the focus ring to snap the shot, a flare from the sun arcing through the frame to create an interesting lensing effect through the softer tissues of the under-wing beneath the harder shell of the elytra, like a small halo, the garden and sky a turquoise-and-lime blur in the background. I'll have to wait until the film is developed to see how the shot turns out though. Like I said. Old school.

I see the shadow of my mother through the screen door, Zoe peering out, but not joining us on the sunny patio, preferring to stay indoors. Can't say I blame her. Some days I feel the same way. Some days I refuse to get out of bed. Some days I think I'd be better off dead… I know my brother wouldn't want that though, for me to be so sad I can't even enjoy the beauty of the day. I don't call to my mother. I know that tomorrow it can just as easily be me, unable to face the beauty of the day, life going on even after one life came to a stop. Today I am determined to enjoy what joy there is to be had while the getting is good. Besides, we'll all be dead eventually, what's the rush?

Out on the lake, with Zeamus.

Paddling paddling paddling. Once we get out of the shallows Zeamus drops the outboard motor and the engine propels us over the surface of the lake, cresting the peaks of each waves. Beautiful day. Quintillions of ovoid refractions of light, sparkling like rising campfire embers in the sun. The wind whips my hair in a frenzy, so I gather the loose strands at the back of my head, the stretchy elastic fabric of the band held in my lips. I've lost more than one Jays cap to the drink, and Zach's are too precious to me to risk losing—we've already lost so much to this lake. But this lake, it is our life, it is our home, intellectually I know the sparkling surface holds no malice, on the contrary, Zelda always says the land loves us.

"She is our mother. She loves us."

But maybe it is all physics? Atoms colliding like a game of pool, and if the angle is just right, the particle will sink. Math and geometry, no emotions required. Is a world of indifference less lovely than a world infused with relationality? No. It's definitely just as lovely. That doesn't make it any less painful. Or deadly. If you sink beneath the waves, you'll drown. If it is -30 the blood will freeze in your veins. Facts. No gills. Physics. Not love.

Once we hit the open water past the floating islands off Drinker's Point, Zeamus cuts the engine and we drift with the islands, bobbing as the sunlight drenches us. Photons like a physical force. Zeamus pulls out his papers and rolls himself a doob with a rustling of dry organics. The heady smell of marijuana drifts across, pang-inducing, the way Zoe's savoury *Mooz à la Bourguignonne* elicits hunger. It's like *Boeuf à la Bourguignonne* except with moose meat instead of beef. Mooz is the Ojibwe word for moose, which is basically the same word since the English borrows the word. Not many moose in Europe. I don't usually like pot, it makes me too anxious. It just doesn't have the same effects that Zeamus describes. Euphoria, relaxation, and calm. When Zeamus offers I take the smallest possible hoot and quickly pass it back. Microdose.

"Do you ever get tired of living here?" I ask.

Zeamus raises his hands, palms open, and twists as if to take in the surrounding beauty, his silver eyes looking over the edges of his purple-tinted John Lennon glasses, twist of greying goatee sprouting from his chin like a mini wizard-beard.

"I mean—don't you get tired of being the only one? Don't you want live in the big city with all those city gays?" And Zeamus laughs.

"There's more of us around than you'd expect."

"Really?" I raise an eyebrow. The rez isn't exactly Gay Central Station, though traditional values actually celebrate sexuality and gender. Christian values hadn't left our territory entirely unmarked; there are as many close-minded folks both on the Rez and in the town of Cheapaye as there are in any other rural town.

"Don't worry about me, I do alright."

"Really, who are you dating then?" I couldn't believe the gossip industry hadn't kept me in the loop.

"Well *dating* might be too strong of a word…."

"Who?"

"Well, there's that Fanon fellow." The skin at the corners of his eyes crinkle in crow's feet, silver eyes twinkling through purple lenses.

"Ogers? Edna's nephew?"

"Yep."

"Haanh. But not dating-dating?"
"Weeell. We'll see."

Zilpah passed. I miss her. I miss her blaring TV. So loud it makes the walls shake. I miss the way she shouted to be heard over her own deafness. The smudges emanating from underneath her bedroom door and the homemade quilts she churned out with the output of a factory. Our home feels a lot quieter. A lot sadder.

My mother Zoe retreats into her own crafts, her beading and sewing, her online marketplace where her customers place their custom orders for earrings and moccasins and medallions and other assortments of beaded bling.

"*Land Back* and *Baby Yoda* are all the rage," she says with a close-mouthed smile.

After a month-and-a-half grandma Zeph goes back to her nursing job at the hospital in Cheapaye. "I need to work" she says, "I need to keep busy—otherwise I just play those damn video games all day." Overnight Zephyr has become the new matriarch of our little witchy family, she has the goth part down at least, though she isn't used to being the one in charge. Zilpah had always been around, Zilpah knew everything, Zilpah always had a word or two of advice, an opinion to opine on any given subject.

Two months after her passing, Zephyr announces her need for a change, "There's this nursing conference in The City." *As if there is only one.* "It might be nice to have a change in scenery, would either of you like to come with me? Zoe? Zaude?"

"It might be nice to get away." Zoe looks up from the gold and brown hummingbirds she's beading. "It's been a while since I've left the Jiibay."

"I don't know," I say, my eyes stray to the cherry blossoms in the yard. "I think I'd rather just stick around here."

I have the place to myself for two whole weeks. I can't remember the last time I've been this alone.

And as for me? I have my camera. Well Zach's camera. What had been Zach's camera when he was still alive. I walk through the house taking pictures of anything and everything that reminds me of my great-grandmother Zilpah.

Her abandoned walker, still standing by the front door. The plants she would overwater until they turned brown. The ticking of the ancient wind-up clock she'd gotten from who-knows-where. The x's she'd drawn on the kitchen power outlets so it was easier for her to find the holes for the prongs on the cord of the electric kettle. The small shelf she'd screwed to the wall, the underside of which she'd affixed the smoke detector so she could reach it without having to climb up a stepladder to reach the ceiling. Her adaptations and inventions are everywhere.

I slide aside the panes of the double-glass sliding doors and step out onto the porch Zeamus, Zeke and I had built. Trickle of water from the creek. Sway and shift of the leaves in the trees. There is the tarnished silver bowl balanced precariously on the edge of the railing, just where she'd last left it. The bowl is empty. I wonder if the spirits feel abandoned now that Zilpah isn't around to leave her offerings. Her twists of tobacco, her pinches from whatever she was eating on her plate. Do they wonder where she went? Are they angry that she no longer pays tribute? Those spirits. Those manidook?

Sunlight sparkles on the silver, the refraction of light causing a glow, like the lensing of light through a ladybug's inner wing. I raise the camera strapped to my chest and snap a photo. My mother blinged-out the leather cord from which it dangles with beaded lightning. Purple, lime-green, and gold. Won't know how it turns out until I get the film developed. That's part of the fun. The excitement of not knowing and waiting to see the results. Photography is always an experiment.

I sit in the den watching re-runs of old horror movies. I've never seen the original version of *The Fly* before. What should I watch next? I click through some of my options. *The Burbs. Night of the Living Dead. Fright Night. Candyman. Creature from the Blue Lagoon*. I briefly consider inviting my cousin Zeke over, or his father Zeamus, but I dismiss the idea. This is my first chance in a long while to be really alone, and I don't want to go and spoil it out of loneliness. This is my first night to myself, there are still another fourteen days if I really need to fill the vacuum with the sound of other living voices. For now the TV will keep me company. And Zilpah's quilts. And horror movie screams. And spaghetti.

That's when I hear it.

Clunk

It sounds exactly like a bird hitting the window. It's happened before, but usually at that twilight stage between day and night, dawn or dusk, when the glass hardly appears to be there at all. It has something to do with the quality of light, which is also the reason why it's the best time for still photography. Since then we've been careful to keep the curtains drawn, hang a few crystals and ornaments for visibility.

Then it comes again.

Clunk

Two birds? I wonder. How likely could that be?

One stone, my stupid brain immediately rejoins.

"OKAY. OKAY," I say outload to myself. Throw off great-grandma Zilpah's quilt, grab an iron poker from the mantle before the fireplace, slip on my fur-trimmed boots at the front door and head back through the kitchen to investigate the source of the sound. The curtain is drawn, vetoing my two-birds theory. I flick on the exterior light, and peer out the sliding glass. Nothing seems out of the ordinary. But everything beyond what the light reaches opaques the backyard into an impenetrable sphere. Bugs instantaneously manifest, swirling about the exposed bulb. If I open the door, I know those damned skeeters will get in and they'll be hounding me all night with their high-pitched whine. Zaagimeg. Bloodsuckers.

Feeling magnanimous, I slide the doors open, iron poker raised prominently like a sceptre. Whoever is around I want them to know who they are dealing with, that I am armed, and I am a queen.

I eye the deck for avian corpses but don't any see any ruin of feathers. I grip my scepter tighter. The night seems ordinary. Nothing seems out of place. Lawn chairs and patio furniture are in the same arrangement as when I last saw them. Hummingbird feeder is swaying. Hunh. Swaying. The hummingbird feeder is shaped like a spinning top, a bulbous round part to hold the sugar water, a cork plug in the top, and a curved bit of metal like the kind in a hamster cage but with a red-tipped nozzle that is meant to attract the eye. "Hummingbirds are attracted to the colour red," Zoe told me.

I know the winged beings to be positively mad for the sweet stuff Zoe fills the feeder with, some kind of faux nectar, at least when she remembers to keep the reservoir full. Wings beat so fast they blur. Faster than the human eye. Hovering like helicopters.

Are hummingbirds nocturnal? I don't recall ever seeing the hummingbirds come by after dark. I mull this over in my head, consider checking the Internet, the encyclopediac answer for everything you've ever wondered. I pull out my cell and lean the iron poker against the brick wall. Punch out the question with my thumbs.

ARE HUMMINBIRDS NOCTURNAL?

Answer: hummingbirds are diurnal. Meaning they are only active during the day, though they might also feed during twilight.

Hunh.

"Well, it's well after twilight now," I say, eyeballing the feeder as the rotation wobbles from entropy as the energy available for continued momentum slowly unwinds.

I shrug, glare once more at everything within the field of my vision, deck chairs, haunted hummingbird feeder, and the overgrown grass in the backyard.

Could have been anything. Skunks. Raccoons. Squirrels. Wolverines. There are always plenty of animals around. And at least some of them are nocturnal and might have liked to test out the taste of the sweet water.

I slide the doors shut and lock them. Leave the security lights on. Head back into the den, my lazy boy, and my quilted blanket.

Back to the debate: what should I watch? Should I abandon the whole enterprise of watching a horror movie alone—that's never really bothered me before. Usually they just make me laugh rather than frightening me. Twisted sense of humour I guess. Sometimes I laugh at the most inappropriate moment. Sometimes I'm the only one laughing, and I think *maybe my brain just doesn't work like other people's anymore.* And so what? maybe it doesn't.

Clunk

Thump

Thump

"What The Actual Fuck!" I know I am not imagining it this time. What am I, *living* in a horror movie? I throw Zilpah's quilt off my legs, jam my feet into my boots, sceptre ready. Peer out at the illuminated yard. Nothing. Step out the sliding glass doors. Crickets. Flowing water. Toads making their raucous of blurbs and blargs into a patchwork of song.

I reach back through the sliding glass to flick off the light, waiting for the spots to recede from my vision, and for my night vision to kick into gear. Waiting for my pupils to enlarge so they can gather in more of the available light. Light from the moon, and the stars, and whatever residual light pollution that might exist from our nearest neighbours who are all quite far away. The residential allotments. Zilpah had successfully campaigned for a lot on the river where her family had always made their summer camp.

"Zeke? Zeke is that you?" I make out the form of my cousin standing at the edges of Zoe's garden. My eyes seem to slide away from his face, I can't seem to focus in the darkness, the edges of things blurry. Without definition. But there is his omnipresent hoodie, basketball shorts, and flashy name-brand sneakers. He's even holding a basketball the exact same way as I'd last seen him. Though that had been in his driveway shooting hoops. "You little perv," I tease, "what the hell are you doing skulking around my backyard after dark?"

"Water finds a way. Water still flows." His voice is all buzzing and wheezing. Not at all like his usual baritone. Kid is only fourteen. Much too short for basketball. Should give up on his dreams of NBA and join the choir. That's what he's suited for. Too ugly for theatre. A voice for the radio.

"Are you high?" Jesus. I step closer to the railing, trying to make out his face, but his hoodie is up, throwing his features into shadow. His face is a dark hole.

"Raindrops. Creaks. Streams. River. Lake." Buzz. Buzz. Buzz.

"Ok, Zeke I'm calling your dad!"

Zeke whorls around like an ancient Greek statue of an Olympic athlete throwing a discus and whips the basketball at my head. *What the Heck!* I duck, and the ball bounces off the brick wall of the house, bounces off the railing, and rolls out into the foliage of the trees surrounding the yard. I look back towards where Zeke had been standing. He's gone. I scan the rest of the yard, but he's nowhere to be seen.

I flick the security light back on as I squeeze through the sliding glass doors. I've accidentally left it open a few inches. I know those zaagimek are going to eat me alive now and it's all Zeke's fault. Back in the den I sit in the comforting glow of the television, the movie poster artwork of *Fright Night* leering at me out of the clouds. Glowing green eyes and too many teeth. The house looks nothing like ours. *What had all that been about?*

I sit staring at my phone wondering if I should tell Zeamus what happened. We'd always been pretty close. Closer than Zeke and I who was technically closer to me in age. Just entering his teenage years as I was leaving mine. Zephyr so proud of being a 43-year-old grandmother; Zeamus had continued the family tradition of having a child while still being a child himself, managed to knock up his girlfriend at age fourteen before he had all his sexuality sorted out. A father at fifteen, he was almost a decade younger than my mother Zoe. Though Zeamus is my uncle, he is only seven years older than me, and he's always felt more like an honourary brother. But I don't want to alienate the younger generation—I don't want to be that "uncool" aunt that tattles on her nephew. I want to be a cool aunt.

I click on Zeke's number instead and send him a text.

GETTING INTO YOUR
FATHER'S STASH?

I wait. A few minutes later the dot dot dot, dot dot dot, dot dot dot … … … of a forming text message appears.

BORED ALREADY?
I GOT PLENTY TO SPARE
MY OWN GREEN
NOTHING ELSE TO DO
ON THIS REZ

Kid was shaping up to be a lot like his father. I smile. I know he's been given all the same lectures on birth control.

WHAT WAS ALL THAT ABOUT?

HUNH?
WHAT WAS WHAT ABOUT

THAT STUFF ABOUT
RIVERS LAKES STREAMS

...

... ...

... ...

???

AND THROWING
BASKETBALLS AROUND
MY YARD

DON'T KNOW WHAT
YOU BEEN SMOKING 🤣
WASN'T ME

Hunh.

YOU WEREN'T JUST IN
MY YARD?

...

TWASN'T I

Hunh.

GHOSTS

"Ha!"

MAY-BE

Ok. So maybe it wasn't Zeke. I never saw his face. It didn't mean it was a ghost necessarily. But still. Weird. Creepy. Spooky. I look back at the *Fright Night* movie still displayed on the TV.

"How about a comedy?" I click over to the titles listed under humour. Rom-Coms aren't usually my deal. Maybe an animated cartoon? "Something a bit more light-hearted." *The Last Unicorn. Coraline. The Dark Crystal. 9.*

"Something with talking rodents maybe?" *The Secrets of NIHM. An American Tail. Ratatouille.*

I scroll through more kids' titles. *The Peanut Butter Solution. The Goonies. Jacob Two Two Meets the Hooded Fang.*

Geesh, when did kids' movies become so terrifying?

Ping

I look up from my search.

"O-kay what was that?" My ears are strained, listening. Waiting for the other pin to drop.

PING

There it is again. Louder this time. Like a wine glass that's been clinked against something. Or a heavy coin dropped on cement.

Cling

Ping

Ding

The quiet, irregular chime continues as I drag myself to the glass partition and peer out to the halo cast by the security light. Slide the double doors apart and step out onto the porch.

Moths and other winged insects swirl about the bulb casting shadows with their bodies.

I take an assessment of the scene. Lawn Chairs. Patio furniture. Deck railing with Zilpah's silver offering bowl still resting precariously on the edge, and beyond that the freshly-turned earth of the herb garden, and the rusted metal O-ring of an old tire rim that we use to contain campfires. Everything appears as usual.

At the very edge of the circle of light, where the shadows are too thick for the security light to penetrate, I see the outline of a shape. A figure. A boy standing at the edge of the light. Hood down, but it's too dark for me to make out his face. Jeans instead of basketball shorts. Not Zeke this time. But oh so familiar. The slant of his shoulders, the weight of his stance. No, not Zeke. ZACH. It looks like my brother Zachaeus, but I know that that's impossible. Zach is dead. He's been dead for over a year now. It can't be Zach. I'm trembling. The iron poker I'm holding up at a defensive angle is shaking. There's no strength in my muscles. Tears blur my vision; I feel wetness on my cheeks. My stomach has dropped. It's down at my feet. My blood sugar has dropped like I haven't eaten anything, like I skipped lunch and dinner and I just need the quick rush of sugar. I'm hunched. Curled in on myself. I can barely stand. Can't breathe. Barely speak. Gasping.

"Zach?!" I say. "Zach? Is that you?" I'm sobbing now. I can't believe my own eyes. There's Zach, my little brother, my little brother, my little brother standing there in the yard. I can see him more clearly now, though he's still standing in the shadows.

"Tribute," the voice wheezes out. Buzzing. "Tribute must be paid. The river flows."

It's not him. It's not him. The relief is like a flood, a dam that's broken open, releasing all the emotions which have been held back, contained. That's not Zach's voice. That's not how he sounds. It's not him. It's not him.

He turns and I can see his ear. See where his ear used to be. It's all blood and puss with white maggots crawling around in the wound. Eating the dead flesh. When they found his body, he'd been missing an ear. He moves into the shadows and he's gone, erased.

My eyes fall on the silver tray. Zilpah's spirit plate for offerings.

Tribute must be paid.

Mii'sa Minik
The End

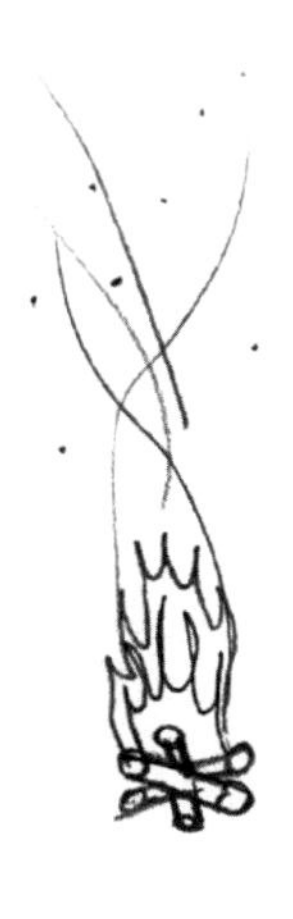